TAILCHASER'S SONG

TAILCHASER'S SONG

Tad Williams

CENTURY
LONDON SYDNEY AUCKLAND JOHANNESBURG

First published in Great Britain in 1992 by
Legend Books
20 Vauxhall Bridge Road, London SW1V 2SA

3 5 7 9 10 8 6 4

Century Hutchinson South Africa (Pty) Ltd
PO Box 337, Bergvlei 2012, South Africa

Random House Australia Pty Ltd
20 Alfred Street, Milsons Point, Sydney, NSW 2061
Australia

Random House New Zealand Ltd
PO Box 40-086, Glenfield, Auckland 10
New Zealand

The catalogue data for this book is available from the
British Library

Printed in Great Britain by
Cox & Wyman Ltd, Reading, Berkshire

ISBN 0-09 995 9402

ACKNOWLEDGMENTS

Special thanks to John Carswell, Nancy Deming-Williams, and Arthur Ross Evans for their assistance in the preparation of this book. Good dancing to them all.

Lao-tzu translations reprinted with permission of the publisher, Bobbs-Merrill Educational Publishing. Wing-tsit Chan, trans., *The Way of Lao-tzu* © 1963 Bobbs-Merrill.

Stevens, Wallace, from 'Thirteen Ways of Looking at a Blackbird' and 'A Rabbit as King of the Ghosts,' reprinted by permission of the publisher, Alfred A. Knopf, Inc., from *The Collected Poems of Wallace Stevens*.

Barker, Eric, lines from 'A Troubled Sleep,' reprinted by permission of *Yankee* magazine.

Dacey, Philip, lines from 'Villanelle for the Cat,' reprinted with permission from *Cat Fancy*.

Toomer, Jean, lines from 'Carma' are reprinted from *Cane* by Jean Toomer by permission of Liveright Publishing Corporation. Copyright © 1923 by Boni & Liveright. Copyright renewed 1951 by Jean Toomer.

Turner, W. J., lines from 'India' reprinted with permission of the publisher, Sidgwick & Jackson from the volume *The Hunter and Other Poems* © 1916 by the author.

Rutledge, Archibald, lines from 'Lion in the Night,' reprinted with permission of Irvine H. Rutledge from the volume *Deep River: Complete Poems of Archibald Rutledge*, copyright © 1960 R. L. Bryan Co.

Alighieri, Dante, from *The Inferno* by Dante Alighieri, translated by John Ciardi. Copyright © 1954 by John Ciardi. Reprinted by arrangement with New American Library, New York, New York.

Jacobsen, Josephine, excerpt from 'Bush,' from *The Shade-Seller* by Josephine Jacobsen. Reprinted by permission of Doubleday & Company, Inc.

Barker, George, lines from 'Elegy: Separation of Man from God,' reprinted from *The Golden Treasury of the Best Songs and Lyrical Poems*, edited by Oscar Williams. © 1953 and 1961 by Oscar Willi-

For I will consider my cat . . .

For at the first glance of the glory of God
in the East he worships in his way.

For this is done by wreathing his body seven
times around with elegant quickness . . .

For having done duty and received blessing
he begins to consider himself.

For this he performs in ten degrees.

For first he looks upon his fore-paws to see
if they are clean.

For secondly he kicks up behind to clear away there.

For thirdly he works it upon the stretch with
the fore-paws extended

For fourthly he sharpens his paws by wood.

For fifthly he washes himself.

For sixthly he rolls upon wash.

For seventhly he fleas himself, that he may
not be interrupted on the beat.

For eighthly he rubs himself against a post.

For ninthly he looks up for his instructions.

For tenthly he goes in quest of food . . .

For when his day's work is done his business
more properly begins.

For he keeps the Lord's watch in the night
against the adversary.

For he counteracts the powers of darkness by
his electrical skin and glaring eyes.

For he counteracts the Devil, who is death,
by brisking about the life.

For in his morning orisons he loves the sun
and the sun loves him.

For he is of the tribe of Tiger.

For the Cherub Cat is a term of the Angel
Tiger . . .

For there is nothing sweeter than his peace
when at rest.

For there is nothing brisker than his life
when in motion . . .

For God has blessed him in the variety of
his movements . . .

For he can tread to all the measures upon
    the music . . .

– Christopher Smart

INTRODUCTION

In the Hour before time began, Meerclar Allmother came out of the darkness to the cold earth. She was black, and as furry as all the world come together to be fur. Meerclar banished the eternal night, and brought forth the Two.

Harar Goldeneye had eyes as hot and bright as the sun at the Hour of Smaller Shadows; he was the color of daytime, and courage, and dancing.

Fela Skydancer, his mate, was beautiful, like freedom, and clouds, and the song of travelers returned.

Goldeneye and Skydancer bore many children and raised them in the forest that covered the world at the beginnings of the Elder Days. Climbfast, Wolffriend, Treesinger, and Brightnail, their young, were strong of tooth, sharp of eye, light of foot and straight and brave to their tail-ends.

But most strange and beautiful of all the countless children of Harar and Fela were the three Firstborn.

The eldest of the Firstborn was Viror Whitewind; he was the color of sunlight on snow, and of swiftness . . .

The middle child was Grizraz Hearteater, as gray as shadows and full of strangeness . . .

Third-born was Tangaloor Firefoot. He was as black as Meerclar Allmother, but his paws were red like flame. He walked alone, and sang to himself.

There was rivalry among the Firstborn brothers. Whitewind was as fast and strong as a cat could dream of being – none could overmatch him at jumping and running. Firefoot was as clever as time; he solved all puzzles and riddles, and made songs that the Folk sang for generations.

Hearteater could not match his brothers' exploits. He grew jealous, and began to plot the downfall of Whitewind and the humiliation of the Folk.

So it came to pass that Hearteater raised up a great beast against the Folk. Ptomalkum was its name, and it was the last spawn of the demon-hound Venris, whom Meerclar had destroyed in the Days of Fire. Ptomalkum, raised and nurtured with Hearteater's hatred, slew many Folk before it was itself slain by the gallant Whitewind. But Viror Whitewind received such wounds that he soon wasted and died.

Seeing the downfall of his schemes, Hearteater was afraid, and crept down a hole and disappeared into the secretive earth.

There was great lamentation in the Court of Harar at the death of Whitewind, the best-beloved.

Firefoot his brother fled the Court in heartache, renouncing his claim to the Mantle of Kingship, and wandered the world.

Fela Skydancer, Whitewind's mother, was ever after silent, all her long life.

But Harar Goldeneye was so full of rage that he wept, and swore great oaths. He went howling into the wilderness, destroying all before him in his search for the traitorous Hearteater. Finally, unable to bear such great pain, he fled to the bosom of the Allmother in the sky. There he still lives, chasing the bright mouse of the sun across the heavens. Often he looks down to earth below, hoping to see Viror running once more beneath the trees of the World-Forest.

Countless seasons turned and the world grew older before Firefoot again met his treacherous brother Hearteater.

In the days of Prince Cleanwhisker, in the reign of Queen Morningstripe, Lord Tangaloor came to the assistance of the Ruhuë, the owlfolk. A mysterious creature had been pillaging their nests, and had killed all the Ruhu hunters who had come against it.

Firefoot laid a trap, clawing away at a mighty tree until it was near cut through, then lay in wait for the marauder.

When the creature came that night, and Firefoot felled the tree, he was astonished to discover that beneath it he had trapped Grizraz Hearteater.

Hearteater begged Firefoot to free him, promising that he would share the ancient lore that he had discovered beneath the ground. Lord Tangaloor only laughed.

When the sun came up, Hearteater began to scream. He writhed and screeched so that Firefoot, although fearing a trick, liberated his suffering brother from beneath the pinioning tree.

Hearteater had been so long beneath the earth that the sun was blinding him. He clawed and rubbed at his steaming eyes, howling so piteously that Firefoot looked about for a way to protect him from the burning of the day-star. But when he turned away, the blinded Hearteater dug himself a tunnel, more swiftly than any badger or mole. By the time the startled Firefoot bounded over, Hearteater had disappeared back into the belly of the world.

It is told that he still lives there, hidden from the eyes of the Folk; that he works foul deeds underground, and aches to return to the World Above. . . .

PART ONE

CHAPTER ONE

... make no mistake
We are not shy
We're very wide awake,
The moon and I!

               – W. S. Gilbert

The Hour of Unfolding Dark had begun, and the rooftop where Tailchaser lay was smothered in shadow.

He was deep in a dream of leaping and flying when he felt an unusual tingling in his whiskers. Fritti Tailchaser, hunterchild of the Folk, came suddenly awake and sniffed the air. Ears pricked and whiskers flared straight, he sifted the evening breeze. Nothing unusual. Then what had awakened him? Pondering, he splayed his claws and began a spine-limbering stretch that finally ended at the tip of his reddish tail.

By the time he had finished grooming, the sense of danger was gone. Perhaps it had been a night bird passing overhead . . . or a dog in the field beneath . . . perhaps . . .

Perhaps I am becoming a kitten again, Fritti thought to himself, *who bolts in fright from falling leaves.*

The wind ruffled his newly groomed fur. Piqued, he leaped down from the roof into the tall grasses below. First he must attend to hunger. Later it would be time to go to the Meeting Wall.

Unfolding Dark was waning, and Tailchaser's belly was still empty. His luck had not been dancing.

He had held motionless, patient watch at the entrance to a gopher hole. When an eternity of near-silent breathing had passed, and the inhabitant of the burrow had still not presented himself, Tailchaser had given up in frustration. After pawing in annoyance at the hole mouth he had gone in search of other game.

Luck had been completely absent. Even a moth had eluded his pouncing attack, to fly spiraling up into darkness.

If I can't catch something soon, he worried, *I shall have to go back and eat from the bowl that the Big Ones put out for me. Harar! What kind of hunter am I?*

A faint wisp of scent brought Tailchaser to an abrupt halt. Absolutely motionless, all senses straining, he crouched and sniffed. It was a Squeaker – downwind, and very close.

He moved as delicately as a shadow, carefully picking his way through the undergrowth, then froze again. There!

A jump and a half before him sat the mre'az he had scented. It squatted, unaware of Tailchaser, and pushed seeds into its cheek – nose twitching nervously, eyes rapidly blinking.

Fritti lowered himself to the ground, his upraised tail lashing back and forth behind him. Hunkered, he drew himself up on his hind legs and poised for the strike – unmoving, muscles tensed. He leaped.

He had misjudged the distance. As he landed short, paws flailing, the Squeaker had just enough time to give a chirp of terror and then drop – *floop!* – into its hole.

Standing over the escape route, Fritti bit his own foot with embarrassment.

As Tailchaser licked the last scraps from the bowl, Thinbone bounded onto the porch. Thinbone was a wild tabby, gray-and-yellow patchwork, who lived in a culvert across the field. He was a little older than Fritti, and made much of it.

'Nre'fa-o, Tailchaser.' Thinbone leaned over and sharpened his claws lazily on a wooden pillar. 'Looks like you're being fed well tonight. Tell me, do the Big Ones make you do tricks for your supper? I've often wondered how it worked, you understand.' Fritti pretended to ignore him, and began cleaning his whiskers.

'I notice,' Thinbone continued, 'that the Growlers seem to have some sort of arrangement: they carry things for the Big Ones, and leap around a great deal, and bark all night for their dinner. Is that what you do?' Thinbone stretched nonchalantly. 'I'm just curious, you understand. Some night – oh, I admit it's not likely – some night I might be unable to catch dinner, and it would be nice to have something to fall back on. Is barking very difficult?'

'Be quiet, Thinbone.' Fritti snarled, then gave a sneeze of laughter and leaped on his friend. They wrestled for a moment, then broke apart, batting at each other with their paws. Finally, tired out, they sat for a moment reordering their fur.

When they had rested, Thinbone sprang away from the porch and bounded into the darkness. Fritti put one last patch along his flank straight, then followed him.

The Hour of Deepest Quiet was just starting, and Meerclar's Eye was high in the sky above, remote and unblinking.

The wind shivered the leaves on the trees as Tailchaser and Thinbone made their way across fields and over fences – pausing to listen to night sounds, then galloping across wet, glimmering lawns. As they came under the eaves of the Old Woods that flanked the dwellings of the Big Ones, they could smell the fresh scents of others of their kind.

Over the top of the rise and past a stand of massive oak trees lay the entrance to the canyon. Tailchaser thought happily to himself of the songs and stories that would be shared by the crumbling Meeting Wall. He thought also of Hushpad, whose slim gray form and arching, slender tail had been on his mind almost constantly of late. It was fine to be alive and of the Folk on Meeting Night.

Meerclar's Eye cast a mother-of-pearl light on the clearing. Twenty-five or thirty cats were assembled at the base of the Wall – rubbing against each other in greeting, sniffing the nose of a new acquaintance. There was much mock fighting among the younger Folk.

Tailchaser and Thinbone were greeted by a gang of young hunters who stood casually about on the edge of the throng.

'Great you're here!' cried Fleetpaw, a young fellow with thick black-and-white fur. 'We're just about to have a game of Hop-in-the-Air – until the elders arrive, that is.'

Thinbone jogged over to join, but Fritti lowered his head politely and moved toward the crowd to look for Hushpad. He could not locate her scent as he slid through the milling group of cats.

A pair of young felas, barely out of kittenhood, wrinkled their noses at him flirtatiously, then ran away, sneezing merriment. Ignoring them, he bowed his head respectfully as he passed Stretchslow. The older male, who lay majestically prone at the base of the Wall, dignified him with a lazy blink of his huge green eyes and a desultory ear-wiggle.

Still no Hushpad, thought Fritti. *Where can she be?* Nobody missed a Meeting Night if he could help it. Meetings were only on those nights when the Eye was completely open and at its brightest.

Perhaps she will come later, he thought. Or perhaps even now she was walking with Jumptall or Leafrustle – extending her tail languidly for them to admire. . . .

The thought made him angry. He turned and cuffed a juvenile tom who had been prancing and capering at his heels. It was young Pouncequick, who gave him such a look of dismay that Fritti immediately felt sorry he had done it – the rambunctious kitten was often a nuisance, but well-meaning.

'I'm sorry, Pouncequick,' he said, 'I didn't know it was you. I thought it was old Stretchslow, and I was going to teach him a lesson.'

'Really?' gasped the young one. 'You would have done that to him?' Fritti regretted his joke. Stretchslow would not find it very funny.

'Well, anyway,' he said, 'it was a mistake, and I apologize.'

Pouncequick was charmed at being treated as an adult. 'I certainly will accept your apology, Tailchaser,' he said gravely. 'It was an understandable mistake.'

Fritti snorted. Giving the young cat a playful bite on the flank, he continued on his way.

Halfway through Deepest Quiet the Meeting was well under way, and Hushpad had still not made an appearance. While one of the Elders regaled the assembled multitude – now swollen to almost sixty – Tailchaser sought Thinbone, who was sitting with Fleetpaw and the others. The Elder was describing a large and potentially dangerous Growler who was running wild in the area, and Thinbone and the other hunters were listening intently as Fritti approached.

'Thinbone!' he hissed. 'Will you come over and talk to me for a moment?' Thinbone yawned and stretched before ambling over to Fritti's tree-root perch.

'What is it, then?' he inquired amiably. 'Is it time for my barking lessons?'

'Please, Thinbone, no games. I can't find Hushpad anywhere. Do you know where she is?'

Thinbone considered Tailchaser as the Elder droned on. 'So,' he said. 'I thought you seemed a little preoccupied. All this over a fela?'

'We were doing the Dance of Acceptance last night!' said Fritti, stung. 'We didn't have a chance to finish before the sun came up. We were going to finish tonight. I know she was going to accept me! What could have made her miss the Meeting?'

Thinbone lowered his ears in mock terror. 'An interrupted Dance of Acceptance! Skydancer's Whiskers! I think I see your fur falling out already! And your tail is going limp!'

Fritti shook his head impatiently. 'I know you think it's funny, Thinbone, and with your string of tail-waving females you don't care about a real Joining. But I do, and I'm worried about Hushpad. Please help me.'

Thinbone looked at him for a moment, blinking his eyes and scratching behind his right ear.

'All right, Tailchaser,' he said, simply. 'What can I do?'

'Well, I suppose there's not much we can do tonight, but if I can't find her tomorrow could you perhaps come out and have a look around with me?'

'I suppose so,' replied Thinbone, 'but I think that a little patience will probably – ouch!'

Fleetpaw had come up from below and butted his flat head against Thinbone's haunches.

'Come now!' Fleetpaw cried. 'What is all this deep discussion? Bristlejaw's going to tell a story, and here you sit like two fat eunuchs!'

Tailchaser and Thinbone bounced down after their friend. Felas were felas, but a story was nothing to sniff at!

The Folk squeezed closer around the Meeting Wall – an ocean of waving tails. Slowly, and with immense dignity, Bristlejaw mounted a crumbled section of the wall. At the highest point he paused and waited.

Having seen some eleven or twelve summers, Bristlejaw was certainly no longer a young cat, but iron control was in all his movements. His tortoiseshell fur, once brilliant with patches of rust and black, had dulled somewhat with age, and the stiff fur jutting from around his muzzle had gone gray-white. His eyes were bright and clear, though, and could bring a sporting kitten to a halt from three jumps away.

Bristlejaw was an Oel-cir'va: a Master Old-singer, one of the keepers of the Lore of the Folk. All the history of the Folk was in their songs – passed on in the Higher Singing of the Elder Days from one generation to another as a sacred trust. Bristlejaw was the only Old-singer within some distance of the Meeting Wall, and his stories were as important to his Folk as water, or the freedom to run and jump as they pleased.

From his position atop the Wall he surveyed the cats below for a long time. The expectant murmurings quieted to soft purring. Some of the young cats – tremendously excited and unable to sit still –

began frantically grooming themselves. Bristlejaw flicked his tail three times, and there was silence.

'We thank our Elders, who watch over us.' he began. 'We praise Meerclar, whose Eye lights our hunting. We salute our quarry for making the chase sweet.'

'Thanks. Praise. Salutations.'

'We are the Folk, and tonight we speak in one voice of the deeds of all. We are the Folk.'

Caught up in the ancient ritual, the cats swayed gently from side to side. Bristlejaw began his story.

'In the days of the earth's youth – when some of the First were still seen in these fields – Queen Satinear, granddaughter of Fela Skydancer, ruled in the Court of Harar.

'And she was a good queen. Her paw was as just in aid of her Folk as her claw was swift to harm for her enemies.

'Her son and coregent was Prince Ninebirds. He was a huge cat, mighty in battle, swift to anger, and swollen in pride for all his youthful years. At his Naming the story had been told of how, as a kitten, he had slain a branchful of starlings with one blow of his claws. So Ninebirds he was Named, and the fame of his strength and his deeds stretched far.

'It had been many, many summers since the death of Whitewind, and none living in the Court at this time had ever seen any of the First. Firefoot had been wandering in the wild for generations, and many thought him dead, or gone to join his father and grandmother in the sky.

'As stories of Ninebirds' strength and bravery began to run from mouth to ear among the Folk, and as Ninebirds began to listen to those ignoble ones who always cling to the great Folk, he began to see in himself the greatness of the Firstborn.

'One day it was told throughout the World-Forest that Ninebirds was no longer content to be Prince Regent at his mother's side. A Meeting was declared to which all the Folk were to come from far and wide for feasting, hunting, and games, and at this meeting he would assume the Mantle of Harar – which Tangaloor Firefoot had declared sacrosanct but for the Firstborn – and Ninebirds would declare himself King of Cats.

'And so came the day, and all the Folk gathered at the Court. While all cavorted and danced and sang, Ninebirds sunned his great body and looked on. Then he stood, and spoke: "I, Ninebirds, by right of blood and claw, stand before you today to assume the Mantle

8

of Kingship, which has gone long unfilled. If no cat has any reason why I should not take upon myself this Ancient Burden . . . ''

'At that moment there was a noise in the crowd, and a very old cat stood up. His fur was shot all over with gray – especially about his legs and paws – and his muzzle was snow-white.

' "You assume the Mantle by right of blood and claw, Prince Nine-birds?" questioned the old cat. "I do," answered the great Prince. "By what right of blood do you claim the Kingship?" queried the old white-whisker. "By the blood of Fela Skydancer that runs in me, you toothless old Squeaker-friend!" rejoined Ninebirds hotly, and rose from where he lay. All the gathered Folk whispered excitely as Ninebirds walked to the Vaka'az'-me, the tree-root seat sacred to the Firstborn. Before all the assembled Folk Ninebirds lifted his long tail and sprayed the Vaka'az'-me with his hunt-mark. There was more excited whispering, and the old cat tottered forward.

' "O Prince, who would be King of Cats," said the ancient one, "perhaps by blood you have some claim, but what of claw? Will you fight in single combat for the Mantle?" "Of course," said Ninebirds, laughing, "and who will oppose me?" The crowd goggled, looking about for some mighty challenger who would fight with the massive Prince.

' "I will," said the old one simply. All the folk hissed in surprise and arched their backs, but Ninebirds only laughed again. "Go home, old fellow, and wrestle with beetles," said he. "I will not fight with you."

' "The King of Cats can be no coward," said the old cat. At that Ninebirds cried in anger and leaped forward, swinging his huge paw at the old gray-muzzle. But with surprising speed the old one leaped aside and dealt a buffet to the Prince's head that addled his wits for a moment. They began to fight in earnest, and the multitude could scarcely credit the speed and courage of the old cat, who opposed such a great and fierce fighter.

'After a long while they closed and wrestled together, and although the Prince bit at his neck, the old one brought up his hind claws and scratched, and Ninebirds' fur was scattered in the air. When they broke apart, Ninebirds was full of surprise that this lean elder could do him such harm.

' "You have lost much of your pelt, O Prince," said the old one. "Will you renounce your claim?" Angered, the Prince charged, and they fell again to fighting. The old one caught the Prince's tail between his teeth, and when the Prince tried to turn and rend his face, the elder pulled his tail from his body. The Folk hissed with astonishment and fear as Ninebirds wheeled bloodily around and faced the old cat once more, who was himself wounded and panting.

' "You have lost your fur and tail, O Prince. Will you not also yield your claim?" Maddened by pain, Ninebirds flung himself on the ancient one, and they wrestled – spitting and swiping, blood and tears glistening in the sun. At last the challenger wedged Prince Ninebirds' hindquarters beneath a root of the Vaka'az'-me.

'As the dirt settled, an excited shock ran through those watching – in the last battling, quantities of white dust had been knocked free from the coat of the challenger. His muzzle was no longer gray, and his paws and legs shone the color of flame. "You see me revealed, Ninebirds," he said. "I am Lord Tangaloor Firefoot, son of Harar, and it is by my command that there is no King of Cats."

' "You are a brave cat, O Prince," he continued, "but your insolence may not go unpunished." With that, Firefoot caught the scruff of the Prince's neck and pulled, stretching his body and legs until they were thrice as long as a cat's are meant to be. He then pulled the Prince loose from the tree root and said: "Tailless and hairless, long and ungainly have I made you. Go now, and come never more to the Court of Harar, you who would have usurped his power. But this doom I lay on you: that you shall serve any member of the Folk who commands you, and so shall all of your descendants, until I release your line from this bane."

'And with that Lord Tangaloor went away. The Folk drove the misformed Ninebirds from their midst, calling him M'an – meaning "out of the sunshine" – and he and all of his descendants went ever after on their hind legs, and do today, for M'an's forelegs have been stretched too far away to touch the ground.

'Ninebirds the usurper, punished by the Firstborn, was the first of the Big Ones. They have long served the Folk, making us shelter from the rain and feeding us when the hunt is bad. And if some of us now serve the disgraced M'an, that is another story, for another Meeting.

'We are the Folk, and tonight we speak in one voice of the deeds of all. We are the Folk.'

His song finished, Bristlejaw leaped down from the Wall with a strength belying his many summers. All the assembled Folk respectfully bowed their heads down between their forepaws as he left.

The Hour of Final Dancing was drawing to a close, and the Meeting broke up into small groups – the cats saying their farewells, discussing the Song and gossiping. Tailchaser and Thinbone hung on for a while, discussing plans for the next evening with Fleetpaw and some of the other young hunters, then took their leave.

As they frisked back across the fields they stumbled on a mole stranded away from its burrow. After they chased it a bit, Thinbone broke its neck and they ate. Bellies full, they parted at Fritti's porch.

'Mri'fa-o, Tailchaser.' said Thinbone. 'If you need my help tomorrow I'll be in Edge Copse at Unfolding Dark.'

'Good dreaming to you, also, Thinbone. You are a good friend.'

Thinbone gave a flick of his tail and was gone. Fritti hopped into the box left for him by the Big Ones, and sank into the sleep-world.

CHAPTER TWO

It is the Vague and Elusive.
Meet it and you will not see its head.
Follow it and you will not see its back.

– Lao-tzu

Fritti Tailchaser had been born the second youngest of a litter of five. When his mother, Indez Grassnestle, had first sniffed him, and licked the moisture from his newborn pelt, she sensed in him a difference – a subtle shading that she could not name. His blind infant eyes and questing mouth were somehow more insistent than those of his brothers and sisters. As she cleaned him she felt a tickle in her whiskers, an intimation of things unseen.

Perhaps he will be a great hunter, she thought.

His father, Brindleside, was certainly a handsome, healthy cat – there had even been a whiff of the Elder Days about him, especially when he had sung the Ritual with her on that winter night.

But Brindleside was gone now – following his nose toward some obscure desire – and she, of course, was left to raise his progeny alone.

As Fritti grew, she lost touch with her early perceptions. Familiarity and the hard day-to-day business of raising a litter blunted many of Grassnestle's subtler sensitivities.

Although Fritti was a bright and friendly kitten, clever and quick-learning, he never fulfilled in size the promise of his hunter-father. By the time that the Eye had opened above him three times he was still no larger than his older sister Tirya, and considerably smaller than either of his two brothers. His short fur had darkened from the original cream to apricot-orange, except for white bands on his legs and tail, and a small, milky star shape on his forehead.

Not large, but swift and agile – conceding some kitten clumsiness – Fritti danced through his first season of life. He frolicked with his siblings, chased bugs and leaves and other small moving things, and mustered his green patience to learn the exacting lore of hunting that Indez Grassnestle taught to her children.

Although the family's nest was in a heap of wood and rubble behind one of the massive dwellings of the Big Ones, many days Fritti's mother would take the kittens out past the outskirts of the M'an-nests and into the open countryside – wood lore was quite as important as city lore to the children of the Folk. Their survival depended on their being smarter, faster and quieter, wherever they found themselves.

Forth from the nest Grassnestle would go, her young forming a straggling, cavorting scout party about her. With the patience passed down through countless generations, she taught her ragged crew the fundamentals of survival: the sudden freeze, the startling leap, true-smelling, clear-seeing, quick-killing – all the hunting lore she knew. She taught, and showed, and tested; then patiently re-taught time and again until the lesson stuck.

Certainly her patience was often stretched thin, and occasionally a botched lesson would be punished by a brisk pawsmack to the offender's nose. Even a mother of the Folk had limits to her restraint.

Of all Grassnestle's kittens, Fritti loved learning most. Inattention, however, sometimes gained him a smarting nose – especially when the family went out into the fields and woods. The tempting whistles and chirps of the fla-fa'az and the swarming, evocative scents of the countryside could set him daydreaming in a moment, singing to himself of treetops and wind in his fur. These reveries were frequently interrupted by his mother's brisk paw on his snout. She had learned to recognize that faraway look.

The dividing line between waking and dreaming was a fine one among the Folk. Although they knew that dream-Squeakers did not satisfy waking hunger, and that dream-fights left no wounds, still there was nourishment and release in dreams unavailable in the waking world. The Folk depended so much on the near-intangible – senses, hunches, feelings and impulses – and these contrasted so strongly with the rock-solid basics of survival needs that one supported the other in an inseparable whole.

All the Folk had exceedingly keen senses – they lived and died by them. Only a few, though, grew to become Oel-var'iz – Far-sensers – who developed their acuteness and sensitivity far beyond even the high median of the Folk.

Fritti was a great dreamer, and for a while his mother harbored the idea that perhaps he had this gift of Far-sensing. He showed occasional flashes of surprising depth: once he hissed his eldest brother down from a tall tree, and a moment later the branch on which his brother had stood broke loose and fell to the ground. There were other hints of this deeper Var, but as time went on, and he began to grow out of kittenhood, the incidents became fewer. He became more prone to distraction – more of a daydreamer and less of a dream-reader. His mother decided that she had been mistaken, and as the time of Fritti's Naming grew closer she forgot it entirely. The life of the hunting mother did not permit brooding over abstractions.

At the first Meeting after their third Eye, young cats were brought to be Named. The Naming was a ceremony of great importance.

It was sung among the Folk that all cats had three names: the heart name, the face name, and the tail name.

The heart name was given by the mother at the kitten's birth. It was a name of the ancient tongue of the cats, the Higher Singing. It was only to be shared with siblings, heart-friends and those who joined in the Ritual. Fritti was such a name.

The face name was given by the Elders at the young one's first Meeting, a name in the mutual language of all warmblooded creatures, the Common Singing. It could be used anywhere a name was useful.

As for the tail name, most of the Folk maintained that all cats were born with one; it was merely a matter of discovering it. Discovery was a very personal thing – once effected it was never discussed or shared with anyone.

It was certain, at least, that some Folk never discovered their tail name, and died knowing only the other two. Many said that a cat who had lived with the Big Ones – with M'an – lost all desire to find it, and grew fat in ignorance. So important, secret and rare were the Folk's tail names, and so hesitantly discussed, that nothing much about them was actually agreed upon. One either discovered this name or did not, said the Elders, and there was no way to force the matter.

On the night of the Naming, Fritti and his littermates were led by their mother to the special Nose-meet of the Elders that preceded the Meeting. For the first time Fritti saw Bristlejaw the Oel-cir'va, and

14

old Snifflick, and the other wise Folk who protected the laws and traditions.

Fritti and his siblings, as well as the litter of another fela, were herded into a circle. They lay hunched against each other as the Elders walked slowly around them – sniffing the air and sounding a deep rumble that had the cadence of an unknown language. Snifflick leaned down and put his nose against Tirya, Fritti's sister, and brought her to her paws. He stared at her a moment, then said: 'I name you Clearsong. Join the Meeting.' She rushed away to share her new name, and the Elders continued. One by one they pulled the other young out of the pile where they lay breathing shallowly with expectation and Named them. Finally there was only Fritti left. The Elders stopped their circling and sniffed him carefully. Bristlejaw turned to the others.

'Do you smell it, too?'

Snifflick nodded. 'Yes. The wide water. The places underground. A strange sign.'

Another Elder, a battered blue named Earpoint, scuffed the earth impatiently. 'Not important. We're here for a Naming.'

'True,' Bristlejaw agreed. 'Well . . . ? I smell searching.'

'I smell a struggle with dreams.' This from Snifflick.

'I think he desires his tail name before he has even received his face name!' said another Elder, and they all sneezed quietly with humor.

'Very well!' said Snifflick, and all eyes turned to Fritti. 'I name you . . . Tailchaser. Join the Meeting.'

Bewildered, Fritti leaped up and trotted rapidly away from the Nose-meet, away from the chuckling Elders who seemed to share a joke at his expense. Bristlejaw called sharply after him.

'Fritti Tailchaser!'

He turned and met the Master Old-singer's gaze. Despite the merriment wrinkling his nose, his eyes were warm and kind.

'Tailchaser. All things in earth's season – only given time. Remember that, won't you?'

Fritti flattened his ears and turned and ran to the Meeting.

The waning days of spring brought hot weather, long trips into the countryside – and Tailchaser's first meeting with Hushpad.

As he drew closer to his maturity the daily company of his brothers and sisters became less important to Fritti. Each day the sun was longer in the sky, and the scents carried by the drowsy wind grew sweeter and stronger. So, increasingly, he was drawn on solitary rambles outside the range of dwellings among which his family lived and slept. During the hottest parts of the Hour of Smaller Shadows – his hunger blunted by his morning meal, his natural curiosity freed – he would range through the grasslands like his brethren of the savannahs, holding imaginary sway over all before him as he stood on a hillside, grass stems tickling his belly.

The deeps of the woods also lured him. He delved at bases of trees for the secrets of scurrying beetles, and tried the strength of outer branches, feeling the intriguing breezes of the upper air swirl through the sensitive hairs of his face and ears.

One day, after an afternoon of intoxicating freedom and exploration, Tailchaser emerged from the low scrub that girdled his woods and stopped to pull a twig loose from his tail. As he sat splay-legged, pulling at the bit of branch with his teeth, he heard a voice.

'Nre'fa-o, stranger. Might you be Tailchaser?'

Alarmed, Fritti leaped to his feet and whirled around. A fela, gray with black striping, sat regarding him from the stump of a long-dead oak. He had been so wrapped in his thoughts that he had not noticed her as he passed, though she perched a mere four or five jumps away.

'Good dancing, Mistress. How do you know my name? I'm afraid I don't know yours.' The bramble in his tail hanging forgotten, Fritti observed the stranger carefully. She was young – seemingly no older than he. She had tiny, slim paws and a softly rounded body.

'There is no great mystery regarding either name,' said the fela with an amused expression. 'Mine is Hushpad, and has been since my Naming. As to yours, well, I have seen you from a distance at a Meeting, and you have been mentioned for your love of rambling and exploring – and here I have caught you at it!' She sneezed delicately.

Her attractive green eyes turned away; Tailchaser noticed her tail, which she held coiled around her as she spoke. Now it rose, as if of its own volition, and waved languorously in the air. It was long and slender, ending in a tender point, and ringed from base to tip with the same black accents as her sides and haunches.

This tail – whose lazy beckoning instantly captured Fritti's admiration – was to lead him into more troubles than even his own bounding imagination could conceive.

The pair romped and talked all through the Hour of Unfolding Dark. Tailchaser found himself opening his heart to his newfound friend, and even he was surprised at what spilled out: dreams, hopes, ambitions – all mixed together and hardly differentiated from each other. And always Hushpad listened and nodded, as if he spoke the dearest kind of truth.

When he parted from her at Final Dancing, he made her promise to meet him again the next day. She said she would, and he ran all the way home leaping with delight – arriving at the nest so excited that he woke his sleeping brothers and sisters and alarmed his mother. But when she heard what it was that made him squirm and tickle so that he could not sleep, his mother only smiled and pulled him to her with a gentle paw. She licked behind his ear and purred, 'Of course, of course . . . ' to him over and over until he finally crossed into the dream-world.

Despite his apprehensions of the following afternoon – which seemed to pass as slowly as snowmelt – Hushpad was indeed there to meet him when the Eye first appeared over the horizon. She came the day after, too . . . and the one after that. Through all of high summer they ran together, and danced and played. Friends watched them and said that this was no mere attraction, to be consummated and then ended when the young fela finally came into her season. Fritti and Hushpad seemed to have found a deeper congruency, which might ripen later into a Joining – a thing rarely seen, especially among the younger Folk.

Tailchaser was picking his way through the litter of the dwellings of the Big Ones, in the fragmented darkness of Final Dancing. He had spent the night roaming the woods with Hushpad, and as usual his thoughts lingered with the young fela.

He was struggling with something, but did not know what it was. He cared for Hushpad – more than for any of his friends, or even his siblings – but her companionship was somehow different from the others': the sight of her tail twining delicately behind her as she sat, or held delicately upright when she walked, tickled a part of his imaginings he could not put a name to.

Deep in these deliberations, for a long while he did not heed the message that the wind carried. When the fear-smell finally reached his pondering, puzzling mind he started with sudden alarm and shook his head from side to side. His whiskers were tingling.

He leaped forward, galloping toward home, toward his nest. He seemed to hear terror-cries of the Folk, but the air was still and quiet.

He clambered across the last rooftop, down a fence with a scratch and bump – and stopped short in amazement and fear.

Where the pile of rubble that had been his family's nest had stood . . . there was nothing. The spot was swept as clean as wind-scoured rock. When he had left his family that morning his mother had been standing atop the heap, grooming his youngest sister, Soft-whisker. Now they were all gone.

He darted forward and fell to scratching at the mute ground, as if to unearth some secret of what had happened, but it was M'an-ground, and could not be broken by claw or tooth. His mind felt blurry with conflicting passions. He whimpered, and sniffed at the air.

The atmosphere was full of cold traces of fear. The smells of his family and nesting place still hung, but they were overlaid with the awful scents of fright and anger. Although the impressions were much jumbled by the action of time and winds, he could also sense who had done this thing.

M'an had been here. The Big Ones had lingered for a long time, but had themselves left no mark of fear or anger. Their reek, as always, was nearly indecipherable of meaning – more like the busy ants and borer beetles than like the Folk. Here his mother had fought them to the end to protect her young, but the Big Ones had felt no anger, no fear. And now his family was gone.

In the next days he found no trace of them, as he had feared he would not. He fled to the Old Woods and lived there alone. Eating only what he could catch with his still-clumsy paws, he grew thin and weak, but he would not come to the nests of other Folk. Thinbone and other friends occasionally brought him food, but could not persuade him to return. The elders sniffed sagely and kept their peace. They knew wounds of this type were best nursed in solitude, where the decision to live or die was freely made, and not regretted later.

Fritti did not see Hushpad at all, for she did not come to visit him in his wild state – whether out of sorrow for his situation or indifference he did not know. He tortured himself with imagined reasons when he could not sleep.

One day, almost an opening and closing of the Eye since he had lost his family, Tailchaser found himself on the outskirts of the dwellings of M'an. Sick and debilitated, he had wandered out of the protection of the forest in a kind of daze.

As he lay breathing raggedly in a patch of welcome sunlight, he heard the sound of heavy footfalls. His dimmed senses announced the approach of M'an.

The Big Ones drew near, and he heard them cry to each other in their deep, booming voices. He closed his eyes. If it was fated that he should join his family in death, it seemed appropriate that these creatures complete the job that their kind had begun. As he felt large hands grasp him, and the smell of the M'an became all-pervading, he began to pass over – whether to the dream-world or beyond, he did not know. Then he knew nothing at all.

Slowly, cautiously, Tailchaser's spirit flew back to familiar fields. As thought came back he could feel a soft surface beneath him, and the M'an smell still all about. Frightened, he opened his eyes and stared wildly about.

He was on a piece of soft fabric, at the bottom of a container. It gave him a trapped, terrified feeling. Pulling himself onto his unsteady paws, he tried to climb out. He was too weak to jump, but after several attempts he managed to get his forepaws over the edge of the container and scramble out.

On the floor below he looked around, and found himself standing in an open, roofed-over area attached to one of the dwellings of the Big Ones. Although the smell of M'an was everywhere there were none in sight.

He was about to hobble away to freedom when he felt a powerful urge: hunger. He smelled food. Casting his eye about the porch, he saw another, smaller container. The food smell was making his mouth water, but he approached it cautiously. After sniffing the contents suspiciously, he took a tentative bite – and found it very good.

At first he kept an ear cocked for the return of the M'an, but after a while abandoned himself completely to the pleasure of eating. He bolted down the food, cleaning the container to the bottom, then found another full of clear water and drank. This gorging on top of his enfeebled state almost made him sick, but the Big Ones who had put the meal down, perhaps foreseeing this, had provided only modest amounts.

After he drank he wobbled out into the sunlight and rested for a moment, then rose to make his way up to the forest. Suddenly, one of his captors walked around the corner of the bulky M'an-nest. Fritti wanted to bolt, but his body's fragile health would not permit it. To his amazement, however, the Big One did not seize him, or kill him where he stood. The M'an merely passed by, leaning to stroke the top of Tailchaser's head, and then was gone.

So began the uneasy truce between Fritti Tailchaser and the Big Ones. These M'an, on whose porch he had found himself, never hindered his coming or going. They put out food for him to take if he wished, and left the box for him to sleep in if he so desired.

After much hard thought, Fritti decided that perhaps the Big Ones were a little like the Folk: some were good, and meant no idle harm, while some were not – and it was this second kind that had brought ruin to his family and his birthing-place. He found a kind of peace in this balance; thoughts of his loss began to recede from his waking Hours – if not from his dreams.

As health came back to him, Fritti once more found pleasure in the society of the Folk. He found Hushpad also, unchanged in whisker or tail. She asked him to pardon her for not visiting him during his upset days in the woods. She said she would not have been able to bear the sight of her playfellow in such distress.

Pardon her he did, and happily. With his strength returned, they once more ran together in the countryside. All was as it had been, except that Tailchaser was more given to silences, and a little less to happy chattering.

Still, his time with Hushpad was now even more precious to Fritti. They talked now, from time to time, about the Ritual that they would enter when Hushpad came to her season, and Tailchaser became a hunter.

And so their high summer waned, and the wind began to sing autumn music in the treetops.

On the last night before Meeting Night, Fritti and Hushpad climbed the hillside overlooking the M'an-dwellings. They sat silently in the dark of Deepest Quiet for a long while as the lights below flickered out one by one. Finally, Tailchaser raised his young voice in song.

> 'So high
> Above the waving treetops,
> Above the teeming sky –
> We speak a Word
>
> Side by side
> Upon the rugged world-back,
> Beyond the sun and tide –
> This voice is heard. . . .
>
> We are traveling together
> With our tails in the wind

20

We are voyaging together,
We are sun-redeemed and warm.

Long now
We have danced within the forest.
Looking only straight ahead –
Lacking but the Word.

Soon, though,
We will understand the meaning
In our whiskers and our bones –
Now that we have heard. . . . '

When Tailchaser finished his song they again sat quietly throughout the remaining Hours of the night. The morning sun rose to scatter the shadows and interrupt them, but when he turned to rub Hush-pad's nose in farewell, an unspoken promise hung between their commingling whiskers.

CHAPTER THREE

They who dream by day are cognizant of many things
which escape those who dream only by night.

> – Edgar Allan Poe

The morning after Meeting Fritti awoke from a strange dream, in
which Prince Ninebirds of Bristlejaw's song had taken Hushpad and
was running away with her in his great mouth. When Fritti's dream-
self had tried to pull her free, Ninebirds had seized him and given a
savage yank. He had felt his dream-form painfully stretching, stretching, becoming as thin and attenuated as smoke . . .

Shaking himself all over, as if to scatter the dismaying fantasy,
Tailchaser rose and performed his early-morning grooming – smooth-
ing down the sleep-ruffled fur all along his body, coaxing errant
whiskers into place, and ending with a fillip that put his tail tip in
perfect order.

Walking through the tall grass behind his sleeping porch, he could
not shed the sense of foreboding that his dream had cast over the
day. It seemed important, for some reason he could not remember.
He should not – and could not – forget the dream. Why?

Practicing paw swipes at an accommodatingly bouncy dandelion,
he remembered. Hushpad! She had not been at the Meeting. He
must go and look for her, discover what had happened.

He felt a little less apprehensive than he had the previous night.
After all, he decided, there were many possible reasons for her
absence. She did live in a M'an-dwelling; they might have closed her
in, prevented her leaving. Big Ones were capricious that way.

Tailchaser made his way across the field of grass and through a
copse of low trees as he skirted the Old Woods. It was some distance

22

to where Hushpad lived, and the journey took him a good part of the morning. At last he came in sight of the M'an-nest, standing by itself in the solitude of surrounding fields. It looked strangely empty, and as he approached he could find no trace of familiar smells.

Calling, 'Hushpad! Tailchaser here! Nre'fa-o, heartfriend!' he jogged closer, but was met with silence. He noticed the entrance hanging open, as was not usual in the nests of M'an. Reaching the dwelling, he cautiously poked his head inside, then entered.

Not only was the M'an-dwelling empty of life, to Tailchaser it seemed empty of everything. The floors and walls were bare, and even his soft footfalls echoed as he moved from room to room. For a fearful moment the emptiness reminded him of the disappearance of his family – but something was different. There were no smells of terror or excitement; no trace of anything upsetting having occurred. Whatever reason the M'an had for leaving, it seemed a natural one. But where was Hushpad?

A top-to-bottom search revealed nothing but more empty rooms. Curious and puzzled, Fritti left the dwelling. He decided that Hushpad must have run away when the M'an left. Perhaps even now she was hiding in the forest, needing his company and friendship!

All that afternoon he roamed the wooded places, calling and hallooing, but could find no trace of his friend. When evening came he went to Thinbone for help, but the two of them had no more luck than Fritti alone. They ranged far and wide, and asked all the Folk they met for tidings, but none could help. In this way ended the first day of Tailchaser's search for the lost Hushpad.

Three more sunrises passed without any sign of the young fela. Fritti found it hard to believe that she would simply leave the area, but no trace of violence had been found, and the other Folk had not seen or heard anything out of the ordinary. Day in and day out he continued searching for her – tired, but with a terrible, relentless need. First his family and his birthingplace, now this.

Even Thinbone gave up after the third day.

'Tailchaser, I know it is a terrible thing,' his friend said, 'but sometimes Meerclar calls, and we go. You know that.' Thinbone looked down, searching for words. 'Hushpad has gone. That is that, I'm afraid.'

Fritti nodded his understanding, and Thinbone went off to join the other Folk. Tailchaser, however, did not plan to give up his search. He knew what Thinbone said to be true, but felt strongly – in a manner he did not fully understand – that Hushpad had not gone to Meerclar, but was living somewhere in the fields of earth, and needed his help.

A few days later Fritti was sniffing his way through a hedge of privet in which he and Hushpad had played many games of Roll-and-Pounce when he met Stretchslow.

The older hunter made less noise than the wind-tossed autumn leaves as he approached, his tawny body moving with confident economy. When he reached Fritti – terribly self-conscious in the presence of the mature male – Stretchslow stopped, sat back on his haunches and gave the young cat an appraising stare. Trying to bob his head respectfully, Tailchaser caught his nose on a privet twig and let out an embarrassed mew of pain. Stretchslow's cool observation softened into a look of amusement.

'Nre'fa-o, Stretchslow,' said Fritti. 'Are you . . . mmm . . . are you enjoying the sun today?' He ended with an awkward gesture, and since the day was quite gray and overcast he suddenly wished he had said nothing at all – perhaps even stayed underneath the privet bush.

Seeing the younger cat so discomfited, Stretchslow sneezed a laugh and sank to the ground. He reclined there lazily, head held high and his body appearing misleadingly relaxed.

'Good dancing to you, little one,' he responded, then paused for a magnificent yawn. 'I see you're still hunting about for what's-her-name . . . Squashpod, was it?'

'Huh-Hushpad. Yes, I'm still looking.'

'Well . . . ' The older male looked about for a bit, as if searching for a tiny, insignificant thing he might have dropped. Finally he said: 'Oh yes . . . that was it. Of course. You'll want to come to the Nose-meet tonight.'

'What?' Fritti was flabbergasted. Nose-meets were for elders and hunters, and were reserved for important business. 'Why should I go to the Nose-meet?' he gasped.

'Well . . . ' Stretchslow yawned again. 'From what I understand – though Harar knows I have better things to do than keep track of all the comings and goings of you youngsters – from what I gather, it seems there have been many disappearances since the last Meeting. Six or seven, including your little friend Peachpit.'

'Hushpad,' Fritti corrected him quietly – but Stretchslow was gone.

*

Above the Wall, Meerclar's Eye hung and gleamed, framing a sovereign wink against the black of the night.

'We have had this problem also, and some of the mothers are getting very worried. They aren't pleasant to be around at all, lately. Suspicious, you know.'

The speaker was Mudtracker, who lived with another colony of the Folk on the other side of Edge Copse. They had their own meetings, and seldom had more than passing contact with Fritti's clan.

'What I mean is,' continued Mudtracker, 'well, it isn't natural. I mean, we lose a couple of kittens every season, of course . . . and the occasional male who decides to move on without telling anyone. Fela troubles, usually, if you sniff my meaning. But we've seen three disappear in the past pawful of days. It's not natural.'

The visiting cat from the far side of the Copse sat down, and there was a rustle of low hisses and whispers among the gathered clan leaders.

Fritti's excitement at being at Nose-meet with the adults was beginning to fade. As he heard the stories that the others told of mysterious absences, and saw the way the sage, wise cats around him shook their heads and scratched their masks in puzzlement, he suddenly began to wonder if they would be any help at all in finding Hushpad. It had seemed to him that as soon as the older cats had acknowledged his problem, it could be solved – but look there! The brows and noses of the clan's protectors-of-tradition were wrinkled with worry. Tailchaser felt a sense of emptiness.

Jumptall, one of the youngest present – though older than Fritti by several seasons – stood to speak.

'My sister . . . my nest-sister Flickerswift had two of her kittens vanish just Eye-last. She is a watchful mother. They were playing at the base of that old sirzi tree at Forest's Edge, and she had turned for a moment because her youngest was having a difficult furball. When she turned around again they were gone. And no smell of owl or fox, either – she looked everywhere, as you can imagine. She's very upset.' Here Jumptall paused awkwardly, then sat down. Earpoint rose and looked around the gathering.

'Yes, well, if no one has any more of these . . . stories . . . ?'

Stretchslow raised a grudging paw. 'Pardon, Earpoint, I do believe . . . where is he . . . ah, yes, there he is. Young Tailchaser there has something to report. If it's not too much bother, I mean.' Stretchslow yawned, showing his sharp canines.

'Tailchewer?' said Earpoint irritably. 'What kind of name is that?'

Bristlejaw smiled at Fritti. 'It's Tailchaser, isn't it? Speak up, youngling, there you go.'

All eyes turned to Tailchaser as he rose.

'Um . . . well . . . um . . . ' A sickly expression made his whiskers droop. 'Well, you see . . . Hushpad, she's my friend, she's a . . . she, Hushpad is . . . well, she's disappeared.'

Old Snifflick leaned over and stared at him keenly. 'Did you see anything of what happened to her?'

'No . . . no, sir, but I think . . . '

'Right!' Earpoint leaned over and gave Fritti a brusque pawpat on the top of the head, nearly upsetting him. 'Right,' continued Earpoint, 'very good, yes, thank you, Tail . . . Tail . . . well, it was a most useful report, young fellow. Now, shall we get on with it?' Fritti sat down hastily and pretended to search for a flea. His nose felt hot.

Wavetail, another elder, cleared his throat – puncturing several moments of uncomfortable stillness – and asked: 'But what are we going to do?'

Another moment's pause, and then the gathered Folk all broke out at once.

'Alert the clans!'

'Post sentries!'

'Move away!'

'No more having kittens!'

This last was from Jumptall, who – seeing the others all staring at him – was suddenly plagued by Tailchaser's flea.

Old Snifflick climbed ponderously up onto his paws. He looked severely at Jumptall, then gazed around at the waiting Folk.

'First,' he growled, 'we had better begin by agreeing not to go yelling and leaping about in this manner. A chipmunk with a bumblebee in its tail would make less noise – and to more effect. Now, let's review the situation.' He stared impressively at the ground, as if mustering deep thought. 'First: an unusually large number of the Folk have gone missing. Second: we have no idea what or who may be causing this. Third: the best and the wisest cats from around our woods are here tonight at Nose-meet, and cannot solve the puzzle. Therefore . . . ' Snifflick paused to savor the effect. 'Therefore, although I agree that guards and such need to be discussed, I think it important that wiser minds than – yes, even ours – should be let to know of this situation. Baffling and affrighting as it is, we have no choice but to inform Certain Others about these events.

'I suggest we should send a delegation to the Court of Harar. It is our duty to inform the Queen of Cats!' Entirely pleased with himself, Snifflick sat down as consternation and surprise whirled about him.

'To the Court of Harar?' breathed Mudtracker. 'None of the Folk of Behind-Edge-Copse have been to the seat of the First for twenty generations!' There was more excited rumbling.

'Neither have the Folk from this side of the Woods,' said Bristlejaw, 'but I think Snifflick is right. We have heard these stories all night long, and no one has the slightest idea of what to do. This may be beyond us. I agree to a delegation.'

The crowd quieted for a moment; then two of the assembly blurted out at the same instant: 'Who will go?'

This started another uproar, and Earpoint had to shoot his claws and wave them around purposefully before things were quiet again. Snifflick spoke.

'Well, it will be quite a long and dangerous journey. I suppose that as I am Senior Elder my knowledge and wisdom will be needed. I will go.'

Before anyone could react to this, there was a sudden snarl from the back of the gathering, and Twitchnose was striding forward. She was Snifflick's mate, had borne innumerable litters by him, and she was a taker of no nonsense. She marched straight to Snifflick, and stared him in the eye: 'You aren't going anywhere, you old mouse-gummer. You think you're going to sail out into the wilderness and sing your horrible hunting songs all night while I sit here like a hedgehog?' she hissed. 'Think you're going to find some slender young fela at the Court, do you? By the time you mount her with those tired old bones she'll be as old as I am, so what's the difference? You old villain!'

Trying to save Snifflick, Bristlejaw quickly said: 'That's right, Snifflick! – I mean, you shouldn't go. The Folk here need your wisdom. No, a long journey of this kind calls for young cats, cats who can travel in the wintertime.' He looked around, and as his eye passed over Fritti the young cat felt a moment of impossible excitement. Bristlejaw's gaze moved on, though, and settled on Earpoint. The weathered old tom rose under the eye of the Master Old-singer, and stood, waiting.

'Earpoint, you have seen many summers,' said Bristlejaw, 'but you are still strong, and wise in the ways of the Outer Forest. Will you lead the delegation?' Earpoint inclined his head in assent. Bristlejaw then turned to Jumptall, who leaped to his feet and stood, seeming to hold his breath.

'You go also, young hunter,' spoke the lore-singer. 'Be aware of what an honor there is in your choice, and behave accordingly.' Jumptall nodded weakly and sat down.

Bristlejaw turned to Snifflick, who had been carrying on a near-silent thumping match with Twitchnose. 'Old friend, will you pick one more emissary?' he asked.

Snifflick returned his attention to the Nose-meet once more, and looked cannily around the circle. The assembled Folk held their breath as one while he deliberated. Finally he beckoned to Streamhopper, a youthful hunter of three summers. Tailchaser felt a pang of disappointment, although he knew he was too young to have had a chance. As Snifflick and Bristlejaw instructed Streamhopper on his great responsibility, Fritti felt a curious frustration gnaw at his heart.

When the three delegates were assembled, Earpoint stood forward to receive the message that they would carry to the ancient Court of Harar. Snifflick rose again.

'None here has traveled where you must go,' he began. 'We have no sure knowledge to guide you, but the songs that tell of the Court are known to all.

'If you are able to discharge this duty, and reach the Queen of the Folk, tell her that the elders of the Meeting Wall – this side of Edge Copse, under the eaves of the Old Wood, on the fringe of her domain – pledge their fealty, and ask for her help and guidance in this matter. Tell her that this plague of disappearance has visited not just the kittenry and questing males, but – Harar curse it – the entire tribe. Tell her we are bewildered, and can find no wisdom in this matter. If she will send a message, you are charged to bring it back with you.' He paused.

'Oh, yes. You are also hereby bound to help and aid your companions – up to, but not including, the failure of your charge . . . '

Here Snifflick halted again, and in a moment was once more the oldest cat of the Meeting Wall Folk. He looked at the ground for a moment, and scrabbled his paw in the dirt.

'We all hope that Meerclar will watch over you, and keep you safe,' he added. He did not look up. 'You may tell your families, but we wish you to leave as soon as possible.'

'May you find luck, dancing,' Bristlejaw said, then, after a moment: 'This Nose-meet is ended.'

Almost all the Folk who were present rose and pushed forward –

some to talk excitedly among themselves, others to get a last sniff or offer a last word to the three delegates.

Fritti Tailchaser was the only cat who did not stay for at least a moment with the brave delegation. He climbed away from the Wall buzzing with unfamiliar feelings.

At the lip of the hollow he stood scratching his claws through the rough bark of an elm tree, listening to the murmur of the crowding cats below.

Nobody at the Nose-meet cared about Hushpad, he thought. Nobody would remember her name when the delegates reached the Court. Stretchslow couldn't even remember it now! Hushpad didn't mean a jot more to any of them than the scruffiest old tom – yet he was supposed to wait patiently while Jumptall and the rest went parading off to the Court of the Queen, in the hope that she would solve the problem! Heavenly Viror, what nonsense!

Fritti growled, a noise that he had never made before, and ripped off another skein of bark. He turned and stared into the sky. Somewhere, he felt sure, Hushpad was staring up at the same Eye, and no one cared but him whether she was in danger or not. Well then!

Tailchaser felt hot determination as he stood on the hillside, head and tail arched. The orb of Meerclar hung above him like a shaming parent as he made an impassioned pledge:

'By the Tails of the Firstborn, I will find Hushpad, or my spirit will fly my dying body! One or the other!'

After a moment – when he realized what he had promised – Fritti began to shiver.

CHAPTER FOUR

And sings a solitary song
That whistles in the wind.

– William Wordsworth

Fritti was finding it more difficult than he had expected to leave his porch box and food bowl. The anger and frustration of the night before seemed less moving in the thin sunshine of Spreading Light – he was, after all, a very young cat, not yet a full-grown hunter. He was not really sure exactly where to begin a search for his lost companion, either.

Nosing the tattered fabric of his sleeping box, fabric that was full of familiar smells, he wondered if it might not be better to wait another day before setting out. Surely a little hunting and a frolic or two with some of the other younglings would help to clear his mind. Of course. It seemed more sensible somehow . . .

'Tailchaser! I heard all about your leave-taking! How astonishing of you! I am quite taken aback.' With a thump and skid, Thinbone leaped breathlessly onto the porch. He eyed Fritti with comical puzzlement. 'Do you really mean to do it?'

At that moment – though all his spirit pulled against it – he heard himself say: 'Of course, Thinbone. I must.'

Once he had spoken these strange words, he instantly felt as though he were rolling downhill. How could he stop himself now? How could he not go? What would the others think? Mighty Tailchaser, strutting about in front of the Wall, telling all who passed by about his quest. *Oh, to be older*, he thought – *and not so stupid!*

Surprising himself, he leaned forward and licked his paw with a calmness calculated to impress his friend. Part of him was fervently

30

hoping Thinbone would tell him not to go – maybe even come up with a good reason.

But Thinbone only grinned and said: 'Harar! Fleetpaw and I are very jealous. We'll miss you while you're gone.'

'I'll miss you all very much, also,' said Fritti, then turned his head away suddenly, as if to bite at fleas. After a moment's silence he looked back around. His friend was watching him with a strange expression on his face.

Another moment's silence, then Thinbone continued: 'Well, I suppose this is farewell, then. Fleetpaw and Beetleswat and all said to say an especial good luck from them. They would have come by, except there's a big game of Bob-Tag blowing up, and they have to hunt out some more Folk.'

'Oh?' said Fritti miserably. 'Bob-Tag? Well, I don't suppose I'll have much time for that sort of game for a while . . . never really liked it much, you know.'

Thinbone grinned again. 'I suppose you won't have the time, will you? What adventures you'll have!' Looking around, Thinbone scented the air. 'Did little Pouncequick ever come by?'

'No,' said Tailchaser. 'Why?'

'Oh, he was asking when you were leaving, and where from. Seemed quite concerned, so I supposed he was going to try to catch you and say good-journey. He looks up to you quite a lot, I think. Well, I suppose he's going to miss you.'

'Miss me?'

'Yes. Spreading Light has almost turned, and you wanted to leave before Smaller Shadows. Wasn't that right?'

'Oh yes. Certainly.' Tailchaser's legs felt as if they were made of stone. What he really wanted to do was crawl back into his box. 'I suppose it's time for me to be on my way . . . ' he said with lame cheeriness.

'I'll walk you to the edge of the field,' his friend replied.

As they walked – Thinbone bounding and chattering, Fritti plodding and scuffing – Tailchaser tried to remember and save each smell of his familiar grounds. He bade a silent and somewhat overblown goodbye to the shimmering field of grass, the tiny, nearly dry creek, and his favorite privet hedge. *I shall probably never see these fields again!* he thought, and: *They'll all probably forget me in a season or less.*

For a moment he felt very proud of himself for his bravery and sacrifice . . . but when they reached the end of the sea of waving grass, and he turned back and saw the faint shape of the M'an porch where his box and bowl sat, he felt such a burning in his nose and eyes that he had to sit for a moment and paw at his face.

'Well . . . ' Thinbone was suddenly a little awkward. 'Good hunting and good dancing, friend Tailchaser. I shall think of you till you return.'

'You are a good friend, Thinbone. Nre'fa-o.'

'Nre'fa-o.' And Thinbone was loping swiftly away.

Half a hundred steps into the Old Woods, and still in the comparatively sunny and airy outer reaches of the forest, Fritti already felt himself to be the loneliest cat in the world.

He did not know he was being followed.

As the sun rose to midday, Fritti continued into the forest depths. He had never been through it to the other side, but it seemed likely that a fleeing Hushpad would go that way – rather than closer to the dwellings of M'an.

Although the sun was high, his keen night vision stood him in good stead, since the trees grew thickly together in these parts. Passing through the thickets and undergrowth, he stared up in wonder at these trees of the inner forest, trunks curved and twisted, frozen into writhing shapes like the hlizza, whose bodies lashed on after they had been killed. Every now and then he stopped to test his claws on one that was unfamiliar to him: some had bark harder than M'an-ground, others were wet and spongy. Some of the larger ones he sprayed with his huntmark – more to reassert his own existence among these tangled branches and deep shadows than out of bravado.

Above, he could hear the songs of the different fla-fa'az that lived in the uttermost heights of the Old Woods. There was no other sound of life but the padding of his own near-silent paws.

Then, in a moment, even the birds were silent.

There was a single sharp rapping noise, and Tailchaser froze in his tracks. The sound echoed briefly, then faded, absorbed swiftly by the leafy clutter of the forest floor. Then, startlingly, came a rapid clatter of these noises – *tok! – tok-tok! tok-tok! . . . tok-t-t-tok!* – from high above him. The crescendo of knocks spread from tree to tree, passing from a point over his head to farther into the forest. Then silence fell again.

Apprehensively scenting the air, whiskers stiff, Fritti moved slowly forward, darting glances into the light-spotted reaches of the thick foliage above him.

He was cautiously stepping over a decomposing log when there was another sharp *tok!* – and a moment later he felt a stinging blow to the back of his head. He whirled, shooting his claws, but found nothing behind him.

Another sharp blow to his right foreleg spun him around again, and, turning, he felt a third harsh pain in his flank. Twirling about from side to side, unable to find the source of the painful blows, he was hit by a barrage of small, hard objects that struck him from above. Backing away – snarling in fear and discomfort – he met another fusillade, this one from behind.

Panicking, Fritti broke and ran, and immediately the loud rapping commenced again – from what seemed like all sides at once. The stinging missiles began to fly thick and fast. Trying to duck his head and protect his eyes as he scrambled away, he ran directly into the gnarled base of a live oak and tumbled to the loam, where he was immediately bombarded by the fiercest shower yet. As he cowered, he could see the missiles bouncing away – rocks and hard-shelled nuts. The pelting became too much for him once more. As if surrounded by stinging gnats, he crashed away into the undergrowth. When he tried to turn one way, a deluge of chestnuts and small stones would push him back – always in the same direction.

As he dove into the shelter of a bramble bush, he felt his paws come down astonishingly on unsolid air. Losing his balance, he toppled forward.

As he slid over the precipice – and caught a swift glimpse of a dry stream bed a fatal distance below – he twisted his body sharply, managing to catch the bramble bush and slow his headlong plunge. Grappling the prickling branches with all four legs now, and teeth and tail, he found himself dangling precariously over the drop – only the brambles between him and a long, long fall.

He hung for a moment, maddened with surprise and terror. *Tok! . . . tok-tok-a-tok!* – and another shower of nuts and stones hailed down on him. Fritti began to yowl piteously.

'Why are you – ow! – hurting me – ow!' he cried, and was rewarded with a hazelnut on his sensitive pink nose.

'I have done nothing to harm anyone here! Why are you hurt – ow! – hurting me?'

There was another swift series of knocks, followed by quiet. Then, from the trees above, came a shrill, chittering voice.

'No harm it says-says!' The voice was high-pitched and angry. 'Liar-liar-liar! You-you! Are killer! Coming here, here hunt and kill. Liar-cat-liar!'

Although it spoke in a fast-paced and excited way, Fritti could understand its Common Singing. He struggled for a better grip on the roots.

'Tell me what I have done!' he pleaded, hoping for time to regain the edge of safety just a paw-reach away. Angry chattering that he could not understand came from all the trees at once; then the rapping noise quieted the voices again.

'We are not stupid nut-droppers, no-no. Bad, so-bad cat, the people of the Rikchikchik not for you, for you to tease and fool, oh no no!'

The Rikchikchik! The squirrel-folk! Even hanging at clawtips from a bramble bush, Fritti felt a moment's wonder. It was known they would hiss and scold intruders, and even fight viciously when cornered – they were among the strongest and bravest of the Squeaker-folk. But band together to attack one of the Folk, one who had not even been stalking? It was incredible!

'Hear me, O Rikchikchik!' Fritti cried. His claws were beginning to feel the strain. 'Hear me! I know your kind and mine are enemies, but that is honorable! We are as we are made. But I promise that I do not intend to molest you, or harm your nests. I am searching for a friend, and I will not eat or hunt here! I swear by the First!' He waited tensely for a reaction, but the trees were silent.

Then a large brown squirrel made his way down the trunk of an aspen – headfirst and slowly – and stopped not two jumps away from Tailchaser's precarious position. The Rikchikchik looked angry, its lips pulled back from long front teeth, but it was only one-quarter Fritti's size. He had to admire its bravery.

'Tails, teeth, lies. This is-is what cats is!' The squirrel still spoke angrily, but more slowly, and was easier to understand. 'Can trust? No. Cat has got-got Mistress Whir. So-bad cats!'

'I haven't harmed anyone, I swear!' cried Fritti plaintively.

'Many tooth-and-claws attack nests! Even now, now, killing cat has caught my chiknek, my . . . mate. Caught! Spoiled seeds – unburied nuts! Terror, terror!'

Pains were shooting up Tailchaser's legs, and he was finding it hard to think. He extended a paw carefully to the cliff's edge, to relieve the pressure on his hind legs. A stone from a tree above struck the questing paw – he almost lost his grip as he pulled the injured foot back. A shrill chorus of squirrel voices in the foliage above called out for blood.

He tried to concentrate on what the brown squirrel was saying.

'Do you mean that a cat has your mate right now? Nearby?'

'Bones of birds! Horror, woe! Poor Mistress Whir. Caught, caught she is!'

Fritti seized at the opportunity. 'Listen to me! Please, throw no rocks down. I am at your mercy. I will try to save your mate, if you only let me get up from this place! You don't have to trust me. Go back into your trees, and if I try to escape, or harm you, you can drop boulders on me, pumpkins, anything! It's your only chance to save her!'

Tail erect and trembling, the large brown squirrel fixed him with a bright eye. For a moment all was frozen in the tableau: the stone-still squirrel and the small orange cat, grimacing in pain and hanging from a bush above a steep fall. Then the Rikchikchik spoke.

'You go. Save chiknek and you free-free. Word of Master Fizz. Sacred Oak-promise. Follow, we lead you, lead you.'

With a leap and scrabble, Master Fizz was gone into the leafy branches above. Tailchaser carefully pulled himself up to where he could get a better grip, then got his back paws up against the bramble roots for leverage and jumped to safety. He was weaker than he thought. His muscles trembled as he clambered up onto solid earth, and he lay for a moment panting. The Rikchikchik made excited noises among the leaves. He got painfully to his feet, and their chirruping voices led him forward.

On the outskirts of a grove of black oaks the Rikchikchik came to a halt. Tailchaser could see what had happened.

One of the old trees had fallen over long ago, forming a huge arch. He could hear the frightened crying of a squirrel from beneath it, and smell the scent of one of the Folk. The sheltering oak shielded the cat so that it could finish its game in peace without being disturbed by the stones and nuts of the vengeful Rikchikchik.

Fritti crept slowly and cautiously around the mop of dead roots that extended from one end of the fallen tree. However he was going to persuade the other cat to give up its rightful hunt-prey, he would have to begin with deference and care. So as not to startle, he called, 'Good dancing, hunt-brother,' as he walked under the arching trunk. He stopped short.

Mistress Whir, her eyes bulging with panic, lay pinned beneath

35

the paw of a large, sand-colored tom. The hunter raised his head inquiringly as Fritti approached. It was Stretchslow.

'Well! Young Tailchaser.' Stretchslow did not rise or move his paw from the terrified squirrel, but gave a nod of greeting that was not unfriendly. 'Isn't this a surprise! I was expecting you through this area eventually, but waiting is so boring.' He started to yawn, then caught himself. 'Well, now that you've arrived, would you like to share my catch with me? She's a nice fat one, as you can see. Had quite a bit of fight in her, too – at first. Stimulates the appetite.'

Things were happening too fast for Fritti. 'You were waiting . . . for me?' he asked. 'I don't understand.'

Stretchslow sneezed humorously at Fritti's bewilderment. 'I expect you don't. Well, plenty of time for all that after a toothsome bit of Rikchikchik. Sure you're not hungry?' Stretchslow raised his paw to deal the squirrel a killing blow.

'Stop!' Fritti cried.

Stretchslow was now the one to look surprised. He squinted at Tailchaser with keen interest – as if Fritti had grown a second tail.

'What's wrong, youngling?' inquired the older male. 'Is this some strange sort of poison squirrel?'

'Yes . . . no . . . oh, Stretchslow, could you let her go?' asked Fritti weakly.

'Let her go?' The hunter was genuinely astonished. 'Heavenly Viror, why?'

'I promised the other squirrels that I would rescue her.' Fritti felt as if he were turning to dust under the curious stare of the other cat, dust that would blow away in the next strong breeze. After a moment's careful scrutiny of Fritti, Stretchslow gave an immense huff of laughter and rolled onto his back, waggling his paws in the air. The she-squirrel did not move, but lay still, breathing shallowly, her eyes glazed.

Stretchslow rolled to his stomach and gave Fritti an affectionate thump with a large forepaw. 'Oh, Tailchewer,' he wheezed, 'I knew I was right! Going on quests! Saving squirrel maidens! Whoof! What a song yours will be!' Stretchslow shook his head from side to side with merriment, then turned his attention back to the huddled Rikchikchik. Fritti's nose burned. He did not know if he was being praised or mocked – or both.

'Very well, then,' Stretchslow said to Mistress Whir. 'You heard Master Tailchaser. He has interceded for your life. Go now, before I change my mind.' The squirrel lay still. Fritti began to move forward – afraid Stretchslow had inadvertently broken her back – when she suddenly bolted between them, sending chips of bark flying, and disappeared from beneath the oak-tree arch.

'I wish I had the leisure to hear your story of how you came to be making promises to squirrels, but there are things I still must do before the Eye appears.'

They were walking together beneath the giant trees – Fritti moving quickly to keep up with Stretchslow.

'However, I need to have more important talk with you. I was sure you would decide to leave on your own, but I miscalculated how soon you would set out. So, I have been searching for you since the beginning of Smaller Shadows.'

'Stretchslow, I am afraid I do not understand you at all. Not in the least, and I beg your pardon. What could you possibly have to say to a silly youngling like me? And how did you know I would come searching for Hushpad alone? And how did you know which direction I'd choose?' Fritti was gasping faintly as he struggled to maintain the older cat's pace.

'Many questions, little hunter. Not all can be answered now. Suffice it to say that I do not learn all I know at the Meeting Wall. I have wandered far in my day, and sniffed many, many things. I do admit that nowadays I derive a great deal of pleasure from sun-soaking – certainly I do not hunt as far afield as I once did. But, still, I have my ways.

'As to your other questions,' he continued, 'well, even a M'an-fed eunuch could have smelled your every intention, little quester. I have known since before Nose-meet – since before you knew yourself – that you would be striking out after little Marshbat.'

'Hushpad,' puffed Fritti. 'Her name is Hushpad.'

'Of course, Hushpad. I know,' said Stretchslow with impatience – and perhaps a touch of fondness. 'It is my way,' he added simply.

Stretchslow stopped suddenly, and Tailchaser fumbled to a halt beside him. Fixing Fritti with his great green eyes, the hunter said: 'There are strange things afoot, and not just in the Old Woods. The Rikchikchik and the Folk making bargains is not the strangest. I cannot sense what is happening with certainty, but my whiskers tell me bewildering stories. You have a part to play, Tailchaser.'

'How could I . . . ' Fritti began to protest, but Stretchslow silenced him with a paw gesture.

'I have no more time, I fear. Smell the wind.'

Fritti inhaled. Indeed, the breeze did carry a strange smell of cold and damp earth, but his senses could make nothing of it.

'You must learn to trust your feelings, Tailchaser,' said Stretchslow. 'You have some natural gifts there that may aid you where your lack of experience leads you into trouble. Remember, use the senses that Meerclar gave you. And be patient.'

Stretchslow sniffed the air again, but Fritti could no longer smell anything unusual. The older cat then rubbed his nose on Tailchaser's flank.

'Keep your left shoulder to the setting sun when you leave the forest,' he said. 'That should put you in a profitable direction. Do not hesitate to speak my name as recommendation on your journey. In some fields I am well remembered. Now, I must leave.'

Stretchslow trotted forward a few paces. Fritti, overwhelmed by events, sat watching him go.

The big cat turned around. 'Have you had your Initiation to the Hunt, Tailchaser?'

'Umm . . . ' Disconcerted, Fritti needed a moment to assemble his thoughts. 'Umm, no. The ceremony would have been the Meeting after Eye-next.'

Stretchslow shook his head and loped back to him. 'There is not time, nor proper surroundings, for the Hunt-singing,' he said, 'but I shall do the best I can.' In a daze, Fritti watched as Stretchslow settled back on his powerful haunches and closed his eyes. Then, in a voice much sweeter than expected, he sang.

> 'Allmother, the hunt-gifts
> We praise now,
> We praise now.
>
> Keep us in your Eye;
> Our true-tails
> You compass us.
>
> The sun is but fleeting,
> The Eye is of Always . . .
>
> Allmother, listen us
> We pray you
> We pray you.

Claw, Tooth, and Bone
Is our pledge to your light.'

Stretchslow sat with his eyes tight shut for a moment, then opened them and sprang to his feet again. No trace of the slowspeaking, slow-moving cat that Fritti had known seemed left but the cool gleam in his eyes. He appeared charged with purpose and energy; as he approached, Tailchaser involuntarily shrank back.

Stretchslow, however, only reached out and touched his paw to Fritti's forehead. 'Welcome, hunter,' he said, then turned and sprinted away – pausing briefly at the edge of a facing thicket to call: 'May you find luck dancing, young Tailchaser.' With that, Stretchslow vanished into the undergrowth.

Fritti Tailchaser sank to the ground in amazement. Had all this really happened? He had been gone less than a day from his home, and yet it seemed forever. Everything was so astonishing!

He brought his hind foot up and began to scratch behind his ear – an outlet for the conflicting blur of emotions. As he scratched wildly, eyes half closed, he sensed movement all around. He leaped to his feet, alarmed.

The surrounding trees were full of flicker-tailed squirrels.

One of the larger ones – not the squirrel he had spoken with earlier – had shinnied down an elm trunk to his own eye-level, and it clung there and looked at him.

'You-you, cat-thing,' it said. 'Now come along-come. Now you talk-talk. Time you talk with Lord Snap.'

CHAPTER FIVE

The difficulty to think at the end of the day,
When the shapeless shadow covers the sun
And nothing is left except light on your fur –

– Wallace Stevens

Fritti was climbing high into the treetops. The Rikchikchik who had summoned him stayed several branches ahead, leading him upward. Behind and all about, the rest of the squirrel party were leaping and chattering in their own tongue. He felt as though he had been climbing for days.

In the dizzying upper levels of the great live oak the procession halted for a moment. Fritti sat on a none-too-wide branch and waited for his breath to come back. Like all cats, he was a good climber, but he outweighed his squirrel companions manyfold. He had to cling tighter and maintain better balance than they, especially up here where the branches were getting thinner: from time to time a limb had swayed dizzyingly under him, forcing him to climb quickly to a sturdier one.

They stopped in one of the last trunk crotches: several large branches flaring out from the trunk of the oak. They had climbed so high that Fritti could no longer see down to the earth below through the overlapping limbs. The fetching party, augmented by scores of other Rikchikchik, watched him from a safe distance and squittered between themselves in amazement at the sight of a cat in the Lord's tree.

His legs aching, Tailchaser was again forced to rise and follow his hosts. After ascending a few more feet up the central trunk, spiraling upward on radiating branches, they turned out along a wide outreaching limb. Away from the trunk the bough's circumference became rapidly smaller, until Fritti balked for fear that it would not hold his weight. The Rikchikchik urged him on, though, and he edged forward until he was forced to lie on his stomach and cling. He would go no farther.

As he lay – swaying gently in the breeze – the squirrel who had led the party chirped a brief signal. The tok-tok-tokking noise that he had heard earlier resumed. Craning his head, Fritti could see several of the Rikchikchik with nutshells clutched in their forepaws, banging them sharply against the tree's trunk and branches in organized, staccato bursts.

From the other side of the treetops a new round of raps answered.

On a branch perpendicular to Tailchaser's, separated from his by several jumps of empty air, a slow and dignified procession was moving – dignified by squirrel standards, although perhaps a little brisk and hoppy in comparison to the sinuous grace of the Folk. Fritti thought he recognized Master Fizz and Mistress Whir near the front of the procession, which contained several pawfuls of Rikchikchik.

Leading the strange parade was a large squirrel with grayshot fur and an exultantly bushy tail. The old squirrel's eyes were as black as obsidian, and they studied Tailchaser intently as the line of tree-dwellers stopped and crouched.

After eyeing the cat imperiously for a moment, the old one turned to Mistress Whir.

'This cat-cat-folk who saved?'

Mistress Whir looked demurely across at Fritti, who clung gamely to his branch. 'Is most yes cat, Lord Snap,' she shyly affirmed.

Tailchaser could not help but notice how the Rikchikchik had protected their leader from him, an untrustworthy cat. Out at the end of this wand-thin limb he had no leverage by which to spring; even if he could manage to, the distance separating his and Lord Snap's branches was too great. Not that he had the urge to spring at anyone at this particular instant – still, he admired the Rikchikchik's cleverness.

'You, cat,' said Lord Snap sharply.

'Yes, sir?' answered Fritti. What did this old fellow want, anyway?

'Cat-folk, Rikchikchik not friends. You help Mistress Whir. Why you do, so-strange cat?'

Fritti had not quite puzzled it out yet himself. 'I'm not sure, Lord Snap,' he answered.

'Could have sheltered with chiknek-stealer under log, under log!'

41

broke in Master Fizz suddenly. 'Didn't,' he added significantly. Lord Snap lowered his head and gnawed meditatively on a twig, then looked at Fritti again.

'Always hunt, fight-fight with cat-folk. Moon-last four cat climb great tree. Steal chiklek . . . steal younglings. Steal many. Who cats?'

'I don't know, Lord Snap. I entered the forest only today. Did you say four cats? All together?'

'Four so-bad cats.' Snap affirmed. 'One each leg Rikchikchik have. Four.'

'I do not know, my lord, but it is unusual for my Folk to hunt in such large numbers,' said Tailchaser thoughtfully.

Snap deliberated for a moment. 'You good-cat. Keep-keep promise. Sacred Oak binds. First time Rikchikchik owe cat-folk favor since Root-in-Ground. T-t-t-teach you thing – you need-need help, Rikchikchik give. Yes?' Fritti nodded, surprised. 'Good-cat have troubles, sing: "*Mrikkarrikarek-Snap*," get help. Sing!'

Fritti tried: 'Mreowarriksnap.' Lord Snap repeated the phrase, and Fritti tried again, troubled by the difficult squirrelish sounds. Over and over he repeated it, tasting the odd chattering feel. All the Rikchikchik leaned forward, encouraging him, showing him how to make the noises.

If Stretchslow saw this he'd really have a laugh, thought Fritti.

Finally he approximated it closely enough to satisfy the old squirrel-lord.

'In my so-so-nice forest, you use for help. Also sing for certain in trees of brother, Lord Pop. Further . . . Snap-knows-not.'

The old squirrel leaned forward and fixed Tailchaser with his gleaming eyes. 'Other thing. You hunt Rikchikchik, no help. Promise gone-gone. Rule of Leaf and Bough. Agree, good-cat?' Snap looked at him cunningly.

Fritti was taken by surprise. 'I . . . I suppose so. Yes, I promise.' A gasp of pleasure went up from the attending squirrels, and Lord Snap beamed with delight, showing his worn incisors.

'Good, most-good.' He chuckled. 'Is bargain-bargain.' The Rikchikchik chief gestured with his tail to the squirrel who had brought Tailchaser. 'Master Click, take cat-folk down tree.'

'Yes, Lord Snap,' said Click. Fritti – sensing the end of his interview – began to inch backward along the narrow tree limb. The squirrels chattered brightly behind him. He thought he heard Whir and Fizz bid him good-journey.

As he descended behind the brisk and efficient Click, Tailchaser reflected with chagrin on the bargain he had just struck with the Rikchikchik.

All I have to do is meet the King of the Birds and the King of the Field Mice, he thought sourly, *and I'll most likely starve to death*.

The waning moments of Stretching Sun had turned the sky above the great forest into flame. The glow of the setting sun reached through the tangled branches and speckled the leafy ground at Tailchaser's feet. On the eve of his journey's first night he padded on, deeper and deeper into the ancient secrecy of the Old Woods.

He was hungry. He had not eaten since Final Dancing of the previous day.

Suddenly, as if it had been swallowed up by the Venris Hound, the light disappeared. In the half-moment it took his eyes to adjust, Fritti was blinded.

He paused, and as his night vision compensated for the sudden darkness, Tailchaser shook his head and shivered. To live always in darkness! Harar! How could the hole-dwellers and burrow-sleepers stand it? He thanked the Allmother for having brought him into the fields as one of the Folk, who enjoyed all their senses.

Continuing on his way with the effortless stealth native to his race, Tailchaser noted the nighttime life of the great woods in its first flowering. His whiskers received the faint heat-pulses of small creatures cautiously emerging to test the evening. All their movements were tentative, though – careful and hesitant. Fritti himself was a factor most of them were already aware of. The small animal that charged headlong from its huddling place at first dark did not usually live long enough to pass its foolishness along to offspring.

Thinking of food now, Fritti moved with control, each step coming down on packed ground that would betray no sound. He wanted to find a place where the air currents moved in more favorable ways, or did not move at all: he was going to effect a trap. He had walked hungry for too long, and did not want to wait for a chance kill.

Besides, Grassnestle, his mother, had taught him hunting lore, after all. He was not going to be forced into digging up Squeakernests for newborns on his first night out!

He would make a clean kill.

Night birds wheeled and soared above. He could feel the presence of the Ruhuë in silent overflight. They were not hunting, he guessed:

the Ruhuë preferred to search and swoop over flat ground. More likely they were leaving nests in the nearby forest.

Just as well, he thought. The nearness of an owl would freeze the forest creatures and make it that much harder to find dinner.

Other night-rising fla-fa'az whistled and piped in the trees, up in the farthest reaches where the Folk were too heavy to travel. Fritti dismissed them without a second thought.

Hopping down into a dry, rock-strewn gully, Tailchaser got a sudden and surprising whiff of cat-scent. He turned, muscles tensed, but the smell was gone. In a moment it was back again, and he breathed it long enough to note some familiarity in the odor. Then, oddly, it disappeared once more.

Fritti stood perplexed by this bewildering phenomenon, hackles raised and nose twitching. The scent had not changed in intensity from movement or wind failure – it had simply vanished.

When the scent returned to him he recognized it. No wonder it had seemed to have a familiar tang to it – it was his own scent.

His nose wrinkled delicately as he sampled the air, confirming his suspicions. He had walked into a night-eddy: a slow, barely detectable whirlwind. The rocks in the dry creek bed, heated by the sun during the day, were warming the air above them. Contacting the cool night air descending, trapped and rerouted by the walls of the gully, the resultant swirl of air made lazy circles . . . carrying his own scent back to him. If he had not paused for a moment, he would not have been in place long enough for it to circle around!

Pleased that he had solved the puzzle, he leaped up to the far side of the stream bed and was moving away when an idea tugged at him. He turned back and inspected the gully wall for several jumps up and down on both sides. He found what he had been looking for – the half-concealed entrance to a Squeaker-burrow.

He knew that the sunwarmth would dissipate eventually. He also knew that the trick would work only once. Carefully, he set himself in place: lying atop the gully wall three or four jumps down the stream course from the burrow opening. He tested the edge of the stream-bed wall on which he lay, and found a spot that would not crumble under movement and send a shower of earth down to betray his plot. Then, working the catechism that his mother had taught him, he stilled himself into immobility to wait.

Unwilling to move his head, he sensed, rather than saw, that Meerclar's Eye had moved but a short distance. When he was finally rewarded by a faint movement at the tunnel mouth, it seemed as if he had waited several lifetimes.

Carefully, so carefully, a nose appeared from the hiding hole and sniffed the air. The rest of the Squeaker followed. It sat frightened-eyed on the lip of the tunnel for a moment, every movement showing a readiness to run at the first sign of danger. Crouched, with nose wrinkling, it tested for hazard. It was a field mouse, brown-gray and skittery.

Without awareness, Fritti began to flick his tail back and forth.

The Squeaker, scenting nothing immediately dangerous close by, moved a cautious distance away from the hole mouth and began to search for food. Its nose, ears, and eyes were constantly trained for predators. Never straying more than a quick leap away from its hole, the Squeaker scavenged from side to side of the dry stream trough.

Fritti found that it took all of his control to not leap down on the mouse that seemed so close. His stomach clenched silently with hunger, and he could feel the impatient trembling of his hind legs.

But he also remembered Bristlejaw's admonition to be patient. He knew that the little Squeaker would be back down its bolt-hole at the first sign of movement.

I will not be a kitten, Fritti told himself. *This is a good hunt-plan. I will wait for the proper moment.*

Finally, he judged that the mre'az was as far from the burrow as was necessary. When the mouse turned its back on his position for a moment, Tailchaser brought up his forepaw and dipped it slowly over the edge of the gully wall, halting and freezing if the mouse seemed about to turn his way. Gradually, with great care, he stretched his paw down, until he felt the faint currents of the night-eddy ruffle the fur of his extended foot.

The eddy carried the scent around – down the gully walls to circle slowly back up to the mouse from a point seemingly near its own tunnel.

As the cat-smell reached it the rodent went stiff, nostrils flared. Tailchaser could see the bound, shivering tension of the mouse as it scented a mortal enemy – apparently between it and the escape route. The Squeaker remained frozen in place for several heartbeats as the eddy carried Fritti's scent past it. Then, in an agony of confusion, it made a half-hearted lunge away from the hole mouth, toward Tailchaser.

All the cat's pent-up energy was discharged at once. His tight-coiled muscles took him over the edge of the stream bed in one motion. As soon as his hind legs touched the ground, he was airborne again. The mouse did not even have a chance to utter a noise of surprise before it died.

Following his left shoulder in the way Stretchslow had directed him, Fritti thought about his strange encounter with the older hunter.

He had always seen Stretchslow at leisure – an aloof, unapproachable figure – but he had not acted like that today with Tailchaser. He had been different, animated and energetic. Even more strange, he had treated Tailchaser with great kindness and respect. Although Fritti had been very careful not to offend Stretchslow in times past, he had certainly never done anything to merit respect from a mature hunter. There was a riddle there that he could not solve as he had the night-eddy.

Such a day! How the others back at the Wall would laugh and call out at the story of one of the Folk learning Rikchikchik language in the tree of a squirrel-lord.

But he might never return to Meeting Wall to sing his song. He was of the Folk, and his oath would bind him. And now he was a hunter – sung and blooded.

Still, the hunter felt very sad and small.

Past the midpoint of night he began to feel a continuous weakness in his tired muscles. He had walked far by the Folk's standards; even farther for one his age. Now he had to sleep.

Nosing about for a sleeping place, he selected a grassy indentation at the base of a large tree. He sampled the breeze carefully, and found nothing to prevent him from bedding down. He turned three times around in the small hollow – honoring Allmother, Goldeneye and Skydancer, the life-givers – then curled up, covering his nose with his tail-tip to save warmth. He was asleep very quickly.

Dreaming, he was under the ground, in darkness. Fritti was struggling, scrabbling at dirt that gave way under his paws, but always there was more dirt.

He knew something was hunting him, just as he hunted Squeakers. His heart was racing.

His scraping paws at last broke through, and he fell through a wall of earth into the open air.

There, in a forest clearing, were his mother and siblings. Hushpad stood there, too, and Stretchslow and Thinbone. He tried to warn them about the thing that was chasing him, but his mouth was full of dirt; as he tried to speak, dust fell out onto the ground.

Looking at Tailchaser, his friends and family began to laugh, and the more he tried to indicate the danger they were in from the following-thing, the thing that hunted him, the more they laughed – until the sneezing, high-pitched sounds swarmed in his ears . . .

Suddenly, he was awake. The laughter had become a high-pitched barking. As he listened, stockstill, he could hear it clearly. It was quite close by, and in a moment he identified it: a fox, yipping in the darkness beyond the trees.

Foxes were no danger to grown cats. Fritti had relaxed back into his sleeping position when he heard another sound – the unhappy mewing of a kitten.

He leaped up instantly to investigate, springing out of the copse and down a tree-crowded slope. The barking and snarling became louder. He leaped onto a crest of rock that jutted from a welter of underbrush.

Many jumps downslope from him an adult red fox had backed a small catling against a hummock. The young cat's back was arched, all the fur puffed out from its small body.

Still not a very daunting sight, thought Fritti, not even to one of the Visl.

As he jumped down from the rock, Fritti noticed something unusual in the young cat's posture: it was injured, somehow, and despite all its loud hissing and spitting, was obviously not in much shape to fight. Fritti felt sure that the Visl knew this, too.

Then, shockingly, Tailchaser realized that the fox-cornered catling was Pouncequick.

CHAPTER SIX

> . . . cats in their huddled sleep
> (Two heaps of fur made one)
> Twitch their ears and whimper –
> Do they dream the same dream?

> – Eric Barker

'Pouncequick! Little Pouncequick!' Fritti loped down the shrub-spotted slope. 'It's me! Tailchaser!'

The youngling, from his sagging defensive posture, turned a drooping eye in Fritti's direction, but showed no sign of recognition. The fox turned sharply to look at the oncoming Tailchaser, but gave no ground. When Fritti drew to a halt a jump or two away, the Visl barked a warning.

'Come no closer, bark-scrabbler! I will do for you, also!'

Tailchaser could now see that the Visl was a female, and despite her ruffled hackles, not much bigger than he. She was thin, too, and her legs were trembling – whether from anger or fear, Fritti could not tell.

'Why do you menace this cat, hunt-sister?' sang Fritti, slowly and soothingly. 'Has he done wrong to you? He is my cousin-son, and I must stand for him.'

The ritualistic question seemed to calm the fox a little, but she did not back off. 'He menaced my pups,' she said, panting. 'I will fight you both if I must.'

Her pups! Tailchaser understood the situation better. Fox mothers, just as the matriarchs of the Folk, would do anything to protect their litters. He looked at her protruding ribs. It must have been a difficult autumn for mother and young.

'How was your family menaced?' Tailchaser inquired. Pouncequick, a jump away, was staring fixedly at the Visl, seemingly unaware of Fritti's presence.

The she-fox looked at Fritti appraisingly. 'In the morning-dark, I had taken the pups out prowling,' she began, 'when I smelled predators – large ones. The scent was unfamiliar, but it had something of badgers, and something of cats. I hurried the pups down to the den and lay on them to keep them quiet, but the danger smell did not go away. So I decided to lead whatever lurked out there away from the nest. I told the pups to stay where they were, then broke from a second burrow entrance.

'The smell was very strong – the predators were near. I showed myself briefly and ran. After a moment, I heard something following. I took them down-ravine, and up the basin's edge. I even exposed myself to sight on the long meadow, in hopes of getting a moon-glimpse of what pursued me –'

'What were they?' Tailchaser interrupted. The Visl glared at him, and her hackles bristled. *Patience!* Tailchaser chided himself.

'I don't know, *cat*,' she said harshly. 'They were too smart to follow out onto the grassland.

'When they didn't appear, I had to double back, for fear they had given me up and gone back to seek the den. As I said, though, they were cruelly clever . . . they were waiting for me when I reentered the scrub wood, and I had to run like Renred to get away. They kept to shadows and underbrush, though. I don't even know to a certainty how many there were. More than three, I think.'

Fritti admired the fox mother for her bravery. He wondered if he would be as selfless in a similar situation. The Visl spoke again.

'Anyway, I ran and ran – far enough that I felt safe for my young – and finally left them in a gorse thicket with a few false scents to chase . . . I hope you're listening very carefully. I seldom speak to cats, and I *never* repeat myself for them!'

'I am listening with great interest, hunt-sister.'

'Very well.' The fox looked somewhat mollified. Fritti hoped that they could settle whatever kittenish mistake Pouncequick had made without resorting to claw and tooth.

'Well, after taking a confusing route back, I arrived at my nest to hear my pups making a terrible noise: barking and yelping and calling for me. I found this little monster in the nest with them. Obviously, the others had led me off, and he had then snuck in to do harm to my young!' Again she bristled. Tailchaser was about to say something calming when Pouncequick cried out shrilly. Fritti and the fox turned to see the kitten starting forward, panting.

'No! No! I was hiding! Hiding!' cried Pouncequick piteously. 'Hiding from *them!*' The kitten began to shiver uncontrollably. Fritti, worried for his little friend, began to move slowly toward him.

'Hunt-sister, in your understandable concern for your litter, I think you have mistaken another victim for one of the wrongdoers.' He was at Pouncequick's side now. The little cat buried his nose miserably in Tailchaser's flank and whimpered. The fox pinned Fritti with a shrewd gaze.

'What is your name, cat?'

'Tailchaser, of the Meeting Wall Clan,' he replied respectfully. His soft singing seemed to have prevented conflict.

'I am called Karthwine,' said the fox simply. 'I will allow you to take your cousin-son without malice. You, however, must take the responsibility for keeping him out of the dens of my Folk. If I find him again near my pups, there will be no compromise.'

'That is more than fair, Karthwine,' said Tailchaser, giving a little head-dip of acceptance. The she-Visl looked him up and down, then turned a final glance to Pouncequick, whose face was hidden against Tailchaser's belly.

'You sing well, Tailchaser,' the fox said slowly, taking care with her words. 'But do not think to rely on that alone in this world. We foxes sing, too, and we know many things. But we *also* teach our pups how to bite.' She turned and stalked away in great solemnity.

The dawn was breaking above them as Tailchaser lay with a shuddering Pouncequick, singing quiet songs of reassurance. After a while, when the kitten's terror had subsided, Fritti led him back to the sleeping tree and curled up around him. As the morning sun rose, covering the woodland floor with criss-crossed shadows, they fell asleep.

The heat of Smaller Shadows woke Tailchaser. Pouncequick was no longer nestled against him.

Fritti raised his head and saw the young catling up and frolicking, soft fur aclutter with pine needles and dead leaves. When Fritti rose and stretched he discovered a great soreness in his muscles. Watching the gamboling kitten with envy, he decided that he would have to set an easier pace until he became more accustomed to this steady traveling.

Pouncequick, still cavorting happily while Fritti sunned his aching legs and paws, seemed to have recovered completely from the terrors of the night before. When Fritti asked him about what had happened, however, a shade of disquiet came into the youngling's eyes.

'Can we talk about it after we eat, Tailchaser?' he asked. 'I'm very hungry!'

Fritti assented, and the next part of the afternoon was spent in a none-too-effectual hunt – spoiled in a large part by Pouncequick's tendency to squeak when excited. They did manage to capture a couple of beetles, which – strangely ticklish going down – were at least filling. After finding a still but drinkable puddle of water, they settled down in the shade to digest.

The long, sleepy silence was broken only by the lulling whir of unseen insects. Then, as Fritti felt himself drifting into sleep, Pouncequick began to talk.

'I know I shouldn't have followed you, Tailchaser. I'm sure I'll be a burden, but I want so much to help you. You have been kind to me many times, when Fleetpaw and the rest just cuffed me about, or teased me.

'I knew you wouldn't let me come, though, so I hid until you set out, and then I tracked you. All by myself!' he added proudly.

'Ah. So that's why you were asking about my leave-taking among the Folk.'

'That's right. I wanted to know where you were leaving from. I'm not *that* good a tracker,' he added a little morosely, then brightened. 'Anyway, I kept my nose to the ground and followed. Everything went fairly well until midday or so; then I became confused.

'For a while it seemed like your trail had turned into someone else's, and then it doubled back on itself, and up and down trees – at least it smelled that way. I got very confused and wandered around for a while; when I found the track again, your traces were barely cold. I followed as best I could, but it was getting dark, and I was hungry. Actually, I still am. Could we go find a few more beetles or something?'

'Later, Pouncequick,' snorted Fritti. 'Later. First I want to hear the rest of your song, little cu'nre.'

'Oh, yes. Well, I was trying to make up ground on you – hoping you would stop to sleep, or something – when I heard the most awful noise. It was a huge group of birds, and they were all twittering and shrieking at the same time. I looked up, and there were hundreds of them – a whole cloud of fla-fa'az – all flying like mad around this tree, and making a terrible fuss.

'I went to the base of the tree, naturally, to see what was going on.

'It must have been horrible up top. There were piles of dead fla-fa'az, ripped and bitten, and feathers everywhere, floating down from the upper branches. And when I looked up, I could see *eyes!*'

'What do you mean, "eyes"?' Fritti questioned.

'Eyes. Big, pale-yellow ones – like nothing I've ever seen. There were too many branches in the way for me to see anything else, but I know I wasn't mistaken. Then whatever it was made a hissing noise at me, and I ran. I think it came down the tree after me, Tailchaser, because the birds stopped making that terrible ruckus – but I didn't look back to find out. I just ran.' Pouncequick paused for a moment with his eyes closed, then continued. .

'I think that there might have been more than one, from the sounds I heard. They were fast, and if I wasn't small – able to get under bushes and such – they would have caught me. I have never been so frightened – not even when a Growler was after me.

'Finally, I could barely run anymore. I was slowing down. I couldn't hear anything behind me, though, so I stopped to listen more carefully.

'I was standing there with my ears up, and something reached out from under a rock and *grabbed* me!'

'From under a rock?' said Tailchaser incredulously.

'I swear by the First! It grabbed my leg! Here, see these scratches!' Pouncequick displayed his wounds. 'You won't believe this either, Tailchaser, but the thing that grabbed me, *whatever* it was . . . it had *red claws!*'

'Well, you said that something was killing the birds you saw. It was probably blood.'

'After half an Hour of chasing me over dirt and brambles? It would have come clean. Besides, this wasn't dried blood. This was bright-red.'

Puzzled, Fritti gestured for the young one to continue.

'I shrieked like a jay, of course, and managed somehow to pull away. I went into a tangle bush as deep as I could, hoping they were too big to come in after me. I couldn't run any farther. They didn't make any noise, then, but I could sense they were still there.

'Then I smelled fox, and suddenly they were off. After I'd waited awhile, I staggered out from the bush and found the den-burrow. I supposed I'd go down just inside, where I'd have some defense if they came back for me. Then the Visl returned. I guess you know the rest.'

Fritti leaned forward and gave the youngster a nose-rub on his forehead. 'You were very brave, Pouncequick. Very brave. So you never saw what it was that chased you?'

'Not quite, no. But I shall never forget those eyes. And those red claws! Phoof!' Pouncequick shook himself from nose to tail, then turned to Tailchaser, anxiety melted away. 'All that talk of fla-fa'az has made me ravenous. Did I mention that I was hungry?'

'I think you did,' laughed Tailchaser.

They rested through the afternoon, and set out again at twilight.

Tailchaser had some misgivings about keeping young Pouncequick with him, but decided that he really had no other choice: he couldn't send the little cat away – back through the dangerous woods – and he himself could not give up his quest for Hushpad.

They made a fairly good pace. Pouncequick tended to trot ahead for a while, then lag behind, fascinated by a butterfly or a shiny stone. It seemed to even out, more or less, and their progress was steady. Pouncequick even managed to curb his squeaking a little, and the hunting improved.

Several days passed. They fell into a routine of alternating walks and rests – a long sleep at midday, when the sun was high, and another at Final Dancing, lasting until sunrise. They hunted as they traveled, catching the odd beetle or small bird hidden in the brush, and hunted bigger game only before the lying-in time of Smaller Shadows.

One afternoon, Pouncequick caught a Squeaker all by himself. It was a young mouse, and a very stupid one at that, but Pouncequick caught it without help and was justifiably proud. Moreover, Fritti decided, it tasted just as good as the cleverer sort.

Their companionship eased the tedium of the journey for both cats, and the days flew swiftly by. Although Pouncequick's incessant bounding and capering occasionally drove Fritti to snarling and swatting, he was still very glad to have the little cat for company. As for Pouncequick, he was delighted to be adventuring with an admired elder. The shadow of his first night in the wild seemed to have vanished, leaving no trace.

The forest seemed to change around them as they traveled – now thick and knotted, choked as tangle-bush, then open and airy as Edge

Copse. Then, at the end of their fifth day in the woods, the trees began to appear successively smaller and farther apart.

Topping a jutting rock that stood out among the treetops like a fela above her kittens, Tailchaser and Pouncequick stood and watched the sun of their sixth day rise. The forest below them stretched away another league or two, becoming steadily sparser, then dwindled to an end. Beyond it lay rolling green downs; clusters of trees sat in the hollows between their rounded sides.

The downs stretched on into the distance, their farthest reaches shrouded in early-morning fog. Beyond that might lie more hill land, or forests . . . or anything. No one Tailchaser knew had ever spoken of what lay beyond the Old Woods.

The two companions scented the breeze, drinking up the smells rising on the warming air. Pouncequick looked down, then butted Fritti's side.

Below them, on a subordinate peak of the outcropping, stood another cat. It was a strange sight, all muddy, with tangled fur and wild eyes. As Tailchaser and Pouncequick stared the unknown cat looked up at them with a strange, unfocused gaze. They had only a moment more to wonder at its ragged pelt and crooked tail; then the stranger leaped down from the rock, landing unsteadily on a wide limb, and vanished into the foliage. Where it had passed, the leaves bobbed for a moment, then were still.

CHAPTER SEVEN

'Oh, you can't help that,' said the Cat: 'we're all mad
here. I'm mad. You're mad.'
'How do you know I'm mad?' said Alice.
'You must be,' said the Cat, 'or you wouldn't
have come here.'

– Lewis Carroll

Tailchaser was doing a lot of thinking. The long days of walking had
given him time to do that, and he was adding up facts in a very
careful way.

Pouncequick's story of pursuit fit in with the other things he had
heard: the disappearance of some of the Folk; the Rikchikchik's tales
of cat raids.

Lord Snap had mentioned four cats: the number alone made Fritti
believe someone other than Folk was responsible for the raids on the
squirrel-nests. And Karthwine the fox had said that the beasts had
smelled part badger, part cat. Perhaps the creatures just looked
enough like cats to lead small animals like the Rikchikchik to a false
conclusion.

Even Stretchslow had said that something strange was in the air.
A new kind of marauding beast? Pouncequick's descriptions of eyes
and claws came back to him, and he shuddered.

With a sudden start, he thought of Hushpad – could those things
have gotten her? But no, he had smelled no fear at her empty nesting
place. They might have caught her in the forest, though! Poor Hushpad! Such a big world, and so full of dangers . . .

His attention was diverted by Pouncequick, who was annoying a
badger. The great digging beasts could be savage when they needed
to be. Tailchaser threw over his pondering and hurried to extricate
the youngling from a potential disaster.

Dragging Pouncequick away by the scruff of the neck, Fritti mumbled an apology to the nettled badger. The beast grunted scornfully at him as he retreated, then waddled off, striped sides huffing.

A lecture failed to dampen Pouncequick much. Soon they were off again, heading toward the outer edge of the Old Woods.

Waking from his midday nap, Tailchaser felt eyes upon him. Across the clearing stood the strange cat they had seen at the jutting rock. Before Fritti could untangle himself from the snoring Pouncequick the cat was gone, leaving no trace. It seemed to Fritti that the odd creature had been about to speak to them – there had been a strange yearning in its eyes.

That evening, as they were crossing a stand of aspens, the cat again appeared before them. This time it did not run away, but stood gnawing its lower lip nervously as they approached.

Seen up close, the cat was a fantastic sight. Its original color was long since hidden under the dirt and mud that caked its fur and twined the hair into swirls and tangles. Sticks and leaves, bits of tree lichen and evergreen needles, all manner of odd clutter festooned its coat from head to tail-tip. It had bent whiskers, and its eyes looked sad and puzzled.

'Who are you, hunt-brother?' asked Fritti cautiously. 'Do you seek us?' Pouncequick hung close by Tailchaser's side.

'Who . . . who . . . who . . . the Ruhu . . . ' the stranger intoned solemnly, then fell to chewing his lip again. His voice was deep and male.

'What is your name?' Fritti tried again.

'Ixum squixum . . . hollow and hellioned . . . how so?' The strange cat looked vaguely into Fritti's eyes. 'Eatbugs is me, I am . . . I ran, so I am . . . so you see . . . '

'He's mad, Tailchaser!' squeaked Pouncequick nervously. 'He has the dripping-mouth sickness, I'm sure of it!'

Fritti signaled him to hush. 'You are called Eatbugs? That is your name?'

'The same, the same. Grass-gobbler and stone-chewer . . . isky pisky squiddlum squee . . . oh! No!' Eatbugs whirled around, as if something were creeping up behind him. 'Aroint thee!' he cried at the empty air. 'No more of your dandly dancing out of earshot, you hugger-mugger hiss-mouse!' He turned back toward the cats with a wild look in his eyes, but as they stared, a change seemed to come over him. The crazed look was replaced by one of embarrassment.

'Ah, old Eatbugs gets confused sometimes, he does,' he said, and scuffed the ground with his grimy paw. 'He don't mean no harm, though – never would, you see . . . '

Pouncequick hissed with alarm. 'He *is* mad – did you see him? We must go!'

Tailchaser was also a little nervous, but something about the old cat touched him. 'What can we do for you, Eatbugs?' he asked. Pouncequick stared at him as though he, too, had gone quite mad.

'There you are,' the stranger said. 'There you be. Old Eatbugs were just lonesome for some talk. It's a big world – but precious few there are to speak with.' The old cat scratched distractedly at his ear and dislodged a small seed pod, which fell to the ground. Eatbugs bent and sniffed it eagerly, then a moment later swiped at it angrily with his paw and sent it rolling away.

'That's your world, now isn't it? That's your world,' he mumbled, then seemed to remember the others. 'Your pardon, young masters,' he said. 'I do wander a bit, betimes. Might I walk with you a ways? I do know some stories, and a game or two. I was a hunter when the world was a pup, and I catch a fair bit of game still!' He looked hopefully at Fritti.

Tailchaser did not really want another companion, but he felt sorry for this scruffy old tom.

Ignoring Pouncequick's frantic 'no' signals, he said: 'Certainly. We would be honored to have you accompany us for a while, Eatbugs.'

The mud-splattered old cat leaped up and cut a caper in the air so ridiculous that even Pouncequick had to laugh.

'Piglets and pawprints!' cried Eatbugs, then paused and looked quickly around. He leaned toward his companions. 'Let's be off!' he added, his voice a conspiratorial whisper.

Eatbugs was not a bad traveling companion. His occasional fits did not prove dangerous in any way, and after a while even Pouncequick accepted him without too much trepidation. He kept up a constant stream of songs and strange poetry all through the evening. When Fritti – wanting a little peace – finally asked him to quiet down a bit, he became silent as mud.

When they stopped to rest at Final Dancing, Eatbugs was still not speaking.

Fritti felt badly about how the old cat had taken his admonishment – he had not wanted to silence him *completely*. He walked over to the stranger, who was lying on the ground with his eyes in that odd, unfixed gaze.

'You told us that you knew some stories, Eatbugs. Why don't you give us one? We'd enjoy it.'

Eatbugs did not immediately respond. When he raised his head to look at Tailchaser, his eyes were filled with a great and terrible sadness. At first Fritti thought that he had been the cause, but a moment's observation showed that the old cat wasn't seeing him at all.

The look suddenly passed from Eatbugs' begrimed mask, and his eyes focused on Tailchaser. A weak smile came to his mouth.

'Ah, what, lad, what?'

'A story. You said that you would tell us a story, Eatbugs.'

'Yes, I did. And I know plenty – ramblers and tumblers and bottom-droppers. What do you want to hear about?'

'One about Firefoot. His adventures!' said Pouncequick eagerly.

'Oh . . . ' said Eatbugs, shaking his muddy head. 'I'm afraid I don't know any good ones, kitling . . . not about Firefoot. What else?'

'Wellll . . . ' Pouncequick pondered, disappointed. 'What about Growlers? Big, mean Growlers – and brave cats! How about that?'

'By the Sniffling Snail, I do happen to know a good one about the Growlers! Shall I sing it for you?'

'Oh, please do!' said Pouncequick, wiggling in his fur. He had missed stories.

'All right,' said Eatbugs. And he did.

'Long ago, when cats were cats, and rats and mice sang "mumbledy-peg, mumbledy-peg" in the brush at night, the Growlers and the Folk lived in peace. The last of the devil-hounds had died out, and their more peaceable descendants hunted alongside our ancestorous ancestors.

'There was a prince – O, such a prince – named Redlegs, who had suffered great unhappiness in the Court where his mother, Queen Cloudleaper, ruled. He went whispering and dancing into the wilderness to hugger-mugger with the rocks and trees, and to have Adventures –'

'Just like Firefoot!' squeaked Pouncequick.

'Hush!' hissed Fritti.

'Well,' continued Eatbugs, 'one day, when the sun was high in the sky and hurt his eyes, Redlegs came upon two giant piles of bones lying on either side of his path at the mouth of the valley. He knew that he was at the gates of Barbarbar, the City of the Dogs. Growlers

58

and Folk had no quarrel at this time, and Redlegs was anyway a prince of his people, so he entered into the valley.

'Around him he did spy every manner of Growler: tall and small, fat and flat; who leaped and bounded and barked, and dug holes, and carried bones hither and yon. But most of the bones were being carried to the pillars of the gate, where the yapping and yelping crews clambered up the piles and laid them on top. As the day wore on, the shinnying Growlers had more and more difficulty getting to the top – where they were trying, dry-nosed and gasping, to join the pillars into an arch.

'Finally, a huge and majestic mastiff appeared, barking commands; the Growlers jumped and gyrated in their efforts to please him, but at last nothing further could be done to join the pillars at the apex. Every leg-sprightly pup of the dog city was sent up to fill the last small gap – which was but one bonelength wide – but none could climb to the top of the curving pillars . . . '

Tailchaser had an unusual feeling. As he lay, eyes tightly shut, listening to Eatbugs' song, he found that he could *see* the events in a way that he had never been able to at Meeting Wall. In his mind's eye, he witnessed the leaning towers of bone, the efforts of the Growler-folk and their mastiff leader, as clearly as if he had been present. Why did he feel this way? He licked his foreleg and washed his face, concentrating on the old cat's words.

'Now,' Eatbugs was saying, 'in those days dogs had not become the lick-M'an, drunk-slobber wretches we see today, but the Folk have *always* found them amusing – unless in direct battle, you see. So, as Redlegs watched the parade of frightened doglings shinnying up the gate arch, only to come cowering down in defeat a moment later, he could not help laughing.

'At the sound of this the huge mastiff turned in anger and gullet-growled: "Who are you that laughs so, cat?"

'Redlegs stilled his merriment, and said: "I am Redlegs, of the line of Harar."

'The mastiff looked at him. "I am Rauro Bite-then-Bark, of these dogs the King. It is not meet or seemly that I should be mocked in this way!" At this the dog-king puffed out his chest and goggled his eyes in such an important way that Redlegs almost laughed again.

' "How long have you been building your gate, O King?" he asked.

' "Full three seasons it has been," replied Bite-then-Bark, "and we but lack one bone to make it complete."

' "So I see," said Redlegs, and suddenly he was of an inclination to play a trick on the puff-puddle-pompous King of the Dogs. "Your Majesty, if I can finish your gate for you, will you grant me one favor?" he asked.

' "What would that be?" inquired the King suspiciously.

' "If I can do your task, I would like a bone for my own."

'The King, thinking of the thousands of bones that he held sway over, yapped with delight at the cheapness of the request and said: "You shall have any bone you desire in my kingdom, only you do this for me."

'So Redlegs agreed, and, taking the last bone-piece of the gate in his mouth, climbed carefully and skillfully up the swaying arch. When he got to the top, he carefully pushed the final piece between the tips of the two curving towers, where it fit like the last scale Meerclar put on lizards. Then he walked down again while all the Growlers barked and harrumphed with pleasure to see their work completed, and their mighty gate standing finished.

'While all stared upward, ears flopping and tongues lolling in glee, Redlegs walked to the base of one of the gate towers. He searched scrupulous careful for a moment, then leaned forward and tugged out one of the bones that was therein piled.

'Nothing happened for a few hiccoughing heartbeats – then waver, wail, and wallow, the gate bent a little to this side, a little to that side . . . then collapsed, with a noise like all the dancing dead.

'When King Rauro Bite-then-Bark, drooling with shock and horror, turned to look at Redlegs, the Prince only said to him: "See, I chose my bone, as you stipulated!" and began to laugh.

'Looking from Redlegs to his shattered gate, the eyes of the King became red with fury, and he woofed: "G-g-g-get that c-c-c-c-ursed c-c-c-cat! K-k-kill him!" And all the Growlers of Barbarbar leaped up at once, and did sprint after Redlegs, who was nonetheless too fast for them and made his escape.

'Over his shoulder as he ran, he called back: "Think of me, O King, when next in your pride you gnaw at a hipbone on your unburied dunghill throne!"

'So it is that these days We Cats and Those Dogs are enemies wherever we meet in these fields we know. They have never forgiven the humiliation of their King, and pledge they never shall – till the sun falls from the sky, and snakes learn to fly on the morning breeze.'

When Eatbugs finished his song Pouncequick was already asleep, rumbling softly. Fritti felt the strange feeling of true-seeing leave him. He wished to question the muddied stranger-cat, but Eatbugs was in a staring trance, half asleep, and would not respond. Finally, Tailchaser also succumbed to the voice of sleep, and crossed over into the fields of dreams.

The morning sun had risen high into the sky when Tailchaser was ousted from slumber by the kneading pressure on his chest and stomach.

Pouncequick, still dozing, was treading softly with his paws as he lay curled against Fritti. The kitten, only recently weaned, was probably dreaming of his mother and nest. Tailchaser again felt a prick of worry over exposing his young companion to the dangers of the quest. The Folk were normally solitary hunters and adventurers once out of kittenhood; responsibility felt a little unnatural.

Of course, he thought, *many unnatural things have been happening of late*.

As Pouncequick continued his sleepy milk-tread Fritti was reminded of his own mother . . . and was suddenly glad for the security of another warm, furry body to curl up with in these strange environs. He licked the soft fur of Pouncequick's inner ear and the sleeping kitten rumbled happily. Fritti was just drifting back down into sleep when he heard a voice.

Eatbugs was up and stalking around, talking to himself. His eyes had the faraway look that Fritti had already seen. He carried his tattered, grime-spattered body erect and tensed.

' . . . Pounding and pumping and trapped . . . here we are . . . trapped! Pinned beneath this wall, this wiggly-woggly wall and all . . . ' Eatbugs mumbled vehemently as he paced back and forth before Fritti's fascinated stare.

' . . . The birds and the shrieking, shriking, jelly-eyed red ones . . . laughing and dancing – can't get out! . . . scratch at the door, where is it? . . . must find it . . . '

Suddenly the old cat went all abristle, as if surprised by sound or smell. Fritti sensed nothing. Hissing and spitting, claws shot, Eatbugs flattened himself against the ground and snarled in a voice forced out between bared teeth: 'They're here! I feel them! Why do they want me? Why?'

He yowled, looking wildly from side to side, as if surrounded by enemies. 'They need me, and it . . . hurts . . . Ahhh! . . . the Vaka'az'me . . . forgive . . . Ah! There's a crack! A crack in the sky!'

With this, Eatbugs squirmed and shook all over, then sprang away

61

into the underbrush. The commotion of his flight quickly receded into the distance.

At Tailchaser's side, his young companion had awakened.

'What was that?' he yawned sleepily, and stretched. 'I thought I heard the most terrible ruckus.'

'It was Eatbugs,' Tailchaser responded. 'I think he's run away. He was having one of his fits – he seemed to think that something was following him.' Fritti shook his head from side to side, trying to shed the weird image of Eatbugs.

'Well, I expect it had to happen,' said Pouncequick matter-of-factly.

'He may be back,' Fritti pointed out.

'Oh, he's not a bad sort, really. Mad as a mockingbird. Tells good stories, though. I quite like the one about Redlegs. Who was Redlegs, anyway, Tailchaser? I've never heard Bristlejaw sing of him. Or of Queen Cloudleaper either, for that matter.'

'I really don't know, Pounce,' said Fritti, and was about to suggest a hunt for breakfast when he finally noticed that the birds had stopped singing. The forest air was completely silent.

Suddenly, as quietly as grass growing, several large cats appeared out of the surrounding vegetation: stranger cats, every one as silent as a shadow. Before the startled Fritti and little Pouncequick could say a thing, or make a move, the strange cats had drawn themselves into a wide circle around the pair.

Pouncequick began to whimper in fright. The strange cats stared at them with cold, cold eyes.

CHAPTER EIGHT

My body translates mysteries with ease.
My body is the Book of How to Go.
I swear my ways are as deep as water's ways.

I send a message with my arching spine.
But keep back more a message than I show.
I lift my paw and give a secret sign.

                      – Philip Dacey

A moving ring now surrounded Fritti and his companion. The strangers circled them, passing each other with sinuous shrugs, sniffing and sniffing and not making a sound. The ring drew tighter, until finally the strangers were nosing Tailchaser and Pouncequick.

Fritti could feel the small cat growing ever more frightened. The strange cats could sense it, too. Tension hummed between the outer circle and the inner core of two.

Finally, Tailchaser could not stand it anymore. As one of the strangers brushed by, snuffling at Pouncequick, Fritti hissed and struck him with the flat of his paw. Instead of attacking, or leaping away in surprise, the strange cat merely nodded his head and stepped back a pace.

He was all black. His muscles rippled glossily beneath the short fur of his coat. His eyes were narrow slits, chinks of smoldering color, but he did not seem to be angry. This cat was not angry at all, but terrifyingly calm.

'So,' said the black cat. His voice was like gravel sliding. 'Now we know where we stand. Good.' He lowered himself to the ground in front of Tailchaser, his ears back, his eyes low-burning embers. Tailchaser – caught in a reflexive response – found himself crouching in mimicry.

The black one spoke again. 'I was wondering how long it would take mela-mre'az like you to respond honorably.' With this remark, the black cat paused and looked at Fritti expectantly, as if waiting for him to say something. Tailchaser – already terrified – had no idea what he was supposed to do.

'Do . . . do you want me to surrender?' he asked tentatively. The black cat looked at him appraisingly. A moment passed.

'Well? Get on with it!' said the stranger.

'Well . . . well . . . I won't give in to you!' blurted Tailchaser, in an agony of fear and confusion.

'Excellent!' boomed the black cat. 'Now we're getting somewhere!' All four of the black one's companions now drew back from where he and Fritti crouched.

'I am Quiverclaw, Thane of the First-walkers,' proclaimed the black cat, tail lashing back and forth hypnotically behind him. 'Offer your face name, trespasser!'

'I am Tailchaser, of the Meeting Wall Clan . . . and I am no trespasser!' finished Fritti. He was angry now.

Quiverclaw seemed pleased by this, for he nodded, but nothing but readiness showed on his face. Hugging the ground even more closely, the black cat's haunches began a slow, rolling motion, and his tail thrashed wildly. Tailchaser unconsciously adopted a similar pattern. Their eyes locked and held.

Fritti suddenly realized that Quiverclaw was almost half again as big as he himself was – but as he stared into the stranger's eyes, it didn't seem important. What was important was that slinky black tail, lashing this way . . . and that way . . .

'Well met, Tailchaser,' hissed Quiverclaw. 'I commend your ka unto the bosom of the Allmother.'

'Tailchaser!' cried Pouncequick, his voice full of panic. Fritti turned and pushed the kitten away from his side and out of danger.

'Be quiet, Pounce.' He turned to the black one again and stared hard at the almond eyes. 'Do not be so quick to neglect your own ka, Thane of Bullies.' Fritti leaped forward. A whoop went up from the other cats, overwhelming Pouncequick's bleat of fear.

Everything seemed to happen at the same moment. Fritti felt a shock of impact as Quiverclaw sprang. Then he was on the ground, thrashing, trying to get away from the claws of the bigger cat. He rolled onto his back, bringing up his back feet to pummel the belly of his opponent.

Quiverclaw pulled back slightly, and Tailchaser was able to slither away and climb onto his feet. But it was only a moment's respite, and then the black cat was on him again.

Over and over they rolled – clawing at one another, yowling in sliding, swooping discord. Tailchaser gave as good as he got for the first few seconds – kicking at Quiverclaw's stomach, biting and scratching at legs and chest – but he was young and inexperienced. The black one was big, and obviously a veteran of many battles.

The two combatants pulled apart for a moment, and circled each other, hissing. They both felt the pull, though, the need for resolution; after a heartbeat they threw themselves together again.

Pinned beneath Quiverclaw, Fritti managed one final effort – writhing and twisting in the larger cat's grip, then wriggling free long enough to bite down hard on the black cat's ear and draw blood. Then his strength was gone, and he was again crushed beneath Quiverclaw's weight. He felt the jaws clamp down on the back of his neck.

'Do you cry "enough"?' growled the Thane into Fritti's neck fur. Fritti was trying to catch his breath long enough to surrender when suddenly the jaws were gone from his neck and an ear-deafening yowl was echoing through the clearing.

Tailchaser rolled weakly onto his back in time to see Quiverclaw – leaping and twisting like a demon-cat – batting with his paws at Pouncequick. The kitten was hanging on grimly, needle-sharp kitten-teeth sunk to the gums in Quiverclaw's shiny black tail.

Finally able to dislodge the young cat, the Thane slid to the ground in pain and exhaustion less than a jump from where Fritti lay. Quiverclaw licked his wounded tail and stared reproachfully at Pouncequick, who haughtily returned the look.

The other cats surrounded Pouncequick, growling angrily, but Quiverclaw caught his breath long enough to wave them off, saying: 'No, no, leave him alone. His protector fought bravely – and he, too, is courageous enough for his age. Not too wise in his choice of enemies, perhaps . . . well, no matter. Let him be.'

Seeing Pouncequick safe, Tailchaser rolled onto his back with his paws in the air. First he saw myriad tiny spots floating above his eyes, and then for a time he saw nothing at all . . .

When he awoke, Fritti found that Pouncequick had become the center of attention.

The group of strange cats were huddled around him with expressions of surprise and amusement on their faces. Pouncequick was apparently telling them about Eatbugs; Tailchaser saw Quiverclaw laughing as Pouncequick attempted to duplicate one of Eatbugs' capering leaps.

Drawing himself quietly up into a sitting position, Fritti surveyed the cluster of strange cats. They seemed friendly enough, now – they had certainly put Pouncequick at ease – but Tailchaser was not so quick to trust. Who were they?

It was obvious that Quiverclaw was the leader. Even laughing, lolling on the ground, he had a look of controlled power and command. Beside him sat a fat, grizzled old tom, orange-and-black body striped like summer lightning, his stomach flattened against the ground between his stocky legs.

On the Thane's farther side were two more cats: one gray, one patched in black and white. Neither was as large as Quiverclaw, or the old tiger-stripe, but they were lean and well-muscled, with the quiet look about them of successful hunters.

The fifth cat, crouching along outside the perimeter of Pouncequick's audience, was very different. Seeing him, Fritti went cold all over.

The fifth cat was white as ice – thin, too; as slender as a birchtree branch – but this was not what disturbed Tailchaser.

He had strange, frightening eyes: milky-blue, and larger than any cat's eyes that Fritti had ever seen. Tailchaser remembered Pouncequick's story. For a moment he wondered if they were in some sort of cruel, slow trap.

But no . . . Pouncequick had told him of terrifying eyes, but Pounce must have seen this white cat.

Look at him, thought Fritti. *If those were the eyes that frightened him, would Pounce be cutting capers for them? And not a red claw among them . . .*

As Fritti looked from paw to paw, Pouncequick finally noticed him and called cheerily: 'Tailchaser! Are you all right? Hangbelly said you would be. I'm just telling the First-walkers about our adventures!'

'So I see.' Fritti walked forward to join the group. No one stirred to make room for him except Pouncequick, so he squeezed in beside his small friend. Quiverclaw looked over to him with snake-slit eyes, but bobbed his head in affable greeting.

'Well met, Tailchaser. Did you have good dreaming?' he asked.

'I did not dream,' Fritti replied. He gave Pouncequick an affectionate nudge.

'Well now, well now . . . ' said large Hangbelly, shifting his huge paunch to look Fritti over. 'Here's the young warrior. You fought right well, nestling. How old do you be? Seen six Eyes, have you?'

'I shall have my ninth Eye in a few more sunturns.' He looked at the ground, embarrassed. 'I am small for my age.'

There was a moment of awkward silence, broken by the soft rasp of Quiverclaw's voice.

'No matter. Courage counts no Eyes. There is precious little enough, without we fail to acknowledge it. You answered the challenge, and fought as the Old Laws command.'

Tailchaser felt he did not quite understand. 'I didn't believe I had much of a choice.' Hangbelly laughed at this, and Quiverclaw's lips curled in amusement.

'You *always* have a choice, laddie-kit,' said Hangbelly, and the others bobbed assent. 'Every day you have a choice, and if you want to, you can lie down in your fur and die anytime. But a First-walker never does y'see? And we respect your choice, too.'

'I was protecting my friend.'

'Very fair, very fair . . . ' said Quiverclaw. 'By the way, I would be doing a disservice to everyone if I did not offer face names. You and I have met through challenge, but my hunt-brothers are strange to you. Hangbelly you have spoken with.' Hangbelly bared his teeth teasingly.

'This is Bobweave.' A nod from the gray as he and Fritti sniffed at one another. 'The fine, amusingly spotted cat – whom the Squeakers do not find at all laughable –' the black-and-white tom inclined his mottled head – 'is Scuffledig. And the proud fellow who sits by himself is Eyeshimmer.' The white cat turned and made the tiniest inclination of the ears toward Fritti, who took it as a greeting and returned a nod.

Scuffledig piped up, 'When he isn't being mystical, he's been known to catch a vole or two himself.'

'He is our Oel-var'iz. Eyeshimmer is Far-senser to the First-walkers.' Pride was in Quiverclaw's voice, and respect. Fritti was impressed. What an unusual cat Eyeshimmer must be, to earn such regard from a natural leader like Quiverclaw!

'I am afraid that I am only Tailchaser,' he said quietly. 'I am not particularly special – and, I am afraid, rather on the small side . . . as I mentioned.'

Hangbelly leaned over and nudged him with his broad head. 'Here, then, nothing wrong with being small. Our Lord Firefoot was the smallest of the First!'

'Speaking of the First – with all respect –' said Tailchaser, 'may I ask why you are called the First-walkers?'

'Ah, yes, there are many things that you young cats do not know,' said Quiverclaw.

'And do you always hunt in a . . . *pack*, like this?' Fritti asked.

'Well . . . ' began the black cat.

Pouncequick eagerly chimed in, 'And what can Eyeshimmer do?'

Bobweave yawned enormously, then said in a disgusted tone: 'They certainly are good with questions. I'm going to go kill some breakfast.' He bounded lithely away.

Quiverclaw watched him go, then turned back to Tailchaser.

'Bobweave is not patient – but he has other qualities that more than compensate. I will try to answer *some* of your questions.'

Hangbelly snorted behind him.

'The First-walkers,' Quiverclaw began, after darting a glance at the hulking tom, 'are the last pure line of those Folk who ran with our own Lord Firefoot in the days of the First. My blood ancestor, Lungeclaw, served him during the time of Prince Blueback.

'We are sworn to a paw-and-heart oath to guard that heritage. The days of valorous combat and oath-bonds and truth will never completely die, as long as the First-walkers survive.' Quiverclaw looked solemnly at Tailchaser and Pouncequick. 'If the Rules and Commands are not obeyed, life becomes scrabble and scrape; without dignity. We First-walkers keep the laws of the First, and give them life. It is not always easy . . . many whose blood runs true cannot live with our discipline.'

The black head turned slowly past the assembly, then faced away into the forest. 'Our numbers have dwindled,' Quiverclaw said.

'And smaller still will those numbers shrink,' said a delicate, high-pitched voice. Quiverclaw and the rest turned to look at Eyeshimmer, who still crouched some distance away.

'So you have said. So you have said,' rasped the Thane wearily.

'And maybe that's not such a bad thing, now,' rumbled Hangbelly, a touch of anger in his voice. 'There are some 'walkers about now as I, for one, could do without!'

Fritti was still curious. 'Do you always travel in such great packs? Strange, indeed!'

Scuffledig and Hangbelly laughed at this. Quiverclaw hastened to explain.

'No, of course not. Strange it would be for the followers of Tanga-loor Firefoot – who most often walked alone – to go a-roving like a great clump of Growlers. No, there are too few of us to walk all together. All told, there are only a pawful of other thanes, besides myself. Each one of us has his territory, and though we meet on the night of the Eye with one or two of our closest neighbors, we usually move alone.'

'But there are five of you here!' commented Pouncequick.

'Ah, but this is an exceptional time. We have been called to the territory of my Thane-brother Sourweed. All the First-walkers who have heard will gather there. There have not been so many of us together since my father's day.'

'We shall dance, and sing, and tell lies,' chuckled Scuffledig. 'Quiver-claw will wrestle with Sourweed, and Hangbelly will sniff too much catmint and embarrass us all!' He dodged a blow from the old tom.

'Yes,' grated Quiverclaw gently, 'but unhappy purposes demand this meeting, and there is more to think of than merriment.'

'Aye, that's true,' growled Hangbelly, 'like what dung-dog it was that did for poor Brushstalker.'

Quiverclaw nudged him. 'You are a fearsome hunter, old friend, but your mouth sometimes out-runs your eyes. The fate of Brushstalker is not a pretty song for young innocents like these.' He indicated Fritti and Pouncequick with a gesture. 'Let us leave this talk now.'

It was obvious to Fritti that sparing their feelings was not Quiverclaw's only reason for throttling the conversation. The wily black Thane was no more willing to abandon all caution and discretion at first meeting than Tailchaser himself had been. Fritti found himself once more admiring Quiverclaw's control.

'Well, I think that it's high time we followed Bobweave's example and knocked down some breakfast.' The Thane got to his feet. Pouncequick bounced up also.

'Will you tell us more later?' the kitten asked. 'About your meeting – and Eyeshimmer?'

'All things in earth's season, young Pouncequick,' said Quiverclaw affectionately. The expression, which Fritti had heard before from the mouth of Bristlejaw, echoed in Tailchaser's thoughts as the cats separated to hunt.

Breakfast finished, the group scattered around the edges of the clearing to attend to grooming and napping. A light rain had begun to patter down, and Tailchaser watched the drops raise little puffs of dust from the powdery ground. The tapping sound of the broad leaves over his head lulled him. He could feel his eyes becoming heavy.

A presence tickled his whisker-tips, and he looked up. Eyeshimmer was sitting beside him, rain-sparkle on his snowy fur.

'The first rains of the year bring out many strong impressions, do they not?' Eyeshimmer's high voice was deceptively careless.

'I'm sorry, I don't understand. What impressions?'

'Impressions. Dream-stuff. Recognition and guide-tailing. I find that the early rains . . . well, as I said.'

Eyeshimmer's presence, and his strange conversation, made Tail-chaser nervous. 'I'm afraid I don't know much about those sorts of things, Eyeshimmer.'

The Oel-var'iz looked at Fritti with amusement. 'As you wish,' he said, 'as you wish.' He walked off as if bearing a secret joke balanced on the tip of his long tail.

Quiverclaw watched the Far-senser's departure from across the clearing. He rose and stretched, then ambled around the perimeter, stepping over a drowsing Hangbelly. Watching him walk, Tailchaser was again struck by the harnessed power of the black cat.

'You look disconcerted, young Tailchaser. Did Eyeshimmer cast a disturbing fortune for you?' The Thane relaxed to the ground beside Fritti.

'No. No, he was just being sociable, I think, but I didn't quite get what he was saying. I hope I didn't offend him.'

'I would not worry overmuch. The Far-sensers are a strange breed, you see. Brilliant, quick as a wet skink, but a little moody and odd. It's the way they're raised, you know. While the rest of us are learning to catch Squeakers, the Oel-var'izë are taught to read the weather in snail tracks, and sing salamanders out of the mud, and suchlike. Or so it's said. Anyway, they're all a bit daft – and Eyeshimmer not the worst by a long stretch.'

Fritti sensed that the Thane was playing the fool a bit for his benefit, but couldn't help enjoying the First-walker's droll manner.

'By the by,' Quiverclaw continued, 'I did want to find out exactly where you and your little friend are bound. We would be happy to escort you, if your path lies with ours.'

'Actually, I was just thinking about that earlier,' said Fritti, stretching languorously. He stopped in midextension, suddenly self-conscious about showing such indulgence in the presence of the Thane. 'I suppose I will have to decide rather soon,' he finished quietly.

Quiverclaw showed no sign of noticing Fritti's embarrassment. 'Sadly, we cannot take you with us to the Thane-meet. There are strong feelings about outsiders, you understand . . . '

Tailchaser sat silent. The task of finding Hushpad loomed once more. How difficult it was being responsible! He missed the simple pleasures of kittenhood. How could he discover her? Every idea that ran through his mind turned out, under examination, to be useless.

'I suppose,' he asked the Thane finally, 'that Pouncequick told you why we are abroad in these woods?'

'He did, young hunter. And a right brave and proper thing it is to do. I wish I could give you some wise words about where to find your fela, but alas, it is a large world. She is not the first to suffer from mysterious happenings, though, but more I cannot say. I am bound to hold silence until the Thane-meet.' The black cat lifted his leg and scratched reflectively behind his ear.

'I, too, have heard many odd stories,' agreed Tailchaser. 'As a matter of fact, my clan sent a delegation to the Court of Harar to seek help in this situation. I suppose I should go and meet them there, and see what they have learned. I'm afraid I had not given the whole subject much more than a sniff and a lick when I decided to set out. Yes, I suppose I must try to reach the Court.'

A strange look flickered across Quiverclaw's slitted eyes.

'The Court, eh?' he grunted. 'Well, each hunter must set his own paws to the path. Unfortunately, when we get to Woodsedge in a day or two's time, we must part ways. Sourweed's territory lies Vez'an-ward — to the east — and your path must take you toward Va'an. We will give you good directions, though . . . and good wishes.' Quiverclaw rose. 'Take some sleep, now. I wish to set off again after Smaller Shadows.' The black hunter paced sinuously off.

The rain had steadied into a drizzle that matted the fur and muddied the paws of the travelers. Through the gray afternoon and evening they marched on across the failing fringes of the old forest. Pouncequick – being the smallest and least fastidious – fell into several puddles, not always by accident.

They reached the final line of trees at the threshold of the downs as the sun was disappearing over the horizon. Quiverclaw decided that they should stop and spend one last night beneath the shelter of the trees.

Bobweave and Scuffledig scouted up a relatively dry spot on a rise beneath a stand of pine trees, and after an unimpressive hunt the party repaired to their sleeping place.

For a long time they lay quietly watching the growing rivulets of water snake past them, each trickle seeking its own path to low ground. Pouncequick and Scuffledig played Hide-and-Swipe across

Quiverclaw's back for a while – until an errant paw took the Thane on the side of the head. Ears back, he snarled the restless pair into uneasy stillness. Then, realizing that it was a losing battle, the chief of the First-walkers turned to Hangbelly.

'Old friend,' said Quiverclaw, 'it looks to be a long night. How about a little entertainment – if only to save my aching head from any more Hide-and-Swipe?'

'A grand idea!' shouted Scuffledig. 'Tell the story of Bobweave and the hedgehog!'

Bobweave looked at Scuffledig with a grimace of distaste. 'Certainly,' he said sourly. 'Then we must have the story of Scuffledig's first gopher hunt.'

Scuffledig looked over in alarm. 'Perhaps we *should* save the hedgehog story for another time,' he conceded.

Quiverclaw smiled. 'Why not a song or a poem?' he asked. 'Mind you that it's proper for our young friends.'

Hangbelly sneezed a laugh and rolled over onto his stomach, which spread impressively beneath him. 'I have just the thing,' he chortled, 'as long as *some* folks as I could name remember their manners and pay attention, like.' This brought Pouncequick – who had been sneaking up on Scuffledig – sheepishly back to lie next to Fritti. Hangbelly sat up, almost bumping his stripy head on a low-hanging branch, and sniffed importantly.

'This,' he said, 'is a small verse as is called "Snagrat and the Spirit-Mouse." ' He hummed for a moment, then sang.

> *'Snagrat was a cat who liked his rats*
> *An' he liked 'em sweet, an' he liked 'em fat*
> *Sing: Hey-crack, derry-crack, liked his rats.*
>
> *Snagrat, ye know, would a-hunting go*
> *In the summery sun and winter snow*
> *Sing: Hey-crack, derry-crack, hunting go.*
>
> *One day he spied by the riverside*
> *A Squeaker plump, rat-mother's pride*
> *Sing: Hey-crack, derry-crack, rat he spied.*
>
> *At the rat he jumped, with a leap and bump*
> *To take the beast in its hiding clump*
> *Sing: Hey-crack, derry-crack, leap and bump.*

> But beneath his claws no rat he saw
> And he gaped a gape from dangling jaw
> Sing: Hey-crack, derry-crack, no rat saw.
>
> Then he heard a squeak, and a rat did speak
> But he could not find it however did seek
> Sing: Hey-crack, derry-crack, rat did speak.
>
> Said the voice: "Dear cat, I'm the spirit-rat
> And I will haunt you and hunt you flat!"
> Sing: Hey-crack, derry-crack, haunt you flat.
>
> Snagrat's head spun at the spirit's dun
> And up he leaped and away he run
> Sing: Hey-crack, derry-crack, leaped and run.
>
> No more Snagrat is a mousing cat
> Now he feeds on beetles and bark and sprat
> And . . . here and there a low-flying bat
> But he has no taste for mouse or rat!
>
> Sing: Hey-crack, derry-crack
> Yow-meow-a-derry-crack
> Hey-crack, derry-crack, eats no rats!'

The end of Hangbelly's song was followed by much laughing and cheering. Tailchaser noticed that even Eyeshimmer had a look of honest amusement on his ascetic face.

73

CHAPTER NINE

Wind is in the cane. Come along.
Cane leaves swaying, rusty with talk
Scratching choruses above the guinea's squawk
Wind is in the cane. Come along.

– Jean Toomer

Sunrise brought a temporary end to the rains. After a morning meal, the party made its way to the edge of the forest and paused for a while to sift the breeze. The downs stretched out into the distance, shrouded in mist. Tailchaser wondered how far away home was.

As Quiverclaw and Hangbelly argued over routes, Pouncequick hopped and danced on the dewy grass. The catling's pleasure at being out from under the brooding weight of the forest was understandable; Fritti wished that his heart, too, could be so light.

If this forest is the worst place we pass, we'll be exceptionally lucky, he thought. *It's nice to be out in the open, but there seem precious few hiding places on the downs. That's one thing that does speak well for dense woods.*

The Thane of the First-walkers approached him, the rest of his party gathered behind in a semicircle.

'I take it you still mean to head for the Court,' Quiverclaw rasped. Again it seemed that disdain was in his voice, but Fritti's mind was too full to give it much thought.

'Yes, Thane, I think it best.'

'Well,' said Quiverclaw, 'we must turn east here, along the rim of the Old Woods. I think that some directions would help you, would they not?'

'Certainly,' said Fritti. 'We've come this far on some very slight information given to us by Stretchslow, but he said we would need help once we were through the forest.'

The black cat leaned forward with an inquiring look. 'Did you say *Stretchslow*?'

'Yes. He is a friend of ours from Meeting Wall. He gave me my hunt-singing!' Fritti added proudly. The Thane wrinkled his nose and smiled.

'Is he a big, tawny fellow?' Quiverclaw asked. 'Always acting as though he'd just wakened up?' Fritti nodded.

'Stretchslow!' came the eruptive bellow from Hangbelly. The stripy old tom wiggled his head in delight. 'Old Stretchslow! Why didn't you tell us, you sly little lizard?'

Fritti was amused. 'I didn't expect you'd know him.'

'Know him?' Hangbelly gurgled. 'Every sniff, every scent! We hunted together in the Southern Rootwood for seasons and seasons and seasons. An excellent cat! Ha! What a whiskerbender!'

Quiverclaw gave an affectionate look to his old friend, who was bobbing like a nestling. 'Hangbelly speaks the truth,' said the Thane. 'You'll earn no enmity from us with Stretchslow's name as a hunt-mark. Well, if you have the sponsorship of such a cat, I feel better on many accounts. Stretchslow would not make a hunt-brother of someone for a game.'

Fritti was again a little bemused. Everyone seemed to find more importance in him than he did himself! 'Well, as I said, Stretchslow didn't sing a very clear song for us about where to go beyond the forest,' he offered.

'Ah,' grated Quiverclaw with mock sorrow. 'To be reminded of my duty by a mere nestling. I think our old comrade sent you from afar to chasten me. I did say I would give you directions, did I not? Very well. Listen closely, for I will give you more than just the path to the Queen's Court.'

The Thane turned and faced out across the rolling landscape. 'Now then: before you stretch the Gentlerun Downs. Follow your nose as it now points – keep the sunset on your left near flank and you won't go wrong. When you cross the Tailwend River you'll be onto the plains, and about halfway to journey's end.

'Keep your nose pointed U'ea-ward, and eventually you'll find the plains rising a bit. When you reach the Purrwhisper, cross to the far bank and follow upstream into the outskirts of Rootwood. You'll know when you've reached it. Can you remember all that?'

Fritti said that he could.

'I'll help him, sir,' said Pouncequick. Everyone agreed that he assuredly would, and the First-walkers gathered around to bid farewell. Even Bobweave came forward and touched noses with Fritti and Pouncequick.

As his companion had a farewell wrestle with Scuffledig, Tailchaser found Eyeshimmer beside him.

'I would like to do a *seeing* for you,' said the white cat. 'I feel possibilities blowing. Do not be afraid.'

Fritti was not sure that he wanted whatever it was that Eyeshimmer was offering, but it was too late to object. The Far-senser had already sniffed his nose, and was scenting down the length of his spine to his tail-tip. Then the white cat sat back on his haunches and closed his eyes.

When he opened them Tailchaser was startled to see that their milky, azure color had changed to a deep blue-black. Eyeshimmer's mouth gaped, and a breathy voice whispered out.

' . . . *The great ones cry out in the night . . . there is movement in the earth . . . the heart's desire is found . . . in an unexpected place . . .* '

The Far-senser shook his head, as if bothered by a loud noise; then the whispering voice continued: ' . . . *everyone flees from the bear, but . . . sometimes the bear himself . . . has bad dreams . . .* ' There was a brief pause, then: ' . . . *when caught in dark places, choose your friends well . . . or choose your enemies . . .* '

After another moment's silence, Eyeshimmer closed his eyes again, and when he lifted his lids his gaze was once more the cerulean shade of a summer sky.

He bobbed his head once to the shaken Tailchaser. 'May you find luck, dancing, young hunter,' he said, and turned away. Fritti sat puzzling over the weird song that Eyeshimmer had sung for him as Quiverclaw approached, Hangbelly stumping along at his side.

'Before we bid you good-journey, friend Tailchaser, I will offer you a word or so of advice,' said the Thane. 'The Court may not be all that you expect. I hope you understand.

'We First-walkers believe it is unnatural, and against the will of our Lord Tangaloor Firefoot, for the Folk to live always in such close proximity to one another. Also, in recent times the place has begun to stink of M'an.'

'You mean that there are Big Ones living near?' asked Fritti, surprised.

'No, of course not, only that the taint of our once-servants has spread even to the Seat of Harar. But I suppose it is not fair to prejudice you. We First-walkers *are* a solitary lot, and many at the

Queen's Seat find us extreme. You will have to be a hunter, and make your own course.' The black chieftain looked down at the dirt.

Hangbelly spoke up. 'The young Prince Fencewalker is not a bad sort, though. If you have need of a friend, he's a good 'un to have. A bit boisterous, but an honest enough cat.'

Quiverclaw looked up and grinned, sharp teeth a-twinkle. 'Come, we have burdened you with enough words to keep a scatter of gray-muzzles pondering for seasons. We must finish our leave-taking.'

The three walked over to join the others. Pouncequick squirmed out from beneath Scuffledig and trotted over to Fritti's side. Quiverclaw waved his paw in benediction.

'Tailchaser and Pouncequick, brave young hunters and friends of our old comrade Stretchslow, we wish you good journeying. Know that you are among the very few outsiders ever permitted to walk with the First-walkers.' Fritti and Pouncequick lowered their heads.

'I will tell you a prayer we speak. If you are in danger, and speak it, any of the First-walkers who may hear will aid you. If there are none about, well, it is no bad idea to call on the name of our Lord the Adventurer – whatever the situation. These are the words:

> *Tangaloor, fire-bright*
> *Flame-foot, farthest walker*
> *Your hunter speaks*
> *In need he walks*
> *In need, but never in fear.*

'Can you remember that? Good!' There was a moment's uncomfortable pause. 'Good dancing to you both,' Quiverclaw added.

Fritti bowed his head. 'Farewell, Thane, and First-walkers. Your kindness is all the more valuable, being unlooked-for. May you also have good journeying and good dancing.'

Tailchaser turned, and without looking back started away toward the downs. After a moment Pouncequick followed.

Long after the First-walkers were out of sight, they still traveled in silence.

The first few days on the downs passed calmly enough. The passage of every Hour or so brought them to the top of a rounded hill, with visibility in all directions. Marking their position from the sun, they had no trouble keeping to their route.

The matted grasses cushioned the tired pads of the two cats, and the green, hilly slopes of Gentlerun were populated in abundance by all manner of edible things and creatures. The downs pulsed to a quieter, more reflective measure than the forest, and even the hunted seemed to accept their status with quiet fatalism. It was not unpleasant, passing across that gently curving country.

Days were becoming colder, though. Autumn was rounding the bend – with winter waiting patiently ahead – and Fritti and Pouncequick could feel the change in the weather as a quiet urging. When they caught themselves lagging, or felt lured by a new sight or smell, the chill down deep in their bones would reach out and give a small, icy squeeze, and send them hurrying back to their path.

Fritti was sad to see Pouncequick's good spirits dampened by the hard traveling. Tailchaser, too, was melancholy, but his responsibility to the brave little cat gave some purpose to the bleaker Hours of the journey.

One gray afternoon the cats were hunting for their midday meal across the broad, green side of a hill. A small scrub growth of forest crowned the hummock, and from below it had seemed a likely place to search for game.

Nosing around the fringes of the copse, the two cats flushed a young rabbit from the undergrowth. As it bolted across the curving sward they leaped in pursuit, splitting off to either side of the fleeing Praere to box its escape.

The rabbit froze in place so suddenly that the surprised hunters also halted, and at that moment a shadow passed over their heads. The Praere, immobile but for twitching nose, panic in its staring eyes, disappeared in a rush of brown feathers that dropped from above.

The hawk barely touched ground as it stooped to the rabbit, grasping it with horny talons, breaking its back. Beating its wings heavily for a moment, the Meskra rose, dangling the limp body. Then, catching the wind, it vaulted upward, leaving the two cats gaping after. Neither bird nor prey had made a sound. The hill was suddenly bare and empty in the weak sunlight.

After a moment Pouncequick turned to Fritti. His teeth were bared in fright. 'Oh, Tailchaser,' he whimpered, 'I want to go home.'

Fritti could think of no response, and led Pouncequick down the hill in silence.

Later that afternoon, when Pouncequick finally fell asleep, Fritti sat and watched the clouds creeping across the low sky.

*

Eight days had passed on the downs since the pair had left the eaves of the Old Woods; Meerclar's Eye had waxed full and begun its closing. From the tops of the higher hills they could now see a dull shine in the distance, snaking a tarnished course through the hummocks of the far country.

Fritti was pleased to see it. He was fairly sure that it was the Tailwend River, and Quiverclaw had said that it would mark the halfway point of their journey to the Court.

They marched onward with a little more enthusiasm, but at first the gap did not seem to lessen very rapidly; the Tailwend remained just a shimmer on the horizon. The downs had begun to slope toward the river basin, though, and the patches of trees that dotted the surrounding countryside were more widely separated.

On their thirteenth night out of the forest they could finally hear the muted sound of the river across the meadowlands. It was a soothing noise – from this distance very much like that of the creek that ran past Meeting Wall after the spring thaws. Before sleep that night the pair played a game of Stalk-and-Spring, and Fritti laughed for the first time since they had parted company with the First-walkers.

They came down the shallow basin to the river's edge on the morning of the fifteenth day on Gentlerun Downs. The mist hung on the grass, and the sky smelled of rain to come. Approaching Tailwend, which was high on its banks, was like coming down off the plateau into a world of water and cool air.

The rushing, gurgling river had a vitality and energy completely unlike the shy, hidebound forest streams of their home. The Tailwend splashed and laughed, carrying river willows and grass stems along in a rush, only to send them spinning off into quiet eddies along the bank where they would float lazily. Then the river would cat-and-mouse them back into the current and carry them out of sight.

Fritti and Pouncequick played on the banks until the sun rose into the sky above their heads and shone through the mist to chip glimmers off the hurrying water. They took turns swiping at sticks that floated in close to the river's edge – darting their paws out, daring each other after twigs farther from shore. It was only when Pouncequick, in a moment of riotous abandon, came close to falling in – caught at the last moment by the nape of the neck – that Fritti began to turn his mind to the problem of crossing the wide, energetic Tailwend.

They walked farther upstream, tracing the coves and inlets, and the water sounds became harsher and more percussive. Around a bend in the river's course they discovered the reason. Here the Tailwend narrowed slightly and lunged past a group of rocks that stood upright in the foaming water like broken teeth. As they drew closer, the top of one of the rocks moved slightly, then turned to look at them with wide eyes.

It was Eatbugs, perched like an owl in midstream.

The Tailwend rushed and hissed past the mad cat. He stared at the two companions for a moment, then rose to his feet, fur starting out spiky-stiff all over his body. Without a word he teetered in place for a moment, then bounded out to another stone farther into the river. He was looking for the next safe spot to jump to when Fritti called out to him above the roaring of the rapids.

'Eatbugs! Is that really you? It's Tailchaser and Pouncequick! Do you remember us?'

Eatbugs turned to gaze imperturbably back at them.

'Please come back! Eatbugs!' Fritti raised his voice. 'Please cross back over!'

Eatbugs hesitated for a moment, then leaped back to the stone he had left. As the two friends watched, he laboriously made his way back across the river, finally hopping off the last stone onto the grassy bank. Regarding them warily for a moment, Eatbugs crouched at river's edge.

Finally, recognition seemed to dawn. He appeared to speak, but Fritti could not hear him above the din of the Tailwend, and signaled that the old cat should follow them up the bank.

Some distance from the river, they stopped.

'It's good to see you again, Eatbugs!' Pouncequick said cheerily. He seemed to have forgotten any fear he had once felt in the presence of the odd, muddy cat.

With a pleased but worried look on his face, Eatbugs walked around the pair, scenting their presence.

'Wurra-wurra-wurra,' he said finally, 'it's the tail-waggers, the shinky-shanky ones themselves!' He cocked his head inquisitively. 'What brings you little lubbers tip-tipping down to the riverside? Dost come to moisten thy noses? Ah . . . the real wonder is, how did you escape the burning questions of the demon-cats? Did you grow wings and fly away? It wouldna be the first time,' he added cryptically.

'What demon-cats?' asked Pouncequick. 'We met only the First-walkers, and they were very kind to us.'

'Ach! Ratspatter!' Eatbugs growled and spat. 'They start out nice, true enough, but soon they want things, want things – always pressuring a body.'

Fritti did not take Eatbugs' rambling too seriously. 'Well now,' he said, 'now that we're all here, should we walk together for a while? Once across the river, we're going to be traveling the Sunsnest Plains. We'd admire your company.'

Eatbugs smiled and nodded. 'I shall be passing that way,' he assented. 'I am following a particularly loud and vociferous star' – he lowered his ears and voice – 'but . . . I know where it goes to ground for winter!' Pleased at having shared his secret, Eatbugs did a small cross-step and bit lightly upon the ear of Pouncequick, who took it in good spirit.

'Can you lead us across the stream?' Fritti asked. 'You seem to know the best rocks.'

'Do chipmunks have fur on their stripey behinds? Of course I can!' said Eatbugs.

The terrain changed on the farther shore of the Tailwend. The green-carpeted hills of Gentlerun dwindled and disappeared within the Hour – succeeded only by occasional kitten-hummocks that swelled cautiously up from the waving grass.

Pouncequick and Tailchaser had never seen anything to compare with the plain of Sunsnest. It stretched out and away from them, seemingly endless: a broad, flat ocean of grass and ground-hugging vegetation. It was as flat as nature could fashion, and although the downs rose up behind them, the impression was of walking on a high place. The sky, now flush with the winds and waters of a colder season, hung close above their heads, adding to the sensation. It felt as though they had been raised up onto a vast surface, to be examined by some impersonal force.

Fritti and the kitten were grateful for Eatbugs' company. After their third and fourth sunrises, the monotonous grandeur of the plains began to make them feel very small and purposeless. Eatbugs, though, was a veritable fountain of distraction, brimming with fragments of strange poems and favored sayings that applied to nothing.

Crouching for rest in the waving grass one afternoon, Pouncequick shyly began to recite a fragment of a poem he was making up about their journey to the Court of Harar. It was awkward and unfinished, but Fritti found it appealing. He was surprised to see that it seemed to make Eatbugs very uncomfortable.

Wishing to spare Pouncequick embarrassment he praised the kitten's poem, then turned to Eatbugs to change the subject.

'I've been wondering,' Tailchaser began, 'why exactly this great flatland is called Sunsnest Plains. I see nothing of a nest about it at all, Eatbugs. Do you know?'

Eatbugs turned his mournful eyes on Tailchaser, and absentmindedly pawed a soiled twist of fur out of his face. 'As it happens, little nibbler of Squeaker-toes, I do. I truly do.'

'Well, tell us, please! Is it a song?'

'No, no, not a song, though I suppose it could be.' Eatbugs shook his head sadly. 'It is just a thing I remember hearing when I was a kitling, fewer Eyes behind me than little inkum-dinkum here.'

Fritti realized that they knew nothing of Eatbugs' past. He promised himself to try later to draw the mad, melancholy wanderer out on the subject.

'It is said, it is, by them as should know,' Eatbugs intoned, 'that when Meerclar Allmother first opened her bright eyes there was darkness everywhere. The Allmother had the sharpest eyes of all, naturally, but even though she could see, she was chattering, chafing cold. So she thought and thought, for no cat, even the greatest, likes to be cold.

'After a while, an idea came to her. She rubbed her paws together – her great, black paws – and she rubbed them so fast that they struck a spark of sky-fire. She took the spark and lay down on the earth.

'There she lay nurturing it, protecting it with the fur of her body – and it grew. The spark tried to run away as it became larger, but always the Allmother would reach out and catch it, roll-rolling it back across the earth to where it was born.

'It grew, and waxed large and grand, and when she would capture it and roll it back the land would flatten beneath them where they passed. Bigger and rounder and brighter it became, until its presence in the world warmed all the first animals.

'All creatures came and gathered around the young sun, crowding and pushing to get closer . . . and no beast would do anything else but lie there in that warmth and bask, until all the world became empty and lifeless except that one spot on the great, flattened plain.

'At this, Meerclar Allmother became angry as bitter weather, and threw the sun up into the sky where it would shine equally over all the world, and the dwellers in the earth dispersed again. There in the sky the sun still shines.

'But still, when the sun has burned and warmed as best it can and begins to tire, Meerclar takes it to her furry breast, where it strengthens again. While she has it, the world is cold for a season.

'And now,' Eatbugs finished, 'we are crossing the very spot where the Allmother kept it in its kittenhood, hence the name. Simple as mice for dinner, isn't it?'

Fritti and Pouncequick agreed that it was.

The next day, near the overture of Unfolding Dark, as the sun of which the mad cat had spoken was settling down into the cloudy west, Eatbugs was again seized by one of his fits.

The company was breast-deep in a swaying sea of grassworks when Eatbugs abruptly sat up, whiskers a-jut, and began to mutter.

He did not seem frightened or wary this time, but full of enthusiasm as he muttered: ' . . . There you are. Ha! Lying in the rye, are you? Trickle and tickle beneath my nose, will-you-sir? Ha!'

Tailchaser and Pouncequick sat down to wait, confident that the spell would soon subside, and they could return to journeying.

'Wait! Wait!' cried Eatbugs, and sprang to his feet. 'The star! Don't you hear it flickering? We must be on it, before it sniffs our true colors! Oh, do not let me be too late again! I shall leap the wall!' Suddenly, without warning, Eatbugs was off, calling after the star as if he could see it bounding in front of him. He disappeared into the tall weeds – the companions, dismayed, gave chase. Eatbugs' speed was too great, though, and soon even his voice had faded from hearing.

They waited in the spot all evening, stomachs impatient with hunger, but he did not return. At last they gave up and went hunting.

The morning found them a party of two again, and they traveled on.

CHAPTER TEN

What do they hunt by the glimmering pools of water,
By the round silver Moon, the Pool of Heaven –
In the striped grass, amid the barkless trees –
The stars scattered like the eyes of the beasts
above them!

— W. J. Turner

Now the rains set in.

Moving across the broad back of Sunsnest, the cats at first would run for what scant cover they could find. But as shelter became more scarce and rain more frequent, they were forced to resign themselves to wet fur.

Pouncequick caught a cold, and his sniffling began to intrude on Tailchaser's own private misery. Sometimes the interruption would bring a rush of sympathy for the little cat, and Fritti would strive to say a cheerful word or give an affectionate nudge. Sometimes, though, he responded to Pouncequick's illness and smallness with flashes of annoyance that flared, then quickly faded.

One night, when a scared, cold Pouncequick had climbed onto him during a violent thundershower, all the frustration that Tailchaser had been feeling welled up; he pushed the kitten away, swatting him with his paw. As Pouncequick crawled into a thatch of grass, little crying noises shaking his small form, Fritti felt a sudden wave of terror. Pouncequick would die, and leave him alone in this vast, wild land!

Then, realizing what he had done, he went and caught the small cat by the nape of the neck and brought him back. He licked the kitten all over his wet fur and huddled against him to keep him warm until the rains would cease for a time.

Several days later, still proceeding with flagging determination, Fritti began to feel that something was following them. After the larger part of the day had passed, the feelings had not departed; they had, in fact, grown stronger. He mentioned this as casually as he could to his young comrade.

'But, Tailchaser,' Pouncequick pointed out, 'game has been awfully scarce lately, and we haven't had much to eat. Really, I expect you're just not quite yourself. Who but a couple of madcats would be out and about in this weather?'

It was a canny point, but deep inside Fritti felt that something more than simply a lack of mice was acting on his senses.

That night, in the most secret part of Final Dancing, Fritti sat bolt upright in their sleeping spot.

'Pounce!' he hissed. 'There's something out there! There is! Can't you feel it?'

Pouncequick obviously could: he, too, was now awake and trembling. They both strained their eyes into the surrounding darkness, but could find nothing except the void of night. A creeping, tingling cold was in their whiskers, though, and from somewhere close by the moisture-soaked air carried a scent of blood and old bones.

They passed the rest of the night like the Squeakers they hunted – starting at every sound – but at last the sensations diminished, then were gone. Even in the thin light of morning they did not feel like sleeping. They were on their way without stopping to hunt for breakfast.

The rains increased that day, the skies dark and swollen, and from time to time a wind blew up from the North and sent the water sheeting into their faces as they trudged forward. The feeling of being watched had not departed, and had now spread from Fritti to Pouncequick. So it was that when they finally did run down a small, bedraggled Squeaker in the late evening, they ate hurriedly and standing up, despite their great hunger and weariness.

The last mouthfuls of stringy meat were just passing their lips when from the swirling, rainy darkness beyond them there came a horrible wailing cry that turned them into immobile stone where they stood, stopping their hearts for a moment in midbeat. Another cry – no less terrifying, but a little farther away – choked up from the other side at the two cats.

Hemmed in! The sickening idea came to them both simultaneously. An odd, chuffing sound came from the site of the first howl, and then something crashed toward them through the tall grasses.

Breaking suddenly from his frozen stupor, Fritti turned and butted Pouncequick with his head, so hard that the little cat almost tumbled over.

'Run, Pounce, fast as you can!' Fritti squeaked, trying to keep his voice down. Pouncequick recovered his balance, and the two bolted forward like snakes from beneath an overturned rock. From the other side now, they could hear the rustling and snapping of brush. They ran as fast as they were able, ears tight to their heads, tails straight out behind them. There were sounds of pursuit.

'Oh, oh, it's the same ones, the red claws, oh!' moaned Pouncequick.

'For the love of Whitewind, save your breath and run!' gasped Tailchaser. Behind them a sputtering, echoing cry was raised into the storm winds.

On and on they pelted, rain and darkness surrounding them, wind blowing against them. Fortunately the ground was level, and there were no trees or rocks – they could not have seen their way even if they had found the presence of mind to look. They were tiring rapidly.

Finally, when it seemed as if they had been running forever, the sounds of pursuit began to dwindle, then were gone. Still they staggered forward as long as they could, until finally they felt as though their legs would not carry them across another jump of ground. They slowed to a stumbling walk, listening intently, straining to hear any trace of followers over the pounding of their hearts and their ragged breathing.

At that moment a huge shape stepped from a clump of weeds before them.

'Now we have you!' it said. With squeals of despair the two cats tottered and fell at the feet of the great, dark creature.

Fritti's spirit struggled back to perception. He was tired, and sick to his stomach. It seemed as though the world was bouncing up and down around him. Confused, he wondered where he was and what had happened.

Then he remembered the chase, and the giant, looming shape.

Fritti tried to twist himself onto his feet, but found himself held fast. There was a sharp grip on the back of his neck, and he could feel nothing beneath his paws. Dizzily, he opened his eyes and peered about.

At his side Pouncequick was being nape-carried, dangling unconscious from the jaws of the biggest cat Tailchaser had ever seen. The monstrous gray-green-and-black-striped tom turned an impersonal stare at Fritti. Pouncequick's captor was pacing beside him, but Fritti's feet were touching nothing but air. . . .

Tailchaser slowly turned his head around. He could not see the face of his warder, but he could see the tree-limb-thick legs of the cat measuring out the ground. Fritti was bobbing and swaying in the grip of this beast, as helpless as a three-day-old kitten.

With a rush of panic he threw back his head, wriggling, and then the light faded again.

Some time later, Tailchaser reawakened, but he made no more attempts to break free.

Finally the seemingly tireless beasts stopped. Fritti was dumped unceremoniously to the ground, and beside him he heard the sound of Pouncequick being dropped like a dead Squeaker. A voice spoke, using the Common Singing, and Tailchaser screwed his eyes tightly shut.

'Surely this can't be what we were searching for?' the voice said, displeasure evident in its inflection. Curiosity lost out to fear: Fritti did not open his eyes, but remained crumpled face-down in the grass.

The cat that had carried him was the next speaker.

'They disappeared, like, sir,' it said, slowly and deeply. 'One moment they was there, and the next – they wasn't. Right strange.'

'Strange – I'm with you, there. And more than a mite disturbing,' said the first voice thoughtfully. 'Where did these two whelps come from?'

'Ran right into us, they did, sir. Shrieked like snagged squirrels and fell down flat. We thought we should bring them in. Been running, they had.'

There was a moment's pause. Tailchaser felt recovered enough to lift an eyelid fractionally. Beside the vast, fuzzy shapes standing over Pounce and him, there was a smaller shape. Smaller, but still considerably bigger than Fritti himself. He shuddered.

'Did you spot anything interesting before they disappeared, Nightcatcher?' the smaller shape asked Pouncequick's guard. Fritti heard no reply, but some kind of response must have been made, for the smaller blur spoke again.

'I know. I was only hoping. Tails and Nails! Too many questions, not enough answers.' The speaker sat quietly for a moment as the two big cats patiently waited, then rose and walked to Pouncequick and sniffed him.

'Just a kitten!' it said. 'Odd place for an apprenticeship.' It turned toward Fritti, who immediately squeezed his eyes shut and went limp down to his last tailbone. The voice came next to his face – it took all his courage not to bolt and run.

'And this one hardly seems a hunter himself. P'raps they've lost their mother?' The speaker leaned closer and sniffed Fritti's ear, then howled so suddenly and loudly that Tailchaser rolled head over heels from the shock: 'I am *Prince Fencewalker*, and I *order* you to wake up and be questioned!'

Tailchaser – panting, ears ringing, claws sunk into the earth for something to hang on to – swayed in place and shook his head.

Fencewalker? he thought. *Where have I heard that name?*

He opened his eyes to find a large, shaggy cat staring at him curiously. The cat's pelt was as red-golden as autumn leaves. The Prince, for so he was, wore an expression of pleasure, his tongue poking out from between his front teeth. He appeared very gratified by Tailchaser's response.

Fencewalker turned to the large brindle that had carried Fritti, and now wore a lopsided grin. 'Nothing like authority,' the Prince said. 'Right, Dayhunter?'

'No sir,' responded the big cat.

The mad humming of Tailchaser's nerves began to subside. He remembered now that Hangbelly had mentioned Fencewalker as a good friend to have at Court.

Looking at the chortling Prince and his two monstrous companions, Fritti wondered if he would be able to survive such a friendship.

By the time that the sun had begun to warm the grasslands around them, Pouncequick had joined Tailchaser in consciousness. Still sick, tired and frightened, the little cat did not move or speak much, but lay listening as Fritti finished telling the Prince of their journey. The Prince asked many questions, and was very interested in the chase of the night before – even more so with Pouncequick's scarlet-clawed thing in the Old Woods. He would have probed the kitten on the subject, but Fritti – worrying about his young companion's weakened state – managed to intercede. Fencewalker reluctantly agreed to postpone the interrogation until later.

Prince Fencewalker then explained that there had been disturbances of a similar kind all along the outlands of the Court of Harar. He and his massive companions, Dayhunter and Nightcatcher, twin sons of an old Court bloodline, had taken on the assignment of bringing the malefactors to bay. They had found no luck, however.

'It makes a cat wonder,' said Fencewalker grouchily. 'They're here, they're there, then they're gone. We three just can't keep up with them. I suppose it's a good thing the First-walkers are taking an interest – we could use some more paws on this.'

'But you're the Prince!' said Fritti, surprised. 'Can't you find all the help you need at Court?'

Fencewalker glowered. 'It doesn't work out that way,' he said, shaking his red-gold mane. 'Nobody will take this sort of thing seriously. Everybody's got something more important to do. Nothing matters to anyone if it's not gnawing at his own tail. Even Mother and the Prince Consort more or less said: "Go ahead and scout around if you enjoy it." Hah! Serve them right if these cat-badgers – or whatever they are – come climbing out of the trees and chew their ears off!'

This set Tailchaser to worrying in silence for a while. What if there was no help at the Court? How would he proceed in his search for Hushpad? The memory of her waving tail and black-trimmed nose came forcefully back to him.

If no one else cares what happens to her, he thought angrily, *all the more reason why I must continue the search.*

His reverie was interrupted by the sound of little Pouncequick being sick. His young friend's poor health was another problem. The rains were here to stay, and Pouncequick would be in bad shape if he didn't get to shelter and food soon.

'Prince Fencewalker, will you be returning to Court now?' he asked.

'I hadn't really decided yet,' muttered the Prince. 'I suppose we might as well try to scare up another cat or two. Why do you ask?'

'My companion is not well, as I'm sure you can see. If you would help us get to the Queen's Seat, we would be grateful.' Fencewalker looked thoughtful.

'The little scuffler isn't doing none too good, sir,' offered Dayhunter helpfully. 'He probably needs to get warm-like.'

Fencewalker passed over to Pouncequick, who was shivering miserably on the moist grass. 'We'll get you to a place you'll like, little fellow,' said the Prince in his bluff, friendly manner, 'if we've got to kitten-carry you all the way. We'll get you to the Court.'

Pouncequick was carried the last leagues across the Sunsnest Plains

89

by Dayhunter and Nightcatcher, but Fritti was strong enough to walk. He found himself enjoying the company of Fencewalker and his hunt-mates.

The Prince was garrulous, telling hunting stories of great length and interminable detail, and frequently interrupting his narrative to check details with Dayhunter. It was particularly hard on continuity when the Prince's huge companion was taking his turn transporting Pouncequick.

' . . . Now I believe,' the Prince would say, 'I believe, and I really should be able to remember, that *that* was the day after we had run down a simply magnificent grouse. Or perhaps it was a cock pheasant? Do you remember, Dayhunter? Was that a cock pheasant?'

'Mmmff!' Dayhunter would reply through a mouthful of Pouncequick.

'Pardon? Grouse, did you say?'

'Mmmf-mmmff.'

'Oh, a pheasant? You're sure?' And so on.

The Prince was a cheerful soul – full of rough good humor, and an affection for sudden, surprising shoves that sent companions tumbling. The companion would then be helped to rise by a guiltily solicitous Fencewalker, who would promise not to do it again without suitable warning.

The twins were so alike as to be indistinguishable in outside appearance, although they could be told apart by scent. Dayhunter was not a clever cat, but goodhearted and very chatty. His brother, Nightcatcher, was very quiet.

After traveling with the three for a day, Fritti finally realized that Nightcatcher's stolidity was involuntary. He was mute, and communicated only in the soundless ways given to the Common Singing. Fencewalker explained to Fritti that Nightcatcher had sustained a throat wound while protecting the Prince from a maddened fox, and had been unable to make a sound since.

'He did it for me, Harar keep 'im,' said Fencewalker. 'These are my true hunt-brothers, don't you see.' Nightcatcher beamed with permanently quiet pride.

The plains began to slope uphill. Fritti knew from Quiverclaw's instructions that they were reaching the outer fringes of Sunsnest. The grade was slight but constant, and at the end of a day's walk Tailchaser's back legs throbbed.

At last they reached the banks of the Purrwhisper. It was a much quieter stream than the Tailwend, gentle and gurgling. Its bed was covered with many-colored stones, and above these could be seen the flashing dart of shiny fish.

They stopped to drink, and even Pouncequick clambered down to lap up the chill, clear water. It was sweet and refreshing, and when they had finished, Pouncequick and Tailchaser lay side by side on the stream bank and shared a silent feeling of hope for the first time in a long while.

Pounce is still a very sick kitten, though, thought Fritti. He was moving closer to warm him when Fencewalker approached.

'Well, here we are at the Purrwhisper. Just a hop and a stumble to go now, little chap!' he said to Pouncequick. 'See that line of shadow there?' The Prince indicated with his chin a ribbon of darkness running along the horizon, just visible against the gray skies. 'That's the outskirts of Rootwood – the biggest, grandest forest in the world. If we follow the Purrwhisper here in a ways – and none too far a way, either – do you know where we'll be?' Fencewalker looked down at the two companions. 'Firsthome! *That's* where – and warm and fat and dry as can be!' He grinned. 'I certainly wouldn't want to spend all my time rubbing fur in the Court, but even *I* admit it's a very nice nest to come back to.'

The Prince gave Fritti a friendly swat. 'I'll bet a couple of outland Folk like you will be amazed. Amazed!'

The following days passed in a sort of walking dream for Tailchaser. Pouncequick was feverish now, and hung quietly in the gentle jaws of the twins. Tailchaser himself was as tired as he had ever been in his short life, but Fencewalker and his companions, close now to their home, were setting a rapid pace. It was all Fritti could do to keep up.

They were moving along the northern bank of the Purrwhisper. Fritti decided that someday he would like to come back and explore the country they were passing – someday when he wasn't exhausted and footsore. All manner of vegetation grew on the shores of the softly splashing river. Sheltered spots and hidden grottoes, protected from the now-constant rain, beckoned invitingly to the weary Tailchaser, and animal and bird noises were calling him to come and investigate. Every whisker of his self-control was necessary to keep him marching on behind his stronger fellows, to shut out the blandishments of the river-world.

At last the small band of cats reached the eaves of Rootwood. Even in his harried condition, Fritti could feel how different this forest was from the Old Woods near his home. There was a feeling of age to this place that made the Old Woods, despite their name, seem kittenlike and fresh. Rootwood looked, felt, smelled and sounded so ancient and established that it seemed inconceivable that any of the great trees about them had actually *grown*. It seemed, rather, as though the world itself had grown up around their roots and trunks.

When Fritti mentioned his feelings to Fencewalker, the Prince nodded. Instead of responding with his usual irreverence, the red-gold hunter merely said: 'Aye. This is the first forest.'

In answer to Fritti's request for an explanation, Fencewalker suggested he wait and ask in the Court.

'There are those who can speak of the forest better than I, and I would not want to give insult by accident.'

Tailchaser had to accept this, for nothing more was offered. But when he asked later about the game of Rootwood, the Prince was again his usual, hearty self and gave Fritti an exacting description of everything that ran, slithered, swam or flew beneath the ancient trees.

The traces and hunt-marks of other Folk became commonplace. Tailchaser was now only interested in ending his journey; he ignored the excited discussions that Fencewalker and his companions had over what the various indicators meant: who had been doing what, and when, and with whom. Pouncequick, now sleeping constantly, was oblivious to it all.

After a day of staggering and limping, Tailchaser himself could walk no more. He and his kitten friend were once more carried side by side in the mouths of the brindled twins.

Sliding in and out of uncomfortable, bouncing sleep, Fritti was dimly aware of voices. The Prince and other cats were calling back and forth, and when Fritti dazedly opened his eyes he could see cat-shapes everywhere – a sea of Folk. It was too much for him to take in, and he closed his eyes again.

He felt himself put down on something soft. As the voices faded away he bounded into the dream-fields.

PART TWO

CHAPTER ELEVEN

... the crowd, and buzz and murmurings
Of this great hive, the city.

– Abraham Cowley

The roof beneath his feet felt hot; it was painful to keep his paws in one place for more than a moment. Treading gingerly up and down, he peered over the roof's edge into the swirling smoke below. He knew he should jump. He should save himself. Behind him was FIRE. The delicate inner linings of his nose were abraded by the fumes, and he could hear the flames booming and roaring below him. Why couldn't he jump?

His family! Somewhere behind him, menaced by the FIRE, were his mother and siblings. They were in danger! He remembered now.

A voice called up from the smoke before him. He stared over into the gray clouds, but could see nothing. From inside the M'an dwelling the terrified voices of his family floated up to him again.

The voice in the smoke was hailing him by name, telling him to jump down to safety. It sounded like Eatbugs, or perhaps Bristlejaw. He tried to tell the voice about his family – about them being trapped and endangered by the FIRE – but the voice kept calling to him: *leap down, forget your family, run, save yourself, run!*

He was caught! He was straddling the edge – the panicky wail of his brothers and sisters behind him; Bristlejaw – or was it Eatbugs – urging him to jump, to escape, to run, run, he couldn't decide, run, oh Harar! run run run . . .

Legs jerking convulsively, Tailchaser fell back into the waking world. The light was very bright. His eyes hurt.

A massive palisade of giant tree trunks stood around him, towering

95

up far beyond his sightline. Jumps and jumps above his head they stretched, branches interlaced like the strands of a mighty bark-hided spiderweb. But Tailchaser could feel warmth on his face. A broad swath of sunlight beamed down unhindered from some far-off sky window in the uppermost branches, making the short, tickling grass on which Fritti lay a summery island in the middle of the ancient cool of the forest.

Fritti felt the tenderness of his paws as he climbed shakily to his feet. He flopped back down and examined them, testing their soreness with his sensitive tongue.

The leather of his pads was cracked, and had probably bled. It had been carefully cleaned, though, and he could find no burrs or thorns – he had picked up many of those in the final stage of the approach to Firsthome, and had not had the strength or concentration to remove them. Someone had cleaned him up.

Fencewalker. Fencewalker had left him here, and no doubt had had his paws seen to. Where was Fencewalker?

Still feeling fuzzy and a little stupid – his heart was just now slowing down to normal after his startling dream – Fritti looked around. There were no other Folk in sight. The clearing amid the towering trees was empty . . . but Fritti could hear the sound of voices. From just far enough away to lend an air of unreality to the sound, the noises of many cats floated to him on the breeze.

Walking slowly and gently on his wounded paws, Tailchaser followed the voices out of the sunlit glade.

Looking up as he paced along beneath the hoary trees of Rootwood, he saw thick, ropy strands of lichen stretching from branch to branch – in some places so thick as to form a natural ceiling. The paths that wandered around the tree roots seemed vaulted, filigreed hallways; sunlight filtered through this canopy, dappling the ground with bright spots, and turning the daylight into a soft, suffusive glow. He could now see some of the Folk whose voices echoed from the bark of old trees and the packed earth of the forest floor.

The forest was alive with cats . . . more than he had seen in all his life since kittenhood, and all in one place. Cats of every size and description: walking, singing, sleeping, arguing – a world of cats at the feet of these powerful, ageless trees.

He stared at the incredible variety, but no one stared back. No one seemed even to notice him as he passed. And so many! Here a fat brindle was chasing a fela with a crook in her tail; there a crowd surrounded a pair of toms wrestling. Some just lay and slept.

Fritti found himself on a wide path: a rut worn into the springy, leafy ground by countless paws. Cats streamed past him coming and going. Those who met his eye gave a brief, strange roll and a twist of their heads. It seemed a neutral-enough gesture, and Tailchaser assumed that it was a greeting of some kind peculiar to Firsthome. Some of the cats that hurried by nudged him impatiently to the side as they passed. Since no one else seemed to take offense – and because he was still so weak and unsure of himself – after it had happened a few times, Fritti paid no more attention than any of the others did.

But, oh! the tremendous amount and diversity of those cats.

However do they manage to get along for any length of time? he wondered.

It was unnatural. It seemed more like a nest of ants, almost. Or the dwelling place of M'an.

'Tailchaser! Stop there! Tailchaser!'

Fritti turned to see Thinbone running up the path behind him. At least it looked like Thinbone . . . but as the cat approached, he saw that this fellow was bigger and glossier than his friend from Meeting Wall, although their coloring seemed identical. He realized with ironic amusement that for a moment it had seemed perfectly natural to see Thinbone here in Firsthome, more leagues from Edge Copse than Fritti could count.

My journeying has accustomed me to strange surprises, he thought.

The gray-and-yellow cat bounded up and stood for a moment trying to catch his breath.

'Nre'fa-o,' said Fritti. 'Have we sniffed before?'

' . . . J-just . . . just . . . moment . . . ' panted the newcomer, and made a comical face as he returned to the business of recovering his wind.

'Forgive me,' he said after a few more moments, 'but I was up, up, up a *terribly* tall tree when you left the healing-spot, and I had to run like dead Uncle Whitewind to catch you. Oh!' he said, looking about. 'I do hope none of Prince Dewtreader's friends or relations heard me say that. It was terribly disrespectful.' He looked at Tailchaser, and gave him such a sly, funny smile of satisfaction that Fritti – who didn't understand the newcomer at all – found himself smiling right back.

'Ummm, you said your name was . . . ?' Fritti ventured after a moment. The stranger sneezed once, convulsively, and delicately stroked his nose with the back of his paw.

'Forgive me,' he said. 'I quite forget myself sometimes. I'm Howlsong. Prince Fencewalker asked that you be, well, not watched over, exactly, but that you have a . . . a . . . ' Howlsong wrinkled his nose, thinking.

'A guide?' offered Fritti.

'A guide! Excellent! That's the sound of it exactly! Yes, so . . . here I am.'

'That was kind of Prince Fencewalker to remember me.'

'He is a fine fellow, right enough. A little too prone to knocking people down, if you know what I mean, but a solid cat. Claws firmly in the bark, we always say. Now, the Prince *Consort* . . . ' Here Howlsong trailed off meaningfully. Fritti, unsure of what to say, nodded his head politely.

'Well then,' said Howlsong suddenly, and fell into a deep fluid-spined stretch. 'Well then,' he resumed, 'let us go and look at Firsthome. The rest of it, I mean. I hear this is your first visit? It's terribly, terribly big and impressive – especially the Court. You'll have to wait to see that until Fencewalker arranges it. Did you really come from across the Sunsnest Plains?'

'From far on the other side, beyond the Old Woods,' answered Tailchaser.

'Incredible. Just amazing!' said Howlsong. 'Do they have trees where you live? I suppose they must, mustn't they?'

They had been walking for only a few moments when Fritti suddenly remembered Pouncequick. Full of worry for his little companion, he questioned Howlsong.

'Oh, they put him in the warmest healing-spot, since he was sicker than you were, and brought him sweet grasses and a little bit of mouse. He's doing much better now,' Howlsong assured him. 'I'll take you to see him later.'

They continued on their way. Howlsong seemed to positively bubble with anecdotes and trivia. He explained to Tailchaser that he was studying to be a Master Old-singer, but that his teacher was very busy because of some kind of Meeting taking place that night – consequently leaving him nothing to do, and making him available to accompany Fritti. He mentioned to Fritti that his 'set' – which Tailchaser took to mean some kind of grouping of young cats – all found Fencewalker to be 'quite an all-right type,' although 'a bit hearty.' Howlsong also explained that the Prince Consort, Prince Dewtreader, was thought of as being 'awfully serious' and 'nearly boring.' Queen Sunback was 'the loveliest cat, of course.' Tailchaser was bewildered by the familiarity with which Howlsong discussed and characterized the hereditary leaders of the Folk – as if they were any group of alley-haunters in the dwellings of M'an!

Customs were just different at Firsthome, it seemed, and it would take him a while to get used to them. Still, much was unfathomable.

'Are there always such an uncountable lot of cats living here?' he asked at one point.

'Blueback's Whiskers, no!' laughed Howlsong. 'Usually less than half this seething throng, I'd guess. They're here for the celebration I told you about.'

'But even if there were only a quarter of these, that's so many! How do you find food? The forest must be Squeakerless for miles around.'

'Oh, we do have to forage a bit far sometimes, it's true,' admitted the apprentice Old-singer, 'but Rootwood is the biggest forest there is – if things get thin, we send out hunting parties to stamp around and herd the game closer back to Court. It's a bit tiring sometimes, certainly – all the extra hunting and such – but it's worth it to live here. I mean, I've never lived anywhere else, and would never want to. Never.'

They walked as they conversed, and now and then Howlsong would interrupt the flow of discourse to point out an important sight: an extra-fine patch of mouse grass, a wonderful old scratching tree, or another cat who Howlsong felt was wretched, or gallant, or clever, or otherwise worthy of special attention. Many of these cats knew Howlsong and called greetings to him, which he cheerfully returned. Tailchaser decided that Firsthome was more like a tree full of birds than the anthill it had resembled at first impression.

After seeing a few more important attractions, and listening to a pair of young felas – 'wonderfully close friends' of Howlsong's – singing a sweet and mournful little song, the twosome at last reached the bower that housed Pouncequick. They found him in a many-jumps-wide path of slanting sunlight. The kitten was awake and talking to a slender gray fela with dark-green eyes and short fur.

'Tailchaser!' cried Pouncequick when he spotted them. 'I'm so happy to see you! I thought you were going to sleep all day and miss the fun. Aren't there ever so many cats here?'

Fritti walked over to him and sniffed the soft kitten-fur. The smell of sickness seemed to be gone.

'I'm very glad to see you, Pounce. I was worried about you.'

'I'm feeling fine!' chortled the youngling. 'Everyone's been grand to me. I've already made friends! Oh, that reminds me, I haven't offered face names. Tailchaser, this is Roofshadow.' He indicated the gray cat, who bobbed demurely. 'She's a visitor, too, as we are,' Pouncequick expanded.

'Nre'fa-o,' said Fritti. 'Good dancing.'

'And to you,' she responded. After a polite head-dip, Fritti turned back to look at his small friend again. Pounce certainly did *look* better, although still a little on the scrawny side. He had eaten very little while he had been ill.

The thought of food made Fritti's mouth begin to water. He suddenly realized that he had had nothing to eat since the day before. He was hungry! Imagine going all afternoon without thinking of food. He really had changed since leaving home.

'Pounce, Howlsong said that they brought you some mouse . . . ' he began.

'Oh, yes, a whole pile of them. They're over there. They were just killed this morning. Help yourself.' Tailchaser began to move toward the heap of Squeakers, then hesitated, looking at Howlsong and Roofshadow.

Howlsong laughed. 'Eat up, cu'nre. Don't even notice me.'

'I'll be going now, I think,' said Roofshadow. 'Perhaps you could escort me, Howlsong? I don't really know my way around yet.'

'I'd be overwhelmed with pleasure. I'll see you two soon,' he said to Fritti and Pouncequick. 'I'll be back to take you to the celebration toward the end of the Unfolding Dark.'

'And I'll return to visit you later, Pouncequick,' added Roofshadow. The two cats walked away with tails curving into the air, Howlsong excitedly describing some phenomenon of Court intrigue to the young gray fela.

Tailchaser had not even waited to watch them leave, but was already up to his chin in mice, with Pouncequick squeaking merrily at the mess he was making.

Afternoon became evening as the two friends sat and talked. Pouncequick had not yet had a chance to see more of Firsthome than was visible from his healing-spot, and was anxious for details. As Tailchaser was describing the many things that Howlsong had showed him or told him of, the rains came again. They could hear the soft patting noise in the leaves above their heads; and occasionally a drop would slip through to plink on the grass or their fur. Most of the rain was stopped by the intermingling branches and hanging lichen, though, and they sat quite comfortably. Eventually they lay down together and napped, the tipping and tapping of raindrops a backdrop for their dreams.

CHAPTER TWELVE

The good die first
And they whose hearts are dry as summer dust
Burn to the socket.

— William Wordsworth

Near the end of the Unfolding Dark, as he had promised, Howlsong returned to the bower.

'Up now, up now, you silly snoring cats!' he cried. 'There's far too much to do and see! We must get to the celebration!'

Full of mice and drowsiness, Fritti slowly bestirred himself. 'Is Pouncequick well enough to come with us?' he asked the apprentice Oel-cir'va.

'Of course! Don't you want to come see the terribly exciting things, Pouncequick?' Howlsong asked the sleepy kitten.

'Yes, I think I would – I mean I would,' said Pouncequick, rousing his diminutive form into a stretch. 'I feel just fine, Tailchaser.'

Absolutely splendid,' laughed Howlsong. 'It's all settled then. Let's be off. I shall have my tail most brutally pulled if we're late.'

As they wound through the tree galleries of Firsthome they found themselves caught up in a stream of Folk, most apparently headed in the same direction.

'Are we going to the Court itself, Howlsong?' queried Pouncequick breathlessly.

The gray-and-yellow tabby looked back over his shoulder as he hurried along. 'No, actually the Celebration is being held in the Meeting Glade. It's the only place where all the Folk will fit at the same time. Cats come from all over Rootwood and beyond, even, just as you two did – think of that! – to be here for the Celebration.

Hello, Smackbush! Your pelt looks extremely glossy tonight!' he called out to someone he recognized.

'What exactly *is* this Celebration?' Tailchaser asked. 'I mean, is it like Meeting Night?'

'No, no, quite different. Well, fairly different, anyway. . . . Glideswallow! Ho there!' he hailed another acquaintance. 'How's Pawgentle? Good, wonderful!' he cried cheerily, then turned back to his two wards. 'Glideswallow is doing the Dance of Acceptance with the most *unfortunate* little black-and-white fela . . . where was I? Oh, of course, the Celebration. I suppose you don't have anything like it back home, do you? Well, the full name is the Celebration of the Song of Whitewind. We always have it at the first opening of Meerclar's Eye of the wintertime.'

'What's it all about?' questioned Fritti. 'I don't mean any disrespect, but I've never heard of it.'

'Well, you *do* know who Whitewind is, don't you?' Fritti nodded. Howlsong continued: 'I'm not too sure that I understand all the deeper parts myself, but Prince Dewtreader – Fencewalker's father, you know – takes the whole thing dreadfully seriously. He tells a story, sort of, and we sing songs. It has something to do with Death, and the Fields Beyond, but I don't pay too much attention, myself. It's just about nearly boring. Most of us come for the chance to see everybody in the Court, especially the Queen's family. And the catmint, of course. Everyone likes catmint.'

'Will the Queen be there?' gasped Pouncequick, fighting to stay abreast of the two bigger cats.

'No, she never attends, for some reason that's slipped my mind. Poor me, so awfully much to think of. Being a Master Old-singer's not falling down a gopher hole, you know. It takes work! Ah hah! There you are, Dandlegrass! It's me, Howlsong!'

The Meeting Glade was in the center of a large forest clearing. Overhead, so high as to be almost beyond sight, the titanic branches of the old trees crossed and tangled into a vaulting roof.

The Glade itself was a wide, shallow bowl, covered in short grass and tree leaves. It sloped up on the end farthest from the approaching trio, ending in a sort of jutting promontory with a broad, flat top. Fritti could see two or three cats already crouching on this hilly point.

The bowl below was rapidly filling with purring, buzzing, nose-rubbing cats, streaming into the Glade from all points of the forest.

They roamed about in small groups, knots of Folk forming and breaking apart, calls sent out across the Glade to friends and relations.

Pouncequick, stunned by the profusion of cats, sat taking in the spectacle, his eyes shining with wonder. Fritti, though, felt faintly uneasy; his fur was tingling and tickling as though trying to stand out from his body – trying to give him more room. It felt unnatural, inexplicably wrong, for the Folk to gather together in such numbers. Gathering occasionally at Meeting was one thing: almost everybody liked company from time to time. But to live together like this, day in, day out – put down your paw and step on someone's tail . . . well, kind as the cats of Firsthome had been to him, he wouldn't stay much longer than he had to.

As the threesome found themselves a spot near the middle of the bowl, a fat, round-headed cat made his way up to the front of the promontory that overlooked the Glade. He was black-and-white, and the shagginess of his fur made him appear even stouter than he was – which was very stout. He looked out over the gathered Folk, and the level of noise dropped.

'That's Rumblepurr, the Court Chamberlain,' said Howlsong in a low, excited whisper. 'He's ever so important. Likes his Squeakers a bit much, and his naps, but don't be fooled. He's old, but he's quick as a tumblebug.'

Rumplepurr made a low coughing noise, then spoke, in a voice as sonorous as the wind blowing down a mountain pass.

'Good dancing, good Folk. On behalf of Her Bewhiskered Majesty, Queen Mirmirsor Sunback – direct descendant of Fela Skydancer, and true ruler of the Folk – and on behalf of the Prince Consort, Sresla Dewtreader, I bid you welcome to the Celebration of the Song of Whitewind. The Prince Consort and Prince Fencewalker will be here very soon.'

Rumblepurr bowed, making himself look – if possible – rounder than before, and returned to the back of the promontory. The noise of the gathered cats swelled again. Howlsong looked at Pouncequick, who was still staring openmouthed from side to side. The apprentice singer grinned and nudged Fritti. 'Nothing like this back at the nest, eh?' he said. As he spoke, another cat approached, calling Howlsong's name in greeting. Howlsong turned away, as if his attention had been drawn to something behind him, and waved his tail in the limpest kind of greeting. The newcomer paused for a moment, uncertain, then padded away.

'I absolutely loathe that Bandyleg,' Howlsong confided to Tailchaser. 'There's something about him that just doesn't set well with me. Hmmmph,' he continued, looking around the Glade, 'I suppose no one interesting will show up until the Celebration starts. At least we didn't have to listen to one of Rumblepurr's long, rambling stories. He's an old dear, and quite clever – as I mentioned, I think – but he can spin the most excruciating tales.'

A hush had fallen over the assembly, and all eyes now turned to the promontory. Fencewalker – with the ever-present twins – was mounting the hill. A group of rowdy young hunters in the first row began shouting up to him: 'There he is! Fence! Who groomed *you*, old boy? Hah! Good old Fencer!'

For a moment the Prince tried to pretend that he couldn't hear them, but was given away by the expression of embarrassed pleasure that crept onto his face as he moved out onto the promontory. He found his place and sat back on his haunches, his huge companions looming up on either side. A few other cats, whom Howlsong described as Court functionaries, were trailing up onto the overlook. Then, finally, Prince Dewtreader appeared with Rumblepurr waddling along behind him.

Dewtreader took his position at the front of the promontory. The young hunters at the front made a few last jibes at the grinning Fencewalker. Silence descended on the assembled Folk. Those who were still looking for a spot to lie down stopped to watch as the Prince Consort spoke.

Dewtreader's coat was a sandy beige, darkened at paws, ears, and tail to a deep brown. A sort of mask of brown also extended up from his nose, just past the upper ends of his slanting, sky-blue eyes. He had the look of a cat who had seen many strange places and things, and regarded them no differently than he did the sun and the leaves. His narrow head turned from side to side as he surveyed the Folk with almond-shaped eyes.

Something about him is very strange, thought Fritti. *He looks like he's seen so much that he doesn't enjoy looking at things anymore.*

'Greetings from the ancient Court of Harar.' Dewtreader's voice was soft and musical, but there was a hard edge hidden underneath. 'I have something to share with you, before the dancing and all begins. I know you would rather dance than listen to me, so I will be short-winded.' There was a quiet hum of amusement from the gathered Folk.

'I would like to tell you something I have been thinking about, and the Song of Whitewind is part of it. Before I begin, could we sing the Song of Thanks? I would feel happier if we did. Come, sing with me.'

Dewtreader began in a careful, melodic voice. After a moment, others joined in, until a whole chorus of voices swelled, rising up to the dome of trees and the starry sky beyond.

> *'Who passes by*
> *so softly gleaming?*
> *Is it just the falling snow?*
> *Watches us*
> *in quiet dreaming —*
> *winter quiet, sweetly slow?*
>
> *Whitewind with his*
> *coat a-beaming,*
> *where the stars*
> *are dancing, gleaming,*
> *where the winter winds*
> *are streaming —*
> *gentle Whitewind*
> *there will go. . . .*

Since he did not know the words, Tailchaser looked around at the singing multitude. Even Howlsong had his head thrown back in close-eyed rapture. Pouncequick sat beside him in respectful, awed silence, listening. All around the sibilant melodies of the Higher Singing rose and hung in the night air.

> *'If the darkness*
> *calls us sweetly,*
> *if the day is gone*
> *completely,*
> *we will give it all*
> *up meetly,*
> *only, Whitewind, tell us so. . . . '*

Something about the song bothered Fritti. Whitewind had been very brave and beautiful, but he had been gone since the earliest days of all. The song they sang spoke of the Firstborn as if they could smell him, see him. He looked about at all the solemn, uptilted faces and shivered. The song ended. Staring over the sea of ears and whiskers and bright eyes before him, Dewtreader began to speak.

'On this mysterious night, when we remember the sacrifice of Viror Whitewind, I would like to speak of another cat who suffered long, long ago.' The Prince Consort's voice was slow and measured, and even the bravos near the front were listening.

'Prince Ninebirds, long ago, was punished by Whitewind's brother Lord Tangaloor Firefoot. Changed and deformed into the creature we call M'an, he was cast forth into the world to serve the Folk as punishment for his pride. And he suffered. For good reason? Perhaps.

'For generation upon generation his descendants served our ancestors, venerating them and caring for them. Through eons, the Folk and the M'an became closer. Many of the Folk became dependent on the M'an to provide the things that we Folk have always provided for ourselves.'

This talk interested Fritti. Quiverclaw said that the influence of M'an was on the seat of Harar – Dewtreader seemed to be discussing it before all these Folk gathered for the Celebration.

'Many who live today say that the Folk have become weak,' Dewtreader continued, 'that many of us have come to rely on these strange, hairless, upright cats as if they were our own parents. Some say this shows a decline, a weakness in our lives. I am not so sure of that.' Dewtreader fixed his inscrutable stare on the Folk below.

'What was the sin of Ninebirds? Pride. Now, all the Folk are proud, of course – are we not the summit, the very tail-tip of creation? Do we not know the complicated dance of the earth best of all? Are these not reasons enough for pride?

'Perhaps. But was it not the pride of Hearteater, his passion to be Lord of All, that led to the death of Viror Whitewind? Does the world's music not forever lack that pure, white tone?

'Perhaps this M'an, this pathetic, oversized beast who clusters with his fellows in papery wasp nests, who goes unclawed and unfurred through the world, perhaps this object of scorn can teach us something?'

The audience was growing restless, although respect for Dewtreader's eminence discouraged noise. There was a great deal of squirming and whispering.

Tailchaser was thinking about what Dewtreader had said. It struck a subtly sour chord in him, like the faintest smell of decay. Pouncequick, though, seemed enraptured. Howlsong was craning his neck from side to side – not listening, but looking for friends.

' . . . For if we, in our pride,' continued Dewtreader, his slanted eyes glowing with reflected light, 'if we find ourselves kept and fed by these most humble of creatures, well, who is to say that it is not for the best? Perhaps the Allmother intends that we should learn humility, we prideful hunters . . . '

Howlsong suddenly leaped up. '*Harar!*' he whispered excitedly. 'I had completely forgotten! My teacher, Volenibble, must sing one of the old stories tonight, and I must help him prepare! Ay! Forgive me, you two, but I *must* run. Oh Skydancer, he'll bite my nose off!' Without waiting for a reply, Howlsong was leaping away, bounding over the surrounding forms.

When Fritti turned his attention back to the front of the glade, he saw that Dewtreader had finished speaking. The audience had instantly begun talking among themselves. Fritti turned to his companion.

'What do you think of all this, Pounce?'

Pouncequick, jerked out of a reverie, stared blankly for a moment, then said: 'Oh, I don't know, really. It's all so grand. I was just thinking about the things Dewtreader was saying, and I felt as if there were some kind of light I needed to reach just ahead. It wasn't exactly what he was saying, but something he said sort of brought it on . . . it was an extraordinary feeling, but I'm afraid I can't explain it very well.'

'It rather bothered me,' said Fritti, 'but I can't get *my* claws into the reason, either. Well, I suppose it's beyond outlanders like us, but Dewtreader's folk didn't seem to be taking it all that seriously.'

The pause in the proceedings continued, the little groups chatting and conversing animatedly. Fencewalker had come to the leading edge of the promontory and was talking to his friends in front.

'It doesn't look as though anything will happen for a while. I'm going to go and make me'mre. Do you want to stay here and wait for me?'

'I think I'll just lie here for a while and watch, Tailchaser.'

Fritti threaded his way through the crowd and out to the forest beyond the rim of the Glade. When he had finished, and covered his hole, he strolled around the edge of the bowl, enjoying the smell of the rain-washed air.

As he was padding along with head high, an exotic odor crept into his nostrils. He stopped for a moment, nose whiffling. The scent was heady and exciting. He followed it forward.

Just behind the promontory where the Queen's family sat he found

108

a small stand of plants with tiny white flowers. This was the source of the tantalizing smell, and for a moment Tailchaser merely stood and drank it in.

It made him feel warm all over, and weak in his knees. It inflamed and then soothed him; made him itch and tingle. He stepped forward and pulled off a leaf with his teeth. He rolled it around in his mouth for a bit, then swallowed it. The taste was slightly bitter, but there was something about it that made him want more. As if in a dream he pulled off another green leaf and gulped it down . . . then another . . .

'Here now! What are you after, there?' The voice was loud and startling. Fritti leaped back from the flowering plants. A large cat was standing behind him.

'You're not to be into those yet,' said the stranger disapprovingly. 'And what are you doing eating so many?'

Fritti felt light-headed and stupid. He could feel himself swaying from side to side.

'I'm sorry . . . I didn't know . . . what are they?'

The stranger stared suspiciously. 'Are you trying to tell me that you've never seen catmint before? Come now, kit-my-lad, I wasn't whelped just sunlast, you know! Get along with you, now. Go on! Point your paws away from here.' The big cat made threatening gestures, and Tailchaser ran. He felt very strange.

Catmint, he thought. *So this is catmint.*

The trees above him seemed to bend as he passed, and the ground felt uneven beneath his pads, although it was level to the eye.

Perhaps my legs have gone all different lengths? he wondered.

As he made his way back into the bowl – reeling past strangers, whiskery faces looming up before him and then receding – he began to feel panicky. Where was Pouncequick? He must find Pouncequick.

Finally he spotted the kitten. Although it seemed to take a terribly long time for him to cross the distance between them, eventually he reached the small cat's side. He tried to speak, but a wave of nausea moved through him. He could dimly see an expression of alarm on Pouncequick's face. The youngling's voice sounded leagues distant.

'Tailchaser! What's wrong with you? Are you sick?'

Fritti tried to nod an answer, but his face felt so hot and his head so heavy that he slumped to the ground. Rolling onto his back, he heard the faint sounds of singing as the surrounding Folk lifted their voices together.

Pouncequick was standing over him, nudging him with his

nose . . . then the kitten's face was dropping away as if falling down a hole, a black tunnel caving in around Tailchaser's vision.

Pouncequick stood over his friend. Hard as he nosed, loud as he called over the singing crowd, still Tailchaser lay like one dead. Pouncequick was all alone. His friend was sick – maybe dying – and he was all alone in a vast sea of strangers.

CHAPTER THIRTEEN

Oh, breathe not his name! let it
Sleep in the shade,
Where cold and unhonored his relics are laid.

— Thomas Moore

Pouncequick ran through the deserted grottoes and paths of First-home in a panic, stumbling over roots and veering from looming tree-shapes. The fish-cold gleam of Meerclar's Eye bled through the chinks in the leaves and branches above.

In the Meeting Glade, with Tailchaser unconscious at his feet, he had called wildly and vainly for help. All around cats were singing and dancing, and moving in chattering groups out of the Glade to hunt up the catmint. Fencewalker was gone from the grass-covered butte, Howlsong was nowhere in sight, and no one noticed the fright-ened kitten mewing beside his friend. In terror for Tailchaser's life, he had fled the din of the Glade to search for someone or something to help him, to advise him.

But the byways of Rootwood were empty, and as he drew farther away from the Celebration – away from the noise and light – the age-old forest began to look very, very grim. At last he stopped, his breath coming in harsh little gasps. He could do his friend no good if he became lost in the woods, he realized. What a fool he was! he chided himself – what a foolish, contemptible kitten. He must go back and find aid for Tailchaser. If the celebrating cats would not help him, well, he would go and drag the Queen herself out by the tail, if he had to!

Turning, he scampered back toward the faint sounds of the Glade.

In the last line of trees crowning the rim of the Celebration place, he

111

ran smack into Roofshadow, the gray fela who had befriended him that morning. She had apparently been stealing away from the festivities, but she gave him a pleasant greeting.

Pounce yelped. 'Oh, oh, Roofshadow, oh, I'm so glad . . . quick! Come and help!' he stuttered with excitement, 'Come and help . . . oh, Tailchaser's, he's . . . oh!'

Roofshadow waited patiently. When Pounce finally calmed down enough to tell her of Tailchaser's mysterious ailment, she nodded worriedly and followed him down into the bowl-shaped Meeting Glade.

The Celebration had begun in earnest now; the assembled cats were leaping and singing beneath the soaring tree-roof. Circles of dancers spun about hypnotically, tails and paws swooping and pointing in the diffused light of the Eye. Many had eaten of the valerian, and the sound of strange singing and unrestrained humors was in the air.

They found Fritti where Pouncequick had left him, curled into a ball like a newborn kitten. His breathing was shallow, and he did not respond when Pouncequick called his name. Roofshadow looked at him for a moment, then delicately trailed her whiskers over his chest and face. Crouching on the grass beside him, she smelled his breath. She stood up, shaking her silvery head grimly.

'Your friend is either a glutton or a fool – or both. He stinks of catmint. Only a mad one would eat enough to make him reek like that,' she told Pouncequick.

'What will it do to him?' the little one cried. Roofshadow looked down at him and her face softened.

'I do not know with surety, youngest hunter. It is known that too much of the catmint leaf and root will frighten and speed the heart, but he is young and strong. What it does to the spirit, though, that is a difficult question. A little lightens the ka, and brings out song and happiness. Much more and the taker grows strong and fell, full of odd dreams. As much as your friend has had . . . Harar, I do not know. We must have patience.'

'Oh, poor Tailchaser!' sniffed Pouncequick. 'What will I do, what will I do?'

'I will wait with you,' said Roofshadow quietly. 'That is all we *can* do.'

Fritti Tailchaser was falling, floating down into infinite blackness.

The forest that had throbbed and bent and billowed around him was gone . . . everything was gone . . . and he fell through emptiness.

Time lost all meaning as he fell; there was no sensation of wind or air passing to indicate how fast he was moving. But for a sickening feeling of motion deep within, he might well have been standing still.

After an indeterminate span of time . . . terror wearing away at his smoldering thoughts . . . he saw – or felt, at first – a faint glow. The glow became a flicker, then gradually resolved itself into a patch of cold, white light. To his amazement, a form could be seen in the center of the light, and as it drew gradually nearer he discerned the shape of a great white cat . . . a tailless cat, revolving slowly in a vast black sphere.

It approached, and the glare flamed more brightly. The eyes of the spirit-cat stared in his direction, but those eyes were unfocused; blind.

The white cat spoke, in a cold, whispery voice that seemed to come across a great distance. 'Who is there?' it cried. 'Who passes?' Its cold tones rang with a grief that passed Tailchaser's understanding. He tried to speak but could not, despite great effort. Straining for speech, Fritti felt a sudden heat on his forehead, as if the star-shaped patch there had become a real star . . . as if it had caught fire.

The white apparition spun silently near for a moment, then spoke again.

'Wait. I think I see you now. Ah, little spirit, you are far from your nest. You should be suckling at the bosom of the Allmother – dancing in the skies above the Glad Fields. Bitterly will you regret straying into these warmthless shadows.'

Tailchaser felt terror and loneliness. He could neither move nor speak, but only listen.

'Long have I run in these black spaces, but I can find nowhere to slip through into the other side,' intoned the stranger in a dead, emotionless voice. 'Long have I sought to find my way back to the light. Sometimes I can hear singing . . . ' it said, with cold wistfulness. 'Always the door is just beyond reach, just around a corner . . . something prevents me. Why can I not go to that rest, that quiet rest that is promised?'

Despite his fear, Tailchaser felt great pity well up in his being at the terrible desolation of the white cat.

'Little star, I sense something strange about you. What is it?' asked the sorrowful, distant voice. 'Do you bring a message, or are you merely lost . . . as I am? Do you bring tidings from my brother? No, it would only be a cruel trick! The cold is too great, the night is too hollow . . . leave me alone, the thought of the living burns me . . . it burns me! Ah, such pain!'

With a muffled, echoing wail, the apparition began to spin faster and faster, and fell away from Tailchaser's sight.

He was surrounded by darkness once more.

Suddenly, he felt matter beneath his paws, although the impenetrable dark had not abated. He tried to cling, to bury himself in this tangible, solid thing. It was like the earth, it was something to touch – and it was the only other thing besides himself in this gigantic, black stillness. For a moment. Until he felt a presence.

Somewhere, out in the lightless reaches, something was searching for him. He could not tell how he knew – could not name the sense that told him – but he knew. Something huge and slow and relentless was stalking him . . . in a questing silence that was far worse than any sound could be in that comfortless waste.

His forehead felt warm again. Did it shine? He felt nakedly obvious; exposed. His brow burned, and he felt that it was signaling his presence to the hunting thing, as light draws the eyes from the forest. Tailchaser tried to cover his face with his paws, to bury the burning mark . . . but could not reach his forehead. His head had stretched away – no, it was his legs that were shrinking! He could feel it now, feel them dwindling away – tingling for a moment, then gone – and now he was lying helplessly on his stomach, unable to run, although every nerve screamed at him to flee. The presence was reaching out, now, groping blindly . . . touching closer and closer. All sense of unreality was submerged in horror. Something had sensed him – and it wanted him.

He shut his eyes tight, like a kitten – hoping something that he could not see would not see him – but in the infinite blackness it was a cruel mockery to exchange one darkness for another. It was almost upon him, probing . . . and now it seemed that he could smell it: rank, foul, and older than stone. The heat on his forehead pulsed like a heart of fire.

Then something seized him and began to shake, and shake, and shake . . .

For a brief instant he thought he sensed a terrible gust of disappointment from the darkness; then he was rising. A spot of light appeared above, shining down like the sun. In the middle of this hole in the blackness he saw a strange, tall shape – a form like a tree with no branches, entirely surrounded by water.

As his eyes blinked at the brightness the upright form took on the lineaments of Howlsong, shaking him and shaking him . . .

Tailchaser fell back into normal sleep, and when he awoke later he found himself in Pouncequick's bower. Howlsong, Roofshadow and his young friend were all in attendance.

'Well, here he is!' said Howlsong. 'We were all terribly, terribly concerned for you. I suppose that they just don't make catmint like that where you come from – I mean the *real thing*. We're so pleased to see you feeling better.'

Pouncequick leaped forward and licked Fritti's face. The gray cat stayed in the background, but measured Tailchaser with her eyes.

Trembling, he thanked them for their attentiveness. He did not feel completely normal yet: the light beaming down through the trees had an odd, refracted quality – a shimmering – and all the sounds that came to him echoed slightly. He felt very light and insubstantial.

Howlsong stood. 'Well, I know you have been awfully ill, but we *have* been lying in all morning, and I have ever so many things to do. I hope you will not hate me if I run off and attend to some of them.'

As he was leaving he turned and added: 'Oh, of course, I almost forgot! The Prince has made an appointment for you at Court for tonight, at the beginning of Deepest Quiet. If you are not well enough to go, well, I suppose a change could be made – but they do take protocol pretty seriously up by the Queen's Seat. Not to harry you into going, that is, if you don't feel up to it. . . . '

'I think I will be able to receive that honor,' Fritti said after a moment's pause. 'I have come a long distance to speak with the Queen, and . . . ' He paused again. 'And, well, yes, I will be there.'

'Good. I will come back to fetch you in plenty of time,' said Howlsong. The patchwork singer bounded out of the glen.

Fritti lay back for a while, pondering the odd, lingering sensations as Pouncequick contentedly groomed him. After a short time Roofshadow spoke up.

'Are you sure you feel strong enough to go before the Queen, Tailchaser?' The slim gray cat watched him as she waited for his reply.

'I think the sooner I get on with this, the better.' he said. He found it difficult to articulate what he was feeling. 'As I told Howlsong, we've come a very great distance. I've made a promise, and I've sworn an oath to it . . . but this Firsthome, I don't know, it makes everything feel sort of unimportant – I mean, you could just lie here day after day, if you wanted to, and think about nothing but waterbugs. Not *chase* waterbugs, mind you,' he tried to explain, 'just *think* about them. You could spend your whole day, every day, just wondering and pondering about waterbugs, and talking to others about waterbugs . . . and before you realized it, you'd be old. One day you'd realize that you'd never actually *seen* a waterbug . . . but by then you wouldn't want to, because it would spoil all your lovely ideas.

'I'm afraid I'm not explaining this very well,' he continued, 'but I feel that if I'm going to find my friend Hushpad then I'd better get on with it, because . . . I'm sorry, I just can't express it properly . . . '

Roofshadow walked over to Fritti and looked at him carefully. She sniffed him – not in a suspicious way, but in an interested one – then sat down.

'I think I sense your meaning, Tailchaser – but, of course, I am a stranger here also. I don't think Howlsong and the others would understand you.'

'They probably wouldn't,' admitted Fritti. He looked down at Pouncequick, who had finished grooming him and was nestling happily against his body listening to their talk. 'What do you say, Pounce?' he asked.

Pouncequick looked up solemnly. 'Well,' he said, 'I am not sure that I understand everything you just said, but I do think that *some* of the thinking that Folk do here is important – at least it makes me want to ask what seem like important questions . . . although I don't really know what makes them important. *There*, do you see?' chortled the kitten. 'I am an even worse explainer than my wise old friend Tailchaser. I think we should answer these dull matters with some food. It's far past breakfast time!'

'I agree, cu'nre.' Fritti smiled, although he himself did not really feel up to eating yet. 'Would you like to come hunt with us, Roofshadow?' he asked the quiet fela.

'Honored.'

All that day they explored the forest maze of Firsthome, discovering brush-choked passages and long-neglected pathways.

The Folk of Firsthome and Rootwood seemed very quiet on this day after Celebration. Most were napping, or lying on their sides chatting lazily with friends. Many had left after the festivities, and the byways of Rootwood were nearly empty.

Roofshadow paid much attention to Pouncequick, leading him into games and coming over to look when he found something that interested him.

She was friendly with Tailchaser, but somewhat reserved. This was fine with Fritti, who was still feeling the effects of his experience the previous night. Most of his waking symptoms had dwindled, but he could not shake loose from the odd feeling of detachment. His companions' conversation seemed distant; he felt himself full of brooding stillness as he passed beneath the old trees like a spirit.

Later, in the early evening, Roofshadow left, with promises to return. Pouncequick, who had bounded like a bumblebee all afternoon, and Fritti, who was still a bit shaky, returned to the healing-spot to have a rest before their appointment at the Court.

Howlsong came for them, full of suppressed excitement at the solemnity and grandeur of his role. They followed him like sleepwalkers down the twisting corridors of Firsthome.

They slipped through a tight-knit fence of silvery birch trees and down into a small canyon. There, in the reflected light of the single wide beam of Eyeshine that fell down through the tangled forest roof, they saw the forms of many cats crouched around the bottom rim of the tiny canyon, round eyes throwing back the light. A large shape came hurrying up from out of the shadows.

'Here now, is this the pair, then? They'll have their time soon enough.' It was Rumblepurr, the massive Chamberlain, his head nodding like a willow in the breeze as he spoke. 'Never do to have them just go charging up – there is a procedure, y'know. You, Howlsong, leave them with me – there's a good fellow. You can wait for them at the back.'

Howlsong seemed a little disappointed, but shrugged and bade them good luck. They followed the bobbing, mumbling Court Chamberlain, who led them to the base of one of the walls of the canyon – near the front, and the light.

'Just you stay here until I call you. Don't make a squeak till then. There's others here who're before you, and Her Softness' time is very important. Just be still, little ones.' Rumblepurr hurried off, his wide body rocking from side to side.

Fritti's gaze followed Rumblepurr across the tiny box canyon. The Chamberlain moved into the center of a cluster of shiny, exquisitely groomed cats who were probably – Fritti guessed – the important Folk of the Court. Before them sat several others of diverse appearance. One – a large, proudly-striped fellow – had an easy and confident grace, even at rest, that reminded Fritti of Quiverclaw.

On a raised plateau of grass at the head of the canyon, roofed over by the limbs and leaves of an enormous oak tree, Fencewalker and Dewtreader sat side by side, the former wearing such a look of barely contained boredom and restlessness that Fritti smiled to himself in the dark. How this sort of thing must grate at the Prince's roving soul!

Beside Fencewalker lay the Prince Consort, his serene countenance full of quiet humor, but his eyes troubling and distant as an approaching storm.

In the center of the plateau, in the middle of the shaft of light, sat Queen Mirmirsor Sunback, illuminated like some dream-creature.

As Fritti first glimpsed her he thought of a fountain, a forest spring. She was clear, shining white, and her long, soft fur started out from her body in all directions like the puff of a dandelion. Beside her was a small earthenware bowl, brought somehow from the dwellings of M'an. Before Tailchaser's gaze the scioness of the line of Harar sat with her back curled and her head forward, one leg pointed outward – the paw thrust in the air like the graceful branches of the birch trees surrounding her Court.

She was nipping delicately at her hind end.

CHAPTER FOURTEEN

To that high capitol . . .
his pale court in beauty and decay . . .

                   – P. B. Shelley

Through the long Hour of Deepest Quiet audience was held in the Court of Harar. Queen Sunback, crouched in the hollow of the great oak – the Vaka'az'me – listened calmly to all who came before her. Tailchaser watched with flagging interest as a procession of claimants presented themselves before the Seat. Matters of territory took up the larger part of the audience, but there were also Naming confirmations, and blessings for expectant felas. Through it all the Queen presided, as remote and unblinkingly bright as a star.

At last all the petitioners had disappeared, pleased or disappointed, into the night. The Queen stretched a long, graceful yawn, then signaled with her tail. Rumblepurr bustled and tumbled up onto the small plateau and leaned over her. The Queen whispered languorously into his piebald ear, and he bobbed his head assiduously.

'Yes, m'lady, that's right, right enough,' wheezed the old Chamberlain.

'Well, then, shall we not hear from him?' asked Queen Sunback in a voice like cold, clear stream water.

'Of course, Your Furriness,' grunted Rumblepurr, and hurried to the front of the plateau. He squinted his old eyes out into the darkness of the canyon and trumpeted: 'Thane Squeakerbane of the Firstwalkers, you may approach the Vaka'az'me!'

The proud-looking, many-striped hunter who Fritti had noticed earlier rose, stretched, and calmly approached the leveled mound.

He paused for a moment at the edge of the rise, then vaulted effortlessly up into the circle of light.

'A First-walker! Like Quiverclaw and Scuffledig!' piped Pouncequick excitedly. Fritti nodded absently as he examined Squeakerbane. In the Eye-light that surrounded the Oak-seat the Thane's wiry body showed traces of many old, whitened scars beneath his short fur. Stripes and scars gave Squeakerbane the look of weathered wood.

'At your service, as ever, O Queen,' said the First-walker, touching his chin respectfully to the ground. Sunback looked down with cool amusement.

'We do not often see the First-walkers here at Court,' she said, 'even those of you who haunt the Rootwood near Firsthome. This is an unexpected honor.'

'With all due respect, Your Exaltedness, the First-walkers do not "haunt" the Rootwood.' Squeakerbane spoke with rough, but quiet, pride. 'As you know, however, we do prefer the solitude of the wild. The Court is too . . . crowded for our tastes.' He sang the word 'crowded' with a subtly disdainful inflection that brought a look of wintery humor to the face of Dewtreader.

'So we are told, Thane,' fluted the Prince Consort, 'but I have heard it whispered that a vast meeting of the First-walkers is assembling east of Gentlerun Downs. Will your comrades not find so much society fully as depressing as our Court?'

Squeakerbane glowered and Sunback sneezed delicately and curried her tail. The Thane spoke with obvious restraint.

'The Thane-meet is occasioned by the same matters that bring me here. The Prince Consort, undoubtedly with good reasons known only to His Highness, seeks to open old wounds. I will not be tail-tweaked. There are graver issues at stake here.'

Rumblepurr, who had remained standing, now huffed uncomfortably and went to sit near Prince Fencewalker, who was showing an interest in the proceedings for the first time all night.

'I wish you all would stop squabbling for a while,' grumped the Prince. 'It would be nice to speak of something important for a change.'

Queen Sunback regarded her son for a moment, then flicked her ears twice and turned to Squeakerbane. 'Brash and bumptious though he may be, Fencewalker has spoken well. You must forgive our rudeness, Thane. I realize your concerns must weigh heavily on you, and you do not have our taste for badinage.' She sent a cold stare in

Dewtreader's direction, which the Prince Consort returned imperiously. 'Speak on, Squeakerbane, please,' the Queen said.

The battle-scarred First-walker stared at her for a moment, then bowed his head low again and held it there for the space of several heartbeats. Then, lifting his gaze, he spoke.

'As Your Regal Softness is aware,' he began, 'we First-walkers are few in number, and our thanages are widespread. I myself have jurisdiction over much of the Sunsnest Plains and this part of Rootwood – excepting Firsthome, of course,' he added, with a sly smile for Dewtreader. 'The territories U'ea-ward, north of the Caterwaul, were formerly the protectorate of my cousin, Thane Brushstalker. Now, he is dead.' Squeakerbane paused significantly. The Queen leaned forward, curiosity in her bright eyes.

'We are sad to hear of the passing of Brushstalker from these fields, of course,' said the Queen thoughtfully. 'He was a brave and canny hunter. But we still do not understand the purpose of your embassy. The First-walkers have always determined their own succession without recourse to our Court.'

Squeakerbane sat back and scratched impatiently. 'And so we shall continue to do, O Queen. It is not Brushstalker's legacy but the manner of his passing that brings me here. Brushstalker was attacked by an unknown enemy and *torn to pieces*. The other Walkers of his thanage have disappeared.'

Queen Sunback, crouched in the split-bark hollow of the Vaka'az'me, gave a shudder of distaste. The pearly inner wood of the trunk framed her white form as she peered out at the Thane.

'How horrible!' she said.

Dewtreader stepped toward the Thane on silent pads. 'What beast committed this act?' he demanded. 'And what can *we* do about it, that you have come to us with this story?'

Fritti, seated among the few remaining onlookers, felt Pouncequick go tense like a bent sapling at his side.

So this is what had brought Quiverclaw and the others up from the South! he thought.

'None of the Folk can say, Majesties,' answered Squeakerbane grimly. 'It was a powerful creature, indeed, if it was only one. If it was a hunting pack it is no less disturbing. Brushstalker was savaged.'

Sunback had regained her aplomb. 'Why do you come to us, though, to make us uneasy?' she asked. 'Brushstalker's fate is terrible to hear of, but Ratleaf and the northern area have long been dangerous, forbidding places. Why do you bring us these upsetting stories?'

'I do not bring these portents just to upset the tranquillity of Firsthome,' spoke Squeakerbane, scarred head proudly erect. 'I come to alert you to peril, because I think the Court is in a hazardous state of complacency. This is not an isolated incident. I know that, and so do you. Your son has been patrolling the borders of Firsthome because of troubles closer to nest.'

'Now we're getting to it!' said Fencewalker, pleased, but Dewtreader raised a slender paw and interrupted him.

'There have been marauders on our borders, but it is nothing to raise hackles over,' said the Prince Consort in his musical voice. 'Wild Growlers, perhaps, or a sickened Garrin – there could be many explanations; so also with the lamentable death of Brushstalker.'

The battered old Thane eyed Dewtreader with quiet contempt. 'The massive Garrin can be dangerous, of course,' he said, 'but they are winter sleepers, and these developments began during the last snows. I think that they will continue through this year's snow, when the Garrin have again gone to ground.' Dewtreader met his stare, but said nothing. 'Whatever is lurking in the northern territories – and beginning to spread out – is not a natural child of this world, as many can attest. The earth has a great forgiveness for its creatures. I have lived in the high places and the deep places, but I have never seen anything like this.'

'What do you mean, Thane?' questioned Queen Sunback. 'I am afraid we do not understand.'

'Something strange has settled in the area across the Hararscrape. The forest creatures of Ratleaf are migrating outward, fleeing the area in swarms. The birds who nest there at this season are flying away across the Bigwater. Of all the Folk, you in Firsthome should know why that portends dangerous times.'

'Make your point, First-walker,' said Dewtreader, his voice cold.

'It should be obvious. Here, around Firsthome, is the greatest concentration of the Folk to be found anywhere: a hungry, hunting mob constantly beating the brush for fla-fa'az and Squeaker. Yet those creatures still remain – having bigger litters and hatchings than in other places, perhaps, but still living out their lives here. Rootwood is their ancestral home as much as it is ours. We Folk – and the ones on whom we prey – all dance together. That is how it should be.

'Whatever has taken up the northern flats, though, and raised a *mound* – a pile of tailings near as big as all of Firsthome – that is something that the creatures of Ratleaf cannot live with. This is a danger we would all do well to regard.'

'Bravo!!' shouted Fencewalker. 'Leaping Harar, but it's good to hear somebody has some sense around here!'

Queen Sunback seemed about to speak. Fritti and Pouncequick – indeed, all those assembled – leaned imperceptibly forward to hear her pronouncement. Dewtreader, however, rose and yawned.

'Well,' he said calmly, 'there is much in what you say, Thane, and much of it is new to us. The mound, in particular, sounds a very strange thing indeed – we shall have more discussion of it later. For the moment, however, we do not find it meet to go kitten-paddling off after rumors, and mounting uninformed expeditions into what *you yourself* have said is very evil territory.' Squeakerbane seemed about to protest, but Dewtreader whipped his brown-tipped tail from side to side and the First-walker held his peace.

'*However,*' continued Dewtreader pointedly, 'we are *not* insensible to danger. The Queen's son, the gallant Prince Fencewalker, has our permission to levy what Folk he deems necessary, with an eye to safeguarding the borders of our territory. He may begin at once.'

'Wonderful!' The Prince leaped excitedly to his feet. 'I'm so pleased!' he burbled – a little inappropriately, Tailchaser thought – and with a leap and a bound, Fencewalker was gone into the darkness.

'Now,' continued the cold-eyed Prince Consort, 'we will also ask that when you have met with your fellow First-walkers, Thane, you return and do us the courtesy of sharing your conclusions with the Court of Harar. Is that possible?'

'Certainly, Your Highness!' said Squeakerbane, somewhat taken aback, 'I hope we can continue to cooperate on this . . . '

'Of course, of course,' said Dewtreader. 'Those are the Queen's wishes. Am I correct, my many-whiskered Queen?' he asked, turning to Sunback. The Queen, lulled by the familiar sound of Court routine, only waved her tail distractedly in assent.

'Very well, then, I suppose that brings an end to the night's audiences. We thank you again, Thane Squeakerbane, for bringing these matters to our attention. Please extend our heartfelt sorrow to the friends and relations of Brushstalker.'

Dewtreader had actually begun to leave the plateau when Rumble-purr spoke up distractedly.

'Err . . . hmmm . . . um, begging your pardon, Lord, but I believe there was one more . . . umm . . . waiting their turn . . . if you see what I mean.' Dewtreader returned to the grassy knoll wearing a look of annoyance that was swiftly muted into bland indifference. The Queen was paying no attention at all – in fact, she was grooming her flank as she reclined between the spreading roots of the Vaka'az'me.

'Very well,' said the Prince Consort, 'where are they? Bring them forward.'

Fritti and Pouncequick, totally unprepared, were urged forward by Rumblepurr. The chubby tom leaned forward and whispered to Fritti: 'Try to keep it short, youngling. Their Eminences are a trifle out of sorts.'

Nervous Fritti could see this clearly. Pouncequick was almost completely overcome by shyness, and trembled silently beside Tailchaser as they stood before the Great Oak.

'What are your names and why have you come before us?' asked Prince Dewtreader impatiently.

'I am Tailchaser, and this is my companion Pouncequick. We are of the Meeting Wall Clan, from the far side of the Old Woods. We are seeking a friend of ours named Hushpad.' Fritti's voice was weak.

The Queen finally seemed to notice the two small cats.

'Do you think she is here in Firsthome?' she asked, turning her gleaming eyes on them. Pouncequick, keyed up to a fever pitch, gave a whimper of despair and buried his head in Tailchaser's hip. Fritti swallowed and spoke.

'No, great Queen, we do not think so. We do think it is possible that she has been taken by the creature or . . . creatures of which Squeakerbane spoke. Many of the other Folk of the Meeting Wall Clan have also disappeared mysteriously. The elder sent a delegation to this Court for that very reason,' he finished hurriedly.

Sunback yawned widely, showing sharp teeth as white as her pelt and an impossibly pink tongue. 'Have we received such a delegation?' she asked Rumblepurr. The old Chamberlain pondered for a moment.

'Can't say as we have, Your Softness,' he said finally. 'Don't think I've heard of the Meeting Wall Clan before this, and it's a dead-rat certainty that no embassy has arrived from there.'

'There you are, then,' said Dewtreader. 'I'm afraid that the doings of the big, wide world sometimes pass this little Court right by. I'm truly sorry that we couldn't help you. Feel free to stay in Firsthome as long as you need to. Perhaps, if you're interested in all that, you could be of help to Fencewalker. You are past your hunt-song, aren't you? Well, no matter. Mri'fa-o. The Queen's audiences are at an end.'

Howlsong, who had fallen asleep at the outer edge of the canyon while he waited, led them silently back through the forest. Fritti, full of vague resentment and gloom, had no conversation to offer, either. After a long stretch of unspeaking travel, Pouncequick finally broke the stillness.

'Just think, Tailchaser,' he said, 'we've actually been to see the Queen of Cats!'

CHAPTER FIFTEEN

I do not know which to prefer,
The beauty of inflections
Or the beauty of innuendoes,
The blackbird whistling
Or just after.

— Wallace Stevens

The days passed swiftly in Firsthome. Outside the sheltering vastness of the Rootwood winter had come.

Fritti and Pouncequick chased away time beneath the great trees, exploring, hunting, becoming fat and glossy of coat. Roofshadow, still polite and reserved, spent a great deal of time with them. She seemed, in particular, to enjoy accompanying Pouncequick on his various expeditions.

One dark afternoon, when the kitten and the gray fela were out wandering the mazes of Firsthome, Tailchaser found himself alone. Howlsong was on an initiation stalk, prior to his Oel-cir'va ceremonies, and would be gone for two sunrises. As the other residents of Firsthome, very few of whom Fritti even recognized, bustled to and fro on secret errands and assignations, Tailchaser strolled beneath the trees by himself. It had been a long time since he had gone anywhere without the accompaniment of a chattering voice or even the presence of a companion.

He meandered to the southern edge of Firsthome, where the trees gave way to the edge of Sunsnest — walking at his own pace, listening to his own inner songs. He wandered out beyond the forest's eaves and down a grassy, sloping meadow sprinkled with feathery early snow. He was so tightly wrapped in thought that he did not hear the icy burblings of the Purrwhisper until he stood on its banks.

Crouched on his haunches, fur ruffled against the chilly wind and fluttering snow, he watched the river splash past — passing out of his sight to the east, Vez'an, where it would eventually join the Cater-waul. Farther, much farther still, was the place of his nesting and kittenhood, and the forest and fields where he had run with Hushpad through the bright-sky summer.

He slit his eyes against the cold breeze as he stared out across the plain; he thought about going home. Rootwood would never be a home to him. Somewhere out there, beyond the winter lands, was the Meeting Wall. Somewhere out there were his friends.

But not his family. Not Hushpad.

For some long time he sat, tail curled around his paws, then rose and walked back up the steep meadow, with the laughter of Purrwhisper diminishing behind him.

'Tailchaser!' chirped Pouncequick. 'We've been looking about for you. Did you go exploring? Roofshadow and I have something impor-tant to tell you!'

Fritti stopped to wait as the kitten bounced up the trail toward him. 'Good dancing, Pounce,' he said, 'and to you, Roofshadow.' The fela looked brooding and preoccupied. 'I have some news myself. Let's go back to our tree, and out of the wind.'

In the bower, as the wind shook the treetops high overhead, Fritti addressed his friends in a serious tone. 'I hope you will understand what I am going to tell you, and will think well of me. I have been thinking about it quite a lot, today. The decision was not so hard as wondering how to tell you.

'I have to leave Firsthome. I have stayed here too long already, and I am losing my purpose – but the promise I made is just as important as it was when I made it. I cannot winter here quietly while Hushpad is undiscovered.

'After going to the Court, and hearing all that was said, I have concluded that no further help can be expected here. It seems that something is happening in the North, and I believe that is where I must go to continue my search. I am quite frightened, really, and every one of my whiskers is atwitch at the prospect, but I must go. Harar knows, sometimes I wish . . . I . . . Pouncequick, are you *laughing*?'

Pouncequick was indeed laughing, snorting little giggles and thum-ping Roofshadow with his paw.

'Oh . . . oh . . . oh, Tailchaser,' he said between sneezes, 'of course we must go. That's what Roofshadow and I were talking about today. And several other days, also. But Roofshadow said you had to decide for yourself when to leave.'

Fritti was taken aback. 'We? But Pounce, it's the cold season. I *can't* take you along with me. It's not *your* oath, *your* ridiculous promise. And besides, forgive me, you're awfully brave, but you're still just a kitling. This may be terribly dangerous – don't you see?'

'I know that.' Pouncequick had a more serious expression, but was still enjoying Tailchaser's discomfiture. 'I think that between you and Roofshadow, you'll manage to keep me out of harm. And perhaps we can do the same for you.'

'Roofshadow?' Now Fritti was astonished. 'Roofshadow, you must not understand how risky this all is. Keep Pounce here, I beg of you. Harar! Have you both gone as mad as old Eatbugs?'

Roofshadow stared at Tailchaser with cool, deep eyes.

'I, too, wish the young one didn't insist on going – but he does. Who am I to know the way of Meerclar? She calls the Folk to many different purposes. As for me, well, I do not fault you for not knowing . . . but others beside yourself have scores to settle – and promises to keep.'

'But . . . ' Fritti began. The gray cat cut him off.

'Tailchaser, before you ever came to Firsthome I stood before the Vaka'az'me, asking for help. I got no more assistance than you did. I, too, had thought about striking north to seek answers – and was about to set off when you two arrived and broke my resolve. Now, I am ready again.'

Fritti stared, uncomprehending.

'I come from the far side of Rootwood,' Roofshadow began. 'My birthing-place is separated by many leagues and countless trees from the Seat of Sunback. My sire was Slipwhisker, one of the elders of the Forest-Light Clan. He was a respected hunter, and I had many brothers and sisters.

'As a young fela I scorned the young males in our tribe – they were overbold and self-satisfied. When I came into my season I made sure to be far away from the clan, so I would not be betrayed by my nature into bearing a litter that I did not yet desire. I found that I *enjoyed* being by myself; enjoyed the solitary way of the hunter.

'I wandered far afield, usually alone. Sometimes I would take my little nest-brother, Snufflenose. He was one of the few Forest-Light Folk whose company I cared for.' Here Roofshadow looked away into the forest heights for a moment. When she turned her gaze back to Fritti, her face was as calm as before.

'Slipwhisker, who sired me, would sometimes tease me about whether I was a fela at all, or instead a small and slender tom. I think he was proud, though. I could hunt as well as any of the young males – and bragged about it a good deal less.

'One morning I had resolved to go exploring E'a-ward into the Rootwood. I asked little Snufflenose if he wanted to come, but he was not feeling well. He asked me if I would stay and keep him company around the nest, but the smell of the morning was strong, and there were new and exciting currents tickling my whiskers. I left him behind, and went out on my own.

'I will not grieve you with a long tale. I returned well after Deepest Quiet – and found a horror such as I could scarcely believe. Most of my clan were dead: torn as if attacked by a fik'az pack. Snufflenose was one of them. No dog pack could ever have caught the entire Forest-Light Clan by surprise. Those whose bodies were not scattered about the forest were gone with no trace. Slipwhisker was one of those who had disappeared.

'For many days I was as mad as a fla-fa'az who has eaten poison berries. When my dreams were in the sunlight again I came through the forest to Firsthome. I waited long for an audience, and when I was seen they told me it was the brawling Garrin, the honey-lovers, who had destroyed my folk. I know better.

'When I saw you and Pouncequick I knew that our paths had come together for a reason. Pouncequick is much like my brother Snufflenose, and now he is my friend. And you, Tailchaser – I am not sure why, but I feel drawn to you, also.' Roofshadow averted her eyes as she said this last. 'Anyway, these are my sorrows, and now I think you understand my desires. We will go together.'

After long moments of silence, Fritti turned to Pouncequick. 'Did you know all this?' he asked weakly.

'Some,' the kitten replied. 'But not all. Why are such terrible things happening, Tailchaser?'

'I can't say, Pounce.'

Roofshadow looked up. The fires that had been kindled in her eyes during her story had abated. She looked cold and tired.

'We had best leave soon, or we shall not leave at all,' she said flatly. 'The winter is killing fierce in this part of our fields.'

As if in answer, the wind sounded a whistling call through the branches above.

CHAPTER SIXTEEN

The long light shakes across the lakes
And the wild cataract leaps in glory.
Blow, bugle, blow, set the wild echoes flying
Blow, bugle; answer echoes, dying, dying, dying.

– Alfred, Lord Tennyson

The snow fluttered and swirled through the columned byways of Rootwood. A near-silent group of cats, Fritti and his companions among them, wandered in straying disorder through the trees. Scattered pawprints slowly filled with powdered snow behind them.

Fencewalker and his group of conscripts were moving out to the northern border of Firsthome; Squeakerbane was accompanying them to forest's edge, where he would turn Vez'an for Sourweed's thanage.

When Tailchaser and his companions had asked to come along, Fencewalker had been surprised and Squeakerbane a little suspicious, but neither had offered objections.

'Why in the name of Blueback's Hindbristles you want to go padding around in the U'ea territories at this season – and with a fela and a youngling besides – I don't var. But it's your pelt, my catling,' the Prince had grumped.

Fencewalker's conscripts were mostly a mixed lot of young hunters and battered old toms who were not finding favor with the felas. One or two, like young Snaremouse – and, of course, Dayhunter and Nightcatcher – looked as though they would prove reliable in troublesome situations, but Tailchaser had doubts that the rest would be much use around Pouncequick's 'red-clawed monsters.' The ragged band showed none of the discipline that had been evident among the First-walkers – they meandered far afield as the group passed through the forest, each reluctant to perform the uncatlike role of staying with

130

his fellows. As a result, when the group stopped to sleep or discuss directions it took ages for the stragglers to come trooping in; quite often the missing would have to be searched for.

In the coldest parts of Final Dancing the band would huddle together for warmth, bodies piled and sprawled piecemeal like fallen leaves. A sudden movement usually meant a paw in someone's eye or nose, and there was endless scuffling.

Of the three companions, only Pouncequick seemed to find any pleasure in the journey. Tailchaser and Roofshadow were often quiet, deep in thought – the fela, especially, remaining aloof from Fencewalker's fractious crew.

So the strange group traveled on through the tree-beamed halls of outer Rootwood . . . over the thin blanket of new snow. . . .

Fifth Eye-rise out from the Court of Harar the travelers noticed the Rootwood beginning to thin. Soon Squeakerbane, Tailchaser and his companions would separate from Fencewalker's caravan to go their own ways.

In honor of their last night together the Folk halted early that evening. They found a sheltered copse – out of the wind, and with only the faintest wisp of white on the earthen floor. They split up to hunt; one by one they returned, after varying degrees of success.

Roofshadow and Tailchaser did not hunt, but instead took a silent walk through the woods. Side by side they paced, unspeaking, their noses filled with the crisp bite of winter, the delicate crunching of their pads on the snow the only sound.

Watching the gray fela move gracefully beside him, Fritti more than once felt the urge to speak, to elicit some reaction from the calm, silent Roofshadow . . . but he could not bring himself to break the stillness.

After they had paused to watch the bright points that speckled the night sky, they walked back to the copse as quietly as they had come.

Pouncequick, puffed with chill and excitement, had also just returned. He had gone hunting with the Prince, and had apparently kept his squeaking to a minimum: they had been successful.

'Isn't it cold?' he piped. 'Fencewalker's an awfully good hunter. You should have seen us! Here he comes now!'

The Prince approached, passing through a gaggle of other Folk who were wandering back – some licking their muzzles. Fencewalker approached the trio and dumped a plump Rikchikchik on the ground before them.

'I hope you will do me the honor of sharing my kill,' he said, with more than a touch of pride. Fritti's stomach rumbled as he watched his companions fall to, but he remembered his oath to Lord Snap.

This promise-keeping seems a me'mre of a way to go about things, he thought ruefully.

Fencewalker looked up, his muzzle steaming with squirrel blood. 'Here now, Tailchaser old fellow, what are you waiting on?' he asked.

'It's too difficult to explain, O Prince. I am honored by your kind offer, but I just can't eat right now.' Fritti's resolve seemed stronger than his hunger, but he did not feel comfortable it would last long. He moved away from his companions.

'Well, let everyone groom himself, I always say,' muttered Fencewalker philosophically, and returned to the fast-disappearing Rikchikchik.

Later, after all the hunters had returned, the group gathered itself into a close-pressed circle, backs against the breeze that swept through even this well-protected stand of trees. They took turns boasting and telling stories. Many of the Folk that Fencewalker had brought from Firsthome proved quite adept at relating funny songs and tales.

'Chances are they're better storytellers than they'll ever be fighters,' muttered Thane Squeakerbane to Furscuff, the only First-walker who had accompanied him from his thanage to the Court.

After a while young Snaremouse got up – after much urging from his fellows – and did a dance. He bobbed and crouched, now sliding on his stomach, now leaping in the air as if he were being pulled into the sky by his black nose. At times only his tail would move, forming strange and hilarious curves as Snaremouse stood stock-still with a look of intense concentration on his face.

The party whooped with glee when he was done. Overheated, he ran off to roll in a small snowdrift.

Squeakerbane – who, despite himself, had enjoyed Snaremouse's dance – rose and stretched. One of the Firsthome cats called out for him to tell a story. The rest of the assembly agreed, and pressed him for a tale.

'Very well,' the Thane said, closing his eyes in thought for a moment, 'a story I shall give you. Do not take offense if I tell you that we prefer stories with a little less fluff and a little more bone, we First-walkers.' Opening his eyes, Squeakerbane shook his scarred, bristly body and sat back on his haunches.

'What your esteemed Prince Consort, Dewtreader, said about Ninebirds and his deformed progeny has put me in mind of something. Do you all know how M'an, the servant, and Az-iri'le, the Folk, first fell out? It is an old story – but not much told around the Court, I'll warrant.'

None but Fencewalker and one or two of the older toms had ever heard of this tale. The Prince said he could not remember how it went.

'Ah, but we First-walkers make a practice of remembering things like this,' said Squeakerbane with a brief smile.

> 'In the wildness
> Always walking
> Passed Lord Firefoot
> Lone and homeless . . . '

he chanted in a singsong voice.

> 'Many seasons
> Forth from Firsthome
> Had he traveled
> Seeking, searching
>
> In the wastelands
> Under strange skies
> Where the Folk
> Had never wandered.'

After a pause, the Thane began his narrative.

'In the time of Prince Strongclaw, in the long and felicitous reign of Queen Windruffle, our Lord Firefoot hunted deep into the farthest reaches of Southern Rootwood. He had been many winters in the wild, and had seen no Folk for many a season-turn. He had run with the Visl, wrestled with the ponderous Garrin and raced the fleet Praere. He missed the company of his own kind, but he had vowed never to return to the Court of his father until Whitewind was avenged.

'One afternoon he met another cat walking on the edge of Rootwood – the most beautiful of the Folk he had ever seen:

> 'Tail like summer
> Warmly waving

133

Finest fur
In breezes blowing

Clear of eye
And lithe of paw-step
Like a spirit
For Lord Firefoot.

'The beautiful one was the color of grain swaying in the broad fields beyond the Qu'cef; as soft and downy as the cloudcats over Sunsnest.

' "What is your name, lovely one?" asked Lord Firefoot.

' "My name is Windflower," replied the newcomer in a voice as sweet as a tiny stream. "Who are you?"

' "Do you not know me?" asked the Firstborn. "I am Tangaloor Firefoot, child of Goldeneye and Skydancer, hunter and wanderer of the First Blood!"

' "That sounds nice," said Windflower, raising a wonderfully tapered paw. "Would you like to walk with me awhile?"

'Lord Firefoot was overcome with admiration for the beauteous Windflower, and they walked together.

'Long they wandered
Leaping, laughing
Firefoot and
The soft Windflower.

Most enraptured
Was the Firstborn
Till he learned
The dreadful story.

' "Windflower, do you have many brothers in your home?" asked Firefoot after a while.

' "No, I live in a dwelling of M'an. No other Folk share my nest."

' "That is odd, then, because I scent a strange tom – although very faintly. Could we be followed?" Firefoot looked inquiringly about as he padded along on his fiery red paws.

' "I do not think so," spoke Windflower sweetly. "You are the only tom – besides myself – that I have seen all day."

'Lord Tangaloor whirled about, stunned. "Are you not a fela?" he

134

yowled. "But how can that be? You seem in all respects unlike a male!" The Firstborn was terribly upset.

' "Oh," said Windflower, embarrassed. "I suppose it is because of what the M'an-folk did to me."

> 'Startled Firefoot
> Hard did gaze, then
> Saw the truth of
> Windflower's speaking
>
> All his tomhood
> Had been taken,
> Changed he had been
> To half-fela.

' "M'an!!!" howled Lord Firefoot. "Treacherous brood of Nine-birds! They have defiled the Folk! I shall be revenged upon them all, someday!" So saying, he ran into the forest, departing forever the crippled Windflower.

> 'So spoke Firefoot,
> Cursed the Big Ones,
> Out-of-sun
> They are forever.
>
> Now the servants
> Make them masters
> But the True-Folk
> Ne'er are vanquished.

'And so the First-walkers, by the word of our Lord Firefoot, never will walk in the shadow of M'an.'

Squeakerbane, having finished his story, lay down again between Furscuff and Fencewalker. There was a moment's strained silence, and then the Prince spoke.

'Well, now, I've never held much with those stretched, hairless folk myself. Quite a story, quite a story.'

Everyone relaxed, and many of the group congratulated Squeakerbane on his tale. More riddles and songs followed, and eventually even the over-excited Pouncequick was tired enough to fall asleep.

Fritti, too, his head full of Hushpad and Firefoot and red claws,

135

finally crossed the borders of the dream-fields. The furry tangle of Folk drowsed and grumbled away the waning Hour of Final Dancing.

The Hour of Smaller Shadows found the travelers descending to the Rootwood fence, the final stand of conifers and aspens that separated the ancient forest from the bluffs overlooking the Hararscrape canyon. Here the Prince's party would establish their border watch, and the others would go their own ways. The sun shone brightly, although the weather was chill.

Stopping at the fence, they could see the sparsely foliaged flatlands – shrouded in the merest sprinkling of snow – stretching away before them to the edge of the mighty canyon.

Turning to the First-walkers Squeakerbane and Furscuff, Prince Fencewalker bobbed his head in farewell. 'Well met and good dancing, Thane,' he said. 'Be sure to see me first when the Thane-meet is finished – before wasting your news on those old sit-on-tails back at the Court. Know that I, for one, will value your words.'

'Many thanks to you, O Prince,' said Squeakerbane gravely. 'It is good to know that true hearts still beat in the ancient home of our Folk.' The First-walker looked over to Tailchaser and his two companions. 'These three Furscuff and I will accompany for a short while – until our paths separate. Go in the watchfulness of our Lord Firefoot, Fencewalker.' He and Furscuff then moved a respectful distance apart as Fritti, Pouncequick and Roofshadow came forward to say their farewells.

On the verge of departure into the unknown but seemingly ill-starred territories, Tailchaser found himself reluctant to part company with Fencewalker. He knew he would miss the bluff, warmhearted Prince very much. When he tried to speak, no words came forth, and he had to pretend tc dislodge a burr from his tail while Roof-shadow stepped forward and thanked Fencewalker for his aid.

'Good dancing, Prince,' added Pouncequick. 'I saw ever so many fascinating things at Firsthome that I will always remember. You've been wonderful to us.'

'Pounce speaks for me, also,' said Fritti quietly. 'We owe you much.'

Fencewalker laughed. 'Marsh mud! I'm in your debt, also – for information about the E'a-ward territories, if nothing else. Stay out of trouble, and that will be my reward.'

The others in Fencewalker's party crowded forward now, and said their raucous farewells. As Tailchaser and the others walked away, Fritti found his words and called back to the Prince.

'Prince Fencewalker! You, also – keep yourself safe and happy!'

'Not to worry, little friend!' boomed the hunter. 'I walked these borders before I was old enough to be Named. You need have no fear for us!'

The Prince and his band disappeared back into the outskirts of the forest.

The sun was low in the sky as the five cats picked their way down the sloping plains.

Squeakerbane, with help from Furscuff, was describing the terrain that they could expect to find ahead. 'Actually,' he was saying, 'you need to proceed north, rather than in the direction we're going now, if you want to get across the Hararscrape. That way lies the ford. But I think you should come with us a bit farther, just to see Grumbleroar. It is worth the extra half-day, and not really very far out of your path.'

As they walked, ever-curious Pouncequick questioned the Thane about the story he had told the previous night, and the First-walkers' attitude toward the Court of Harar.

'After all,' he asked, 'don't lots of the Folk live with M'an, in M'an-dwellings? Why is that wrong?'

The crusty old Thane took the querying in good grace. It seemed that no one ever felt offended by Pouncequick, Fritti noted wryly, except badgers and Visl.

'The wrong, youngest hunter,' explained Squeakerbane, 'is that we are the Folk, not Growlers who need to be led to live; who hunt in packs and fawn on any that give them food. The Folk have always survived on their wits and skill, performing the earth-dance without help. Now half our number live in bloated indolence, emasculated and imprisoned – but uncaring – rising only to eat the food provided them by the children of Ninebirds.'

Though he strove to maintain calm, the scarred visage of the Thane revealed the depth of his feeling. 'And now,' he continued, 'even in the Court where our Lord Firefoot once lived, this poison has crept in. Dewtreader and his wearying mysticism and fatalism! It is wrong! Anyone can see that a cat must run, must hunt. And the Queen! Tangaloor forgive me, she *eats* from a *bowl* – as if she belonged to one of those hulking, unintelligible brutes that we cast out untold generations ago. The Queen of the Folk does not even hunt!' Squeakerbane was trembling with suppressed rage, and after a moment shook his head. 'I should not allow myself to become angry,' he said, chagrined, 'but in our time of great danger, to see those mewing sycophants lolling about while our kin are being destroyed . . . forgive me.' The Thane lapsed into silence, and for a long time the others imitated him.

The travelers approached Grumbleroar near the end of Stretching Sun. Here, on the rim of the Hararscrape, the cold air was thick with swirling mists. A muted rumbling was all around.

Squeakerbane, who had not spoken for some time, suddenly showed a brightened aspect. 'This is something you may pass along in story to litters yet unborn,' he said to Roofshadow.

At the canyon edge the sound grew louder, until it was a deafening clamor. Fritti winced. It was obvious that the name Grumbleroar was well chosen.

The mists were so thick at this spot that Squeakerbane decided to lead them across the Purrwhisper near its descent over the edge of the Hararscrape. As they traversed the slippery, water-slimed rocks, and the Purrwhisper – no longer the gentle stream that flowed past Firsthome – frothed below them, Fritti felt a moment of regret for all the times he had allowed himself to be led since he had left home.

A fitting end to this whole ridiculous trip, he thought: pounded and splashed to death by the safest river in all of Meerclar's fields.

But they made it across, even Pouncequick avoiding disaster. Back at the cliff's rim they could see the Purrwhisper pounding over the precipice, plummeting down the canyon's edge in a foaming white surge to churn and plunge off the rocks into the mighty Caterwaul far, far below. The water rose up from the swiftly flowing river at the bottom of the Hararscrape, and from where they crouched the setting sun, shining through this curtain of mist, tore the sky into glittering gold, red and purple. Grumbleroar falls bellowed like a furious beast, and the cats stared out at its awesome power.

When Unfolding Dark finally mantled the sun, Squeakerbane led them back up the banks of the Purrwhisper – away from cliff's edge. As the roar of the falls faded to a faint booming, they stopped.

Stunned as they were by the magnificence of Grumbleroar, it was some time before Tailchaser and his friends realized that Furscuff and the Thane were preparing to leave them.

'I am sorry we cannot guide you farther,' said Squeakerbane, 'but as it is we shall be several sunturns late for the Thane-meet. My suggestion is that you continue along the canyon wall, as I mentioned before, and cross over at the Slenderleap. It would be well to wait for sun-high before you cross, even if you reach it tonight: it is a treacherous path.'

They said their farewells, then, for the First-walkers were in a hurry to continue onward. 'Remember,' said Squeakerbane as they parted, 'the lands you are walking into bear an evil name these days. Tread warily. I wish there was more that we could do, but you have set your paws onto strange roads – and who knows what may come of that?' So saying, the Thane and his companion took their leave.

For the better part of two more Hours the three companions headed west, following the edge of Hararscrape. All were full of their own thoughts. When they reached the massive tree that stood solitarily on the canyon's rim, marking the near side of Slenderleap Ford, they curled up quietly and went to sleep. Fritti did not dream.

CHAPTER SEVENTEEN

Who wakes in the wilderness when night is done
 Fancying himself lord of all the land
May see what was not there at the set of sun
 And tremblingly will come to understand
The peril that has passed him in the dark –
 Tracks . . . in the sand.

– Archibald Rutledge

The light of day showed the Slenderleap Ford – a narrow, arching natural rock bridge flung over the Hararscrape. The opposite wall of the canyon was so far away that Slenderleap seemed to dwindle into nothingness in midspan.

Pouncequick looked out across the formation apprehensively.

'Well, I suppose we shall have to cross it, won't we, Tailchaser?'

Fritti nodded. 'It's either that or try to go down into the Hararscrape and cross the Caterwaul at the bottom. I don't fancy that much.'

'It's the only way open to us now,' Roofshadow said quietly. 'Squeakerbane said it's leagues and leagues to the end of the canyon. I doubt this will be the worst thing we see, anyway. Shall we go?'

Tailchaser sized the fela up carefully.

I don't think she's as calm as she wants to put about, he thought. *My whiskers tell me she's scared, too. Maybe more than we are. But there are all kinds of bravery, I suppose.*

'Roofshadow's right, Pounce,' he said aloud. 'Let's get to it.'

Once past the giant oak, whose root clusters seemed to anchor one side of the curving bridge, Fritti took the lead. Pouncequick followed him and Roofshadow brought up the rear, keeping a careful eye.

Slenderleap Ford was wider than it appeared from a distance – wide enough that three cats could have walked abreast – and at first the going was fairly easy. The wet weather and chill temperatures had left patches of ice on the stone, though. Tailchaser and his friends walked slowly and very carefully.

When they had moved a distance out onto the span, the canyon walls fell away below them, and the growling and pounding of the Caterwaul rose up to fill the air. The footing became treacherous, and the noise of the river drowned out most sounds. They journeyed over the canyon single-file and unspeaking, like caterpillars on a slender branch.

Near the midpoint of the stone ford Fritti felt the wind that blew down the canyon swirl roughly about him, tugging at his fur. Sudden gusts forced him to take a few shaky steps.

He stopped, pivoting slowly back around to face his companions. Pouncequick was a jump or two behind, and Roofshadow trailed the kitten at a slight distance, a look of grim concentration on her solemn gray face. As Tailchaser waited, Pouncequick also stopped, peering down from the ford into the Hararscrape.

'Tailchaser, Roofshadow!' he keened above the wind. 'I can see a flock of birds below us! *Below* us! We're higher than the fla-fa'az themselves!' In his excitement Pouncequick leaned even farther out to savor the sensation. Fritti's heart raced with fear, and felt as though it had grown to block off his air.

'Pounce! Get away from there!' he snarled. Pouncequick, startled, jumped back from the edge and slipped, skidding on the slick stone. Roofshadow, right behind the kitten now, swiftly seized him by the scruff of the neck. Her bite, sure and hard, drew a squeal of pain from Pouncequick, but she held her grip until his questing paws found a solid hold once more. She then gave Tailchaser a look that caused him to turn around without saying a word and continue on across the span.

On the downward-sloping section Roofshadow herself lost her footing for a moment in a heavy gust of wind, but managed to crouch and hold until the danger was past.

At all times the Caterwaul bellowed and shouted up at them: three tiny little creatures on a thin strand above the mighty waters. When they at last reached the opposite side the trio collapsed to the ground with trembling legs and lay for some time before they could go forward.

The landscape on the far side of Slenderleap was undistinguished and lonely. From the canyon's rim a jumble of rocks and hummocks of earth spotted with brush and clinging shrubbery stretched before them. As they moved away from the tapering span and the rushing of the Caterwaul subsided behind, the cold silence of the land rose around them like a fog.

Except for birds, which from time to time passed silently overhead, there were no signs of animal life. The breeze that whispered past Tailchaser's face and whiskers brought nothing but chill air and faint mist-traces of the river.

Pouncequick also sniffed the wind curiously, then turned to Fritti for confirmation of his senses. 'I don't smell any other Folk, Tailchaser. I don't sense much of anything.'

'I know, Pounce.' Tailchaser looked around. 'It's not the most hospitable place I've ever seen.'

Roofshadow gave Fritti a significant stare and said: 'I am sure we will find life in Ratleaf Forest, if only in the deeper places.' Fritti pondered the look.

I suppose she doesn't want me to frighten Pounce, he guessed.

As they walked, Fritti became aware of a slight feeling of irritation, something unsettling at the very rim of his consciousness. He felt a faint buzzing, or humming – but it was as thin and insubstantial as the noise of a brzz-hive a hundred leagues away. But it *was* there – and very subtly, it was getting stronger.

When they stopped to rest in the wind-damping shelter of a standing stone, he asked his companions if they had sensed it, too.

'Not yet,' said Roofshadow, 'but I expected you would first. It's a good thing you can.'

'What do you mean?' asked Fritti, mystified.

'You heard Squeakerbane. You heard Fencewalker. There's something happening in these wilds, and that's why we're here. Better that we sense it before it senses us.'

'What kind of something?' Pouncequick's eyes were bright and curious.

'I don't know,' said Roofshadow, 'but it is bad. It is *os* in a way that I have not sensed before. I knew that when I found the home of my Folk. If we are going to walk into its territory – and here we are – then we should at least not deceive ourselves on that account.'

As Roofshadow spoke, eyes clear and spine straight, Fritti could not help wondering what she had been like before the death of her tribe. She was a hunter, no doubt of that, but the hard-edged look that she wore seemed to be more from sorrow than other causes. Would she ever dance or laugh? It seemed odd to try to picture it, but he *had* seen her play with little Pouncequick. Maybe someday she would be happier. He hoped so.

They walked for a while into the evening, and when Meerclar's Eye was high above them, stopped to rest. The humming that was not quite a sound seemed closer, more pervasive now, and even Pouncequick and Roofshadow felt something – a current, just below the surface. After hunting for some time without success the three cats conceded victory to the desolate wilderness and curled themselves up together in a furry pile to sleep.

Tailchaser wiggled his nose free from Pouncequick's hind leg and sniffed the air groggily. The Eye had slipped below the horizon, and the dew of Final Dancing was wet on his muzzle. Something had awakened him, but what?

Trying not to arouse his sleeping comrades, he craned his head up from the knot of warm bodies like a hlizza rising up on its coils.

The humming, the strange pulsing that he felt bone-deep, had changed pitch. It was more vibrant somehow – not closer, but sharper.

He felt a strong, piercing sensation. In the darkness outside the circle of warmth something was watching them. Tailchaser froze, holding his head motionless, aware even in his fear that it was an uncomfortable position.

Suddenly, as if he had fallen into cold water, a great wash of loneliness flowed over and through him. It was not his own. Something, some being, was wearing this hideous isolation like a skin – he could sense it as strongly as if the tortured creature were right beside him. He remembered the cat of his dream, spinning forever through the darkness, radiating cold despair. Was this the same feeling?

Even as he thought of the catmint nightmare the feeling was gone. The hum had become a low throb again, and the wilderness around them was empty. Fritti could feel, although he could not say how, that the watcher was gone. When he woke the others they listened blearily to his excited story, but after some time had passed it became obvious that whatever it had been would not return that night. They returned to uneasy sleep.

After marching for a short time in the sunlight of the following morning, they sighted the mound.

They were descending down a rocky plain into a wide, shallow valley. It stretched away before them to the foothills of a range of tall mountains, so far away they seemed only dim shapes against the sky. The snow had begun to fall again, and as it fluttered down to land and cling on their coats they looked across the cracked, gray valley floor to the mushrooming bulge in its center. The mound, low and massive, thrust up from the cold ground like the shell of an enormous dun-colored beetle.

Coming over the low rim of the valley the travelers felt the pulling sensation suddenly increase. Fritti shied back, hackles raised, and Pouncequick and Roofshadow shook their heads as if beset by an unpleasant noise.

'That's it!' hissed Tailchaser, feeling panicky and short of breath.

'It is,' Roofshadow agreed. 'We have found the source of many problems.'

Pouncequick had retreated several steps, and now crouched, eyes wide and small body shivering. 'It's a nest,' he said quietly. 'It's a nest, and the things in it will sting us and sting us!' He began sniffling quietly. Roofshadow, walking a little unsteadily herself, went to his side and nuzzled him comfortingly behind the ear. She looked up from the kitten inquiringly.

'What do we do now, Tailchaser?' she asked.

Fritti shook his head in bewilderment. 'I don't have the slightest idea. I hadn't ever expected . . . this. I'm . . . I'm frightened.' He looked down at the huge, silent mound and shuddered.

'So am I, Tailchaser,' said Roofshadow, and the tone of her voice drew his gaze. She met his eyes, and the shadow of a smile passed across her face, the merest twitch of her whiskers. Something else passed between them. Fritti, feeling awkward, padded over to Pouncequick.

'It's all right, little friend,' he said, sniffing Pouncequick's nose. The small cat smelled of terror, his body trembling, his bushy tail curled up between his legs. 'It's all right, Pounce, we won't let anything happen to you.' Fritti was not even listening to his own words – he was staring off again, across the valley.

'Well, whatever we *will* do, now we must move,' Roofshadow pointed out. 'The winds are rising again, and we are completely exposed. And not only to the weather.'

Fritti realized that she was right. They were as naked and unprotected in this spot as a bug on a flat rock. He nodded in agreement, and they coaxed their young comrade to his paws.

'Come on, now, Pounce, let's find a better place to lie up for a while, then we'll have a bit of a think.'

Roofshadow, too, moved to reassure the youngling. 'We will not go any closer, Pouncequick . . . not now. I don't want to spend the Hours of Darkness very close to that *os*-mound in any case.' The youngling, persuaded into movement, walked quietly between them as they began a long march around the outside rim of the valley.

Along the valley edge, circling the mound like small planets orbiting a gray, dead sun, the companions paced quietly and kept close together. As the sun rose into the sky, bringing a sickly light to the valley, stands of trees became visible over the far rim of the great bowl. A vast sea of woodlands reached into the distance.

'That must be Ratleaf,' Roofshadow said. Tailchaser was startled at how loud her voice sounded after their long silence. 'It looks to be quite a long walk,' she continued, 'but it will certainly provide shelter.'

'Certainly,' agreed Fritti. 'Do you see it, Pounce? Think of it! Trees to scratch, Squeakers to hunt – everything!'

Pouncequick gave him a weak grin, and murmured: 'Thank you, Tailchaser. I will be all right.' They continued on.

Toward the end of Smaller Shadows a clutch of large, dark birds flew overhead. One of their number peeled off from the others and swooped down to circle over the cats. He had a bright eye, and feathers of glossy black. He hovered lazily for a few moments quite close above their heads; then, uttering a shrill cry of derision, he soared up to meet his fellows. Croaking, they disappeared from sight.

By the dwindling away of Stretching Sun they had come near enough to Ratleaf Forest to distinguish the spires of individual trees protruding above the edge of the valley. With the night fast approaching, the sensation of malevolence coming from the shadowy hump on the valley floor seemed to increase.

Tailchaser felt the throbbing deep inside himself, and only by repeating the First-walkers' prayer over and over mindlessly was he able to stifle his urge to bolt and run until he would fall down exhausted. 'Tangaloor, fire-bright,' he muttered to himself, 'flame-foot, farthest walker . . . ' Pouncequick and Roofshadow did not seem to be feeling it quite as strongly as he, but they looked strained and worn. The forest was now completely visible, stretching for leagues beyond the bowl-shaped valley. It looked very warm and inviting.

When the sun finally began to set, limning the tips of the trees with golden light, they quickened their pace, pressing their bodies to still greater efforts. As the sun dipped below the farthest horizon of the forest, only its red corona left pressed against the sky, a bitterly cold wind sprang up; it bit at their noses and flattened their fur.

Tailchaser, with Pouncequick and Roofshadow struggling gamely behind him, increased his speed. The buzzing sensation was mounting; he felt quite ill. A vast, formless panic seemed to snap at their heels. One after another, the trio broke into a run.

Up the steep outer slope of the valley wall they galloped, topping it at last to look down on the edge of Ratleaf. Heedless now of anything but the gathering oppressiveness behind them they tumbled down the short rise and dashed across the rocky flat, to vanish at last under the eaves of the forest.

Ratleaf Forest slumbered . . . or seemed to. A murky, stagnant calm hung in the air. As Tailchaser and his companions slunk wearily through the trees the forest's silence weighed as heavily on them as their own fatigue.

Once into the woods, Fritti and Pouncequick were quite ready to collapse where they stood, but Roofshadow pointed out the importance of finding a site that was better protected against cold and discovery. Although the mound was now out of sight, it had not disappeared from their memories: with groans of weariness they acceded to the fela's suggestion and continued deeper into the forest.

Picking their way across the damp loam, past moss and mushrooms, the cats found themselves imitating the silence of their surroundings. Heads down, moving slowly, they stopped frequently to wrinkle their noses at the unfamiliar scents of Ratleaf. Moisture pervaded everything, earth and bark sodden and dripping – the whole forest smelled of tree roots in still water deep underground. The air was steaming-breath cold.

It took the travelers until the end of Unfolding Dark to find shelter: a windbreak provided by a standing granite boulder and the roots of a toppled tree. They promptly fell down to sleep. Nothing disturbed them, but when they woke near the middle of Deepest Quiet – sore and hungry – they did not feel particularly rested.

There were still no signs of any creatures bigger than insects. After a period of fruitless search the cats were forced to settle for a supper of grubs and beetles.

Although they were all feeling poorly, Tailchaser felt especially on edge and upset. The throbbing of the mound, despite its having decreased noticeably when they passed into Ratleaf, still dug at him. Also, unlike his two friends, he had not shared Fencewalker's squirrel and had now gone two full days without any type of meal he would call satisfactory.

As he swallowed his last grub, he snapped: 'Well, here we are, and no mistake about it. I have brought us right to the brink, no question. I hope you are both pleased about following me while I made a complete *M'an* of myself! Perhaps you'd like to follow me into the mound so we can all be hideously slaughtered.' He swatted an oak boll with his paw and watched it carom away.

'Don't say such things, Tailchaser,' said Pouncequick. 'That's not true, any of it.'

'It is true, Pounce,' said Fritti bitterly. 'The great hunter Tailchaser has come to the limit of his quest.'

'The only thing you have said that is true, Tailchaser,' said Roofshadow with surprising vehemence, 'is that we have found what we were looking for. That is something that Fencewalker, Squeakerbane and the others cannot say. We have found the source of the terror.'

'Apparently Thane Brushstalker found it, too – and you heard what happened to him! Meerclar protect us!' Tailchaser was a little mollified, though. He looked up from his sulk to face his comrades. 'All right. The question still remains. What do we do?'

Pouncequick looked at the two elder cats, then said quietly, as if ashamed: 'I think we should go back to the Prince and tell him. He'll know what to do.'

Fritti was about to object when Roofshadow cut in: 'Pouncequick's right. We felt the *os* in that place. We three are too few and too small. To think that it is our place alone to deal with this is an arrogance surpassing Ninebirds'.' The fela shook her head, green eyes thoughtful. 'If we bring others here they cannot fail to discover what we have. Perhaps then the weight of the Court of Harar will be put to some use.' She stood, another shadow in the dark forest. 'Come, let's return to the tree roots until the sun is out. I am certainly not going anywhere tonight.'

Tailchaser stared at the gray fela, admiring her. 'As usual, you speak with quite a bit more reason than *I* have been using. You too, Pounce.' He smiled at his young friend. 'Harar! I'm glad that you two didn't let me go off by my stupid self.'

In the Hour before dawn Fritti was unable to sleep. Roofshadow and

Pouncequick tossed fitfully and muttered, but Tailchaser lay between them and stared up into the dark treetops, nerves as taut as a bent branch. From time to time he would drift off into a brief, dreamy near-sleep, only to find himself suddenly wide awake again, feeling trapped and exposed, his heart pounding.

The night wore on. The forest remained as still as stone.

Tailchaser was wandering along the dream threshold when he heard a noise. He lay listening distractedly for a moment as it grew louder; suddenly he realized that something was charging rapidly toward them through the underbrush. He leaped onto his paws, jarring his friends into groggy wakefulness.

'Something's coming!' he hissed, fur bristling. The din increased. Time seemed to slow, each moment expanding into a smothering eternity. A shape burst out of the undergrowth only a few jumps away.

Spiky and tattered, eyes starting from its head, the apparition crashed out into the open. Highlighted by the Eye beaming down through the trees, it seemed to take forever to reach the companions. Tailchaser, rigid with panic, felt as though he were under deep water.

The bizarre figure skidded to a halt. The Eye-light was full in its face for a moment – full in the face of Eatbugs.

Before Fritti, shocked and startled, could move or say a word, Eatbugs threw back his head and howled like the bitterest winter storm.

'Run! Run!' cried the mad cat. 'They're coming! *RUN!*'

Pouncequick and Roofshadow were bolt upright now. As if to emphasize Eatbugs' cry, a terrible choking scream welled up from the darkness of the woods beyond. With a bound, Eatbugs was past Tailchaser and his companions and gone. Another horrible moan split the air. With unconscious noises of terror, the trio was after him, running headlong into the forest, away from the hideous sound.

Tailchaser felt as if he were in an awful dream – the flickering of Eye-light and darkness nearly blinding him, Eatbugs barely visible before him, rocks and roots rising up around him. The forest seemed to rush past. He could hear Pouncequick and the fela laboring along beside him. On and on they ran, no thought of stealth or hiding, only escape, escape!

Now Pouncequick alone was at his side – gasping, driving himself along on his short kitten-legs in an ecstasy of terror. Fritti was pulling away from him. Without thinking, Tailchaser slowed down, turned to urge him on. There was a cracking sound from overhead, and something sprang down from the trees. Tailchaser felt sharp claws gouging him, raking his back; then he was crushed to the ground and his ka fled into complete darkness.

CHAPTER EIGHTEEN

I saw my evil day at hand. The sun rose dim on us in the morning, and at night it sank in a dark cloud, and looked like a ball of fire.

– Black Hawk

Another jarring impact returned Fritti to the waking world. Bruised and exhausted, he lay with his eyes closed. He could feel the bitter cold rain splashing down on him, matting his fur. The sudden jolt – had he been dropped? pushed? – had knocked the breath out of his chest. As he sucked the air back into his lungs a scent came with it that prickled his skin: cold earth and salty blood – and a deep, penetrating animal musk. His muscles clenched involuntarily, and a bright pain shot across his back and shoulders. He restrained a noise of protest.

Slowly and cautiously he opened an eye. He shut it again immediately as cold rainwater splashed in. After a moment he tried once more. Just beyond the blurry tip of his own muzzle he could see the miserable, bedraggled face of Eatbugs, who was cringing on the ground nearby. Over the arch of Eatbugs' back he could also see a little of Pouncequick's fluffy tail.

'There. I told you the little grub would wake up. Now he can carry his own sun-cursed weight.'

Tailchaser started involuntarily at this speech so near to his head. The voice used the Higher Singing in awkward, halting style, full of dissonant notes and slurs. The harsh sounds resonated with violence.

Ears flattened against his head, Tailchaser turned very slowly to look over his shoulder. Something large and terrible loomed there.

Three cats stared down at Fritti and his companions where they lay on the wet ground. They were big, fully as large as Dayhunter and Nightcatcher, Fencewalker's comrades – but they looked very different: wrong, not the way the Folk were meant to be. Their faces were snakelike, flat brows and wide cheekbones, and their ears lay well back on their skulls. Three pairs of eyes stared from these faces, huge and deep-set, burning with an unsettling fire. The muscular bodies were knotted, low-slung and powerful, terminating in wide, spatulate paws with . . . red talons, hooked nails the color of blood.

Tailchaser felt his heart quicken with fear. One of the beasts approached him, strange eyes glinting. Like the other two he was mostly a sooty black, with a few sickly, pale spots on his underside.

'Get up, me'mre,' he snarled. 'You've been carried long enough. From now on you'll hop along properly or feel my teeth.' He bared the spiky contents of his mouth. 'Do you understand?' With this the creature leaned down toward Tailchaser. His breath smelled of carrion. Fritti felt terror's constriction from his throat to his stomach, and could only move his head weakly.

'Good. Well, you and your miserable friends can get up, then.' Tailchaser, unable to meet those terrible eyes any longer, snuck a glance over to his companions. He could see Pouncequick's face now. The kitten was awake, but wearing a look of shock and numbness. He did not meet Fritti's gaze.

'You there!' Tailchaser turned back. 'Listen, when I say "up," up is where you'd better be. This is Scratchnail speaking, a chief of the Clawguard. You've not still got your miserable guts because I *like* you little bugs. Up! Now!'

Fritti climbed painfully to his feet. He could feel something thicker and warmer than rainwater matting the fur on his back. He wanted desperately to groom, to clean the wound, but his fear was too strong.

Scratchnail hissed at the other two beasts: 'Longtooth! Bitefast! Sun sizzle you, don't stand there – kick these slugs onto their paws! If you have to bite an ear off, go ahead. The Fat One won't much care if they're not so pretty.' Scratchnail laughed, a grating, coughing sound that hurt Tailchaser's ears. The other Clawguard moved forward and pulled the silent Pouncequick and Eatbugs to their feet.

For the first time since regaining the waking world, Fritti took a look at his surroundings. They were still in Ratleaf, apparently – lines of trees extended out on all sides into the night. A drizzling rain spattered down through the branches, and the ground was spongy and sodden.

As the three companions were forced into a slow march, all Tailchaser could think was: *I'm going to die. I didn't find Hushpad, and now I've died trying. Died. Going to die.*

Then, as the Clawguard impelled them along with savage paw-blows to the head and flanks, he wondered: *Where is Roofshadow?*

Although it seemed to Fritti that they had been walking forever, the feel of the air told him that it was still only midway through Final Dancing. Had it really been only a short time ago that he, Roofshadow and Pounce had been curled up together warmly? He looked at his young friend limping along before him. Poor Pounce – if only he hadn't come. Looking at the small, bedraggled form, he felt the first warmth of an unfamiliar emotion: hatred. The huge, deformed beasts that harried them on with cuffs and snarls were all too tangible, but since they were real they could be hated. Where were they going? Where were these creatures taking them? Fritti knew – the mound.

So there was something to know, at least; some face to the evil. It seemed to help a little, although Fritti could not say why. It was pointless to wonder too much, though, because he knew that he was – that thought again – going to die.

Eatbugs, leading the procession, had begun to mumble to himself. Tailchaser could not distinguish any words in the angry murmur, and apparently the Clawguard could not either. After the first moments they ceased paying attention, but Fritti could sense something building in the mad old cat, a gradually swelling tension. It made him apprehensive.

Eatbugs, with a yowl of rage, turned on Longtooth, the nearest Guard. 'Crawler!!' screamed the ragged old cat. 'Your song is sour! I know your dirt and darkness!' Longtooth, lips curling in surprise, started back almost imperceptibly, and Eatbugs leaped past him into the trees. Tailchaser's heart was racing.

The beast of the Clawguard was off balance for only a heartbeat; with a growl he bounded after Eatbugs. He caught him within a matter of moments, knocking the tattered cat skidding in the mud, then leaped onto his back. There came a frenzied yowl – from which of the two Fritti could not say – and then, amazingly, Eatbugs rose up and raked his claws against Longtooth's snout. Eatbugs' mud-matted fur stood out spikily as he pressed forward; for a moment he seemed to grow, to become strong. Then, as Longtooth recovered his wits and charged again, Tailchaser saw that Eatbugs was just what he had been: an old cat, puffed by madness, up against a monster twice his size. Longtooth dealt a crashing kick to Eatbugs' face as they grappled, and the old one dropped limply to the muddy earth, blood running from his nose, and lay silent. The Clawguard, hissing like a hlizza, jumped forward to tear out his throat, but Scratchnail's voice rasped out.

'Stop, or I'll have your eyes!' Longtooth, his glittering stare now opaque with bloodlust, hesitated for a moment. He bared his teeth, then turned to stare at his chief. Scratchnail chuckled, a dry, scaly sound.

'Well,' he said, 'the old drooler made a pretty fool out of you, didn't he?' Longtooth looked over to his leader with undisguised hatred, but moved no closer to Eatbugs. 'Almost got away, too, didn't he?' Scratchnail taunted. 'It was your fault, and now you can carry him for a while. You'd better hope that pathetic old skin-rat is still breathing, because the Fat One wanted this bunch alive – at least until he sees them. What do you think he'd do to you if you interfered, my friend?' Scratchnail grinned. Longtooth, shaken, backed away from the crumpled form of Eatbugs.

'Maybe he'd give you to the Toothguard, eh? Wouldn't *that* be unpleasant!' Longtooth shivered and looked away from his chief. Gingerly, he approached the old cat and sniffed him, then picked him up with his mouth.

'Very good,' said Scratchnail, motioning to Bitefast, who had watched the events without moving. 'Let's go. The Fire-eye will be open soon. We'll have to make double-time to the Western Mouth.'

Fritti and his young friend were harried forward, always in a straight line, with no slackening of pace allowed. The steady rain had thickened, soaking their fur and turning the forest paths into slippery bog.

When it seemed as though things could be no worse for the prisoners, the rain began to turn to hail. Tailchaser, feeling the stinging pelt of the ice-stones, remembered the Rikchikchik and their attack from the treetops. This attack was unceasing, though, and his body was already cold and battered. When he and Pouncequick tried to change their route slightly, to gain more protection from the trees overhead, Scratchnail and his bullies pushed them back onto the path. The beast-cats themselves were not bothered by the hailstones – or did not seem to be – and seemed to be hurrying toward some important rendezvous. Fritti and Pounce, silent and beaten, kept their heads low and kept moving. The first traces of dawn were beginning to blue the edges of the Vez'an sky, and the Clawguard had grown agitated.

Abruptly, at an unintelligible command from Scratchnail, Longtooth bounded forward and vanished into a clump of bracken. Everyone else waited for a moment in the eerie silence of Ratleaf. Then Bitefast's reptilian head reappeared and bobbed once. Scratchnail gave a low growl of approval.

'Now, you miserable Squeakers, into the bushes you go!'

Longtooth, still carrying the silent form of Eatbugs, followed Bitefast into the tangle of brush. After a moment's hesitation – in which he weighed the chances of making a break for freedom, and realized that he would never outrun Scratchnail – Tailchaser followed the Clawguard. Pouncequick, eyes still inwardly fixed, padded after.

I suppose they're going to kill us here, Fritti thought.

Tailchaser felt suddenly resigned to death – almost grateful to be able to give up the struggle.

With the Clawguard chief bringing up the rear, they ducked and twisted their way through the clinging tendrils. Eyes half closed to protect them from looming thorns, Tailchaser almost tumbled headlong into the hole that appeared before him.

The hole was wide and dark, the tunnel quickly bending out of sight into the earth. Pouncequick peered around Tailchaser's shoulder at the tunnel mouth, eyes wide with silent terror. His mouth worked for a moment, but only a weak mew emerged.

Scratchnail pushed through the last of the branches. 'Well,' he said, 'climb in, you surface-creepers, or I shall have to help you.' His distorted form bulked closer, eyes glowing. Fritti felt torn. Perhaps it would be better to die in the open than to be killed like a gopher down a short hole. But as he looked at Scratchnail, some of his hatred came back, and he wanted to live a little longer. Why should the huge Clawguard have to get them into a tunnel to kill them? Maybe the things that the chief had said to Longtooth were true. There was always some hope of escape if they were kept alive.

Well, he decided, *I suppose I have no other choice*.

As he was stepping gingerly down into the dark hole, he looked back at Pouncequick. The kitten was so full of fear that he was pushing back from the tunnel entrance, preparing to bolt. Tailchaser was alarmed. Scratchnail, impatience traced across his brutish face, was about to do something. As Fritti hesitated, unsure of what to do, the chieftain shot his blood-red claws. Shocked into action, Fritti leaped forward, ducking a startled swipe from Scratchnail's talons, and pushed the balking Pouncequick toward the hole. The terrified kitten began to whimper and splayed his legs in resistance, digging his claws into the wet ground.

'It's all right, Pounce, you'll be all right,' Tailchaser heard himself saying. 'Trust me – I won't let them hurt you. Come on, we've got to go.' He hated himself for forcing the frightened youngling into that dark, awful burrow. Butting and tugging with his teeth, he managed to pry Pouncequick's grip loose, and they descended into darkness.

CHAPTER NINETEEN

While, like a ghastly rapid river
Through the pale door,
A hideous throng rush out forever
And laugh – but smile no more.

– Edgar Allan Poe

The walls and floor of the tunnel were damp. Sickly-white roots, and bits of other things about which Fritti did not care to guess, hung down from the earthen ceiling. As they moved away from the entrance the light gradually dimmed, and it would have disappeared completely but for a faint phosphorescence of the soil that lined the burrow. They journeyed downward in faint, ghostly light, like the spirits of cats traveling in the void between stars.

Pouncequick, once underground, resumed his plodding and nearly lifeless mode. The clay beneath their paws stuck and crumbled between their pads. The silence was complete.

After some time they caught up with the other two Clawguard, Longtooth still carrying his soiled burden. So they continued: Fritti and Pouncequick, hemmed fore and hind by red claws, above and below by damp, solid earth.

It was impossible for Fritti to gauge the passing of time. The group, captors and captives, walked and walked, but the featureless soil never changed; the dim, nauseating glow of the tunnel earth neither waxed nor waned. On and on into the depths they passed, with no sound but their own breathing and an occasional incomprehensible exchange between the Clawguard. Tailchaser felt as if he had been in this dark hole forever. He began to slide in and out of a kind of dream. He thought of the Old Woods, the look of sunbeams slanting down to illuminate the forest floor . . . of running through the wonderfully fragrant, ticklish grasses with Hushpad – chasing and being chased, collapsing at last to nap in the summer warmth.

The cold, unexpected wriggling of an escaping worm beneath his paw jolted him back to darkness, and the tunnel. He could hear the harsh rasp of Scratchnail's breath. He wondered if he would ever see sunlight again.

At length Fritti's hunger overcame his reverie completely, and he began to pay more attention to the worms that squirmed through the moist earth of the burrow. After several attempts he caught one, and, with some difficulty managed to down it as he walked. It felt dreadful not to be able to stop pacing while he ate, but he feared the consequences of slowing down. Although it was a tricky business, he felt a little better for having had the morsel, and he caught another as soon as he could and ate that, too. He tried to pass the next one to Pounce, but the kitten paid no attention. After several fruitless attempts to force the wiggling mouthful on him, Fritti gave up and ate it himself.

The tunnel began to slope upward. After a short while the procession came to a small underground cavern, no more than a couple of jumps across, but high-roofed. Inside this cavern the air flowed a bit more freely, and when Scratchnail brought them to a halt Fritti was more than happy just to sit and breathe for a moment, and to rest his sore legs and paws. Wearily, he began to groom the worst of the mud and stones from between his pads, then turned his tongue to the wound on his shoulder. The blood had dried and the fur was matted stiff. It hurt when he cleaned it. Pouncequick sat motionlessly beside him, as if paralyzed; when Fritti turned and began to groom him, he submitted without a sound.

Scratchnail and the other two had been conversing in low tones at the far end of the cavern. Longtooth approached the two companions and dropped the unconscious form of Eatbugs beside them. Then, at a nod from Scratchnail, he turned and slipped away up the tunnel at the far entrance to the cave. Bitefast and the chief stretched their long, corded bodies on the floor of the earthen chamber and stared at their prisoners. Fritti – deciding that the best procedure was to ignore them as much as possible – continued to clean the dirt from Pouncequick's fur and tend to the young cat's many cuts and abrasions. Eatbugs groaned once and stirred, but did not awaken.

Finally, a muffled yowl came from the direction in which Longtooth had disappeared. At the urging of Scratchnail – in the form of a low snarl and a jerk of the head – Bitefast vanished up the tunnel, almost before the echoes had stopped echoing from the limestone walls. There was a commotion up the corridor. Fritti could hear the voices of Longtooth and Bitefast arguing. After a time they emerged into the cave dragging a limp, bulky burden. Scratchnail rose and ambled over on splayed paws to examine what they had brought.

'Found him where the branch tunnel opens upground into the valley wall, chief,' said Longtooth with a tongue-lolling grin. 'Just like you smelled. Caught 'im looking other way, then had to drag 'im down quick, before I got burned by the Fire-eye. By the Master, he's a big one, isn't he?' After all this speech Longtooth turned and self-consciously cleaned a wound on his flank.

Interested despite himself, Tailchaser leaned forward, staring in the dim cavern light. The bundle that the two Clawguard had dragged in was some kind of animal. A low sound of pain issued from the crumpled figure.

Scratchnail looked over at Fritti. 'Come have a gape, little mud-Squeaker,' he said. 'Don't be afraid. This one won't hurt you!' The chief's laugh scraped through the rock chamber. Tailchaser moved hesitantly forward.

Lying on the wet stone floor was a large Growler, bleeding from several wounds on his stomach and face. As Tailchaser peered past Scratchnail, the dog's eyes opened and stared blearily. He was as large as the Clawguard themselves; Fritti was impressed and frightened to know that one of the monster cats could take a fik'az this size by himself. The Growler blinked – vainly trying to keep the blood out of his eyes – and wheezed painfully. Something inside was broken and the animal was dying. Saddened and disturbed, Fritti turned back toward his corner.

Longtooth looked up from his wound-licking and said to Scratchnail: 'We don't have to give any to *these*' – indicating Fritti and Pouncequick – 'do we?'

Scratchnail looked at the pair – Fritti, wary and nervous; Pouncequick, paralyzed and silent.

'We just have to get them to Vastnir alive. We don't have to share our little treats with them.' So saying, Scratchnail shot his scarlet claws and made a swift disemboweling stroke across the belly of the fik'az. Then, although the horrible agonized cries had not stopped, the Clawguard began to feed. Fritti curled up around Pouncequick and tried to ignore the sounds.

When the Claws had finished their meal, covering the cavern floor with grisly debris, they slept. At Scratchnail's canny direction, Bite-fast and Longtooth had dragged their bloated bodies over to the entrances. When they rolled over onto their backs to sleep, legs in the air, they effectively blocked off any route of escape. Tailchaser could only lie next to Pounce and Eatbugs helplessly while the beasts digested their prey.

Fritti had no idea how long he lay beside his two silent companions, listening to the gurgling slumbers of their captors. He drifted into fitful sleep, and was awakened by a strange sound. At first, in his groggy state, he imagined he was dying, and that the carrion birds had come down from the sky to strip his bones. He thought he heard them all around him, bargaining solemnly over the choicest bits. Their voices were harsh, low and cold. . . .

Coming fully awake, he listened to the eerie sounds filling the cavern. These were no great old carrion birds.

Still stretched on their backs, sprawled against cavern walls of moist stone, the Clawguard were singing.

> 'A day will come
> Above the mound
> No light will shine
> Upon the ground –
> And from the deep
> Where Old Ones sleep
> Our Folk will creep
> Without a sound. . . .
>
> No more to hide
> And wait for night
> No more to shun
> The hot daylight
> The sun will die
> And you and I
> Will upward fly
> To hunt and bite. . . .
>
> The Sun, the Sun
> The Sun will die
> And dying slip
> From out the sky
> And in the black

We will take back
All that we lack
The Sun will die. . . . '

On and on it went, the hideous chanting voices groaning out the
song of darkness and hatred and revenge – night creeping over the
world, blood on the stones and earth, and the Folk of the mound
rising up, holding sway over all.

Next to Fritti, Eatbugs' eyes snapped open. He began to rise, then
lay back and listened, unmoving and unspeaking, as the song droned
on. Tailchaser saw him shake his soiled head, wearily, painfully, and
then close his eyes again. The chant of the Clawguard seemed to have
no end. After some time, Tailchaser fell back into oppressive, stone-
heavy sleep.

CHAPTER TWENTY

Lo! Death has reared himself a throne
In a strange city, lying alone
Far down among the dim West . . .

  – Edgar Allan Poe

Beyond the cavern the tunnels seemed to grow warmer. Fritti knew that aboveground it was winter; snow and freezing rain were falling. Here, deep in the earth – *how* deep Tailchaser had no way of knowing – the air was becoming thick with heat and moisture.

Eatbugs was up and moving now. He mumbled quietly to himself as he walked, but otherwise showed no signs of resistance to their captors. Longtooth, his muzzle not yet completely healed from the swipe that Eatbugs had given him, was taking great delight in harassing the old cat, who gamely resisted all attempts by the Guard to enrage him.

Tailchaser, trudging on leaden paws, once again began to feel the throb of the mound. Here, beneath the ground, the sensation was different, the vibration digging deeper into his bones and nerves. The pulse of the mound seemed lower and more basic – all-pervading, but, strangely, more natural. Tailchaser knew that they were approaching their destination.

'You can feel it, can you?'

The harsh croak made Fritti jump. Scratchnail was following close behind, watching him, the unpleasant yellow eyes observing his every movement.

'I see that you've started to hear the song of Vastnir. You're a sharp-sensing little bug, aren't you, star-face?' The chief moved up to Tailchaser's side. The massive, thick-muscled form looming over him intimidated Fritti, and made it difficult to speak.

'I . . . I feel *something*,' he stammered. 'I felt it before . . . above ground.'

'Well,' Scratchnail leered, 'aren't you the clever-quick one?! Don't you worry . . . there'll be some Folk who'll pay plenty of attention to a smart young tom like you where we're going – more attention than you'll like, perhaps.' With a cold, bleak grin that exposed few teeth, the Clawguard chief dropped back to pace behind Fritti once more. The skin around the young cat's whiskers itched and crawled. He didn't want anyone or anything more interested in him than was already the case. He hurried forward to catch up with Eatbugs and Pouncequick. The earth throbbed.

Soon the tunnel began to broaden. Every hundred or so jumps now, the company passed branching tunnels or caves – it was difficult to tell which, since they were just dark holes in the wall of the main shaft. The air continued to warm, a damp heat that made Fritti and his companions feel sluggish. Eatbugs twitched his head from side to side as if to throw off something binding.

'Here now, back to the holes – never do, never do . . . ' The mad old tom looked imploringly, first at the unresponsive Pouncequick, then at Fritti, who could only shake his head. 'All this bim-bam bashing and gnashing . . . can't . . . can't . . . ?' Eatbugs rolled his eyes and subsided into muttering. Tailchaser pushed at Pouncequick gently with his head.

'Did you hear him, Pounce? What do you think of all this, hmmm? Get your whiskers up, does it?' Fritti waited vainly for a response, then tried again. 'What a story this will make when we get back to Meeting Wall, won't it? D'you think the Folk will believe us?' After a moment, Pouncequick raised his head and looked at Fritti plaintively.

'Where's my friend Roofshadow?' he asked. His voice was so quiet that Tailchaser had to cock his ears forward to make out the words.

'We'll find her, Pounce, I promise. I swear on my tail name – we'll get away from here and find her!'

The kitten looked at him for a moment with a puzzled expression, then lowered his gaze to the ground once more.

Skydancer's Ears and Tears! Fritti cursed himself. *When am I going to stop making promises I have not the slightest chance of keeping? Still,* he thought, *I had to say something to Pounce. He has the look of someone who's going to lie down and float to the Fields Beyond any moment. At least I got a word or two out of him.*

Now Tailchaser noticed that the sound of the tunnel had changed.

Below the near-silent padding of their paws, he thought he could discern a thin wash of voices – cat voices, but very distant.

Bitefast, the nearest Guard, turned and hissed: 'We'll be home, soon. *Your* home, too – for a short while, anyway.'

Finally the underground path widened again and turned downward. The pulsing had become constant and almost familiar, and the voices Fritti had noticed earlier sounded louder and louder. Then, when it seemed as if any moment they must come upon the source, Scratchnail stopped the procession.

'Now,' he said, fixing Fritti and his comrades with a hard stare, 'we are about to enter Vastnir by one of the Lesser Gates. If you make any movement to escape I will tear you to ribbons, and be pleased to do it. And just in case you decide to try your luck' – here he narrowed his gaze on Eatbugs, who turned his eyes away uncomfortably – 'even if you're fast and tricky enough to get by me – which I doubt – you'll come to wish you'd died at my claws, I promise you. The Clawguard are not the worst who home in the Vastnir Mound.'

Scratchnail turned to his fellows. 'And you two. Remember, no one is to interfere – especially not the Toothguard. The prisoners stay with us until I say otherwise, understood? It had better be.'

They all followed Scratchnail downward, and shortly rounded a bend in the tunnel to find themselves in a wide entranceway before the gate. Silhouetted at the end of the tunnel by a fitful blue-green light stood two massive Clawguard, silent and terrible, bigger even than Fritti's captors. On either side of the entrance they guarded, on small piles of raised earth, were skulls. One was of an enormous Growler, the eyesockets dark as sorrow. The other was the skull of a large horned beast. All four of these sentries looked down pitilessly on Tailchaser and his companions as they were led through.

As he passed beneath the arched tunnel mouth into the depths of Vastnir, Fritti felt a strange sensation. As he had in his catmint nightmare, he began to experience a burning feeling on his forehead. Whatever it might be, though, neither his friends nor the Clawguard took any notice of him.

Beyond the threshold was a vision that would stay with Tailchaser as long as he lived.

Before them sprawled a vast cavern, the roof as high above as the treetops of Rootwood. It was lit by the luminescent earth they had seen in the tunnel, and also by the faint blue glow of stones that protruded down through the ceiling rock. The phantom light rendered all in the cavern into spirits and vaulting shadows.

Below, on the cavern floor, countless cats moved back and forth like termites in rotten wood. Most of them appeared to be normal Folk, although their faces were so full of despair and pain that they seemed almost a different race. Among them moved the Clawguard, lumpish and huge, directing the streaming, insectlike hordes as they crept to and fro.

It's like some horrible dream of Firsthome, Fritti thought.

The stench of fear and blood and unburied me'mre rose up on the hot air currents and filled his nostrils, choking him. With a snarl, Scratchnail herded them down to the cave floor, across the jutting rocks and warm, moist soil. They maneuvered among the lines of cats, brushing past Folk who did not even look up, but only plodded on toward whatever grim destination the ubiquitous Clawguard were leading them to.

As they passed one group Fritti saw a smallish cat, eyes and ribs bulging, who appeared to be sick. He coughed and staggered, then collapsed to the stones. Before Fritti could move to help him, a Clawguard shouldered his way past and bent over the sick one. Then the brute picked him up by the neck and shook him violently. Tailchaser could hear the sound of bones snapping; the Claw flung the broken body to the side with an impatient head-flip, and the line of cats moved on. Tailchaser stared after them, then over at the crumpled body lying unnoticed and unmourned in the dirt. His hatred flared, then settled into a low flame, banked deep inside himself. He, also, turned away.

As Scratchnail's procession reached the far side of the great cavern and was approaching the gaping maw of another tunnel, a thin, piercing voice called out: 'Ssscratchnail!' The sound seemed to come from one of the innumerable caves in the rock wall before them. The chief halted the group as a dim shape appeared in the darkness of a cave mouth.

'What do you want of me?' Scratchnail snapped angrily. His voice held an odd intonation.

'Hissblood wants to sssee you, Sscratchnail,' the thin voice said, sibilant and mocking. As the shape in the grotto spoke, Fritti could see the gleam of its teeth, but no reflected shine of its eyes.

'That's a laugh!' the chief snarled. 'Why should I care anyway?'

In the dark grotto the teeth were bared again. 'Hissblood wantss to know who your prissonerss are. There wasss to be no more taking of captivesss. That was the understanding, no?'

'My business is between the Fat One and myself, and there's no room for you crawlers to go sticking your hairless snouts into it. If Hissblood wants to have any dealings with me I'll be in the Lower Catacombs later on.' Scratchnail pivoted and walked away.

'He will meet you there,' said the thin voice, and the sound of deathly merriment came from the shadowed cave.

Entering the huge tunnel in the cave wall, Longtooth hissed at Scratchnail: 'What do the Toothguard want with these, anyway?'

The chief turned on him with a growl. 'You keep your muzzle shut!'

Longtooth asked no more questions, and they went some distance down the tunnel in silence. Scratchnail finally halted the group at a widening of the way. The chief pushed Eatbugs and Pouncequick roughly to one side, then turned to Bitefast.

'You and this dribbling me'mre,' he barked, indicating Longtooth, 'take these two down to the Middle Catacombs. They're not to go anywhere else until I say so. Me, no one else!' Bitefast nodded. 'Good. I'm going to take the clever one here for a special audience. I think you-know-who will be interested in him. Now move!' With this he propelled Tailchaser up the tunnel, and the other Clawguard herded Fritti's companions off toward a side tunnel.

Tailchaser turned as he was pushed forward and called back over his shoulder: 'I'll be back for you, Pounce, don't worry! Take care of him, Eatbugs!'

Scratchnail dealt him a stinging paw-blow to the side of the head that brought moisture to his eyes.

'Fool!' rasped the beast.

The winding way led farther down into the earth. The tunnel they traveled was strewn with rocks and bits of bone, and wet things that made Fritti wince when he stepped on them. He had to scrape against the dirt walls to avoid contact with the terrifying Claw chief.

Now the shaft pitched down steeply. The faint glow of the walls was interrupted by splashes of blue-and-purple light that seemed to be reflected from farther down the tunnel. Stepping along the sloping pathway, Tailchaser also noticed a change in the air – it was becoming much colder. Within twenty steps the chill had sharpened, and the ground underneath his pads seemed hard, perhaps frozen. With Scratchnail beside him, he ducked to pass beneath the low roof.

When he raised his head again he found that they had passed into a great chamber – the Seat of Vastnir. They had come to the Cavern of the Pit . . . the heart of the mound.

The cavern was high-domed, the ceiling dark and distant. Around a central pit fissures in the ground spewed forth indigo light, stark beams glaring up through the mist of the cavern floor. The walls above were honeycombed with grottoes and tunnels, and everywhere dark shapes streamed in and out, bustling around the wide rim of the pit and climbing up the jagged stones to disappear into the holes above.

Fritti could see the plume of his breath in the icy air. Cold like this so far underground was terribly wrong – but what was not in this nightmare place?

Moving forward at Scratchnail's harsh insistence, he looked now to the pit, and the massive shape that rose from it, dominating the subterranean chamber. As he neared, wonder turned to horror.

Up from the dark mist-shrouded center of the pit rose a squirming mass, a heaving pile of small bodies that protruded above the edge of the huge hole in the cavern floor like a volcano rising in a deep canyon. The squirming mountain was a mass of animals – tortured, dying, many already dead. Cats and fla-fa'az, Squeakers, Praere, Growlers and Rikchikchik, the heap of writhing beasts gave forth a million ghost-faint sounds. Many of the creatures were maimed or dismembered; closer to the bottom, most were not even moving. The stench penetrated Tailchaser's nose, and he gagged. He slumped to the cold ground, the mist billowing up around him, hiding for a moment the terrible sight. Scratchnail leaned down and butted him with his wide, flat head.

'Step up, now, you simpering beetle. You're about to meet His Lordship.'

Weak in the knees and stomach, Fritti was prodded and dragged forward to the edge of the pit. He wanted to close his eyes. Instead, repulsed yet fascinated, he stared out at the squirming mountain, at the thousands of blank eyes and mindlessly sagging mouths puffing little jets of vapor.

The Clawguard stepped up beside him. 'Your Mightiness! Your humble servant has brought you something!' Scratchnail's voice grated and echoed from the towering walls.

'Oh. You have, have you . . . ?' bubbled a grotesque, suety voice. 'Throw it in with the rest . . . I'll eat it later.' A gigantic, dark shape

– heretofore invisible at the top of the pile of bodies – turned its head and opened vast, eggshell-white eyes. Blind eyes.

Tailchaser gave a bleat of fright and leaped backward against the stone-hard body of Scratchnail. Cowering between the Clawguard's legs, Fritti forgot for a moment even his fear and hatred of the chieftain – the thing atop the pit blew all else from his mind like a screeching wind.

It was a cat. Twenty, fifty, a hundred times bigger than himself, Tailchaser could not tell; its swollen body was so massive that its tiny legs could not reach past to lift it. It lay, bloated and supremely powerful, on the peak of the wriggling flesh-mound.

'No, Great One, it is not to eat . . . yet.' Fritti heard Scratchnail's voice, distant, unimportant. 'This is one of the ones you sensed, Great One. Do you remember?'

The hideous creature pivoted its neckless head until the blank, dead eyes were facing the shivering Tailchaser. The nostrils flared.

'Oh, yes . . . ' said the voice slowly, a sound like mud splattering on stone. 'We remember now. Did it have companions? Where are they?' The voice took a sharper tone.

'He had two, O Lord.' Scratchnail sounded nervous. 'A kitten, Lord, a little mewling kitten, and a crazed old tom, filthy as sun and flowers. But this one, this is the one you want. There's something *to* this one. I'm . . . I'm sure of it.'

'Ahhh,' burbled the giant, and rolled back slightly onto its side, as if to think. It poked its round head down toward the pile on which it lay, but could not overcome its own bulk. A look of annoyance creased the vast brow, and suddenly three Clawguard, who had been watching with dismay from the opposite edge of the pit, leaped down into the hole. They quickly plucked the struggling form of a cat out of the midst of the heap and scrambled up to the monster. As they clambered over his belly he opened his mouth complacently. The wriggling, yowling cat was dropped in. Crunching sounds were heard as the great cat began to chew, and a look of contentment crossed the blind face.

As Tailchaser looked on helplessly, the beast swallowed, then turned its attention back toward him once more.

'Now,' it dripped, 'let us see what kind of Folk threaten our designs.' There was a shocking jolt. Tailchaser felt for a moment as if a huge mouth had picked him up and shaken him. Then came a fiery pain, and something bored into his mind. Digging, burrowing, it tore through his thoughts, knocking them asunder – it waded through hopes and dreams and ideas; it carelessly crushed notions as it passed. An invisible force held Tailchaser to the spot. He contorted and howled as the mind of the beast invaded him.

When it was over he lay stunned and quivering on the icy earth beside the pit. A stabbing pain ebbed and surged behind his forehead. Finally Scratchnail spoke. His voice sounded subdued.

'Well, Great Master?'

The shape above the pit yawned, showing blackened teeth. A brief flare of light empurpled the scabby gray fur.

'This little bug is nothing. There are suggestions, yes – hints – but no power to speak of. It can do nothing. You say its companions are harmless?'

'This was the only one with even a trace of anything different, Lord, I swear it.'

'Well . . . ' There was a bored finality now in the liquid heaviness of the creature's speech. 'Take it away. Kill it, or put it to work digging tunnels – we do not care.'

The Claw chieftain dragged Fritti to a standing position, then forced him toward a doorway out of the cavern.

'Clawguard!' called the bloated thing. Scratchnail whirled and bobbed subserviently.

'Yes, Master of All?'

'Next time, do not so lightly disturb the meditations of Lord Hearteater.' The milky eyes glinted.

Bobbing and choking, Scratchnail hurried Tailchaser out of the Cavern of the Pit.

Stumbling and stupefied, Tailchaser was driven through the labyrinthine corridors of Vastnir. His captor dogged his footsteps and did not speak. Although he felt spirit-broken, still Fritti's mind was awhirl with the thought of what he had seen.

Hearteater! Lord Hearteater of the Firstborn! Fritti had seen Grizraz Hearteater, the ancient enemy of the Folk. He had heard him speak! A fit of shivering wracked his weakened body as he thought of the huge, blind thing lolling in the cavern behind them.

He had to get word to Fencewalker and the others . . . somehow. The Court of Harar must know of the danger . . . whatever good it might do. How could they defend themselves against such power, such terrible minions? Hundreds of the fierce Clawguard were in the main caverns alone – there was no way of knowing how many more lurked in this insect nest of tunnels and caves.

How can I do anything anyway? he thought bitterly. *I'm under sentence of death.*

His mind turned finally to Scratchnail, whose hot breath even now feathered his tail. Tailchaser dimly recalled that Scratchnail had been somehow embarrassed before the terrifying Hearteater. Surely the Clawguard leader would not suffer Fritti to live after that?

Limping, pondering, Tailchaser felt a gust of dry air ruffle his face-fur. He looked up. Here the tunnel was dark, almost lightless. Fritti could faintly see forms moving toward them in the shaft ahead.

With startling swiftness, Scratchnail reached his hook-taloned paw forward and slammed Tailchaser against the side of the passageway. For a moment he had to strain to catch his breath. As he wheezed helplessly he heard a strange rustling, a creaking as of old tree limbs, and suddenly the tunnel was full of whispering shadows.

Several dark shapes passed by. Tailchaser could faintly see tails and ears, but all seemed shadowy and indistinct. The air was full of choking dust and a cloying, sweet smell. Beside him Scratchnail lowered his head respectfully and averted his gaze. A faint sibilance, as of dry, powdery speech, fluttered in the air; then the strange shapes had passed up the corridor.

As Fritti regained his breath Scratchnail stared up the passageway with burning eyes.

'The Boneguard,' whispered the dark beast. 'The Master's closest servants.'

At the mouth of a cross-tunnel – indistinguishable by Fritti from the countless others they had passed – Scratchnail halted.

'I don't know what your secret is,' he growled, heavy brows shadowing his eyes, 'but I know there's something there. I will not make the mistake of taking you before the Fat One again without knowing what it is, but I *will* find out. The Master can make mistakes, and I believe you are one of them.' The chief snorted angrily. 'Whatever your little secret is, I will force it out of you. In the meantime, you can keep your miserable self occupied. Get in there.' Scratchnail extended a malformed paw, indicating the hole near Tailchaser.

Screwing up his courage – apparently he was to live a little while longer! – Fritti asked: 'Where are my friends?'

'Filling the bellies of the Toothguard, if I don't return soon. Keep your nose out. You'll have enough to worry about just saving your own wretched pelt. Now, move!' The chief gave Fritti a fierce shove that sent him stumbling into the opening behind him. He lost his footing on the inclined gravel surface and found himself skidding and tumbling down into deeper darkness. As he rolled to a halt he heard Scratchnail's voice scrape down to him: 'I'll be back to see you soon enough, never fear.' A coughing chuckle bounded down the shaft.

It took some moments for Tailchaser to accustom himself to the almost total absence of light. He was in a chamber of rock; he could see the dark forms of other cats huddled at the extremities of the chamber. The stone cavern walls sweated moisture, and the air was hot and damp.

Scores of emaciated, dead-eyed Folk lay about him. Most, sunk deep in misery, did not even look up at the new arrival. As Tailchaser slunk along the wall – hunting for another exit, or a place to lie down – some of the cats snarled weakly up at him, as if he were intruding on their territory, but it was a perfunctory sort of resistance. The thought of the Folk crammed into this tiny space, forced to live next to and on top of each other in sweltering heat, brought anger to Tailchaser's spirit once more.

As he stepped across the sprawled bodies, Fritti was halted by the tones of a familiar voice. He scanned the faces and shapes of those around him, but saw no one he recognized. Neither could he summon a name to match the memory. He was about to continue across the cavern when his gaze touched on the cat who lay at his feet.

This one was shrunken, thin as a ferret. His sunken, bleary eyes stared hopelessly up at Fritti. It was this mumbling apparition whose voice had stopped him, and now Tailchaser sucked in a deep breath of surprise as recognition swept him: it was young Jumptall, one of the delegates from the Meeting Wall Clan to the Court. He looked on the verge of death!

'Jumptall!' said Fritti. 'It's me, Tailchaser! Do you remember me?' For a moment Jumptall looked on uncomprehendingly; then his eyes slowly focused.

'Tailchaser?' he mumbled. 'Tailchaser from . . . home?' Fritti bobbed his head encouragingly. 'Oh.' Jumptall closed his eyes, weakened, and was silent for a moment. When he opened them a spark of comprehension was there.

'I don't understand,' he said. 'But . . . luckier if you'd died . . . '

Jumptall's eyes closed again; he refused to say any more.

Roofshadow crouched in the shelter of an overhanging rock, watching the flurrying snow. The chill air made her feel dizzy. She wanted desperately to get up; to run and keep running until she was out of this horrible forest – far away from the terrible, throbbing mound that was the source of all distress.

When they had been attacked by night, given only scant warning by the appearance of the crazed woolly cat, she had run with her friends – had run wildly. For all her seasons of hunting, she had been panicked, frenzied. At one point she had almost knocked down little Pouncequick in her overwhelming desire to escape. The shame of that still hurt her more than her wounds.

As they ran, something had seized her, knocking her from her paws – she had grappled with something large, but by scratching and twisting had managed to pull free. Bolting into the deep brush, she had lain hidden for some time, hearing the sound of flight and pursuit carrying on into the night. Not until the first rays of Spreading Light had she forced herself to crawl forth and look for a hiding place out of the cold.

She had been hurt by the thing that had grabbed her: her hind leg was very painful – she could not put her full weight on it, and had limped a long way over frosty ground before locating the windbreak. She had lain for two full nights and days, sick, feverish, too weak to go hunting.

Her companions were gone – captured, probably, or killed – and at this moment all she wanted to do was go far away: to disappear into the southern forests and never think of this terrible place ever again. But at the moment she could go nowhere. Her instincts told her to stay put. She needed to heal.

The thought of Tailchaser and Pouncequick had stirred her for a moment, and she lifted her head and scented the air. Then a shooting pain contorted her face, and she laid her chin back down on the cold earth and pulled her tail over her nose and eyes.

Deep underground, in the mazes of Vastnir, Fritti Tailchaser was learning a few of the secrets of the mound. Jumptall, his acquaintance from nesting days, was too weak to talk much, but with the help of a young cat named Pawgrip he had been able to explain some puzzling things to Fritti.

' . . . You see, the Clawguard are mostly just the bullyboys. They're fierce enough, Harar knows,' said Pawgrip with a grimace, 'but they don't make any decisions. Even their chiefs don't make many, I don't suppose.'

'What do you mean?' asked Tailchaser.

'They can't even hunt unless someone tells them to. Whiskers! No one even makes me'mre in this ghastly ant heap unless somebody gives him permission.'

'And you say that there are others? Other creatures?' Fritti thought of the shadowy Boneguard and shook himself nervously.

'Hissblood and his Toothguard,' whispered Jumptall in a quavering voice. He coughed.

'They're bad, sure enough,' assented Pawgrip. 'They're even uglier – and more *wrong*, if you know what I mean – than the Claws. They just seem to skulk around and keep everybody behaving. Even most of the Clawguard seem scared of them.'

Tailchaser was puzzled. 'But where do they all come from? I've never seen or heard of any Folk like them.'

Jumptall shook his head, and Pawgrip answered. 'No one has. No one knows. But you-know-who . . . ' Here the little cat lowered his voice and looked around. 'You-know-who can do all kinds of things. Mate Folk and Growlers? Worse things than that have happened down here. . . . ' Pawgrip trailed off significantly. Unnerved by the reference to Hearteater, whose presence still loomed huge and frightening in his memory, Fritti got up and stretched. He walked to the entrance of their cell and looked up the shaft.

'But why the digging?' he wondered aloud. Behind him Jumptall raised himself up on his forepaws and swayed weakly.

'Cats weren't meant to dig,' he said with surprising strength. 'Killed Earpoint. Killed Streamhopper.' Jumptall shook his head sadly.

He looks more ancient than old Snifflick, thought Fritti. *How did it happen? He is scarcely older than I am.*

'Always digging they are . . . or rather, *we* are,' said Pawgrip. 'Should think they'd have enough nasty tunnels by now.'

'Then why?' persisted Tailchaser.

'I don't know,' admitted Pawgrip, 'but if they keep digging like they have been, soon all the tunnels will come together. The whole world will fall into their holes.'

'Killed Streamhopper . . . ' muttered Jumptall sadly, 'killing *me* . . . '

CHAPTER TWENTY-ONE

Here sighs and cries and wails coiled and recoiled on the starless
air, spilling my soul to tears. A confusion of tongues and monstrous
accents toiled in pain and anger. Voices hoarse and shrill and sounds
of blows . . . tumult and pandemonium that still whirl on the
air. . . .

– Dante Alighieri

After a long passage of sleepless time for Fritti, several Clawguard
came to the mouth of the prison cave and summoned the captives
out to work. Whining and huffing, they scrambled one after another
up the steep shaft. Fritti was surprised to see many of the Folk
moving at all, let alone making the strenuous climb, but Pawgrip
explained that no one was fed unless he could clamber out. Those
who could no longer manage the ascent would remain in the small
cavern until they died. Jumptall, with help from Tailchaser and
Pawgrip, managed to struggle up the sloping entranceway. At the top
they all made a hurried meal of insects and grubs, then the waiting
Claws bullied them into a straggling line and led them through a
seemingly endless succession of tunnels.

They were delivered over to Snoutscar, a heavy Claw whose fur
clung patchy and sparse over his muscular body. Snoutscar sent the
prisoners, in bands of three and four, down a tangle of short tunnels
that led out from the central underground chamber. Tailchaser found
himself paired with two older cats, both of them so weary and
bedraggled that they could not muster energy for conversation.

As they reached the mouth of their designated tunnel, Fritti turned
and asked, of no one in particular: 'But what do we do?' Snoutscar
wheeled around, smacking Tailchaser with a flailing paw. Fritti
crashed to the ground, and Snoutscar's knobby face, criss-crossed
with the whitened marks of many battles, loomed over him.

'I'll have no sun-worms questioning me! Is that clear?' he raged. His body stank.

'Yes!' quailed Tailchaser, 'I just didn't understand!'

'You'll dig is what you'll do, and you'll dig hard, sun burn you! And you'll be finished when I say that you are. Do you see?' Fritti nodded his head miserably. 'Good,' continued Snoutscar, 'because I'll have my eye on you from now on, and if I catch you shirking I'll have your tongue out. Now dig!'

Fritti ran to rejoin his tunnelmates, who were cringing at the attention that had been turned in their direction. They gave Tailchaser reproachful looks as they all climbed down into the tunnel.

The rest of the day passed in damp, steamy misery. Tailchaser and his two companions scraped away at the end of a small tunnel, using the claws and feet that Meerclar had never intended for this kind of activity to scratch the hard, claylike soil. It was monotonous, spine-bending work. In such a confined place Fritti could find no comfortable position for extended digging, and before the day was half over he began to ache.

They paused briefly at midday. Fritti tried unsuccessfully to clean the packed earth from his sore paws and bleeding, lacerated pads. After what seemed like mere moments of rest they were ordered back into their tunnel.

As time wore on Fritti found himself wanting only to lie down and sleep: if they killed him, what difference would it make? It would happen sooner or later anyway. But when he had almost convinced himself the snarling head of Snoutscar would appear, blocking the entrance to the burrow, eyes glittering and mouth twisted. Tailchaser would redouble his efforts, digging rapidly and painfully long after the head had disappeared again.

The two older Folk at his side had mastered a relentless but unhurried pace; toward the end of the digging time Fritti finally began to imitate them. At last Snoutscar ordered them up from the tunnels. The paw- and bone-weary group shambled back to their prison hole, escorted by harrying Clawguard.

Half-tumbling down the incline, Tailchaser fell almost immediately into a deep, overwhelming sleep.

Deeper in the Catacombs, with hundreds of jumps of earth and rock between themselves and the sun, Pouncequick and Eatbugs had fared no better than Fritti.

As Tailchaser had been led unwillingly away, Longtooth and Bite-fast had shoved and threatened the two remaining companions down into a cave several levels below. There they had been instructed to stay until Scratchnail should return and decide what to do with them. Unlike Fritti in the cave to which he was eventually led, Pouncequick and the old cat found themselves the sole inhabitants of their prison – but cracked and split bones strewn across the dark floor suggested that they were not the *first* inhabitants.

After what had seemed like Hours of solitude a soft snuffling sound broke the cavern's silence. Certain that it was the Clawguard returning to kill them, Pouncequick stiffened himself against the far wall of the hole, ready to resist that final departure.

A strange, pale shape appeared in the entrance of their prison cave. Pouncequick's immediate relief – this was obviously not the Claws – was quickly replaced by a disturbing chill – a strange feeling, like putting one's nose into a nest of scurrying white termites. Eatbugs, in fitful sleep at the other end of the tiny grotto, pitched and quivered as the shape advanced into the chamber. Pouncequick strained to focus on the intruder.

What was wrong with its fur?

The creature had none. Cat-shaped, it was as hairless as a newborn kitten. At first, wildly, Pouncequick thought it must be some kind of monstrous infant – its eyes were sealed shut, as were the eyes of the Folk when they emerged from the womb. The thing turned toward Pouncequick, huge nostrils dilating. Then, in a high, whispering voice, it spoke.

'Ahhhhhhh. The little newcomer . . . how nicccce of you to join ussssss.' Its speech was sibilant, like the voice of a hlizza. As it drew nearer Pouncequick could see that it had no eyes at all, just folds of skin below the brow. He pushed himself farther away, arching his back.

'Wh-what do y-you want with us?' quavered the kitten.

'Ohhh . . . it knowsss the Higher Sssinging . . . ?' The thing gave a sinister giggle which turned to a yawn showing a mouthful of long, thin teeth like ivory pine needles. 'Well, little sssurface-Sssqueaker' – it grinned – 'if you musst know, I have come to take you to Massster Hisssblood, who earnessstly desiress to meet a fassscinating young tom like yoursssself.'

'H-H-H-Hissblood?' said Pouncequick, hiccoughing with fright.

'One of the great lordsss of the Toothguard, yesss. A very great power in the mound. Hisssblood yearnss to know what makess you and your companionsss ssso awfully interesting to Chief Ssscratchnail. You sssee, little worm-friend, Master Hisssblood and your Clawguard friend are, shall we ssay, friendly rivalsss.' Again the eyeless Tooth-guard revealed that thicket of gleaming teeth, and moved toward the terrified kitten, his furless skin bagging and wrinkling as he slouched closer.

'Nipslither!!' boomed a voice. 'I expected your mole-nuzzling master would send you!'

The Toothguard leaped back, startled, large nostrils flaring. 'Ssscratchnail!' he hissed. The Clawguard captain had come silently down the entranceway, and now blocked the only exit from the small cavern.

'Doesn't your master think I know better than to trust those witless minions of mine? Ha!' Scratchnail barked a hoarse laugh.

'Don't try to hinder me, you oaf!' whispered Nipslither. 'I ssshall make you pay for it if you do.' His tone brought the fur up on Pouncequick's back, but Scratchnail only emitted a rasp of disgust and lowered his head as the Toothguard began a slow, circling move-ment. Without warning Nipslither leaped forward, fangs bared, to be met by the rearing Clawguard. There was a great outrush of breath as they came together.

Crouched against the cold stone, Pouncequick watched wide-eyed as the two figures writhed and spat on the floor of the tiny cavern. In the darkness he could only glimpse the combat as it boiled from wall to wall – here a gleam of wicked teeth, there the spotted under-belly of Scratchnail, bared for a moment. The creatures' two tails – one black, the other naked and coiling – twined about each other like maddened serpents.

There was a brief flurry of thumping noises, a yowl of pain, and then Scratchnail was lunging down to catch Nipslither in his heavy jaws, to grasp the hairless beast's throat. The Clawguard chieftain's mighty neck muscle jumped and pulsed – a short, cracking sound – and Scratchnail's enemy sagged. The black beast dropped the body of the Toothguard. It lay, kicking feebly for a moment, then was still.

Scratchnail turned to the cowering Pouncequick. The Clawguard's body was sleek with blood, but he seemed to give it no more notice than rainwater.

'You don't know how lucky you are, little sun-rat!' he grated. 'Hissblood would bring you to a world of sorrow. Now, you and the

176

old dirt-fur' – he indicated Eatbugs, who had slept through everything – 'you just do what you're told. I'll be back to check on you.' Scratchnail disappeared up the entranceway without a backward glance at Pouncequick or Eatbugs or the broken, eyeless thing on the cavern floor.

Many Hours later, Bitefast came to take Pouncequick out to dig. Bitefast's face was swollen: Scratchnail's punishment for laxity. Eatbugs could not be roused from sleep, and the limping Claw, in a foul temper, bit the old cat on his matted ear hard enough to draw blood. Eatbugs still did not wake, although the shallow rise and fall of his chest showed that he still lived. Irked by this failure – and perhaps fearful of more punishment – Bitefast treated little Pouncequick in brutal fashion as he forced him out to labor.

Pounce was assigned to a slave work gang, and spent long periods of hot, breathless time scrabbling at dirt tunnel walls with his small paws.

What seemed like days went by; Pouncequick's world narrowed to a repetitive nightmare of digging, followed by solitude in the tiny cave at the end of the work period. Eatbugs remained in a stupor, not rising either to eat or pass me'mre, and showing only occasional movement. Their Clawguard captors decided that he had given up his will to survive, and left him undisturbed in the small rock chamber when Pounce was harried forth to the excavations.

One day, while being led by Longtooth through the massive cavern that stood behind the Greater Gate of Vastnir, Pouncequick thought he saw Tailchaser. The cat who appeared to be his friend was with a large press gang of slave Folk, and appeared bound for one of the outer tunnels. Pouncequick called out excitedly, but if it was Tailchaser the distance was too great, for the cat with the white star on his forehead did not turn. Pouncequick received a stinging paw-slap across the muzzle from Longtooth, and was kept longer at his digging than usual.

When he was returned to his jail that night, Pouncequick began to seriously consider the fact that he might never see Tailchaser again. He had already lost Roofshadow. He saw no way that he could ever escape from the mound.

Up until that moment he had hoped, deep in his mind, that the whole experience was a bad dream, a phantom. But finally, Pouncequick realized, his eyes were open. He knew now where he was. He knew he would remain there until his death.

There was something curiously liberating about this knowledge. In a way, it was as if somewhere, deep inside, a part of him had been set free to run beneath the sky – leaving only his body behind.

For the first time since being taken by the Clawguard, he slept peacefully.

In the shadow of the trees at the edge of Ratleaf Forest, with the sun of Smaller Shadows dim and remote in the winter sky, Roofshadow looked out across the dim valley at the squat shape of the mound.

Although she was now well enough to travel – the twinge in her hind leg almost gone – she had felt impelled to come for one last look down on the agent of her unhappiness.

Vastnir crouched like a living thing, waiting for its proper moment to rise up and strike. She felt its pulse working in her stomach, nauseating her. Roofshadow wanted nothing more than to turn, now, and go. Somewhere, she knew, there were forests untainted by this blight – clean, deep forests. If the sickness spread, well, there were places it would not reach in her lifetime.

All through the dark afternoon, Roofshadow looked down upon the hated mound. When darkness came she found a hiding place and slept.

At first light she was staring down at Vastnir again. Thinking.

CHAPTER TWENTY-TWO

I feel
The link of nature draw me: flesh of flesh,
Bone of my bone thou art, and from thy state
Mine never shall be parted, bliss or woe.

> – John Milton

In his dream Tailchaser was standing at the very pinnacle of a tall needle of rock, hundreds of jumps above a misty forest. Looking down from his perch, he could hear the sounds of creatures hunting for him in the mists below – thin noises of speech that drifted up into his ears. It was cold on the rock; it seemed as if he had been on it forever. Below, the frozen green sea of forest stretched infinitely into the distance.

Although he knew he was in danger, Fritti felt no fear, but only a sense of the dull inevitable: soon the searchers would exhaust the hiding places in the woods below; inescapably their attention would turn to the spire. The burning eyes would gather at the bottom, then move upward. . . .

Looking out into the swirling fogs that blurred the separation of earth and sky, Fritti saw an odd pattern in the vapors: a strange, spiraling nexus. With the speed and completeness natural to dreams it resolved itself into a white cat, spinning and spinning as it approached his eyrie. It was not the white cat of his Firsthome hallucination, though. As the revolving shape neared it became Eyeshimmer, Oel-var'iz of the First-walkers.

Hovering before Fritti, Eyeshimmer sang out in a high, keening voice: 'Even the Garrin fears something . . . even the Garrin fears . . . '

Suddenly, a great wind blew up, setting the mists dancing. Eyeshimmer whirled off into the blackness. The wind swept through the trees, and around Tailchaser's rock. He could hear sounds of fear and despair from the hunters below. Finally, there were only the rushing fogs, and the roaring of wind and lost voices. . . .

Tailchaser awoke on the hot, moist floor of his prison, mired in the sleeping bodies of his fellow captives. He tried to hold on to the dream-shards that were even now melting away like frost in the sun.

Eyeshimmer. What *had* the Oel-var'iz told him that day, so long ago? They had been taking leave from Quiverclaw and his walkers. . . .

' . . . Everyone flees from the bear . . . but sometimes the bear has bad dreams. . . . ' In the dream, Eyeshimmer had mentioned the Garrin, the bear, also – but what did it mean? Surely nothing about a real Garrin? 'Everyone flees from the bear . . . ' Could it mean Hearteater? Bad dreams . . . was there something that even Lord Hearteater feared? What?

Fritti's thoughts were interrupted by the arrival of the Clawguard. In the ensuing confusion, the reluctant rising and the scramble up the entranceway to a meager breakfast, Tailchaser's dream faded back into his mind, dissolved by cruel reality.

Aboveground an Eye had opened, shut, and opened again since Fritti had come to Vastnir Mound. The brutal routine, harsh punishments, and hideous surroundings had pounded most of the resistance from him. He rarely thought of his friends: his inability to help them or himself was as terrible as his imprisonment; to dwell on it was more galling than to sink into the mud with all the others, to fight over grubs and squabble over a place to eat, and to keep an eye opened at all times for the Clawguard. Or the Toothguard. It was easier not to care; to live from moment to moment.

Once a muted hiss had run through the ranks of the tunnel slaves: 'The Boneguard is coming!' The rustling shadows had come forward from a disused tunnel, and the light had seemed to dim. All of the other captive Folk had thrown themselves to the ground, their eyes tightly shut – even the Clawguard had looked nervous, their fur bristling. Fritti had felt a momentary urge to remain standing, to face up to whatever awful truth scared even their hulking captors, but as the strange voices and the cloying, spicy smell had wafted toward him his legs had become weak, and he, too, had sunk down – not looking up until Hearteater's chosen were gone. Thus, in the large things and the small, little by little, Fritti's spirit was broken to the mound.

Small alliances were made among the captives, the cats' natural aloofness giving way slightly under the strain of the situation, but these comradeships were transitory, gone with the first dispute over food, or room to stretch out for a moment. There were few diversions and very little cheer.

One endless night, though, as the captives lay in their underground cave, someone called for a story. The audacity of this request made several captives look around fearfully for the Claws: it seemed as though someone would move to prevent such a straightforward pleasure as this. When no one appeared, the call was repeated. Earnotch, a battered old tabby from Rootwood, agreed to try. For a long time he stared intently at his paws, then with a last, quick look to the entrance shaft, began.

'Once, long ago – long, long ago – Lord Firefoot found himself on the shores of the Qu'cef, the Bigwater. He desired to cross, for he had heard rumors that those Folk who dwelt on the other side – distaff descendants of his cousin, Prince Skystone – lived in a land of great beauty and plentiful hunting. Well, there he sat on the banks of the Bigwater, and wondered how to reach the other side.

'After a while, he called for Pfefirrit, a prince of the fla-fa'az who owed him a favor from days gone by. Pfefirrit, a heron of great size, came down and hovered overhead – but not *too* close to the great hunter.

' "What may I do for you, O cleverest cat?" he asked. Lord Firefoot told him, and the bird-prince flew away.

'When he returned, the sky at his tail was full of fla-fa'az of every description. At their prince's command, they all flew down close to the Qu'cef and began to beat their wings, making a mighty wind. The wind blew so cold that the water soon froze over.

'Tangaloor Firefoot set out, the fla-fa'az moving before him, turning the Bigwater to ice in his path so that he could walk across. When they reached the far side, Pfefirrit swooped down and said: "That pays for all, cat-lord," and then flew away.

'Well, cu'nre-le, several days later Lord Firefoot had explored all the far country. It was indeed lovely, but he found the inhabitants to be strange and somewhat simpleminded Folk, much given to talking and little to doing. He had resolved to cross back over to his own land, and so he made his way to the water's edge.

'The Bigwater was still hard and frosted, and he moved out onto it to walk home. It was a long way, though – not for kittenplay is it named the Bigwater – and when he was in the middle the ice began to melt. Firefoot ran, but it had been too long, and the Qu'cef melted beneath him, dropping him into the icy water.

'He swam for a long time in the terrible cold, but his great heart would not give up. He struggled on toward land. Then, suddenly, he looked up to find a great fish with a fin on its back – and more fangs than the Toothguard – swimming in circles around him.

' "Well, well," said the fish, "what is this tender morsel that I find swimming about in my home? I wonder if it tastes as good as it looks."

'Now, Firefoot had been in despair when he saw the size of the fish, but when it spoke he was suddenly filled with joy, for he saw a way out of all his troubles.

' "I am certainly good-tasting!" said Lord Tangaloor. "All of the swimming cats are tender in the *extreme*. It would be a shame, though, if you ate me.'

' "And why is that?" said the immense fish, swimming closer.

' "Because if you devour me, there will be no one to show you the sunlit cove where my people live and sport in the water all the time, and where a great fish such as yourself could eat and eat and never have his fill."

' "Hmmmm," mused the fish. "And if I spare you, will you show me where the swimming cats live?"

' "Of course," said Firefoot. "Just let me climb onto your back that I may see the way better." So saying, he clambered onto the fish's huge, finned back and they swam on.

'As they approached the far side of the Qu'cef, the fish demanded to know where the cove of the swimming cats was.

' "Just a little farther, I am sure," Firefoot said; so on they went, until they were very close to the shore. Again the fish demanded to know the place.

' "Just a little closer in," said Lord Tangaloor. They came closer still to the shore, until – of a sudden – the water became so shallow that the giant fish found he was unable to move farther forward. Then he discovered he was too far aground to move backward, either, and could only roar in anger as Firefoot leaped off his back and waded to the sand.

' "Thank you for the ride, Master Fish!" he said. "As a matter of fact, I'm afraid we do very *little* swimming where I come from, but we do like to eat! I am going to find a few other of my Folk, and then we are going to return and dine on you the way you would have on us!"

'And they did. This is why, from that time forward, no cat has willingly entered the water . . . and we eat only those fish we can catch without getting wet.'

The prisoners laughed as Earnotch finished his story-song. For a moment it was as though all the rocks and earth between those Folk and the sky had melted away, and they were singing together beneath Meerclar's Eye.

The mound never slept. Like a hive of maddened insects, the labyrinth of tunnels and caves was alive with strange forms and unheard cries. The pale light of the luminous earth made the main corridors and caverns a shadow-play of teeming, flickering ghosts. Elsewhere there were unlit paths as dark as the spaces between worlds – but even in these black, desolate places unseen shapes moved, and sourceless winds blew.

The mound had not been long in the eye of the sun. Scarcely half a dozen seasons had swept by above since the blistered earth of the valley floor had first begun to rise, swelling like a tree limb seeded with wasp's eggs. Like the wound it resembled, the mound covered on the surface the deeper and more profound disturbance below: leagues and leagues of tunnels stretching out in capillary profusion; passing away through the soil, beneath hill and forest and stream in all directions, like a stupendous, hollow spider's web.

At the center of the web, beneath the blunt dome of Vastnir, the cruel, incomprehensible spider tested the strands, his body gross and immovable, his mind questing out to the limits of his spreading dominion. Grizraz Hearteater – born of Goldeneye and Skydancer, corrupted beneath the earth since the world was young – felt his time approaching. He was a *force*, and in a world scaled down by the passing and lessening of the Firstborn, he was a force to which no other could now compare. In the heart of his mound he lay, and his creatures multiplied around him, spreading outward. The tunnels, too, were spreading, riddling the surface world from below. Soon there would be no place so remote that it would exceed his grasp. And the night was his: his creatures, created in the dark of the earth, ruled the darkness above as well. When the last threads were complete he would also rule the Hours of brightness. All he needed was time, only a slim moment in comparison to the eons he had waited and schemed . . . and burned. What could impede him now, so near to final sunset? His family and peers were gone from the earth without trace, except in myth and reverence. He was a *power*, and where was the power that would come against him?

His inexorable, cold intelligence weighed these arguments and found them solid – but still he was not free of a smallest, most insignificant mote of unease. Hearteater threw his mind outward again: searching, searching. . . .

Since sunrise, Roofshadow had been pacing intently back and forth along the tree-sparse edge of Ratleaf Forest. To her west, across the broad expanse of valley, lay the slumbering presence of the mound.

Back and forth, soft gray paws laid delicately down one after another, Roofshadow walked a careful circuit. Her head was hung low, as if her pacing indicated deep thought or momentous decisions to be made, but in actuality she had already made her choice.

The sun, sparking the cold air and striking diamond gleams from the snowy ground, had passed the meridian and was beginning its winter-rapid descent when the gray fela stopped her careful treading and tipped an ear toward the earth. She was motionless for long seconds – as if the wind from the mountains above had frozen her, fur and bone, where she stood. Then, shaking her head gently, she lowered a snuffling nose, breathed for a moment, then suddenly canted her ear again. As if satisfied, she extended her paw, tapped softly on the crusty snow and began to scrape away the cold white skin of the sleeping earth.

Once through the powdery shell, she lowered her weight onto her back legs and began to dig in earnest. The soil was near-frozen and her paws stung, but she continued her rapid movements, sending flurries of mud and rock up from beneath her tail.

The Hour passed, and Roofshadow began to fear she had sensed incorrectly. The ground was hard-packed and firm; most of her small, slender form was below the hole's rim when, without warning, a spading paw thrust through the bottom of the pit into emptiness beyond.

Warm, fetid air rushed up through the aperture, and she reared back in surprise. This was what she had sought, though. She grimly resumed digging. A short span of scrabbling and she was able to pass her head and whiskers through the opening. When she pulled her front paws through she felt a surge of panic as, for a moment, she was suspended over nothingness, dangling helplessly. The unknown darkness below her became a bottomless abyss. Her weight pulled her back legs past the crumbling rim of the hole. She fell only a moment, then touched lightly down on the loam on a tunnel floor.

She turned her eyes briefly back to the hole above her, which glowed with the light of the setting sun. It seemed a very small hole now, although it was not very far away. It was not far away, but it *was* behind her.

Head down, green eyes wide to gather what little light there was in this dark, unfriendly world, Roofshadow padded silently down into the earth.

CHAPTER TWENTY-THREE

Fear death? – to feel the fog in my throat,
The mist in my face.

– Robert Browning

Limping through one of the immense, stone-arched chambers, the ragged group of cats shuffled slowly toward the digging tunnels. Tailchaser searched the bobbing sea of hopeless animals for Pawgrip. He located the small, wiry cat at the rear of the marching party, and slowed his already leaden pace until Pawgrip caught up.

'Hullo, Tailchaser!' Pawgrip said, a faint echo of his former sprightliness. 'You look a little stronger. How does that shoulder feel?'

'Better, I suppose,' said Fritti, 'but I doubt it will ever truly heal.' He raised and shook his front paw experimentally.

'Well,' said Pawgrip in a conspiratorial tone, 'I got a message to that fellow in the Upper Catacombs. He sent back to say that he hadn't seen your friends, but he'd keep his eyes open.' Pawgrip gave a weak smile that was meant to be encouraging. They were passing beneath one of the huge inner gates now, and had to lower their voices to a whisper. The tunnel walls had become closer, and their speech reverberated in a manner sure to attract unwanted attention.

'Thank you for trying, Pawgrip,' said Fritti. 'How was Jumptall feeling this morning?' The Meeting Wall delegate had refused to rise for work the last two times, and as a consequence had also not eaten.

'Badly, I'm afraid. Just lies there, and says if he moves he'll lose his tail name.'

They walked silently for a moment in the midst of the emaciated, staring-eyed cats. Hulking Clawguard walked the perimeter of the

186

disheartened procession, occasionally moving forward to threaten or prod.

'Jumptall is going to die soon,' said Tailchaser. In the world above he would have been amazed to hear someone say such a thing in so calm a voice.

'He is no longer strong enough to live,' agreed Pawgrip. 'His tail name is all he has . . . '

In a cave on the rock wall above the Greater Gate, Roofshadow looked down upon the charnel life of the mound.

Dulled by the strain of countermanding her instincts, tired and frightened, she had groped her way steadily down into the throbbing center of the mound.

When the tunnel had ended precipitously, on the wall of the Greater Gate chamber, she had suddenly seen the entirety of the wrong, the *os*. The misshapen guards and sick and dying prisoners below, the weird lights and noxious heat of the air – all this had struck her like a blow as she reeled above the cavern.

Unable to catch her breath for a moment, she stumbled back from the lip of the cave and slumped, a shuddering mass, to the darkened floor.

Far behind her, close to the surface, the pale, twitching nose of one of the blind Toothguard had detected a strange thing: an unauthorized tunnel opening to the world above; the soil was newly disturbed.

Escape attempts were frequent, of course, but invariably they failed. This seemed different, though. The keen nostrils of the hairless creature who had discovered the hole perceived a curious fact: something had been digging *in*, not out . . .

Somewhere deep in Vastnir, a shape appeared from one dark hole and entered a darker one. Heat and air currents led the shape to what it sought.

'Master Hisssblood!' it called. There was a pause, then:

'Sssskinwretch, I have long sssince ceassed to be entertained by your annoying presssence. I think I ssshall finally make an end of you.'

Even in darkness, the shape's discomfort was recognizable.

'Pleassse, Lord, don't do anything foolissh. I bring you important newsss!' Another long silence, and Skinwretch could smell and feel Hissblood's approach as clearly as the Folk aboveground could see in the broadest daylight. He resisted the impulse to flee.

'What could you tell me that I might possibly find of value, you old sssslobberer?'

Hissblood's tone suggested imminent, painful death, but Skinwretch recognized his opening and plunged in: 'Only thisss, most wonderful Lord, only thisss: sssomething hass tunneled *in* to Vassstnir! Ssssomething from the sssun-world! I found the place where the thing entered, above the Greater Gate!'

Hissblood approached, until the heat of his breath raked his cowering subordinate.

'And why ssshould *I* care?' the leader of the Toothguard spat – but now there was a subtly reserved edge to his voice. 'I sssuppose you have told everything that walkss, crawlsss or digsss between here and the Lower Catacombss?'

'No, great Massster!' whined Skinwretch, pleased that he had guessed correctly. 'I came ssstraight to you!'

'Fetch me Nuzzledark. You are *sssure* it wass an entrance tunnel? If you have misssled me . . . !'

'Oh, no,' hastened Skinwretch, choking with fright. 'I'm posssitive, Lord. Absolutely sssure.'

'Then I shall call on Basssst-Imret,' said Hissblood in a cold, satisfied voice.

'You will involve the *Boneguard*?' quailed Skinwretch. Hissblood's teeth snapped, drawing blood from the furless skin.

'*Imbecccile!* How dare you even draw *breath* in my presssence? Get out of my ssmell, you lick-sssslobberer. Get Nuzzledark, then go and crawl under a ssstone sssomewhere until I have forgotten that you exissst!'

Gasping, Skinwretch fled back into the lesser darkness. Hissblood licked his naked chops.

Trudging back from the excavations in the company of the other tunnel slaves, a bone-weary Tailchaser looked up to see the dark figure of Scratchnail pacing beside him, cruel smirk thinning his black lips.

'Mre'fa-o, star-face,' said the Clawguard mockingly. 'How are you getting along in your new home?' Tailchaser did not answer, but continued walking. Scratchnail did not seem offended.

'Still have your pride, do you? Well, that, too, will be attended to – I haven't forgotten you. Not at all.' Scratchnail stopped for a moment to stretch, his mottled belly touching briefly on the cavern floor. Finished, he caught up to Fritti again in an easy lope.

'We'll have plenty of time for a chat later,' he grated. 'I just thought I would come by to make sure you were still getting your daily constitutional. Wouldn't want you to get fat and complacent, would we, my little slug?' Scratchnail stared hard at Tailchaser's stoic posture, then continued, in a lower tone: 'Something is going on just now. All of Hissblood's little blind salamanders are dashing about as if their nasty little tails were on fire. I just wanted you to know that I'm going to keep an eye on you, no matter *what's* happening. I have a feeling this may involve you – I don't know why. Don't bother to look innocent, just remember this: I'm going to find out about you. *I'm going to figure out your secret.*' Scratchnail turned. 'Good dancing, sunworm.' The Clawguard trotted off.

Fritti stared at the ground as he heard Scratchnail's heavy feet padding away. He could only wonder what he was going to be made to suffer for next.

In his cave, only the motionless, unconscious form of Eatbugs for company, Pouncequick was in the throes of a waking dream. Although his eyes were closed, he felt as though he were seeing as clearly as ever he had in the world above.

He felt himself standing once more upon the Slenderleap Ford, the Caterwaul roaring and thrashing beneath him. From his vantage point on the rock span he could see the mound in all its squat oppressiveness. A hole appeared in its side and a line of dark shapes emerged. They moved in a strange dance, stiff with malice and alien purpose.

Pouncequick heard a loud, trumpeting sound, as if the sun had found a voice. The dark figures broke apart; they scurried in disarray, then fell to the ground and passed into the earth. The rushing of the Caterwaul became louder now, and from out of the waters stepped a great white form whose outlines were shifting and unclear. It walked across the valley. Where the black dancers had fallen and been swallowed up, trees and flowers burst full-grown from the earth. The white figure moved to the mound, and at its touch the vast cairn opened up, revealing itself as a great black rose, petals shot through with the colors of sunset. In this glowing light the white figure dwindled – no, did not dwindle, but was transformed into a mist, and rose upward.

Suffused with a sense of peace, feeling himself lifted with the dream-mist, Pouncequick did not realize for some time that he was being shaken. He unwillingly opened his eyes and saw the bony, sullen face of Longtooth, mouth asnarl.

'Oh, no, not you too. Bad enough the other one,' the Claw rasped, indicating Eatbugs. 'Get up – let me have a look at you.' He gave Pouncequick a cursory nose-to-tail inspection. Longtooth looked over his shoulder, then turned to the youngling with a sour face.

'Scratchnail wants me to keep a close eye on you. The whole mound's in an uproar because someone got in who wasn't supposed to. I feel sorry for the stupid me'mre when they get their claws on him.'

With a look of distinct pleasure over the probable fate of the intruder, Longtooth settled down on the cavern floor. Pouncequick, although he closed his eyes again, had lost his inspiring dream. Dimly, he heard many creatures passing in the tunnels outside his prison.

Tailchaser looked uncomprehendingly at Pawgrip.

'What?' he asked groggily.

'One of the new Folk wants to talk to you. Don't ask *me*,' said Pawgrip, shaking his head. 'Over by the entrance shaft.'

Pawgrip wandered back to his sleeping spot. Fritti, stretching, felt the ache in his shoulder and the thin pain of hunger in his belly. Stepping as carefully as his tired legs would permit, he made his way through the clutter of sleeping, groaning bodies. Near the front of the large prison-cavern, squeezed against a wall near the tunnel entrance, a small, gray cat was huddled into itself. As Fritti approached he could hear commotion drifting down from the upper levels. The small cat seemed to be shivering.

'Mre'fa-o,' he said to the newcomer, with weak amiability. 'I'm Tailchaser. I heard you . . . ' He broke off in midphrase, whiskers twitching. This new cat looked very familiar, even in the near-darkness.

'Roofshadow!' he gasped. His mind whirled. Had she been here all along, working in the mound? Was it really her?

'Quiet!' hissed the fela.

Still marveling, he leaned forward and scented her nose, her flanks. Roofshadow! As he dreamily sniffed, she flicked him on the nose with her paw. Like an embarrassed kitten he straightened up, looking wildly from side to side. None of the other prisoners were paying the slightest attention. Nevertheless, he hunkered down so close that his whiskers tangled with Roofshadow's, and began ardently grooming her. Quietly, and with a tongue full of fur, he asked: 'How did you get here?'

'I dug into one of the tunnels,' she said. Though she spoke with composure, her sides heaved.

It must have been terrible for her he thought – *lost in this place; searching for one cat in the midst of countless others.*

'How in the name of Meerclar did you *find* me?' he asked, still grooming.

'How did I what? Find you? I don't really know, Tailchaser, I just knew that I had to. I can't explain right now . . . I can't even think . . . Would you stop that?' She bristled, and he ceased cleaning her coat. 'We don't have time!' she continued. 'We have to get out of here – I think they're looking for me.' She stood, and her legs trembled a little. Tailchaser did not comment, but rose also.

'We can't leave without Pouncequick,' he said.

Suddenly, and unexpectedly, he thought of Hushpad – the object of his quest, for whom he had left the Meeting Wall so long ago. Could she be here somewhere, also? Was she still alive? He thought of Hearteater's grisly throne and felt suddenly small and helpless.

'Do you know where he's being kept?' asked Roofshadow. He turned to look at her. She *was* exhausted, and he was no better off.

'Pounce?' he said. 'No, I haven't seen him since they separated us.' He looked apprehensively up the shaft.

'I'm afraid we don't have the time to look for him, then,' the gray fela said calmly. 'We'll be lucky to get out ourselves.' She started toward the shaft.

Tailchaser was shocked. 'But we can't just desert him! I brought him here! He's just a kitten!'

Roofshadow looked back over her shoulder and snarled: 'Tailchaser! Don't be stupid! It might take us days to find him. We have to get out and warn the Folk at Firsthome – otherwise it will be too late for all of us! We'll do him more good if we bring back help than if we're caught and killed ourselves. We have to tell Fencewalker and the others. Come on now!'

Fritti tried to object, but he knew he could never explain the truth to her: about Hearteater, or the Toothguard, or the leagues and leagues of tunnels crawling with hideous earthspawn.

Roofshadow was not waiting to hear, anyway. She was slinking up the inclined tunnel, toward the flickering, sickly light and the sound of harsh voices. Fritti followed her.

The mound was alive with activity. Clawguard bunched in groups, conferring in dull snarls, then broke apart to range down tunnels and storm into prison caves. As Tailchaser and Roofshadow reached the main corridor outside the shaft, the Claws had moved in force into the holding cavern adjoining the one they had so recently quit. Growls of rage and weak cries of pain could be heard echoing up into the tunnel in which they stood. They broke into a run, staying in the deeper shadows close to the corridor wall. Passing several other prison caves, they found an apparently disused tunnel, dark and musty-smelling, and darted in. The din behind them faded a little, and they stopped for a few moments while Roofshadow tried to orient herself. Eyes closed, she let herself be commanded by instinct, reaching into her sense-memory for the way to her entrance hole. After a moment's deliberation, she led them down the tunnel.

They stayed away from the main thoroughfares, taking advantage of spur tunnels and niches and unfinished shafts. Out and up they went, spiraling toward the surface, toward the place of escape.

Several times they were almost caught. Once, on hearing the pad of approaching footsteps, they had to force themselves into a shallow, unfinished tunnel, and then stand frozen in terror, holding their breath, while two Clawguard debated whether their hiding place was worth searching. When the beasts finally decided against it and loped off Fritti found he had trouble catching his breath again.

Finally, they began a last, steep ascent toward Roofshadow's entrance. Peering around a corner, they found the last tunnel completely dark. As they moved quietly forward they caught a glimpse of starlight – the way out, at the far end of the corridor. Fritti had not seen the sky in so long that he felt silly with excitement. Despite the oppressive wet heat of the mound, a chill arched down his backbone and curled his tail. He bounced forward joyfully; for a moment he felt there was grass beneath his feet again, and cool wind in his fur. He heard Roofshadow call his name, softly but urgently. He paid no heed.

Then the starlight disappeared.

At once something struck him, catching him completely unaware. Roofshadow's admonitory call became a yowl of fear. Something was on top of him – some snapping, biting thing.

'Nuzzledark! Don't allow the other one to esscape!' slashed a voice in the dark, and he heard Roofshadow cry out again. The thing atop him drove for his throat with spiny teeth, and as he twisted desperately he felt furless skin squirm beneath his claws. Toothguard! He struggled to pull loose from the grasping creature, and managed to sink his own teeth into flesh for a heartbeat. He was rewarded with a hissing squeal of pain from his attacker. He drove his back legs up and heard the gasp of lost air. In the moment's respite he pulled free, and then dashed back toward where he had last heard Roofshadow's voice. His eyes were finally adjusting to the profound darkness, and he saw another form rear up just in time to avoid the worst of the blow, which still sent him spinning. He came to rest against the cringing mass of Roofshadow.

'Sssslitbelly! Help Nuzzledark with the prisssoners.' Fritti could now make out the owner of the voice, its elongated, hairless body crouched beneath what was to have been their escape hole. Its eyeless head nodded approvingly.

'Sssso,' it said. 'Asss expected, you return to your point of entrance. How niccce. Ssssince you are ssso interested in traveling, now we shall take you to sssee *our* domain, yesss?'

The other two dark shapes now flanked Roofshadow and Tailchaser, and one of them said: 'Why do we not end their livesss here, Massster Hisssblood?'

The Toothguard lord let a long second of silence hang in the dark, damp air.

'You should know better than to quesssstion me, Sssslitbelly – esspecially since you yoursself have proved ssso *inefficient*. These creaturesss have causssed uss all great problemsss, and we shall have to work hard with them to repay the bargain. They will live awhile longer becaussse I wisssh to learn certain thingsss. However, I can learn *nothing* from *you*. Do you sssee my meaning?'

Slitbelly was gagging on his answer when a dark shape hurtled out of the tunnel from behind Tailchaser and Roofshadow, knocking the two Toothguard sprawling like sticks. Not waiting to discover the identity of their mysterious benefactor, Fritti and the fela sprang to their paws and raced back up the corridor. Behind them they could hear snarls and cries, and the sounds of vicious combat. Above it all, the mad voice of Hissblood was screeching: 'Sssstop them! Sssstop them!!'

Time expanded into one dark and everlasting moment as Fritti and Roofshadow fled through the lightless outer halls. Away from the Toothguard, away from Roofshadow's tunnel, away, away – they could think of nothing else. Tailchaser was bleeding from new wounds, and his shoulder throbbed and flamed with each stride.

They raced through nearly complete darkness, relying on their whiskers and keen hearing: these shafts were almost devoid of the luminous earth that lit most of Vastnir. They stumbled against stones and over roots in the floor; several times in their panicked flight they ran into earthen walls, rose, and ran on.

Eventually they had to slow down. They were completely lost, and had passed an uncountable number of branch tunnels in the darkness.

'I think we will be trapped here forever!' gasped Roofshadow as they loped along.

'If we keep our left sides to the wall, and keep turning outward, eventually we must come to one of the exit tunnels – at least I hope so,' wheezed Tailchaser. 'Anyway, it's the only thing I can think of.'

Faint sounds whispered up from holes and cross tunnels. Some were the distant noises of Vastnir rising from the main chambers. Some, though, were unidentifiable – moans and whispers, and once the sound of something large splashing in a deep pit. They walked carefully around the pit, and by unvoiced agreement did not speak of the noise that had wafted up from its depths. They kept turning outward, and the noises of the mound became fainter and fainter with each bend.

The air seemed to be getting chill; when Fritti commented on it, Roofshadow pointed out that they were approaching the surface, leaving the unnatural heat of Vastnir. It did not feel like the cold of winter to Fritti, though. It was a deep cold, but damp and moist. It felt as though they were running through a thick fog. The air near the opening of Roofshadow's tunnel had not felt this way. He saw no sense in arguing, however, and restrained his objections.

Moving down what seemed to their ears and whiskers to be a broad, high-ceilinged corridor, Tailchaser heard a different sound: something that – though faint – sounded like the padding of soft footfalls. He mentioned it quietly to Roofshadow, and they slowed to an almost silent walk, straining their ears. If they were footfalls, they must be quite far back to be so nearly inaudible. The twosome increased their pace slightly.

The hallway, such as it was, narrowed suddenly; they found themselves in a low tunnel so suddenly that Tailchaser cracked his forehead against the roof. This tunnel wound and dipped, then rose again, as if it had been dug among large rocks or other massive obstacles. Fritti and Roofshadow crouched low to the ground and reduced their pace to a near-crawl. Finally, the burrow opened out into another wide, well-planed chamber.

They had progressed several steps when Tailchaser noticed a difference.

'Roofshadow!' he hissed excitedly. 'There's light!'

There was, although it was noticeable only in contrast to the dense blackness through which they had passed. The glow came from around a corner at the far end of the massive hallway, faint and indirect. It did not seem to have the same quality as the luminous earth.

'I think we're near the way out!' said Roofshadow, and for a moment Fritti thought he could see the gleam in her eye. They broke into a fast walk, then a run – able now to see the obstacles, massive tree roots and stones, which loomed black against the faint gleam at the end of the great hall. The air was still chilly, but drier; dust was everywhere, so much dust.

He had bounded ahead of Roofshadow, who reared suddenly, crying: 'Tailchaser! Something is foul here!' Then one of the black shapes between them rose up, and with the movement the air was suddenly full of a sickly, spicy odor. Roofshadow squeaked – a strange, throttled noise – and Fritti stumbled to a halt.

Both cats stood as though paralyzed. A dry voice, like the sound of branches rubbing together, issued from the dark shape.

'*You shall not pass,*' it said. The words were faint, as if spoken from a great distance away. '*You are the Boneguard's now.*'

'No!' boomed a new voice. Unbelieving, frozen with an odd, exalted terror, Tailchaser saw the sunken eyes and malformed face of Scratchnail suddenly appear out of the darkness behind Roofshadow. The gray fela, overwhelmed, sagged in place and lowered her head.

'I took them from Hissblood and his Toothguard. These two are *mine!*' Scratchnail growled, but moved no closer.

'*You have no claim,*' whispered the odd, sighing voice. '*No one may interfere with Bast-Imret. I do the bidding of the Lord of All.*' The Boneguard moved, swaying slightly with a leathery, folding noise, and the Clawguard chieftain quailed, reeling as if he had been struck.

'*Take the fela, if you wish,*' continued Bast-Imret. '*Our business is with the other. Go now. You tread in deep places.*'

Scratchnail, whimpering with some unseen injury, leaped forward and grabbed the unresisting Roofshadow by the nape of the neck, then turned and disappeared down the dark, cluttered tunnel. Fritti tried to call out after Roofshadow, but could not. His joints tingled with the effort as he tried to pull away and run.

The dark form of Bast-Imret turned – cat-shaped, but sunken in clinging darkness, even while facing the glow at Tailchaser's back.

Fritti could not look at its face, at the dark spots that should have been eyes. Head averted, he struggled – and for a moment succeeded. His legs felt like water, but he managed to turn around and crawl agonizingly away from the Boneguard.

'*There is no escape,*' whispered the wind.

No, thought Fritti, *it isn't the wind. Run, you fool!*

'*No escape,*' breathed the wind, and he could feel himself weakening.

Not the wind, must escape, must escape . . .

'*Come with me now*' – it was not the wind, he knew that. He continued crawling. '*I will take you to the House of the Boneguard,*' droned the unfeeling tones of Bast-Imret in the darkness behind him. '*The pipes play always, in the darkness, and the faceless, nameless ones sing in the deep places. There is no escape. My brothers await us. Come.*'

Fritti could hardly breathe. The smell of dust, spices, and earth dizzied him . . . permeated him . . .

'*We dance in darkness,*' chanted Bast-Imret, and Fritti felt his muscles stiffening. '*We dance in darkness, and we listen to the music of silence. Our house is deep and quiet. The earth is our bed . . .*'

The light seemed brighter. Tailchaser had nearly managed to reach the bend in the tunnel. He blinked his eyes, dazed. Without warning, the dark figure of Bast-Imret was before him, blocking the end of the hallway. A dry, poisonous air seemed to blow out from the Boneguard. Choking, Tailchaser sagged to the floor, unable even to crawl. The creature stood over him, faraway voice crooning unfamiliar speech.

Terror surged through him, hot panic, and somewhere he found the strength to lunge forward. As he struck, he felt the dusty fur give against his momentum. Bast-Imret crumpled with a sound like snapping twigs, clutching at Fritti as he tried, with what seemed his last dying strength, to push past. Beyond the tunnel's edge lay a pool of light. He strained toward it, and the freedom it represented.

But the Boneguard clung, and in the darkness the choking dust and sweet smell enwrapped the two of them like another shadow. Fritti felt the paws of the Boneguard – brittle, but strong as tree roots splitting rock – curl about his neck. The flaking, dry snout quested for his throat. With a final squeal of revulsion, Tailchaser lashed out.

There was a hideous tearing sound as he pulled away from the creature. Great, flayed rags of crumbling fur and skin came off in his claws and teeth – and as he tumbled toward the light he could see the dull wink of old, brown bones, and the grinning skull of Bast-Imret.

As he scrambled up the short shaft he felt a searing pain. The space between his eyes throbbed and burned. When he reached the hovering, gray-blue disk of sky, he turned for a moment – and saw the terrible thing behind him. It was standing in the shadows of the tunnel's base, its skeletal mouth slowly opening and shutting.

'*I will remember you until the* stars *die . . .* ' cursed the distant, toneless voice. The fire in Fritti's head flared again, then was gone.

Tailchaser forced himself over the edge of the hole. The light was so bright that spots floated before his eyes. Hobbling, almost falling forward, he struggled away from the hole – away from Vastnir.

The world was white. Everything was white.

Then, everything was black.

PART THREE

CHAPTER TWENTY-FOUR

O magic sleep! O comfortable bird
That broodest over the troubled sea of the mind
Till it is hushed and smooth!

– John Keats

Pain and weariness battled beneath Tailchaser's fur. High in the sky hung the cold, burning stone of the sun. The world was shrouded in snow; trees, stones and earth were mantled in an even, white sheath. Little needles of chill pain pricked Fritti's feet as he stumbled through Ratleaf Forest.

Since recovering consciousness, he had staggered near-blindly, putting distance between himself and the mound. He knew he had to find shelter before Unfolding Dark, when the gruesome shapes would come up from the tunnels below, hunting him . . .

The snow behind him was dotted with red.

Late afternoon found Fritti still in helpless, unthinking flight. He was weakening rapidly. He had not had anything to eat since what must have been the morning of the previous day; that had been – as was usual for the tunnel slaves – barely sustaining.

Tailchaser had now penetrated into deep forest. Columns of trees pillared the forest roof; the ground everywhere was shrouded in ice. Fatigue and glare made his eyes burn and tear, and from time to time he imagined he saw movement. He would stop, hunker down on the cold snow blanket with pounding heart . . . but there would be nothing, nothing: a static world.

The life of the old forest now driven out by the foulness growing near it – or so it seemed – Ratleaf made no sound, but silently heard the crisping of his pads; it made no movement, but motionlessly observed his struggle.

As the day wound forward and the biting soreness in his nose, ears and paws disappeared, to be replaced by a puzzling blankness of sensation, the illusion of subtle movement would not be laid to rest. From the corner of an eye Fritti glimpsed scuttling, shadowy presences; when he turned his head, though, only snow-laden trees met his gaze.

He was beginning to wonder if he was not indeed mad, as shadow-haunted as old Eatbugs, when one of his sudden glances caught the gleam of an eye. It was gone immediately behind the tree branches that had framed it, but it had been an eye: he was sure of it.

When another minute, peripheral movement caught his attention he did not turn but staggered on, watching with a sort of half-deranged slyness. In the extremity of his weariness he did not even consider the possibility that it might be a stalking enemy. Like a kitten playing with a dangling vine – first coy and uninterested, the next moment leaping for the kill – he could only think of the moving object; catching it, putting an end to the game.

Head down, the crimson drops staining the snow more irregularly now, Fritti saw a brief flash of something dark and swift in the trees to his right. Seemingly unaware, he pitched the uneven progress of his march slightly to that side until he was a jump or so from the edge of the copse.

Another flicker of activity just ahead – he had to restrain himself from springing.

Carefully now, carefully . . .

He stopped for a moment; he crouched down and licked one of his bleeding paws, all the time tensing his muscles, ignoring the twinges of pain, waiting . . . waiting for another movement . . . there!

Leaping, half-tumbling, Fritti crashed through the underbrush, paws flailing. Something had been knocked from the low-hanging branches and was scurrying before him. With a surge of strength he sprang.

As his paws made contact he cracked headfirst into a tree trunk and rolled stunned onto his side, something small and warm struggling beneath him. Holding whatever it was down with a forepaw, he rose and shook his head. He did not feel injured, he thought – not hurt, but tired . . . so very tired . . .

For the first time he looked blurrily down on his prey. It was a squirrel, its eyes bulging in terror, lips drawn away from long, flat teeth.

Rikchikchik, he thought to himself. *Something about the Rikchikchik . . . are they bad to eat? Poisonous?* He felt as if his head were buried in snow. *Why so cold? Why can't I think? Squirrels. Something I should say to this one?*

He thought hard. Every idea seemed another difficult step to be taken. Looking down at the small body and trembling, brushy tail, he felt a glimmer of memory. He lifted his paw from the Rikchikchik, who lay motionless, staring up at him with panic-bright eyes.

'Mrrik . . . Mrikkarik . . . ' Fritti tried to remember the sounds. He knew he must say it. 'Mar . . . Murrik . . . ' It was no use. He felt a great, soft burden settling on his back, buckling his legs.

'Help me,' he choked in the Common Singing. 'Help me . . . Lord Snap said to tell you . . . Mrirrik . . . '

Tailchaser collapsed to the snow beside the startled squirrel.

'Now, you-you cat: you speak brrrteek, why say brother name Lord Snap?'

Above Tailchaser's head, clinging upside down to the trunk of a tree, was a chubby old squirrel with a bent tail and glittering eyes. Behind him, showing less courage, a phalanx of Rikchikchik peered down the trunk and between leaves at Fritti.

'Talk now – talk!' squeaked the squirrel-leader. 'How know Lord Snap? Tell-tell!'

'You say Lord Snap is your brother?' asked Tailchaser, trying to clear the cobwebs from his mind.

'Most certain yes!' chittered the squirrel a trifle disgustedly. 'Snap is brother of Pop. Lord Pop is I – you see, so-silly cat?'

Feeling addled, Fritti reflected on this a moment.

'I was supposed to say something to you, Lord Pop – I mean, Lord Snap, your brother, told me to say . . . how did it go . . . ' Lord Pop made an impatient clicking noise. 'I'll try to say it!' Fritti muttered. 'Mrrarreowrr . . . no, that's not it. Mrririk . . . Meowrrk . . . *Harar!* I can't remember it!'

Tailchaser noticed that Lord Pop's retinue seemed to have lost much of their fear of him, and were, in fact, squealing with amusement. Tailchaser was sore and confused and tired, and for a moment his mind wandered. Then, suddenly: 'Dewclaws! I've got it!' Fritti laughed, a painful sound. '*Mrikkarrikareksnap!* That's right, isn't it?' In his moment of exultation, he felt suddenly light-headed, and sagged where he stood. Lord Pop leaned forward and fixed him with an agate eye.

'Is right. Sacred Oak pledge of Snap. We honor. Strange-strange times. You can walk, so-strange cat?'

Limping, Tailchaser followed the Rikchikchik party into the deep groves of inner Ratleaf. Trudging behind the chattering, hurrying squirrels, Fritti absently noticed the red glare of the setting sun. Something rustled in the back of his mind, tried to make him pay heed to the gathering darkness . . . but his head hurt; it was too hard to think. The rising steam of his breath caught his attention. He crunched on through the snow behind the bustling Rikchikchik.

The group halted. Tailchaser stood dazedly by until Lord Pop and two other Rikchikchik descended from the trees to stand beside him. Looking down on their arched tails and round backs, he smiled benevolently and said: 'I've been in the mound, you know.' The squirrel-lord's companions drew back at this, chittering, but Lord Pop stood his ground, bright eyes thoughtful. He soundlessly signaled the others back; together they coaxed Tailchaser into a hollow, lightning-blasted stump. The inside was sheltered, free of snow. After making three stumbling, automatic turns for the First Cats, Fritti collapsed to the ground. A bevy of Rikchikchik brought pine needles and bark, covering him from nose to tail-tip.

'We talk-talk sun next, so-strange cat,' said Pop. 'Now, you make sleep, yes?'

But Tailchaser had already slipped across the border into the dream-fields.

That night a darkness alive with searching shapes swirled harmlessly past, leaving Fritti's sleeping place undiscovered and safe.

In the depths of dream, Tailchaser stood on the edge of a vast plain of water, tempest-stirred, but silent. The broad shiny surface stretched as far as he could see, and the shapes of fla-fa'az wheeled and dove in the gray sky.

When he finally awoke, the short winter day was already half over. By the end of Smaller Shadows he found himself once more facing Lord Pop, who, with his court, had returned to Tailchaser's hollow tree. In his imperious stutter the squirrel-lord indicated that they had waited a long while for their cat-guest to rise, and had eventually given up and gone out to forage.

Tailchaser, feeling infinitely better for the long sleep, was only now discovering how many different parts of his body ached and throbbed.

He was also ravenously hungry. The Rikchikchik may have sensed this, for even Pop showed more restraint than he had the previous day. For his part, Tailchaser fervently wished that he could slip off and do some hunting, but in view of the precarious alliance with the Rikchikchik, his natural prey, he decided it would be better to wait until he could creep off unobtrusively. So, stomach grumbling, he sat and listened patiently to Lord Pop's long summation of the morning's activities.

'So . . . now-now is the time for true-talk, yes?' chirped the portly squirrel-lord. 'Why here, so-sudden cat? Why talk bad place?'

Fritti tried his best to explain the occurrences that had brought him finally to Ratleaf Forest. It was necessarily a long tale, and took a good part of the fading afternoon. When he told of his rescue of Mistress Whir and his subsequent audience with Lord Snap, the listeners responded with shrill noises of approval. The Rikchikchik were then nervously fascinated as he described the swarming cat metropolis of Firsthome. When he finally told of Vastnir, and his awful internment, several of the young females became quite dizzy and had to be fanned with the bushy tails of their companions.

Lord Pop listened in grim quiet, interrupting only for clarification of certain points about the mound and its denizens.

' . . . And then I found you . . . or you found me, rather,' finished Tailchaser. Lord Pop nodded his head. 'What I don't really under-stand,' added Fritti, 'is why you are all still here. I thought everyone had left Ratleaf.' He looked inquiringly at the squirrel leader.

'Many Rikchikchik leave. Many gone-gone,' replied the lord. 'But Pop no leave. Can't-can't. Nest to tribe since Root-in-Ground. Few-small stay, too. Live or die.'

Fritti nodded understandingly, and for a moment the unusual gathering was silent. A brief and surprising foretaste of mortality, borne on the chill breeze, touched Fritti. He remembered his need.

'I have a favor to ask of you, Lord Pop,' he said.

'Ask.'

'I have a message to get to Firsthome – to the lords of my Folk. It must get there soon. I could not travel quickly enough myself. I am still very weak.'

'Rikchikchik will do,' said Lord Pop without hesitation. 'We take word-word. Send Master Plink. Plink so-fast, like nut-fall.' A young Rikchikchik sat up on his haunches, visibly swelling with importance.

'He looks very capable,' said Tailchaser approvingly. 'But he should not go alone. The message is important, and it is a long, dangerous journey to Rootwood. Also . . . ' Tailchaser tried to speak as delicately as he could. 'Also, the cats of Firsthome are not as acquainted as I am with the bravery and goodness of the Rikchikchik. They are liable to . . . have a misunderstanding. To send a large party would be preferable.'

As the import of Tailchaser's words sank in Master Plink was seen to deflate, and two or three of the younger females threatened to become faint again. Lord Pop, however, took it in stride.

'Marvelous Acorn! No worry, cat-friend. Many Rikchikchik go soon. Plink will be small lord!' He chittered briefly at the young male, who looked somewhat reassured.

Fritti gave them the message to be carried, repeating it several times until Plink and the other young bucks had memorized it.

' . . . And remember,' he said seriously, 'if Prince Fencewalker isn't there, it must be given to Queen Sunback *herself!*' The assemblage made little whistling noises of awe, and Pop signaled an end to the conclave.

Fritti's hunting was not tremendously profitable. He caught enough bugs and grubs to take the edge off his hunger, and before bedding down was even persuaded by the now-comradely Master Plink to try a chestnut. Even with the Rikchikchik's help at removing the nut meat from its confounding shell, he did not find it a very satisfying experience; though he thanked Plink effusively, he secretly decided he would not make a very good squirrel.

Winter vented its fury on Ratleaf Forest. Flurrying snowstorms and gale winds drove Lord Pop's small retinue back into their nests. The messengers had left with a great deal of ceremony, and with their departure Tailchaser sank into lethargy. His one pressing need fulfilled, Firsthome now to be alerted, he found himself succumbing finally to the effects of his harrowing time underground. Contact with the Rikchikchik became less frequent. Fritti spent more and more time hunkered down in his tree-stump nest, sheltering and recuperating. Hunting was sparse so he conserved his energy, spending long stretches of time in slumber, the waking hours brief and barely distinguishable from the sleeping. Curled in his lightning-blasted tree, tail curved protectively over his nose, he let his mind wander over the things he had done and seen. As if they were present with him, he summoned up his friends from Meeting Wall: Thinbone,

Fleetpaw, the aloof Stretchslow and kind Bristlejaw. How they would marvel!

Sometimes he thought of Hushpad, the grace of her walk and the soft contours of her neck and head. He would pretend that he had found her and taken her back home; that she listened in awe and respect as he described his adventures.

'For me?' she would say. 'All of that to find me?'

Then the wind would whistle down the stump and ruffle his fur, and once more he would be back in Ratleaf. He would think of those he had left behind, left to awful destinies in the mound.

I suppose that is why I was Named Tailchaser, he thought sourly to himself. *All I have done is follow the closest thing – led on, like a kitten chasing its tail, moving in circles until it exhausts itself.*

One day, nearly half an Eye since he had been found by the Rikchikchik, Fritti was walking back to his nest after a long afternoon of unsuccessful hunting. Not all the life of Ratleaf had been driven out, but most of the creatures that remained were hidden for the long, cold winter. Tailchaser was feeling empty and purposeless. He stopped to drag his claws down the bark of a standing pine tree, relieving a little frustration and sending a shower of powdery snow down from the branches above. He felt a sudden revelation.

His time in Ratleaf was over. The vast, empty forest, snowbound and silent, was a way station – a neutral area. Like the half-sleep between dreaming and waking, it was a place not to remain, but to gather energy to move one direction or the other.

That moment, as he stood with back arched and whiskers washed by the cold air, he remembered the words of one of the Elders at his Naming: 'He desires his tailname before he has even received his face name.' They had laughed, but now he realized there was truth there. He had set out, not just to find Hushpad, but to *gain something*. He had been led, true, but he had chosen to follow. Now, he must turn one way or the other. He could return the way he had come, leaving it to Fencewalker and the others to succeed or fail . . . or he could complete his journey. Not that he, with his own small paws, could make any large difference, but he could finish his journey. His friends were trapped, helpless – he could not save them, perhaps, but they had come with him, and they all belonged together.

For a moment, just a moment, he thought he could understand what it was like to finally hear one's inner voice; to find one's tail name. The fur on his back bristled, and he had a fit of uncontrollable shivering. He dropped back down to his paws and turned back to his nest.

It was not until he had curled himself up for sleep that he realized he was really going back to the mound.

CHAPTER TWENTY-FIVE

The lions pass a thornbush and melt.
Though the whole day is unbroken
the passage of the sun will represent heaven
the bones will represent time.

                       – Josephine Jacobsen

Dawn found Tailchaser moving toward the Va'an-ward border of Ratleaf. He had not gone to say farewells to the Rikchikchik. Despite Lord Pop's honor-bound discharge of Snap's debt, Fritti did not feel he could comfortably involve the squirrels any further. They were already struggling for their own survival. Chance and strange times had made them allies, but Tailchaser knew that the Rikchikchik and the Folk were prey and hunter, and would be those things always. He only hoped that the artificial alliance would hold until the message was safely delivered to the Folk of the Queen's Seat.

As he paced silently through the tree-crowded snowscape he thought of Firsthome and his time there – a halfhearted attempt to keep his mind occupied. The mound would be before him soon enough; there was no reason to hasten his thoughts ahead.

Among the thinned tree rows and bracken near the outer edge of the great forest, Fritti heard a sound from above: the rustling of wings. He momentarily considered darting for shelter, but before he could spring from the open white space in which he was framed, two black shapes dropped from the heights above. Prepared – he hoped – for whatever ill fortune had descended on him, he crouched, hackles raised.

The two dark creatures settled on a branch above with a flurry of ebony pinions. Fritti relaxed . . . somewhat. It was only a pair of ravens – Krauka – one large and one small. Not the most harmless of fla-fa'az, but not strong enough to match talons with the Folk.

Still, he regarded them suspiciously as they in turn stared down at him with glittering eyes.

'Th'art the Tailchaser?' asked the older bird in an unmusical voice.

"Course, Dad, there be the star on's head, now, see?' squeaked the smaller. Tailchaser took a step backward in surprise.

'You can speak!' he breathed. 'You know the Common Singing?'

With a harsh cackle of amusement the larger Krauka flapped his wings, lifting slightly off the branch. Settling down, he preened his chest feathers in a self-satisfied manner, keeping an eye on Fritti.

'There be many who bear no fur, yet speak nigh better'n *cats*!' The large bird chuckled again. 'Those what be long-lived like we, well, they do learn. Aye, even my eldest here' – he indicated the smaller raven – 'though's got no more sense nor a tumblebug.'

'Well,' said Fritti after a moment's consideration, 'I suppose I should by rights be beyond surprise by now. How do you know my name?'

'Those what gossip with squirrels should not wonder that the trees know all they secrets. There be little adrift in this forest what doesn't blow past the ear of old Skoggi, which is me.'

'My old dad beest chief Krauka in these woods!' piped the small bird proudly.

' . . . An' my young Krelli here has not got the brains what the Big Black Bird give to a mushroom.' Skoggi leaned over and pecked the top of his son's head. Krelli cawed piteously and scuttled up the branch, out of reach of the paternal beak.

'Next time, do you think afore opening your dinner-hole!' said Skoggi. 'An' don't be sharing our business with every marmot what gives you the time o' day.'

Fritti was amused in spite of himself. 'But you seem to know *my* business,' he pointed out.

'Like I said aforetimes,' chuckled the raven, 'Rikchikchik is a powerful talky lot. Keep they nuts, but no secrets. It be common knowledge, like, that you come from' – he indicated with his shiny black head – 'from there. The mound, as 'twere. You be well known 'mongst those what hasn't fled the Ratleaf – though that be proper few, now. Where be you going now, Master Tailchaser?'

Although the Krauka seemed harmless, Fritti decided on caution. After a moment he said: 'Oh, actually, I'm just exploring the forest. As a matter of fact, I should probably be on my way.'

'Ah, belike, belike . . . ' rasped Skoggi. He walked a little way down the branch, ruffling his pitchy feathers, then stopped and peered shrewdly at Fritti from the corner of a glinting eye. 'Did it not be so obvious that you were a cat of great smartness, like, with a sharp eye toward preservin' that fine, furry skin you be wearin' . . . well, were it not for this, it would seem like you were wanderin' toward that mound, yonder.'

Fela's Whiskers! Fritti cursed to himself – the Krauka was a clever one.

'But,' countered Tailchaser, 'as you point out, why would I want to go near that terrible place again?'

'True enough. 'Tis a turrible place, 'tis. Evil things what care not where they bite come crawlin' up. It looks a dark and turrible place, 'deed it do – the forest be fair empty now, the things what it harbors be so foul. 'Tis all a poor soul can do to protect his family, and put morsel or two in they sweet young beaks.' He looked over to Krelli with poorly mimed affection.

'Then, why *do* you stay?' asked Fritti.

'Ah, well now,' croaked Skoggi, with a sigh betokening great sorrow, 'this be the only home ever we knowed. It be powerful hard to leave behind the nesting spots of nigh on thousand generation. 'Course' – and here he laughed creakily – 'it has been might easier keepin' the little darlings fed of late. Those creatures what lives below-ground may be right bad, but leasts they leave behind what they don't eat.' Convulsed with laughter, the raven nearly fell from the branch. Tailchaser grimaced. 'Yes, now,' continued Skoggi, still bubbling with mirth, 'no matter who eats, an' who what's eaten, there's always some o' the latter what's left behind. 'Tis the prime advantage of being born to th' Krauken.'

'Be we goin' to eat Master Tailchaser, Dad?' asked Krelli with innocent curiosity. In a flash, Skoggi had fluttered up the tree limb and, with his strong beak, administered a swift and painful tattoo on his fledgling's skull.

'Thou interrupts thy betters again, an' I'll nip off thy pinfeathers and toss you outen yon tree for the mound-cats to munch, ye rockhead! You can't be eating everyone what passes by!' He turned to Tailchaser. 'Now, my fine cat, 'course we both know that you be'n't so addle-pated as to go clambering back into this affrightening mound. So. Be that as it may, *were ye going to*, p'raps I could tender a leetle advice?'

Fritti pondered for a moment, then smiled tightly up at the Krauka. 'Well, since we are speaking of this silly thing, and supposing I *was* in need of advice, what would you want in return?'

Now it was Skoggi's turn to show a look of cold amusement.

'You cats be'n't quite so foolish as ye be sung of. However, this one time, the hy-po-thitical deed which I'd be helping you with'd be reward itself – tho', Black Bird knows, not pufferin' likely of success. Be you interested?' Fritti nodded in acceptance. 'Good, then. Well, let me tell this.

'In days not long passed, when first we saw yon dungheap rise up along our forest, were no tunnels that led out from it. The first 'un was a small 'un, and when they dug out the biggers, this one fell out o' use. Methinks it still be *unguarded*, it having been fair hidden – the mound-cats had not then what sway they do now. Here be how you may find it . . . '

When Skoggi had finished he turned to his son. 'Now, you flipwing clodpoll, mark this well – i' case someday you be called on to relate how you was the last what saw the brave Master Tailchaser alive!' With another croaking laugh, the raven mounted into the air, Krelli wincing as he followed.

'Wait!' cried Fritti, and the two black fla-fa'az stopped and hovered. 'If it doesn't matter to you who eats who, why are you helping me?'

'A fair question, Master Cat,' Skoggi called raucously. 'You see, as I figure it, at the rate they be going, those mound-cats'll have cleared the whole o' Ratleaf by autumn-time. 'Course, wherever they go there'll be food for us Krauka . . . but I be gettin' right old. I prefers to fall out o' the nest of a mornin' and find my breakfast a-waitin'. So, if you find luck, you'll be doin' me a favor to brink your Folk back to the forest!'

With a harsh caw of merriment, the ravens were gone.

'Pouncequick! Please, listen to me!'

Roofshadow walked gingerly across the prison cave and gave the kitten a not-too-gentle prod with one of her smoke-gray paws. Pouncequick let out a murmur of displeasure, but his eyes remained closed; he did not move.

Roofshadow was worried. Pouncequick had been sleeping or lying silent almost all the time since Scratchnail had brought her to the cave. The kitten had barely acknowledged her existence, raising his head only once, some time after she had arrived, to say, 'Oh. Good dancing, Roofshadow,' before lapsing back into his somnolent state. A few times since then he had replied to her insistent questions, but

212

with little interest. In the corner of the cavern, Eatbugs sprawled like one dead.

'Pounce, please talk to me. I don't know how much longer I'll be left here. They'll come back for me anytime.' She thought of Scratch-nail, and fear made her fur crawl. The Clawguard chieftain had thrown her roughly into the prison pit with promises to come back and 'deal with her' after he had made his report to the Lord of Vastnir. That must have been days ago, although the dragging Hours of darkness made it seem an even longer interval. He might return for her at any moment.

'Pouncequick!' She tried again. 'Can't you understand me? We're in terrible danger!' She prodded him again. 'Wake up!'

Groaning, Pouncequick rolled slightly to one side, away from her demanding paw.

'Ohhhhh, Roofshadow, why don't you leave me alone? It's lovely here, and I don't want to . . . ' He lapsed into silence for a moment, his beatific expression twisting into a frown. 'And . . . and . . . I don't want to be where I was before,' he finished sadly.

Roofshadow was exasperated and becoming a little panicky.

'What do you mean? You're dreaming, Pounce.'

The youngling shook his head, the placid look returning to his face. 'No, Roofshadow, you don't understand. I'm with the white cat. Everything is very peaceful. I'm learning things. Please, don't be angry with me. I wish you could *see*, Roofshadow!' he said fiercely, eyes still tight-shut. 'The light . . . and the singing . . . '

Pouncequick fell silent again, and all the fela's efforts could not make him speak more.

The abandoned tunnel mouth was just where the raven had said it would be, hidden beneath a snow-flocked gorse bush at the rim of the woods. Tailchaser pawed suspiciously at the old tailings that ringed the entrance, but detected no recent presences. Ducking beneath the sheltering bush, he scrabbled away at the dirt and debris that had partially blocked the hole. When he had cleared a whiskers-wide opening, he poked his head through and sniffed again. The tunnel interior smelled only of old dirt and a few small animals who had briefly sheltered there.

With only the faintest waver of his newfound resolution, he stepped inside. Above the white forest the sun stood in the Hour of Smaller Shadows.

This tunnel was considerably drier than most of the others that he had walked within the mound. Its air of disuse reassured him, and he made good time, padding boldly down into the depths. The glowing earth shone only fitfully here, but it was enough.

Soon he began to pass cross tunnels, and from some of these wafted hot, moist air. He was approaching the active byways of Vastnir. He knew he would have to be more cautious.

Since the sound was so low-pitched, so subtle, at first he did not notice that the silence of his abandoned spur tunnel had been breached. The subliminal pulse of the mound had been so familiar to him during his long imprisonment that he scarcely noted its resumption. When it finally impinged on his conscious thoughts, he realized that this time it seemed subtly different. That bothered him, and he could not say why. Then he understood.

The noise was growing gradually louder, as if he were approaching the source. Every footfall seemed to be bringing him nearer to the agent of the dull, almost inaudible throbbing. When he had been a captive in the mound it had always sounded the same: remote, yet omnipresent, as if all of Vastnir had been producing a low, rumbling drone.

Now, the sound had begun to take on distinction – booming and hissing, definitely louder; growing more so with every step Fritti took. As he rounded a bend, the shaft sloped steeply down, and a miasma of hot, wet air rolled up out of the darkness at the end of the tunnel. Tailchaser reared back, combing frantically at his face with a forepaw to clear his eyes of the clinging murk.

Still determined, despite a fluttery feeling in his middle, Fritti slit his eyes against the billowing vapors and moved forward. As he legged cautiously down the incline he passed beneath a door or opening of some kind, for suddenly the throbbing became an echoing roar, rattling and reverberating from the walls of a huge cavern that he could not see for the mist-clouds that surrounded him.

Like Grumbleroar Falls, he thought.

His fur was rapidly becoming sodden. He understood that he had stumbled upon some vast underground cataract.

The strange subterranean breezes shifted direction and the vapors swirled away. In the half-light of the glowing soil he could see the giant cavern above which he crouched, insectlike, on one of the shallow ledges that ringed the walls. Below, red-lit and foaming, surged an immense flood of water. The cavern had no floor, only the gigantic, steaming river which passed endlessly through from one

214

ide to the other, filling the great domed cave with fogs and chaotic oise.

Tailchaser felt the heat of the burning river beat up into his face s he peered cautiously over the ledge. The pounding force of the vater as it crashed against the cavern walls and disappeared into the ock beneath him made Fritti feel suddenly dizzy, disoriented by the nagnitude of the spectacle. As the river boomed its way down into he darkness beneath him, flaring comets of spray jetted up, to hang nally motionlesss far above his head, then plummet back to their ource. Fritti backed away from the edge and huddled for a while ear the tunnel mouth.

Finally, the tumult began to sicken him. He pushed forward. around the cavern, near the opposite side, he could see several unnels, coal-black against the shadowed, crimson-brushed rock. Keeping tightly to the cavern wall he headed toward these, walking arefully along the high, clinging path above the surging river.

It was slow going. From time to time, the wind would mysteriously hange and the swirling mists would descend, forcing him to stop nd cling in place until he could see his way again. Inching his way round the perimeter of the monstrous chamber, he kept his eye irmly fixed to the trail before him. Occasionally he would see move-ent in the corner of his vision, but upon looking up find only leaping pray. Once he thought he saw two tiny figures scuttling along one f the pathways criss-crossing the far wall, but as he squinted into he gloom the mists heaved up again. When they had receded, all eemed as it had been.

After an eternity of tortuous progress, he gained the far wall. Picking his way up the steep path, he reached the holes, farther above he roar and crash of the boiling river. The first tunnel that he reached tself fumed and steamed and he hurried past, but the next opening arried a welcome hint of cooler air. Once he was inside the tempera-ure dropped rapidly. Pleased at this good sign, Fritti put distance etween himself and the great cavern.

With several tunnel bends behind him, the sound of the river had decreased to its earlier muted throbbing. He flopped to the floor of he shaft, glorying for a moment in the relative stillness and cool. After a few breaths he applied his tongue to his soggy, matted coat.

'You there!' The voice slashed through the shadowy tunnel. Fritti eaped to his feet, his heart pounding louder in his own ears than the aging water.

'Sssstay!' hissed the voice. 'Sssstay and have wordsss with Sskin wretch of the Toothguard!'

CHAPTER TWENTY-SIX

Ah, yet would God this flesh of mine might be
Where air might wash and long leaves cover me;
Where tides of grass break into foam of flowers,
Or where the wind's feet shine along the sea.

— Algernon Swinburne

Transfixed, Tailchaser stood as slow steps crunched down the tunnel toward him. He could hear the whistling breath of the approaching creature. A nearly overwhelming desire for flight struggled with a dull, unreal feeling of resignation, and he swayed gently in place.

'My companion and I want to ssspeak with you, ssstranger.' Again, the hissing words, closer now.

Companion, Fritti thought. *There are two of them.* His legs trembled, and he drew his tail up between the hindmost pair and waited. From out of the darkness loomed the blind head of the Toothguard. Its nose-skinned body tottered unsteadily. Fritti stared.

Where the huge nostrils had once flared in the Toothguard's eyeless face, there was only a scarred ruin of tattered flesh.

Skinwretch came shakily to a halt not a jump and a half away from Tailchaser, and his damaged snout poked questingly to and fro.

'Are you here?' queried the Toothguard. Tailchaser's heart leaped, and he gave an involuntary squeak of relief. The thing had been wounded! It could not sense him, or at least not well.

'Ahhh,' breathed Skinwretch. 'There you are. I hear you now. Come, don't desssert usss. My companion and I have lossst our way.' The blind thing moved closer, leaning an ear in Fritti's direction. 'What isss your name?'

Tailchaser weighed again the possibility of making a dash for freedom. He decided against it. Here, perhaps, was a situation that could be turned to his advantage. It would be dangerous, of course, bu everything here below the earth would be.

'Um . . . um . . . Tunnelwalker!' he blurted after a moment' hesitation.

'Sssplendid. Your name soundsss asss if you will be aptly sssuite to aid usss. Are you of the Clawsss? Your voice sssoundsss very high.

'I am but a youngling,' said Tailchaser quickly.

'Ahhh,' breathed Skinwretch, satisfied. 'Of courssse. With the fina preparations, even the young are presssed into ssservice. Come, yo mussst guide usss. Asss you ssseee, I am sssuffering from a temporar infirmity.' Mumbling, the maimed Toothguard turned and shuffle up the corridor. Fritti followed a short distance behind.

Final preparations? he wondered. *What is happening?*

'You mussst have come passst the Ssscalding Flume,' Skinwretch called over his shoulder. 'I ssshould never have come ssso clossse The russhing of the water disorients me, I fear. It iss quite incredible is it not?'

'Yes, yes, it certainly is,' assented Tailchaser. 'What brought you out to this lonely part of the mound?' He hurried forward to bette hear the hairless creature's reply.

Skinwretch was quiet, then answered: 'I am afraid that I have ha a bit of a ssetback, you sssee. A youngling like you may not kno it, but there is a great deal of unfairnesss – unfairnesss to folk lik mysself. You ssee, I do not want to criticizzze, oh no, but I wass punished unfairly because a prissoner escaped. But I wasss not eve there – oh no, I merely passsed along some information to my masss ter, Lord Hisssblood. When the essscape occurred, he wasss punishe by the Lord of All. In turn, *I* wass made to sssuffer. Unfairnesss sssuch unfairnesss . . . ' The Toothguard broke off with a little whim pering gurgle. Fritti realized with a thrill of fright – and pride – tha it was *his* escape that Skinwretch spoke of.

After a moment, the Tooth broke off his keening and said: 'My companion iss just ahead. I hope he hasss not left. He too hass sssuffered injusticeness. Ah, I believe I can hear him!' Tailchaser ha forgotten the companion, but now he too could hear the loud, son orous breathing. As they turned a corner he saw a large, dark shape lying flat in the shaft. Skinwretch inched forward, testing before hir with a great wrinkle-skinned paw. He pushed at the big, dark body

'Get up, get up!' he shouted. 'I've found young Tunnelwalker t help usss find our way back. Get up!' As the recumbent creature urned reluctantly over, Skinwretch said to Fritti: 'Perhapsss you two now each other. My friend wasss an important figure in the – '

An all-too-familiar face, blocky and malformed, was revealed as he shape rolled over and cast baleful eyes on Fritti.

'Tailchaser!' howled Scratchnail, rising on his front paws. Before Fritti could move his stiffened body, Skinwretch had leaned over and lung a smacking paw at Scratchnail's face. The impact knocked the Clawguard off balance. He rolled back down onto the ground again, noaning.

'Sssilence, you fool!' snarled the Toothguard, and bobbed his blind head toward Tailchaser, who stood by, shocked into rigidity.

'Don't mind thiss one,' he assured Fritti. 'He isss not right in the head, I fear. The Lord of All dealt harshly with him over the matter of thisss sssame prissoner. Now, he sssees thiss fellow in every sssh-dow. It isss quite sssad, iss it not?' Indeed, Scratchnail was paying no attention to the actual Fritti beside him, but was rubbing his chin in the dirt, moaning Tailchaser's name over and over. Finally he topped, and looked up at the Toothguard.

'Why were you gone . . . so long?' Scratchnail asked Skinwretch. Coming from that powerful body, the pleading tone seemed dread-ully unnatural. Fritti let out his long-held breath. The world under-ground, which had contracted into a stone-cold, heavy skin around him, expanded once more. Incredible! His luck was holding. To be his close to a Scratchnail who did not recognize him!

'Get up, you great lump!' Skinwretch snapped. The Clawguard's rightened mewing struck the lightheaded Tailchaser as almost comi-al. 'I have found sssomeone to help usss find our way back to the nain tunnelsss. We can find food there! Rissse.' Scratchnail pulled his bulk erect.

'He iss not right in the head, asss I told you,' Skinwretch apologized s the threesome started up the corridor. 'He would have died, lessspite all hisss ssstrength, but for me.' There was strange pride in he voice of the Toothguard.

Tailchaser now found himself in the unenviable position of being guide and companion to two creatures who wished him and his kind lead – leading them through tunnels with which he was completely unfamiliar, down to the secret center of the maze.

Scratchnail, although up and moving, still showed no signs of recognizing Fritti. His behaviour veered from simpleminded to unex-ectedly lunatic and vicious. At one point he turned suddenly on Tailchaser, howling, 'Black winds, black winds!' and tried to rend

219

him with powerful claws. At a sharp word from Skinwretch, he was again cringing and crying.

'Not right, not right,' lisped Skinwretch, shaking his scarred head. 'He wasss once a mosst important chief, you know.'

After they had walked a bit farther – Tailchaser relying on minute changes in the air temperature and pressure to guide them in what he hoped was the correct direction – he worked up the courage to try to draw the so-far-amiable Skinwretch out.

'How are the "final preparations" going, eh? I'm afraid I've been involved in some . . . er, rather important things up . . . up aboveground.'

'Nobody tellsss poor old Ssskinwretch much,' complained the Toothguard, 'but I hear many thingsss. Great movementsss, a great uneasinesss . . . I heard two of my brother guardss whisspering not long ago that sssoon the sssurface will be breached!'

The surface . . . *breached*? Fritti did not like the sound of that. Some terrible, imcomprehensible thing was about to happen, and apparently he and a scatter of stuttering Rikchikchik were the only creatures who could do anything about it.

No, thought Tailchaser, correcting himself, *I can do nothing but find my friends, and probably die with them.*

With the mobilization of Vastnir, escape would be unlikely for one, let alone three or four. No, further hope – and a tenuous one, at that – rested on the leaping backs of squirrels, and a jaded, unconcerned Court.

'Star-face! Creeping, skulking star-face! I'll have his heart out!' Yowling, Scratchnail had stopped in his tracks, whipping his black muzzle from side to side. Fritti realized with a start that although Scratchnail was mad and Skinwretch blind, he *did* have a white star on his forehead; he would be easily recognized by any of the mound's more discerning occupants below. As Skinwretch soothed the raging Clawguard, Fritti dipped his head down and rubbed his brow in the dust. Blinking the dirt from around his eyes, he straighted up.

I hope that will hide it, he thought – *or at least obscure it enough that it will pass unnoticed. I will never look like a Clawguard, but at least I can hope to look like a nameless slave.*

The hairless one had coaxed Scratchnail into a walk again, and though the Claw made strange, whining noises, he did not disrupt their course again for some time.

Tailchaser's directional sense seemed to be working. He began to see signs of increasing traffic in the shafts they were following – stronger and more recent scents came from the side passages. Fritti began to think about finding his captive friends. He knew that he could travel quickly and safely only in these outer, mostly unused byways; once he was into the active heart of the mound his deception would be of no use.

The sound of harsh voices came suddenly from around the curve of their path. Scratchnail – as if in some kind of anticipation – chose this moment to lie down, spreading his large, dapple-bellied body across the tunnel floor. Tailchaser looked wildly about, and after a long moment spotted a tiny tunnel in the wall they had just passed. Grating, sneezing laughter echoed up the shaft as he leaped back and squeezed himself into the small space, which turned out to be a crevice – and a cramped one. He heard the laughing voices stop, and the heavy pad of approaching paws. Then they spoke, in the unmistakable snarling idiom of the Clawguard.

'What's this? What's this great load of unburied me'mre doing in the way?' There was a sharp bark of amusement, then another, equally unpleasant voice said: 'It's obvious somebody needs skinning around here, by the Great One! Who's responsible?'

Skinwretch spoke up in an aggrieved tone. 'Pleassse now, massterss. Do no injury! Asss you can sssee, I am in the company of two very important membersss of your brotherhood! Tell them, Tunnel-walker!'

'Two!' laughed the first Claw. 'I see but one – and a great, boneless wreckage he looks to be, too! What do you see, Riptalon?'

'Exactly that. A useless hulk and a little, squirming blind mole. Unless I miss my count, Shredfang, that makes but two. The little Squeaker's *lying* to us!' Skinwretch gave a whimper of fear, and Fritti heard the two Clawguard move closer.

'Lying to Guards on the Lord's business. I think we'll make him jump for that, don't you?'

'Tunnelwalker! Sssave me! Sssave us!' The Toothguard's voice rose hysterically, and Fritti, crouched in his shallow niche, held his breath.

A muffled groan rose up, and then Scratchnail's droning voice: 'Tailchaser! Star-face did it! No, Lord Huh . . . Lord Heart . . . Hearteater, not the burning! My ka . . . no! Ahhhhhhh!' His voice rose into a keening wail. The two Clawguard made sounds of surprise.

'By the Blood-light!' grunted Shredfang. 'It *is* a Claw!'

'It's Scratchnail!' Riptalon gasped nervously. 'He is proscribed! The Lord of All punished him. We should not touch him!'

'Pfauggh! You're right. This place stinks of the unclean! The shame of it! And that mewling blind worm . . . come, let's be off.' The disgust in Shredfang's voice did not disguise the fear that whimpered beneath. Swift, padding footfalls passed by Tailchaser's crevice and faded down the corridor.

Fritti waited for what seemed like a very long time, then stepped gingerly back out into the tunnel. Skinwretch's furless shape was huddled over the supine black form of Scratchnail . . . and for a moment Fritti was oddly touched. Then the Toothguard swiveled his ruined muzzle around, and the sensation vanished in a cascade of revulsion.

'Who'sss there?' Skinwretch called.

Tailchaser made a hesitant noise in his throat, then said: 'Why, Tunnelwalker, of course. I have been off exploring some spur tunnels. I just passed a couple of my fellows. Did you meet them?'

'They threatened usss!' panted Skinwretch. 'They were going to kill usss! Why did you leave?'

'I told you!' said Fritti, feigning anger. 'Now, get up – and get him up too. I have important things to do, and I am only helping you because you are so pathetic and incapable. Now, are we going to get padding or not?'

'Oh, yesss, Tunnelwalker! Come, Ssscratchnail, get up now.'

With Tailchaser leading, and Scratchnail trailing reluctantly, the mismatched threesome moved on into the heart of gathering forces.

CHAPTER TWENTY-SEVEN

> Not with a Club, the Heart is broken
> Nor with a Stone –
> A Whip so small you could not see it
> I've known
> To lash the Magic Creature
> Till it fell
>
> – Emily Dickinson

Strange things were happening in the world above the labyrinth. Distant cries and lights made the night Hours mysterious and unsettling. Felas gave birth to kittens too unusual to survive, and Prince Dewtreader of Firsthome made dire pronouncements. Many Folk were afraid. The ground everywhere felt unsolid – shifting and treacherous.

The Eye opened to its fullest a complete sun-turn earlier than expected, and hung red and swollen in the sky. Meeting Nights were full of unanswerable questions and nameless fears. Blind Night, the night of greatest darkness, was coming. Some whispered that this time the darkness would bring the *os*.

The *os* was on the tongues of many, and in the minds of more . . .

Below the ground, the Great One on his carrion throne of death and dying worked a web of curious forces. Energies beat and pulsed through his seat of power so intensely that sometimes the air itself in the Cavern of the Pit became as solid and resisting as water. Strange images waxed and waned, flickering at the edge of vision like lightning on the eyelids of a sleeper. At times, now, none but the Boneguard could attend the Lord of All, and the Claws would stand muttering in the tunnels outside the Master's cavern.

Even Tailchaser, on the periphery of Vastnir's main arteries, could sense the imminence of . . . something. Scratchnail had ceased talking altogether – mumbling and howling alike – and plodded along with a dull, lifeless sheen on his deep eyes. He stopped incessantly to scratch, gouging at his dark fur with crimson claws until it seemed he must draw blood. Fritti understood. His skin, too, was crawling.

The trio had paused by one of the main passages, looking down a dark, sloping access tunnel to the broad causeway below. Teams of Clawguard marched purposefully by, or harried fainting, stumbling prisoners. At Tailchaser's side Skinwretch cocked an ear to the sounds of pads scuffling endlessly past.

'Aaaahh.' The Toothguard beamed, his scarred face crinkling into a complexity of lines. 'Hear that? Lisssten. Great thingsss are afooot . . . great thingsss.' The naked snout took on a dejected cast. 'The unfairness of it. That a faithful sservant, sssuch asss I . . . ' He made a sniveling sound. Fritti, worriedly watching the Clawguard legions, nodded his head distractedly – forgetting momentarily that the other could not see him.

'I was born to sserve the Lord of All,' Skinwretch lamented. 'How could I have been brought to thiss low essstate?'

The Toothguard's reproachful words finally sank in. An idea began to form in Tailchaser's mind.

'Skinwretch, I have something important to tell you,' Fritti said in a low voice. 'Let's move back up the corridor a bit.'

When they had walked back to stand by the stuporous Scratchnail, Fritti said: 'You say you are loyal to the . . . the Lord of All?'

'Oh yessss!' Scratchnail eagerly affirmed. 'It iss my one purpose!'

'Then I can tell you my secret. Do you promise to keep it?'

'Oh, certainly, Tunnelwalker, mossst asssuredly!' Skinwretch bobbed up and down in a horrible parody of trustworthiness. 'I ssswear by the Foaming Ssstone of the Toothguard!'

'Good.' Tailchaser deliberated for a moment. 'Lord He – the Master – has grave need of information from a certain prisoner. He does not trust his chiefs, though. Some of them, like . . . well, if I must say it, like Hissblood, have shown themselves to be unreliable – if you understand me.'

The Toothguard was jiggling excitedly. 'Of course! I understand. Like Hisssblood! Exactly!'

'Well,' continued Fritti importantly, now warming to the deception, 'he has chosen me to find and observe the prisoner. But *no one may know*! You can see that it would be . . . well, unwise, especially now!' He was a little unclear himself on the logic of this, but Skinwretch seemed enraptured by the idea. 'Anyway,' he added, 'the Lord of All has chosen me, and I am choosing you. You must find the prisoner for me, and no one must know why, or even suspect. Can you do that?'

'Clever Tunnelwalker. Who will sssusspect old crippled Ssskin-wretch? Yesss, I ssshall do it!'

'Good. The prisoner you must find for me is the fela who accompanied the escaping Tail . . . Tail . . . ' He hemmed and hawed convincingly. 'Tailchooser. The one Scratchnail raves about. The fela who was with him survived, did she not?'

'I do not know, Tunnelwalker, but I ssshall find out,' said the blind creature soberly.

'Very well,' said Fritti. 'I will meet you on this spot when three work shifts have passed. Can you find it again?'

'Oh, yesss. Now that the Ssscalding Flume no longer boilss my earsss I can find my way anywhere.'

'Move, then, and take Scratchnail with you – only, keep him out of trouble that will draw attention.' Fritti especially did not want to be yoked himself to the powerful, maddened beast – who would be even more of a danger if his memory returned. 'And remember,' he added, 'if you betray me, you betray your Master. Go!'

Fraught with newfound purpose, Skinwretch hurriedly roused Scratchnail, and the two went trudging away.

Tailchaser stifled an impulsive sneeze of pleased laughter as he watched them disappear. The hardest was yet to come.

With that matter settled, Tailchaser felt his fever-swift thoughts begin to slow down. He was very hungry. This presented a problem. As he stood close to the tunnel wall and watched yet another press gang of captives being herded out to the diggings, he considered his alternatives. He supposed that he could try to stay inconspicuously on the edge of things – stealing a meal here or there, trying to avoid the guards by stealth and speed. Sooner or later, though, he would be caught. There were no free Folk roaming about the mound – at least, none that he had seen. It was courting disaster, and he had a mouthful of trouble already.

Another clutch of prisoners, overseen by a pair of surly Claws, moved along the passage below him. As they passed his hiding place, one of the slaves near the front collapsed. There was a great yowling and snarling as others tried to leap over the fallen one, and collided with their fellows. The two Claws, red talons shot, waded into the flurry.

Fritti seized this chance, bounding out of the tunnel and moving rapidly toward the rear of the line.

It will be easier to escape from one of these gangs than to live like a phantom for very long, he decided. *Also, who would hunt for an escaped prisoner in a prison cave?*

'You little sun-rat!' rasped a voice. Tailchaser looked up into the heavy-jawed face of one of the guards. 'I saw that!' the Claw snarled. 'Try sneaking off again and I'll slit you from gorge to tomhood!'

The crush of tunnel slaves surged forward again, bearing Fritti along.

Life with the slave gang was not as difficult as it had been before. He was stronger after his interval in Ratleaf; though the hunting had been sparse, still he had eaten better than the poor beasts with whom he was imprisoned. It saddened him to see the misery and suffering around him – but this time things were different: he had joined this press of captives by choice; he was operating in secret. Although his heart warned him against foolishness, he could not help feeling a quiet pride. He had a purpose, and so far he was succeeding remarkably. His luck *had* been dancing.

The prisoners, too, could feel the difference in the mound's atmosphere. The stirring, anxious sense of impending events had beaten them down. No prisoners told stories, or sang. Even the arguments were lackluster, dispirited. Collectively the slaves were cringing; they were waiting for the blow to fall.

One of the other captives told Tailchaser laconically of the rumors among their warders: about the lights and noises in the Cavern of the Pit, and of the assembling of Claws and Teeth into bridling, impatient units who were then sent out to farther tunnels. Trying to appear unconcerned, Fritti milked the prisoner – a one-eyed tabby named Fumblefoot – for more information, but the weary cat had no more to offer.

Fritti had been with the tunnel slaves for two work shifts and his impatience was rising: he knew that his time was running out. All he could think of was the danger that his friends were in. Firsthome and the fate of the Folk had faded from his memory as useless abstractions. After he left Fumblefoot, Tailchaser sat humpbacked in the corner of the cave until the guards came to drive them forth.

The dirty, back-bending digging time oozed by as slowly as running sap. Although his paws were cracked and bleeding, Fritti dug as though consumed – striving to obliterate the dragging Hours by main force.

*

When the smirking Claw at the mouth of the tunnel growled down the order to quit digging, Tailchaser and the other weary prisoners began to mount upward. Carefully falling behind, he stopped as the last cat before him strained up over the tunnel rim, then quickly doubled back down the short passage and threw himself to the earth at the end of the hole they had been excavating. He wiggled as far beneath the piles of loose soil as he could and lay quietly.

The sounds of the milling prisoners drifted down from above. For a moment, a burning golden eye looked down into the tunnel, but dirt and darkness hid Tailchaser from all but the closest inspection, and soon he heard the press gang crunching away. He remained silent at the burrow's end while his heart beat many times, then finally crept cautiously toward the surface.

The small cavern from which the tunnel network led was empty. The dim earth-light revealed no movement but his own. Nonchalantly but rapidly he groomed the worst of the dust from his face, legs and tail, then moved silently out into the larger shaft down which his fellow prisoners and their guards had already vanished.

In the cavern where Pouncequick lay dreaming of the white cat, Roofshadow herself was also finally sleeping. The strain of anticipation – waiting for the return of the vengeful Clawguard – and the enforced helplessness of her situation had worn her down until she could no longer muster strength or worry to resist. Chin on paws, she had lain for a long time staring at the peaceful, helpless forms of Pouncequick and Eatbugs, and hopelessness had drifted over her like a warm mist. When the guard thrust his malignant head into the chamber he saw all three of the cats lying in deathlike stillness. With a yellow-fanged grin of approval, he withdrew.

Eatbugs' eyes blinked open. For a moment, while his body still lay slack and motionless, they filled with an intense, cool fire. Then the light flickered in their depths and seemed to die. The lids sagged back into place, and all was still as stone once more.

Skinwretch was waiting for Fritti when he arrived at the spur tunnel. The Toothguard was doing a little dance of anticipation, his furless tail kinking and wriggling like a drowning nightcrawler. Tailchaser, who had spent what seemed like Eyes and Eyes working his way carefully across the mound to this spot, approached as quietly as he could, only to be greeted by Skinwretch's shrill, excited hiss.

'Tunnelwalker! Have you come? I have newsss, newsss!'

227

'Silence!' Fritti himself hissed. 'What news?'

'I have found your prisoner!' said the Toothguard gleefully. 'Ssskinwretch hasss done it!'

Tailchaser felt the pressing of time. 'Where? Where is she?'

Skinwretch grinned, the mouthful of teeth below the scarred snout gleaming crazily. 'Not far from here, oh yesss, very clossse. Oh clever Sskinwretch hass ssserved the Lord of All!'

Trying to keep his patience, Fritti waited with dry mouth as Skinwretch described where Roofshadow was being held. When the eyeless Toothguard had finished, Tailchaser began to back away, planning furiously, then suddenly stopped.

I'd better keep up appearances, he thought. *This creature is a terrible enemy, but he makes a good ally.*

'You have done well,' he told the Toothguard. 'The Master will be pleased. Remember, not a word to anyone!'

'Of coursse not. Not clever Ssskinwretch!'

As he watched the creature's mad caperings, Fritti suddenly noticed something he had missed in his excitement. 'Where's Scratchnail?' he demanded. 'You were to keep him with you.'

A sudden look of fear crossed Skinwretch's ruined features. 'Oh Tunnelwalker, that one. He isss full of *ossss*. He would not stay by me, and I could not make him – he iss very powerful, you know. He ran off into the tunnelsss, crying and ssaying ssstrange thingsss. He wasss punished becausse of the prisoner, and he iss sssick with the *osss*.'

Nothing to be done, thought Fritti. 'Never mind,' he told Skinwretch, who brightened immediately. 'Go on, now, and if I need you I will find you.'

Tailchaser darted out of the spur tunnel and across the main shaft, stopping in an alcove on the far side, shielded by darkness from observing eyes. When he looked back he saw Skinwretch, maimed face in a crooked smile, still leaping and jigging in the shadows.

Hiding in pools of deeper shade, stealing quietly past squadrons of bristling, congregating mound-dwellers, Fritti moved like a spirit-cat through the awakening underworld. The mound-beasts were everywhere – moving, whispering, flexing sharp red claws.

Fritti reached the junction of three tunnels that Skinwretch had described. Looking cautiously around, and seeing no one paying attention, he ducked down the passage that the Toothguard had nstructed him to take. Tail erect, whiskers tingling and every bit of ur puffed upright, he crept downward.

A shaft entrance in the tunnel wall ahead. That was the one! He elt an urge to leap, but controlled himself. Carefully, carefully . . .

He reached the hole and peered cautiously down. In the dim light t the bottom of the shaft he could see . . . Pouncequick! His heart eaped. The young kitling and Roofshadow were being kept in the ame cave! His luck was holding.

Leaning farther forward, he could now see two more shapes. Roofhadow! And was the old one Eatbugs? But why weren't any of them noving? Could they be . . . but no. He could see Pouncequick's sides ising and falling.

Something crashed down on him like a toppling tree. With a yowl f pain he tumbled to the side of the cavern entrance. Standing over im with a massive paw cocked for another blow was a large black hape. The half-familiar face of the Clawguard leered down at him.

'What are you up to, then?' the brute growled.

'N-nothing!' squeaked Fritti. 'M-m-my name is T-Tunnelwalker, nd I've lost my way.' He tried to make himself small against the arth. The Claw leaned closer.

'Is that right?' he snarled, and his hot breath made Tailchaser link. The beast's eyes narrowed. 'Just a moment. You look familiar. What's that mark on your head?'

His head? Forehead? Skydancer's Tears! Fritti cursed himself. He nust have wiped the masking dust from his face when he had emerged rom the slave tunnel.

Fritti made a sudden squirming movement toward escape, but the eavy paw descended on his neck, scarlet claws softly pricking his hroat.

'By the Great One!' said the Claw. 'If it isn't our little escaped un-rat! Isn't that fine!'

In a rush of despair, Fritti recognized his captor. It was Bitefast, cratchnail's former companion, who now bared his teeth at the rapped Tailchaser in a terrible smile. 'Well now,' chuckled the Claw, it's awfully good that I should be the one to find you. Because of ou, they ruined the chief. All because of you!' The paw pushed ruelly down on Fritti's throat. He coughed helplessly.

'Well, I'm the chieftain now.' Bitefast smirked. 'And I'm going to nake sure you get what you deserve.' The black beast squatted, and ushed his deep-set eyes up next to the face of his wheezing captive. The Claw's voice descended to a vindictive whisper.

'I'm going to take you straight to the Fat One!'

CHAPTER TWENTY-EIGHT

Wheresoever thou art our agony will find Thee
Enthroned on the darkest altar of our heartbreak
Perfect. Beast, brute, bastard. O dog my God!

– George Barker

Tailchaser was pushed, prodded, bitten and bullied down the now-crowded corridors by Bitefast. As they passed – the dark and muscular Clawguard driving the small orange cat – some of the mound-dwellers turned to stare curiously after the mismatched pair. There was nothing unusual in the sight of one of the captive Folk being herded to punishment or doom, but the small cat was snarling and balking – resisting! It had been a long time since any had seen the sun-dwellers showing any fight.

Fritti, in a haze of pain, frustration, and anger, did observe an unusual thing: there were no slaves, no work gangs to be seen sullenly treading the roads of Vastnir. Apparently their work was done. No wonder he had been discovered.

Bitefast directed Fritti down through crowds of indifferent Claw-guard and hissing, wrinkle-skinned Toothguard. Down, from level to level, passing beneath the Greater Gate, to arrive at last at the vaulted antechamber to the Cavern of the Pit.

Before the entrance to the Seat of Hearteater stood a group of Clawguard, arguing. The apparent leader, a squat, chunky beast with only a stump where his tail had been, seemed to be trying to restore order. He snapped at one of his minions, who retreated growling, but crept back a moment later with head held low.

'Ho, Crushgrass!' Bitefast called to the tailless one. 'What are you and your pack of mouse-huggers doing down here?'

Crushgrass turned to peer at the new arrivals. 'Ah, it's you, is it Bitefast? Very bad, very bad all this is.'

'What are you whining about?' asked Bitefast with a tongue-lolling grin.

'It's Snapjaw here,' said Crushgrass worriedly. 'He and some of my other fellows have been hearing strange things in the Upper Catacombs.'

'Scratching, like,' said Snapjaw, low-browed and sullen. 'It's no right.'

Bitefast barked a harsh laugh. 'What these fellows need is some sharp teeth put to 'em. You need to keep these shirkers under a firmer paw, Crushgrass.' He laughed again. There was an unpleasant murmuring among Crushgrass' guards. 'And what are you all doing here in any case?' Bitefast continued. 'The Master'll have your eyes!'

Crushgrass winced. 'They were going to come down here without me, if I didn't come. How would that look?'

'Like a mutiny. Now, it's a mutiny that you're leading, my fine stupid friend. Scratching! Hah! Stoneblood and fire! You'll soon find that the Master is worse than any scratching!'

'And what brings *you* here, anyway?' Snapjaw hissed nastily.

Without warning, Bitefast was on him, knocking him to the ground and tearing his ear.

'You can talk to your chief like he's a mewling kit, but don't try it with me!' Bitefast rasped into Snapjaw's bleeding ear in a low dangerous voice, then spoke up to the rest, who were watching avidly. 'As it happens, I've brought an important prisoner to the Lord of All. If you're lucky, he'll be so pleased with me he'll forget to tear your innards out.'

'Important prisoner? This little thing?' asked Crushgrass.

'The only escape we've had, this one,' growled Bitefast. 'He must have had help, right? Stands to reason, doesn't it? And you know what that means, don't you?' The Claw leaned forward for emphasis. 'Conspiracy! Think about that!' Bitefast bared his teeth, pleased.

'But if he escaped, what's he doing back?' queried one of Crushgrass' guards. Bitefast glared at him.

'I've had just about enough questions from your like,' he said menacingly. 'I've got more important things to do than stand about jabbering with you scabby lot. I'm going in to see the Master. Go on, Crushgrass, take your whimperers and their "scratching," and get back to your tunnel. You're got no business here.'

'And you've got no place to order me, Bitefast,' said the other chieftain defiantly, but started away, his mumbling crew behind him. Snapjaw, with a hateful look, followed shakily.

'No backbone,' said Bitefast in a self-satisfied tone.

Fritti had been motionless throughout the exchange, sensing the emanations that beat out from the chamber beyond – the grinding, reaching power of Hearteater. He barely felt Bitefast poking him forward toward the entrance. A mist swam before his eyes, and a blunt throb of pain started up at the front of his skull.

The two guards of the portal, one Claw, one Tooth, bobbed their heads minutely as they recognized Bitefast, but did not turn to watch as he led Fritti by. As they passed below the arch, cold mist swam up to meet them. Tailchaser was already shivering.

In the middle of the cavern the throne of the Impossible One rose up from the pit, the writhing, dying bodies making rippling patterns in the blue-and-violet light. Atop this monolith of pain lolled Lord Hearteater, blind and immobile like an immense, newly-hatched larva. Below him dozens of fevered servitors scurried around the rim of the pit.

Bitefast, his bravado gone now, pulled Tailchaser slowly toward the great beast. As they stood on the great circular precipice – the Claw chief working up courage to speak – there was a commotion at the far end of the cavern, near the main entrance. Fritti could see Clawguard running rapidly through the portal, but the ground-hugging mists made it impossible to tell what was happening.

The creature above the pit turned his head slowly in the direction of the disturbance. Bitefast coughed once, loudly, but the Master only stared away, across the great rock-rimmed cave.

'G-Greatest Lord . . . Mighty One, hear thy slave!'

Bitefast's voice carried out across the pit. The massive head pivoted slowly, turning back at last to fix milk-white eyes in their direction. Both the Clawguard chief and his captive took an involuntary step back from the rim. The Firstborn regarded them expressionlessly.

'Greatest Lord, your servant Bitefast has brought you the escaped prisoner – the star-faced one. See!' The mottled beast stepped back, leaving Tailchaser cowering on the edge of the great pit beneath the unfathomable inspection of Hearteater.

Bitefast, unconsciously shooting and sheathing his claws as he waited, at last could bear the silence no longer. 'Have I done well, Greatest One? Are you pleased with your servant?'

Hearteater turned his head slightly toward the Clawguard. 'You will live,' he said. His voice sounded like centuries of decay. Bitefast made a spluttering noise, but before he could speak the dead, muddy voice added: 'You have done well. Now go.'

Eyes goggling, Bitefast backed toward the entrance, turned and disappeared. Tailchaser sagged to the cold ground; the vapors swirled between him and the pit. When they receded, the Fat One's ancient, blind eyes were focused upward, seeing nothing. The tortured heap on which the thing reclined heaved slightly, as in some strange collective shrug. The Lord of Vastnir appeared not to notice. Suddenly, like a cold, clammy intruder, Hearteater's voice spoke inside Tailchaser's mind.

'I know you.' The thick presence forced its way effortlessly into his thoughts. Tailchaser, in a sick frenzy, rubbed his head against the frost-hard ground of the cavern, but the voice could not be driven out.

'You are no threat. Free or prisoned, quick or dead, you are less than a pebble in my path.' The ageless thing, smothering Fritti's panicked thoughts in flabby despair, droned on: 'But I still need my minions . . . for a while yet. All must know futility. All must know *resistance* is futility. I should render you to particles and set you afloat between the stars . . . '

A terrifying emptiness swept into Fritti's mind, as if he had been suddenly cast into the endless abyss. Somewhere he could hear his body squealing in terror . . . somewhere – remote, unreachable.

'But,' the awful hammering drone began again, 'you are already promised. Bast-Imret and Knet-Mukri – all the Boneguard – have claimed you. You will be taken to the House of Despair, to be entertained there until your ka struggles to fly to the great void . . . '

As if silently summoned, gray mist-shrouded shapes issued forth from the caves high up on the wall beyond Hearteater's pit. A stately, awful progression started down from the honey-combed cavern wall, as slow and relentless as black-ice forming on a winter pond. In the dim indigo light that flickered from fissures in the rock they were indistinct . . . formless. Bright sparks that might have been eyes twinkled.

A thin breeze sighed down from the heights of the chamber and the darkness settled a little closer. The other creatures drew back silently to let the Boneguard pass. A powerful force held Tailchaser pinioned to the earth, and he could only watch as the shadow company approached.

A sudden disturbance at the cavern's far entrance, loud alarums from the Clawguard there, turned all the eyes but those of the blind beast in the pit. The line of Boneguard stopped, their indistinct forms rippling. Beneath Hearteater the dying bodies heaved again; then for a moment all was still.

A lone figure tottered through the entranceway, into the Cavern of the Pit. It was a Toothguard, leathery hide slashed and bleeding.

'We are attacked!' the creature shrieked. 'There isss great sslaughter at the Vez'an Gate! Other placesss, too!' A great cry arose from the gathered beasts, and now sounds could be heard from the tunnels beyond the great cavern.

'What is it? What is it?' cried one of the Clawguard, maddened.

'The treacherous Firssst-walkersss! They have come with the sssunwormss of the Firssthome! Treachery! Attack!' Screeching and whistling, the Toothguard collapsed. The cavern was instantly a place of pandemonium – Tooth and Claw alike leaping, snarling, and screaming, spilling and surging out of the tunnels. From outside the cavern the noises of the struggle were louder, closer. Above the chaos Hearteater lay motionless as a glacier.

Tailchaser, sprawled on the earth at the edge of the pit, watched it all as if he were in a dream. The cries and furor had not touched him, had not penetrated the paralyzing frost that Hearteater had laid on his heart and ka. When a massive wave of struggling beasts poured through the entrance to the cavern, locked talon and fang in mortal combat, he watched the swelling madness with the same curious indifference he had once shown to ripples on a summer pond. Only when several of the figures near the front of the fighting began to look faintly, distantly familiar did he feel a thawing of interest.

A great black cat – like a slender, supple Claw – was laying about in spitting fury in the midst of gnashing Toothguard. Who was that? Why should it matter to him? He felt it important that he remember. Nearby a second tom, crisscrossed with thin scars, wrestled and tore at a Clawguard far bigger than he was. Another one. Should he know him, too?

A huge striped cat thundered through the entranceway, scattering guards before him. As he looked across the cavern from the summit of his detachment, Fritti felt an urge to smile – despite the fact that the swag-bellied tom was fighting for his life.

Why? he wondered. *Why am I smiling?*

Because it's Hangbelly, and Hangbelly is funny.

Hangbelly. Hangbelly, and Squeakerbane, and . . . and . . . Quiverclaw! His friends. His friends had come!

The frost melted from his soul. The Folk had come at last! They had come!

Fritti climbed to his paws with a weak cry of happiness. The fighting was spreading, moving closer to where he stood – and gradually surrounding the pit where the Master lay in inscrutable power. Tailchaser staggered back toward the wall of the cavern, taking the slight refuge of a recess in the stone. The guards had already sprung past him toward the fray.

Slowly, as if by unspoken command, the mound-creatures were edging backward until at last they formed a ring around the misty, violet-lit hole in the cavern's center. The attackers massed and charged, but broke against the line of the pit guards. Struggling shapes plunged howling over the rim, to vanish into the fogs that floated about the Master's throne. The attackers withdrew, poised to throw themselves forward once more. There was a heartbeat of stillness, in which fur could almost be heard to bristle . . . then the mud-and-thunder voice of Hearteater boomed through the cavern.

'STOP!'

Shocked silence, and for a moment nothing but the echoes of that terrible sound reverberated in the air. Quiverclaw, who had scrambled partway up the base of the chamber wall, stared into the dimness of the pit. His raspy whisper, charged with superstitious fear, fractured the stillness.

'Dugs of the Allmother!' Hisses of fear boiled up from the other Folk, and hundreds of backs and tails arched as one.

The voice of Hearteater welled up once more. 'I wondered if the lackeys who worship the memory of my departed brothers would eventually gain the courage to try to take me in my den. Hear me, then, you Firefoot-sniffers and Whitewind-chasers: the last of the Firstborn is not to be dealt with by a mewing rabble like yourselves. You are beyond your depth, surface-crawlers.'

The pressure of his words weighed the attackers down like a tangible thing, but the mound-creatures did not move either, so great was the force of Hearteater.

Finally Squeakerbane stood, his battered old face firm, whiskers straight and proud. 'Words!' cried the Thane of the Rootwood First-walkers. 'We have brought more true Folk than there are stars in the sky, Lord of the Ant Heap – even now they swarm down your Praere-hole. Your day is over!' All around the attackers shook their heads, and purred with wonder and pride, so that a great humming filled the rocky vastness. 'You may sit like a toad on your imitation

Vaka'az'me until the end of time,' cried Squeakerbane, 'but we shall never rub our chins on the ground for you! Your power is broken!'

The laughter of Grizraz Hearteater rolled down like the grinding of an avalanche. 'FOOLS!' he boomed. 'You speak to me of power, with your tiny lives like the tumbling of leaves! What a mockery!' His laughter swelled again. There was a rumbling beneath, and Hearteater's throne-mound pitched sharply. 'You speak of the Vaka'az'me,' he bellowed, and the rumbling grew louder. 'You think you see the throne of Hearteater, but you see *nothing*!!' The Master of the mound shouted with mirth, a noise as chilling as freezing rain. The Folk quailed and would have run, but Squeakerbane stepped forward, and the line held.

Before the Thane could say a word, Hearteater's dark, swollen body began rocking and pitching atop the carrion mound. 'Do you think I perch here to frighten the pitiful, scurrying things that serve me?' the Fat One demanded. 'To put otherworldy fears into the minds of such as you? HA HA HA HA HA!' Hearteater's voice rose to a deafening pitch. 'Like Fela Skydancer who bore me, I am bringing warmth to this pile of squirming flesh. I am giving it *POWER*!'

The rumbling noise from the pit became a tearing, sucking sound. The lights beaming up from the earth flickered crazily. The assembled creatures, Free Folk and Clawguard alike, began to yowl in fear and scramble away from the pit.

A huge shape emerged from beneath Hearteater, as if hatched, or as if forming itself from the vapors of the pit. It made a sound like the crying of uncountable dying things – myriad voices in one soulless cry. Howling and screeching, all who surrounded the pit scattered to the walls of the cavern as the vast thing clambered ponderously forth.

The sickly purple light touched on something monstrous and deformed, dark and unrecognizable. There was a vague, lunatic suggestion of some demon-hound in its slavering muzzle and red eyes. It was formed of the melting, twisted bodies of the pit – dying, piteously suffering beasts melded into the shape of a single great one.

Some of the Folk, courageous to the point of madness, tried to stand and fight. It was on them in a moment, shambling and deadly.

'I have brought it forth!! The *Fikos*! I have brought it forth!' The cavern was full of cries, dead and dying, shouting chaos. As the dog-thing flailed and slew, the voice of Hearteater rose above all: 'Fikos! Your bane! The bane of all that walk on the surface of the world!!'

Tailchaser turned from the awful sight and fled the Cavern of the Pit.

CHAPTER TWENTY-NINE

The fox has a bag of tricks,
the hedgehog one very good one.

– Archilochos

Vastnir was in pandemonium. As Fritti ran through the near-darkness he saw cat-shapes careening by, shrieking and bounding like so many maddened bats.

Tailchaser could think only of his friends; the horror and death behind him were too great. It seemed to be the end of all things – all life, all reason, all hope. He wanted to face it with his companions.

No one heeded him in his flight. Clawguard and Toothguard fought with one another, as well as with the advancing host of Free Folk. Prisoners lured up from their caves by the sounds of chaos swarmed in confusion, scuffling, crying, searching desperately for exits. The thundering, mindless voice of the Fikos rolled through the mound, singing devastation and madness.

Fritti tried to remember the ill-attended directions given him by Skinwretch. Several times in the confusion of sounds and bodies he feared he had lost his way. Finally, he recognized the downward turn. Ears flat, he sprinted down the sloping tunnel.

Roofshadow and Pouncequick were crouching, hackles raised, at the back wall of their cave. At their feet lay Eatbugs – but now his eyes were open. He stared with odd, quiet interest at Tailchaser as he appeared at the doorway. Roofshadow did not appear to recognize Fritti for a moment, then, with a headshake of amazement, she bounded forward, calling his name.

'*Tailchaser!* You're here! What is happening?' She drew near him, sniffing, but he moved past her to Pouncequick.

'Pounce!' he cried. 'It's me, Pounce! Are you all right? Can you walk?'

Pouncequick stared up at him for a moment as if he did not understand, then a soft smile spread over the kitten's features. 'Nre'fa-o, Tailchaser,' he said. 'I knew you would come back.'

Fritti turned around to see Roofshadow staring apprehensively up the shaft. 'Terrible things are happening, Roofshadow,' he said. 'The Folk have come, but they have been met by great danger. We can do no good here. Our only chance is to get out – now, in the confusion. Help Pouncequick up. I'll get Eatbugs.'

Without questioning, the gray fela leaped forward to help the youngling, but Pouncequick raised himself on shaky legs. 'I can manage,' he said. 'I was just waiting for Tailchaser to arrive,' he added mysteriously, then stretched, his body a small, arching bow-shape.

Eatbugs proved more difficult. Though awake, and not actively resisting, he appeared confused. He did not seem to understand the need for haste; he tottered about the cavern, sniffing corners and walls as if he had just recently arrived.

'He has been in the dream-fields since we were captured,' offered Pouncequick. 'This is the first time I've seen him afoot for I don't know how long.'

'I hope he remembers how to use his paws,' grunted Tailchaser, 'because our time is getting short – if it isn't already too late. Come. I'll lead. Roofshadow, bring up the tail-end and help Eatbugs.'

'But where are we going?' asked the fela. 'If the Folk have come to the mound, won't there be guards at all the ways in and out?'

'I think I know a way that will be unguarded,' Fritti replied, 'but it will be chancy. We must go now! I will tell you what I can as we run.'

The procession moved to the exit, Tailchaser sticking a nose out first to make sure the way was clear. The tunnel outside was empty, but sounds of great tumult filtered down from above.

As he reached the exit from the cave, Eatbugs balked for a moment, staring around the chamber in which he had lain imprisoned for such a long time. For the first time since passing the gates of Vastnir, he spoke.

'A poxy, boxy place . . . ' he said softly, then suffered himself to be prodded forth by Roofshadow.

As the foursome coursed through the haunted corridors, Fritti tried to explain all the things he had seen. All about them the dead and dying lay intermingled with the confusion of the living. The luminous soil that lined the chambers and tunnels glowed only fitfully now, and danger seemed everywhere in the darkening mound.

Several times their path was blocked by mound-creatures and they were forced to struggle for passage. Fritti and Roofshadow fought for freedom as though maddened, throwing the Teeth and Claws into confusion: why wouldn't these small Folk be cowed into quick surrender? Everywhere the world of the mound seemed to be fraying apart, and to the terrified mound-dwellers these desperate, ungovernable slaves were only more frightening evidence of normality's eclipse. Time after time the startled Guard fled in dismay to seek more easily subdued creatures.

Eatbugs did not help to resist attackers, but only cringed, mumbling painfully. Pouncequick stood strangely aloof, and would not raise his small paw to defend himself, even when directly menaced. Instead, he stared blandly at his attackers until they shied away, awed by what they could not understand. Tailchaser and Roofshadow, fighting constantly in defense of their small convoy, were wounded in many places. Pouncequick, unhurt and untouched, followed them like a youngling on a day's romp.

'I don't know how we can go on like this much longer,' gasped Roofshadow as they fled the scene of another skirmish. 'Someone will assume control of these creatures soon, and then we may as well commend our kas to Meerclar.'

'I know,' Fritti panted. He had no hope to extend – indeed, the byways they traveled were becoming more dangerous by the moment. He saved his breath, putting it to the better use of haste.

Finally, though, as they followed the outreaching tunnels, they entered the less frequently trafficked areas. The attack by the Folk of the Firsthome had drawn most of the sentries in from the fringes of the mound; as the foursome turned and tracked ever downward, the din of battle began to fade behind them. The light of the mound-earth was fading, too, but Fritti had covered these paths before – more important, he was now following the slowly increasing thunder of the Scalding Flume.

The hissing, roaring noise of the underground river became louder and louder in their ears as they essayed a succession of narrow, low-roofed tunnels. The air was filling with moisture. They emerged from a tight passage into what Fritti remembered as the last high chamber before the cavern of the Flume. Escape seemed possible now, although Tailchaser was sure that behind him the Free Folk were fighting – and losing – a deadly important battle.

He halted the group to explain the dangerous footing ahead, but his warnings remained unspoken. When he turned, Eatbugs was gone.

'Roofshadow!' he called. 'Where's Eatbugs? I thought you were following him!'

The gray fela, licking her wounds, looked back into the empty darkness. A look of shame crossed her green eyes. 'I'm sorry, Tailchaser,' she said softly. 'Pouncequick stepped on something sharp and was limping. I came forward to help him. Eatbugs was right behind us . . . '

Fritti shook his head briskly in frustration and sorrow. 'It's not your fault, Roofshadow. You couldn't have expected it. Here, let me describe the cavern ahead, and the way around the river.'

Roofshadow nodded her head in understanding as he finished. Pouncequick just sat looking quietly at Tailchaser in the growing gloom.

'I hope that I will be able to catch up to you before you leave the Flume,' said Fritti, 'but if not, stay to your right shoulder and bear toward the surface.'

'What do you mean, catch up with us?' asked Roofshadow in confusion.

Seeing the distress on her features, Tailchaser was saddened and could not speak. Pouncequick, unexpectedly, spoke for him.

'He is going back to find Eatbugs,' said the youngling.

Roofshadow was astonished. 'Going back? Tailchaser, you can't. Time is growing shorter and shorter. Don't sacrifice yourself for nothing!'

'It's not for nothing,' Fritti said. 'I must do it. I want you to go. If you can get Pounce and yourself out I will feel better about everything. Now go, please.' He made as if to turn back, but Roofshadow ran and placed herself between Fritti and the tunnel. In her grief she looked more wild than Tailchaser had ever seen her – wilder by far than when she had fought for her own life. She looked as though she had fallen out of step in the earth-dance, and could not find her part.

'Pouncequick!' she cried. 'Tell him not to go. Don't let him just go off chasing Death's tail this way!'

But Pouncequick only looked at her with his old affection, and

242

said: 'He has to go. Don't make it harder for us, please, 'Shadow.'
He turned back to Fritti. 'May you find luck dancing, Tailchaser.
Come back to us if you can.'

Tailchaser had only a moment to marvel at the change in his young
friend. The noises of hatred and conflict winding down the tunnels
brought him to his purpose once more.

'Mri'fa-o, good, good friends,' he said, and would have paused to
sniff them both, but he could not meet Roofshadow's eye. He leaped
past her and ran up the tunnel, back the way they had come.

The outer passages through which they had just passed in relative
safety were again filling with the dark shapes of Claw and Tooth. The
milling beasts seemed to be regaining cohesion, and in Fritti's mind,
this boded badly for Quiverclaw, Fencewalker and the rest. From
above his head – how far above he could not tell – came the scraping,
dragging sound of some huge thing moving in the Upper Catacombs.
This boded far worse. He could easily guess what malign presence
had escaped from the Cavern of the Pit, and was even now shambling
through the upper tunnels. Tailchaser did not suppose that Eatbugs
could have disappeared very far back along the route, but if he
had . . . well, even Fritti's newly found resolve was not strong
enough to take him willingly within reach or sight of the thing above.

Creeping down a cramped passageway – treading softly because of
a group of Clawguard he had spotted, who stood at the forking of
the tunnel not a score of jumps ahead – he was suddenly brought up
short by an unexpected sound: a soft laugh from somewhere close
by. Looking down, he saw a crevice between stone floor and wall. It
was from this that the noise came.

He squatted, keeping an eye on the Clawguard up by the corridor's
splitting point. They were engaged – from what he could discern at
this distance, and in the dim light – in an argument of some sort.
Putting his keen ear down to the crack, Fritti listened closely.

It was not laughter that he had heard, but a strange whimpering.
He pushed his head through into the fissure – his whiskers just fit –
and peered around. A dark shape was huddled down in a small cave
formed in the tunnel wall.

'Eatbugs?' Fritti whispered quietly. If the creature heard him, it
gave no sign. Tailchaser carefully levered himself down into the
cavelet. The darkness inside was nearly complete, and the cave was
so small that Fritti could find no room to stand; he was forced to
crush himself up against the matted, bristly shape.

243

It must be Eatbugs, thought Fritti. *No one else has fur so dirty.*

He gave the sobbing shape a sharp nudge. 'Eatbugs. It's me, Tailchaser. Come on now, I'll get you out of here.'

Fritti prodded the mad cat again, and the whimpering sounds became a disjointed stream of words.

'Trapped, trapped and twitted . . . twitted like the twinkling . . . twinkling . . . oh, there is badness, *os* and f-f-further . . . '

Fritti was disgusted. He might have expected that Eatbugs would have lapsed into this gibbering state. 'Come now,' he said. 'There's no time for this.' His eyes had become better adjusted to the near-absolute blackness; he could just barely make out the tufted, wild-haired form beside him.

' . . . Don't you see, don't you see,' moaned the voice, 'they have suited us with a pelt of stone . . . they have taken the skulls of stones and made us altogether a cage out of it . . . the fitting is too tight. Nether depths, how it *burns!*' On this last, the voice rose until it was nearly a howl. Tailchaser flinched. If this continued they would surely be heard.

His patience now beginning to smolder into fear, Tailchaser seized a mouthful of dirty fur in his teeth and pulled, hard. A paw, with a force like a great stone, pushed him over and pinned him down. His heart leaped. Had he been mistaken? Was this not Eatbugs after all?

That would be the final irony, he thought. *To go following my tail name on a mission of selflessness and then crawl stupidly into a hole with a ravening beast.*

Tailchaser tried to struggle out from beneath the firm grip, but he found he was clutched as securely as a newborn. His efforts caused the thing that held him to turn, and for a moment its face was spotted with faint light from the crevice's opening.

It *was* Eatbugs. The dim light showed his eyes, crazed as cracked ice.

'My blood has called the whirlwind!' Eatbugs shrieked. 'The sucking, spinning thing . . . O, pity me. I am its center, it will never leave me . . . O, even the *void* would be sweet . . . !'

As the last echoes of the cry rolled out into the corridor beyond, Fritti heard the sound of running paws and sharp, questioning voices. They were discovered. He gave one last heave, but Eatbugs – with deranged strength – had caught him fast. He might as well have been pinioned beneath a fallen oak. Helpless. He closed his eyes, and waited for death.

244

Time seemed to slow, as it had before when the Clawguard came out of the night . . . such a long time ago. Drifting, he found something at the edge of his memory, and drew it in to examine. It was the prayer that Quiverclaw had taught him – or, rather, the start of . As his mind lazily examined the fragment of song, part of him still heard the scuffling sounds outside the fissure, and the muffled lamentations of Eatbugs.

The bit of lore floated before his mind's eye . . . Tangaloor, fire-bright . . . yes, that was how it began. How curious, that he should remember it now.

'Tangaloor, fire-bright . . . ' He said it aloud now, and listened to the sweet contrast it made: to the harsh breathing of the beast beside him, and the harsh cries of the beasts without. More of the prayer came unbidden to his voice, more song 'Flame-foot, farthest walker . . . your hunter calls . . . ' What was the last? Oh yes: . . . In need, but never in fear.' That was it.

He sang it again, straight through, oblivious to the gasping of Eatbugs beside him. The Clawguard in the tunnel above were curiously still.

> Tangaloor, fire-bright
> Flame-foot, farthest walker,
> Your hunter speaks
> In need he walks
> In need, but never in fear.

Even with his eyes closed, Fritti was aware of a change. Light was streaming in, shining crimson on the inside of his eyelids. The luminous earth must be aglow again. He opened his eyes . . . but the crevice-glow was as dim as before. Instead, a red brilliance was springing up within the cave itself.

In the darkness, Eatbugs' legs and paws had begun to glow as if they were afire.

Eatbugs began to roll and pitch strangely. The light spread, and the red-lit air itself began to shimmer as if from great heat, but the temperature did not change.

There was a great flash, and a voice like the singing of all the Folk beneath Meerclar's Eye cried out, triumphantly:

'I AM . . . !'

The sheer force of it flung Fritti back; he struck his head against the crevice wall. As he rolled groggily back over he saw that the great light had faded. Eatbugs crouched before him, his body black, nearly invisible – his legs red as fire, red as sunset. The marks of madness and disarray were gone, the fur thick and fine; Eatbugs' eyes stared back at Tailchaser with a wisdom and love and pride such as he had never seen before. There was a sadness, too, that hovered as close as a second pelt. Fritti knew that he was in the presence of all that was great in his race.

'Nre'fa-o, little brother,' Eatbugs said to him – but Fritti knew now that it was Eatbugs no longer: the true ka had come back. The voice was the melody of night, of things that know the old, delicate pattern that earth and her things know. Fritti dropped to his stomach, hiding his eyes behind his paws. He curled himself into a ball.

'No, little brother,' said the wonderful voice, 'you must not do that. You have no need for shame before me – quite the opposite. You have helped me find my way back after a long, dark journey, and in a time of great need. It is I who should bow to you and your efforts.' So saying, Lord Firefoot – for it *was* he – took up Fritti's paw and touched it to his brow. The white star on Fritti's own forehead flared up in the gloom of the small cavern.

'Ah, little one, I followed your special light as Irao Skystone followed the dawn-star into the trackless East,' sang Lord Tangaloor. 'I only hope I have come in time.'

The air in the small place shimmered again, and Lord Firefoot seemed to grow to fill every crevice in the room. 'I must needs settle some old accounts,' he said. 'I have wandered many years, trapped in the prison of my own madness, while my brother nursed his corruption. He has called up powers that the earth was not meant to hold – as I did myself, upon a time. My reasons were better, but still it left me with a wracked shell, and my ka flown far away. Many perversions have been loosed by my brother Hearteater. I must try to put an end to his ways.' The presence seemed to shrink slightly. 'Aahh, and my brother Whitewind must be avenged, too, or never again will his ka rest. Alas, that innocents such as you should be caught up in the doings of the Firstborn. Come now, young Tailchaser, what may I do for you – though naught I try will go far toward equaling my debt? Speak, for soon I must be gone.'

Stunned, Fritti sat for a moment in silence. When he spoke at last he found himself unable to look up at the one before him.

'I wish my friends to escape safely – all the brave Folk who came here.'

The Firstborn was silent, as if staring out over a great distance. When he spoke, his voice was gentle.

'Little brother, many of those brave ones are gone; their kas have fled to the bosom of the Allmother. Even I cannot quicken them, else would have saved mine own brother, who I loved. As for the fela and the youngling, well, I shall try to help, but at this moment they need your presence more than mine. I cannot explain, but it is so.'

Fritti jumped up and scrambled toward the way out, but Firefoot called him back with a laugh.

'It can wait but a moment more, I promise you. I did see something else, another desire that courses strongly in you. You seek someone, although you have lost your search. This search helped lead you to me, so it seems only right that I should aid you.'

Fritti felt as if he were falling into the sky-deep eyes . . . a moment later he was staring wildly from wall to wall: the tiny underground chamber was empty. Then a voice came to him, treading his mind as effortlessly as Hearteater had, but nimbly . . . and with respect.

'*I have given you the knowledge to finish your quest. Would that I could give you more, but I shall have sore need of my resources very shortly. You will be in our thoughts, little brother.*'

The presence was gone, and Fritti was completely alone.

Wondering, he remembered the Clawguard who had been massing outside. When he cautiously lifted his head through the fissure, he discovered the tunnel to be as empty as if it had been undisturbed since the days of Harar. Only several piles of dust, gently sifting in an unexpected cool breeze, spoiled the absolute stillness.

Unable to remember how he had covered the distance or what paths he had followed, Tailchaser found himself mounting the curving path that circumscribed the cavern of the Scalding Flume. The great, boiling river roared as vigorously as ever, and seemed to be striking even higher on the stone walls that penned it. The path before him was masked in mist. Fritti started upward.

The river *did* in fact seem to be leaping to greater heights: the tendrils of water splashed up against the cavern's massive ceiling, then fell back as hissing rain. Despite the poor visibility, Tailchaser moved quickly and surely along the pitted, eroded trail. He had been touched by something far beyond himself, and still felt the buoyant after-effects.

The breeze changed direction, coming about into his whiskers, and

247

in that instant he heard Pouncequick's shrill squeal of fright and
pain.

'Pouncequick, Roofshadow, I'm coming!' Fritti howled. Suddenl
he was leaping along the narrow path, trusting to instincts that h
knew he did not possess in his frenzied hurry to reach his friends
As he skidded around a bend in the narrow trail, scrabbling fo
footing above the booming, steaming waters, he saw his two com
panions ahead. Roofshadow was standing over a bleeding Pounce
quick, struggling fiercely with a great dark creature twice her size
Scratchnail.

The black beast, striped and spotted with blood, turned his ma
eyes toward Tailchaser's approach. A snarling grin curled his wid
face.

'Star-face. Star-face the Tailchaser! I'll kill him someday! I will!
Scratchnail gave out a loud bark of laughter, and Roofshadow fel
back, wounded and panting. Tailchaser bounded grimly forward a
Scratchnail fell into a crouch, thick tail thrashing the air behind him
A rumble from the ceiling stones seemed to pass through the cavern

Fritti pulled up short in the wide part of the path, dropping to
bow-backed hunch several jumps away from the Clawguard. Th
ominous rumble mounted once more above the clamor of the Flume

'Come for me if you want me, Scratchnail,' Tailchaser said, puttin
as much scorn into his voice as he could muster. The Claw-beas
grinned again, and his tail whipped. 'Come for me – if you're throug
fighting kittens, you stone-headed Garrin.' Scratchnail growled an
stood, the short fur on his back rising up like black grass.

'Roofshadow!' Tailchaser cried, above the increasing tumult from
above and below. 'Take Pouncequick and keep moving!'

'He's badly hurt, Tailchaser,' the fela called back. The Clawguar
was moving sinuously down the path toward Fritti, death in eacl
scarlet claw.

'All the more reason to get him to the surface!' Fritti called. 'Thi
is my fight. You've done what you can. Go on!'

Fritti saw Roofshadow and Pouncequick turn and move up th
trail, the kitten stumbling badly. He turned his attention back to th
creature before him.

They faced each other – the small orange cat with the white star
the dark, blood-nailed beast from the earth. Hips and tails wriggling
they stared for a long moment. The Clawguard sprang, and there wa
another great noise from above. In the instant before contact, Fritt

saw showers of small stones come pattering down – then Scratchnail was on him.

Biting and kicking, they rolled over on the narrow causeway, the dark beast's low snarls matched in intensity by Tailchaser's own maddened yowling. They gouged and snapped, then broke apart, walking a constrained circle on their tiny ledge, death-instincts drawing them slowly nearer each other until, leaping, they closed again.

The ritual was repeated over and over. The superior size of Scratchnail was wearing away Fritti's failing strength, but the smaller cat would not let up. They struggled and bit, fell apart, then fell together once more. Both cats moved with the anguished slowness of dark, blind creatures on the bottom of the Bigwater, blind things thrashing in the mud.

Finally, Fritti was overborne, pushed down on the edge of the pathway. His head hung limply, a dizzying drop above the rolling waters. The cavern now reverberated to a ceaseless pounding from the very stones of the roof, as if giant shapes danced above their heads.

Fritti lay motionless. An arching jet of burning-hot liquid shot up past his face. Scratchnail buried his teeth in Tailchaser's nape, gripping tight on the spine. Fritti could feel the mighty jaws closing . . . closing . . . and then the pressure stopped.

The Clawguard had released his hold. He was staring down at Fritti, squat paws on the smaller cat's chest. Something in Scratchnail's eyes changed, and they lost focus.

'Star-face?' he said questioningly. His look of mad hatred seemed to change, to shift into something like fear. 'It really *is* you, Starface?' He seemed to be recognizing Fritti for the first time, as if he had been fighting spirits, shadows that suddenly had become real. Scratchnail's expression began a slow twisting back into hatred.

'You have destroyed me, you little sun-rat,' he snarled. The Clawguard swiveled his head from side to side in confusion, looking up into the farthest reaches of the cavern.

'What has happened?' he screamed. 'What has happened to my . . . '

A hideous, grinding roar, and then a great wave of gray rock passed before Fritti's eyes, obliterating Scratchnail from his sight. Then this too was gone; suddenly, Tailchaser was alone on the ledge. Painfully turning his head, he saw the last of the sliding rocks career down the sloping stone wall below him and, with a great splash, disappear into the swollen river. Of Scratchnail there was not a trace.

Fritti pulled himself upright and clambered laboriously over the broken remains of the avalanche, then went limping up the winding path. The cavern was shaking in earnest now; the water below leaped and danced in mighty spouts that climbed toward the cavern's roof. The heat was oppressive: Tailchaser had to exercise all his resolve not to lie down where he was and not move again.

He reached a tunnel leading out. Behind him, the cavern of the Flume was threatening to shake itself to pieces. He numbly put one foot in front of the other and trudged on until he could walk no farther, then fell prone to the tunnel floor. He could dimly see what seemed by happy fancy to be a patch of sky. The tunnel walls, too, were quivering.

How funny, he thought distractedly. *Everyone knows there is no sky below the ground . . . !*

The last noise he heard was a rending crash from the cavern below. It sounded as if every tree in Ratleaf had fallen at the same time. Then the tunnel collapsed behind him.

CHAPTER THIRTY

Poor intricated soul! Riddling, perplexed
labyrinthical soul!

– John Donne

pring was bursting and crawling, pushing forth irreverent scents
nd smells – the very ground beneath Tailchaser's back was warm
ith activity and renewed life. Soon he would get up and stroll back
o his nest, to his box on the porch of the M'an-dwelling . . . but for
ow he was content to sprawl on the grass. A breeze ruffled up his
ur. He waved his legs carelessly in the air, enjoying the cooling
ffect. Eyes closed, a long day of Squeaker-dandling and tree-scuffing
ehind him, he felt as though he could lie this way forever.

The feathering wind brought a tiny squeak, faint as the gleeful cry
f a vole finding vole-treasure deep within the earth. Deep, deep
ithin the earth. Again the cry came – louder, now – and Fritti
ought he heard his name. Why would anyone want to disturb him?
e tried to recapture his pleasant reverie, but the imploring voice
ecame more insistent. The breeze increased, singing past his whis-
ers and ears. Why should his perfect day be spoiled? It sounded
ke Hushpad, or Roofshadow: felas were all alike, treating you like
n old stoat until they needed you, then following you around and
owling as if they'd hurt themselves. Ever since he had brought
ushpad back from . . . from . . . where had he found her? It hadn't
een more than an Eye ago, since . . .

'Tailchaser!' That cry again. His brow furrowed, but he would *not*
ondescend to open his eyes. Well . . . maybe just to take one quick
ook . . .

Why couldn't he see anything? Why was it all black?

The voice cried out again, sounding as though it were disappearin
down a long, dark tunnel . . . or as if he were falling awa
himself . . . into the darkness . . .

The light! *Where was the light?*

Somebody – or something – was licking his face. A harsh, insister
tongue rasped across the sorest parts of his mask, but when he trie
to pull his head away, that pain was worse. He lay back, resigne
and after a while little spots of light began to appear before his eye
He could make no sense of these swirling, leaping points, but h
nose finally distinguished a scent that was familiar. The floating spec
began to coalesce; like tall grass pushed aside by a paw, the blackne
slid away.

Roofshadow, with a look of fierce concentration, was washing h
muzzle with her rough pink tongue. Fritti could not focus his ey
well – she was very close, and the effort was painful – but her sm
confirmed it. He spoke her name, and was surprised when she d
not react. He tried again, and this time she drew back and stare
then called out to someone he could not yet see: 'He's awake!!'

Fritti tried to greet her, to tell her how glad he was to see her
the fields of the living – if that was where he was – but before I
could do more than make a sound, he slipped back into darkne
again.

When he awoke later, Roofshadow had been joined by a larg
shaggy red cat. It took him a long time to recognize Prince Fenc
walker.

'What . . . what . . . ' His voice was very weak. He swallowe
'What happened? Are we . . . on top of the ground?'

Roofshadow leaned forward, green eyes warm. 'Don't try to tall
she said soothingly. 'You're safe. Fencewalker brought you ou
Fritti felt a weak, irrational stab of jealousy.

'Where's Pouncequick?' he asked.

'You'll see him soon,' she said, and looked up at the Princ
Fencewalker beamed down with bluff good spirits.

'Worried about you. Didn't think . . . just worried, we were. Wh
a row, what a row. Fabulous tussle.' The Prince seemed about
give Fritti a good-natured thump. Roofshadow moved betwe
Fencewalker and his intended victim, who was already tiring.

'Just sleep, and let Meerclar mend,' she said. Tailchaser reluctant
let go his grip on wakefulness. So many questions . . .

*

252

Fritti found healing in the dream-fields. He soon found that he could sit up, although it dizzied him. A determined self-inventory found no serious wounds. His numerous cuts had stopped bleeding, and Roofshadow's patient ministrations had cleaned the worst of the matted blood from his short fur. His eyes were swollen – he had trouble opening them more than halfway – but generally he was in good condition.

Roofshadow did not want to answer his questions yet, and would sit patiently silent as he pressed her for information. Fencewalker dropped by frequently to see Tailchaser as he recuperated, but his roving temperament made it difficult for him to sit and talk long. His visits were hearty, but brief.

Fritti's dreams had not been entirely wrong. The ground *was* warm. The distant reaches of Ratleaf Forest were capped in snow, a white mantle extending into the misty horizon, but the fringe of the forest in which Tailchaser had awakened was green and wet – the thin carpet of grass humid and damp, as though the snow had been suddenly melted away by a hot sun. Roofshadow said that all the area round the mound was that way, but that she thought the snow would return eventually. It was, after all, still the ragtag end of winter.

Days went by, and before long Fritti was up and walking. He and Roofshadow explored the prematurely green forest, padding together through the sodden false spring. Here and there a solitary fla-fa'az could be heard singing bravely in the treetops.

Fritti still had not seen Pouncequick, but Roofshadow promised to take him soon. Pounce, too, was recovering, she said, and should not be excited.

Here and there in the unseasonal greenery the startled faces of other Folk would appear, gaunt and staring-eyed. Most of those who had made their way to freedom during the dying Hours of the mound had lingered only a short while, leaving to search for better hunting or to return to home grounds. No spirit of fellowship seemed to tie these survivors: they drifted off one by one as they became strong enough to travel. Only the sick – and the dying – remained with Fencewalker's band of hunters, and soon even the Prince would lead most of his party back to the wooded bowers of Firsthome. A small guard would be mounted to stay and keep watch on the site.

Seeing these survivors, Fritti wondered aloud about the fate of the uncounted multitudes, masters and slaves, who had not escaped.

253

Hearing this, Roofshadow told Fritti as best she could of the fina[l] Hour in Vastnir.

'When we left you with that . . . beast,' she said, 'I never expecte[d] to see you again. It seemed as if the world was coming to pieces[.] She walked silently for a while. Fritti tried to say something reassur[ing], but she stopped him with a curiously stern look.

'Pounce was half dead, bleeding. I pulled him up the last tunne[l] by the neck. Things were falling, crashing . . . it sounded like gian[t] creatures fighting. Finally, we made it out of that place, out into th[e] valley; it was covered with snow. There were others there, too, millin[g] and crying. We were like lost kas, stumbling, falling in the snow[.] The ground was shaking.'

Their walk had taken them out to the rim of Ratleaf. Before the[m] stretched the rising plain, slick with melted snow, droplets gleamin[g] on the leaves of stunted vegetation. Roofshadow led on, continuin[g] her story.

'I saw someone dashing about, making loud noises and leadin[g] Folk to and fro . . . it was Fencewalker, of course. I caught up wit[h] him and told him what had happened. I'm afraid I was rather ears[t] back at that point, but the Prince understood. He said, "Tailchaser[?] Young Tailchaser?" – Fencewalker's not so very old, but he acts a[s] if he'd like to be. Anyway, he said: "Can't have that, not you[ng] Tailchaser, must do something, by all means!" You know how h[e] talks. Well, he gathered up a few of the healthier Folk and I led the[m] all back to the tunnel. I stayed with Pouncequick, whose . . . wh[o] was very weak and sick.'

'They found you half buried under dirt and rocks, and carried yo[u] out just before the rest of the place shook itself down. I didn't kno[w] you were alive for a very long time. I hadn't been able to bear waitin[g] to find out.'

Fritti was stepping over a twisted root, and missed the expressio[n] on the gray fela's face. Stopping for a moment to shake dry a soppin[g] paw, he asked: 'What do you mean when you say the place shoo[k] itself apart? I'm afraid I don't remember the end very well.'

'I'm going to show you,' said Roofshadow.

They toiled awhile longer up the sloping plain, wrapped in though[t.] At last they reached the edge of the valley in which the mound ha[d] stood.

Where Vastnir had once pushed its brooding head up through th[e] valley floor there was now a wide, shallow basin – the ground sunke[n] as if beneath the tread of a league-wide paw. The soil was as black as the wing of a Krauka.

On the way back to Ratleaf, Fritti asked again to see Pouncequick. He has been with me longer than anyone, 'Shadow,' he pointed out.

She seemed disturbed by his use of the shortened name.

'I never tried to prevent you, Tailchaser,' she said unhappily. 'I just suggested what I thought best. . . . He's gotten very strange,' she added after a moment.

'Who could blame him, after what he's been through?' countered Fritti. 'Who could blame any of us?'

'I know, Tailchaser. Poor Pouncequick. And Eatbugs, too.' Fritti looked at her, wondering, but Roofshadow was shaking her head sadly. 'I haven't asked yet, but I suppose I know,' she said. 'He was . . . well, you were too late to help him, weren't you?'

Fritti balanced his secret and decided to keep it. 'By the time I found him . . . Eatbugs was gone.'

And that is mostly true, he thought.

'Such sad times,' said Roofshadow. 'I suppose I should take you to Pouncequick. Tomorrow, all right?' Fritti bobbed approval. 'I didn't know him,' she continued. 'Eatbugs, I mean. Understand, I intend no disrespect, Tailchaser, but you have the *oddest* friends and acquaintances!'

Fritti laughed. 'I'll race you back,' he said, and they ran like wildfire.

The muted advent of Spreading Light brought Fencewalker and other guests in its train.

Fritti, pulled taut in a walking stretch, spotted the Prince swaggering through the underbrush, moisture gleaming on his shaggy form. At his side stalked the graceful black form of Quiverclaw. A cry of pleasure from Tailchaser was followed by warm greetings all around, and the three cats, two large, one small, sprawled contentedly and conversed.

'I hear that Stretchslow's confidence in you was amply filled, Tailchaser.'

Quiverclaw's grave words made Fritti want to wriggle with pleasure, but the demands of maturity won out over indulgence. 'I am honored that great hunters like the Prince and yourself think so, Thane. I must admit that most of the time I was in that place I would have settled for a quick, painless death. I truly would have.'

'Ah, but you didn't, did you?' crowed Fencewalker. 'That's the nose-biter!'

'And from what I hear, sent for help by squirrel,' smiled Quiverclaw. 'Unusual, but effective.'

This time, Tailchaser's wriggle escaped suppression. 'I thank you both,' he said. 'The main thing, though, is that you came. I saw it; it was wonderful.' Fritti sobered. 'I also saw . . . that thing that Hearteater called up. Horrible . . . it was horrible.'

Quiverclaw nodded. 'Things like that were not meant to be. Already I have trouble remembering what it looked like, so *wrong* it was. The *os* given flesh – I suppose that soon I will be thankful I cannot recall its aspect. But it caused grave loss. Squeakerbane, Harar bless his mighty heart, fell before it – he and others beyond my reckoning.'

'Did . . . is Hangbelly . . . dead?' asked Fritti quietly. Quiverclaw pondered silently for a moment, then lifted his head with a crooked grin.

'Hangbelly? He was grievously injured . . . but he will live.' The Thane chuckled. 'It will take more than even that terror to kill old Bounce-Gut.'

Fritti was pleased to hear of the fat First-walker's survival. Fencewalker smiled, but looked uncharacteristically morose.

'Many, many brave Folk fell,' said the Prince. 'The world will not see a gathering of the Folk like that for many seasons – more seasons than the forest has tree trunks. Many good fellows never came up from the ground again. . . . Bah!' Fencewalker's pink nose twitched in sorrow and disgust. 'Snaremouse, and young Furscuff . . . Pokesnout . . . the Thanes, scrawny old Sourweed and Squeakerbane . . . Dayhunter and Nightcatcher, my fine lads – they died protecting me, you know – they are all down in the cold earth, and we sit in the sun.' Visibly upset, the Prince turned away and curried his tail. Fritti and Quiverclaw stared at the ground between their paws. Tailchaser's nose felt hot and itchy.

'But . . . but what did Hearteater mean to do?' Fritti finally blurted out. 'Why did it all happen? Meerclar,' he breathed, the thought occurring to him for the first time, 'Lord Hearteater *is* . . . gone, isn't he? Dead?' He looked anxiously at the Thane.

'We think so,' Quiverclaw said seriously. 'We have talked about it, the Prince and I. If nothing else, we must be able to tell the Queen of the outcome. Yes, we think Hearteater is gone. Nothing could have survived that final Hour.'

Fencewalker, who had straightened up, said, 'Oh, aye, *that* was a real whisker-bender!'

'What happened?' asked Fritti.

'Well,' intoned Quiverclaw, 'when the Fikos-thing came up from the pit we tried to fight. It was laying about fiercely, though; we were forced to retreat from the cavern.'

'Retreat?' shouted Fencewalker. 'Ran! Tail over whiskers like spooked Squeakers! And who could blame you?'

'Some stayed to fight, my Prince . . . like Squeakerbane.' Chastened, Fencewalker waved a paw for the Thane to continue.

'Anyway, we fell back into the outer chambers. There we met the Prince and his Folk, who had breached the minor gate. The Fikos forced its way out of the cavern, but did not seem to have purpose – it was destroying anything in its path, friend or foe. It seemed mindless. Following some urge, it shambled up one of the main corridors – that was all that saved us from complete rout, I think. Everything was chaos, Folk fighting and dying – '

Fencewalker interrupted, 'It began to get dark, don't forget that.'

Quiverclaw nodded gravely. 'Indeed. It was as though that huge monstrous thing – or maybe Hearteater himself – was drawing in all the light . . . taking a deep breath of light . . . I can't explain. We were fighting in the deepest blackness, then something . . . something like sky-fire, but underground . . . shot through the chamber, burning and crackling as it went by. Straight through, and into Hearteater's cavern, as if it had a will. I have never seen the like.'

Fritti felt a strong joy deep inside himself. 'I wish I could have seen it.'

'From where we made our stand we could see the light bursting from Hearteater's chamber as if the sun had rolled down into a hole in the ground. The earth around us began to shake. There were great hissings and boomings, like . . . like the sky was tumbling down, or the forest was dancing above our heads. Fencewalker shouted out to run, to get all the Folk out – '

'That's true,' the Prince inserted.

' – and everyone went racing for the tunnels leading out. Hearteater's creatures were running in circles like berry-drunk fla-fa'az, screeching and clawing at one another . . . it was a sight that will live before my dream-eyes forever.'

'It was all falling down, then,' said Fencewalker. 'Falling down, and scalding mist and waters coming up through the floors . . . what a tumble that was for the Firstborn, eh? Who would have dared think of it?'

Tailchaser reflected on all he had heard. So much to think about. Should he try to explain what had happened to him? Was he even sure what had happened?

'Why?' he asked, finally. 'What did Hearteater want?'

'We may never know, really,' said the Thane, furrowing his pitchy brow. 'Lord Hearteater, we can suppose, wanted revenge on the descendants of Harar. He had been long beneath the earth, and had been brooding since time beyond tail-tips on bringing the Folk under his sway. He must have been wearying of his poor copies of Meerclar's children, and their bobbing and scuttling . . . but he *was* of the Firstborn, and I do not think his purposes – or madnesses – will be wholly knowable to us. He called on things outside the earth-dance; it seems that a balance was disturbed. The dance is complicated, and a disturbance on the one side creates counter-disturbance.' The Thane laughed. 'I can see Fencewalker staring at me as if I had the foaming-mouth sickness. He's right, you know, Tailchaser – there's not much point in singing the song if you have to guess at the words.'

Quiverclaw was interrupted again, this time by a high-pitched chattering from the treetops. Fencewalker and the Thane exchanged a glance.

'Teats on a tom!' groaned Fencewalker ruefully. 'I'd forgotten.'

'It sounds as if they are aware of that,' said Quiverclaw, as the angry noises resumed. 'Please, Lord Pop!' he called. 'Forgive us our discourtesy and come down. We have been careless of time.'

A procession of Rikchikchik – Lord Pop in the lead, a disdainful expression on his round, toothy face – shinnied single-file down the trunk of a poplar. Although Pop himself wore a look of insulted dignity, the rest of his train appeared goggle-eyed and nervous in the presence of the three cats.

Lord Pop drew the crowd to a halt. His own nose, however, remained pointing conspicuously skyward until Prince Fencewalker made an embarrassed coughing noise.

'Terribly sorry, Pop. Really am. Didn't mean any offense against Rikchikchik. We just forgot, you see.' Fritti wondered if the Prince's discomfiture was due to his mistake, or having to apologize to squirrels.

The Rikchikchik chief eyed the uncomfortable Prince for a moment. 'Only came to tell so-brave Tail-chase cat,' he said, a little huffily. The squirrel-lord then turned to Fritti. 'Pledge kept, you see-

see. Rikchikchik do right. Now, must bring more Rikchikchik back-back. Badness most gone.' Pop performed a jerky head-bob, and Fritti returned it.

'Your folk are very brave, Lord Pop,' he said. 'Is that Master Plink? You did well, courageous Plink.' The young Rikchikchik buck fluffed his tail; the other Rikchikchik chittered admiringly. Lord Pop also clucked approval.

'Squirrels . . . ' mumbled Prince Fencewalker. Pop fixed him with a bright eye.

'Tell Tailchaser what we have declared, Fencewalker,' prompted Quiverclaw.

'Well . . . ' said the Prince, embarrassed again, 'well . . . Dewclaws! You say it, Quiverclaws. It was your idea,' he finished peevishly.

'Well,' assented the Thane, 'it has been declared by Prince Fence-walker, son of Her Befurred Majesty, Queen Mirmirsor Sunback, that in recognition of their service the Rikchikchik may live unhunted by the Folk within the confines of Ratleaf, and that the First-walkers will enforce this ban to the best of their powers.' Tiny whistles of approval came from Lord Pop's entourage. 'Of course, outside the bounds of Ratleaf you had better look to your tail-plumes,' Quiver-claw added in a not unfriendly way. Lord Pop looked at Quiverclaw appraisingly, and made a satisfied clucking sound.

'So,' chirped the squirrel-lord. 'Now all done-done.' He turned back to Fritti. 'Nut-gathering luck, so-strange cat.' Lord Pop faced around and led his rump-bobbling procession back into the branches. Within a moment they were gone.

'I'm sorry, but it just doesn't seem proper,' grumped Fencewalker. 'Squirrels . . . '

When Smaller Shadows arrived, Roofshadow came to take Fritti to Pouncequick. She led him away from Fencewalker's camp into a grove of cloud-tall trees. When he saw Pouncequick's pale, fluffy shape in a patch of sunlight at the center of the stand, Fritti pulled away from her and dashed forward.

'Pounce!' he called. 'Little cu'nre!' Pouncequick looked up at the sound of his voice, and rose – with a grace belying his kittenhood. Tailchaser was on him in a moment, sniffing and head-butting, and Pouncequick's aloofness gave way briefly to pleased wriggling.

'I'm so pleased to see you finally!' Tailchaser declared as he circled his friend, smelling the familiar Pouncequick scents. 'I never dreamed that we could all be together once – '

Fritti broke off, staring gape-jawed in shock.

Pouncequick had no tail! Where his furry plume had once waved there was now only a healing stump, curled tightly against the youngling's haunches.

'Oh, Pounce!' Fritti breathed. 'Oh, Pounce, your poor tail! Harar!'

Roofshadow stepped forward. 'I'm sorry I didn't tell you, Tailchaser. I wanted you to see that Pouncequick was alive and healthy first, or you would have been sick with worry when you yourself were in need of healing.'

Pouncequick pulled a quiet smile. 'Please, don't be so upset, Tailchaser. We all lost things and gained things in that place. When you attacked Scratchnail in the Flume cavern you saved me from worse than this.'

Fritti did not feel comforted. 'If only I'd arrived sooner . . . ' he groaned. Pouncequick met his eye with a knowing look.

'You couldn't have,' said the tailless catling. 'You know that you could not have. We all played our part. A tail is a small thing to lose so that one can find a tail name.' Pounce's face took on a distant expression, and Roofshadow gave Fritti a worried look.

'What do you mean, Pounce?' Fritti asked.

'We freed the White Cat,' said Pouncequick dreamily. 'I saw him. I saw him in his sorrow, and I saw him in his joy – when the mound fell. He has returned to the dark body of the Allmother.' The kitten shook his head as if to clear it. 'We all lost something, but gained something far greater' – he looked pointedly at Roofshadow – 'even if we do not yet know it.'

Fritti stared at his small friend, who was making dreamspeech like a Far-senser. Pouncequick caught his look, and his small mask crinkled with warmth and affection.

'Oh, Tailchaser,' he giggled, 'you look so comical! Come, let us go find something to eat.'

As they walked, Pouncequick spoke raptly of Whitewind.

' . . . There is something, after all, in what Dewtreader said. A fela will sacrifice herself for her kittens; you were willing to give yourself for us.'

'It wasn't that simple, Pounce,' said Tailchaser uncomfortably.

'Viror wants us to be whole, I think,' the kitten continued, 'but Dewtreader . . . well, Prince Dewtreader sees many things, but I think he is too gloomy. Whitewind always loved to run, to feel the wind in his fur – he doesn't want his children to brood and grow mystical, only to remember that if they are not willing to give back the gift he has given them – *at any time* – then the gift will do them no good.'

'I'm afraid that all your dreaming and thinking has put you far beyond my ideas, Pounce,' said Tailchaser. Roofshadow was grimacing.

'But you yourself taught me the most, Tailchaser!' said Pouncequick, amused. He stopped to turn over a fallen branch, sending a startled bug scurrying away. With a leap and a bound the catling had imprisoned the scuttling insect; in another moment he had crunched it up.

'Anyway . . . ' Pouncequick spoke with a full mouth. 'I have decided to go back to stay at Firsthome. There are many wise ones there – including the Prince Consort – and I have much to learn.'

Like cautious parents, Roofshadow and Tailchaser paced silently behind the frisking Pouncequick.

CHAPTER THIRTY-ONE

The best is like water.
Water is good; it benefits all things and does not compete with them.
It dwells in places that all disdain. That is why it is so near the Tao.

— Lao-tzu

While his body slept, packed snugly between Pouncequick and Roof-shadow, Tailchaser met Lord Tangaloor in the darkness of the dream-fields. The legs of the Firstborn smoldered with rosy light, and his voice was music.

'Greetings, little brother,' said Firefoot. 'I find you in better spirits than when we last spoke.'

'You do, my lord.'

'Why have you not then set out to finish your quest? I have told you where you may find what you seek. Your troubled ka tells me that you need to discover this resolution.'

In the shadowy spaces of sleep, Fritti heard the truth in Firefoot's words. 'I suppose it is only because of my friends,' he said. 'I fear that they will need me.'

A low, pleasant laugh welled up from the Firstborn. 'My little brothers and sisters are strong, Tailchaser. Our Folk do not let love bind them that way. The strong meet in strength.' The shadowed form of Tangaloor began to fade away, and Fritti cried out.

'Wait! Forgive me, lord, but I would like to ask you another thing.'

'By my mother!' laughed the Firstborn. 'You have grown passing bold, young Tailchaser. What would you know?'

'The mound. What happened there? Is Hearteater gone?'

The presence of Firefoot was suddenly all around him, comforting and tangible.

'His power is broken, little brother. There was nothing left of him

262

ut hatred, anyway. He had festered in darkness too long; he had no ther purpose. Blind and immobile, he could never have come up rom below the ground – the sun would have burned him away.'

'Do you mean there was no danger, then – to *our* fields?' Fritti sked, confused.

Firefoot's singing voice grew serious. 'Not that at all, little cat. There was great danger. His creations were all too real. The Fikos tself was a creation of pure hatred, birthed to go where he could not - above the ground, to stalk crookedly beneath the sun. . . . Oh yes, t was fell indeed, and would have made the daylight fields a horror hat Hearteater's children alone could have trod with impunity. And ven if they themselves could not, what did my brother care – so ong as no other of Meerclar's creatures could savor the sweet steps f the earthdance?'

The voice of Firefoot was growing faint now; Fritti had to prick orward his dream-ears to make it out: 'Like all ancient, unreasoning atreds, the Fikos was mindless, all-destroying . . . if I had not been rought back from the outer reaches, it would have been beyond the ower of the bravest Folk to halt it.'

'Lord Firefoot!' Fritti called after the vanishing dream. 'Pounce-quick said that your brother was freed!'

' . . . *Lord Viror suffered for eternities* . . . ' murmured the fast-dwindling spark of red. '*Now, the balance has been set right. . . . Look o the skies, little brother. . . . Good journeying!*'

Fritti sat bolt upright. On either side his companions protested sleep-ly. Craning his neck, he gazed up into the sable sky of the Final Dancing. 'Look to the skies,' Firefoot had said. Fritti's spirit sang vith the wonder of it all.

Above the U'ea-ward horizon, couched like a dewdrop on the petal f a black rose, gleamed a star that Tailchaser had never seen before. t burned and shone – a white fire against the belly of Meerclar.

Roofshadow was going back to Firsthome with Pouncequick.

'I wish to see him safely there, at least,' she told Fritti as they took final walk together. 'Also, if any of my clan escaped the destruction f Vastnir they will return to our lands in Northern Rootwood. I vish to see if any of them yet live.'

Fencewalker's party was setting out for the Seat of Sunback at sun-ext. The chill winds of winter had resumed; snow had begun to reep back over the cooling outskirts of the mound.

'If I did not know already of your desire to finish your quest,' said Roofshadow, stopping to look into Fritti's eyes, 'well, then I would ask you to come with me. But I know you cannot.'

As she spoke, Tailchaser watched her proud, fine face. Her whiskers caught the morning brightness.

'I know that Pouncequick may be less needy of our attention than we suppose,' said Fritti kindly. 'I wish I could come with you. It seems strange that our adventures should end this way.'

Roofshadow continued to hold Tailchaser's eye. He felt a deep love for this she-hunter who would not spare her own feelings.

'My name is Firsa Roofshadow,' she said quietly. Surprised, Tailchaser felt his heart beat several times in the silence. She had told him her heart name!

'Mine . . . mine is Fritti Tailchaser,' he said at last.

'Allmother keep you, Fritti. I will think of you often.'

'I hope I can see you again one day . . . Firsa.'

Her heart name! He did not even know Hushpad's!

All the long walk back, Tailchaser's thoughts swirled in confusion.

Prince Fencewalker, impatience treading close in his pawprints, walked back and forth calling out directions and suggestions.

'Come now! Enough grooming, lads! Finish that up and bend leg, Pawgentle. Time to take to our traveling pads!' Many Folk milled about the Prince. The long march back to Rootwood was about to begin.

Fritti had already said his farewells to Fencewalker and the others. The Prince had given them an affectionate head-butt, saying: 'Traipsing off again, are you? Traipsingest little whisker-washer I ever knew! Well, be sure to come see me at the Court. We'll bend the ears of those sit-on-tails then!'

Quiverclaw, who was setting out for the Thane-meet that would name the successors of those fallen in the mound, had also stopped to say a fond good-journey.

Now Fritti sat with his two closest friends, and was suddenly tired of leave-taking. Sniffing Roofshadow's cheek, he rubbed his face against her warm, soft fur and said nothing.

'I will not say I hope to see you, because I know I will,' said Pouncequick. With all his newfound insight, still the little cat looked forlorn. Tailchaser relented and nuzzled him for a moment.

'I'm sure I will see you both,' he said calmly. 'Nre'fa-o, my two friends.'

Fencewalker was bellowing final instructions to the assembled Folk; here was a great murmuring. Tailchaser turned away and walked back toward Ratleaf Forest and the resumption of his own journey. The cold breeze rattled the branches.

Beyond the fringes of the now-dwindling thaw, Ratleaf was still winter-deep in cold. A solitary figure in the endless whiteness of the forest, Tailchaser wondered about the transfiguration of his small friend Pouncequick. His thoughts were accompanied only by the soft plishing of his pads denting the snow mantle.

Pouncequick *had* changed. Although he could still caper and play as a youngling was expected to, and although he certainly hadn't lost his kittenish appetite, still there was a quality of innocence no longer present. Several times while watching little Pouncequick talk like a grizzled elder, his tiny body shortened by the length of a tail, Fritti felt a wave of deep, inexplicable sadness.

The lost tail did not seem to bother Pouncequick as much as it did Fritti. The idea of his small friend being mauled and torn by Scratchnail disturbed him greatly, and he worried the thought like a slow-healing wound.

'It's very strange, Tailchaser,' Pounce had told him, 'but it feels as though it's still there. I don't miss it. I can feel it right this moment curling behind me – I can even feel the wind on it!' Tailchaser had not known what to say, and the youngling continued: 'In some ways, it's better now. What I mean is . . . well, since I can't see it, and nothing can happen to it, it's perfect: pure. And it always will be, too. Can you sense what I mean?'

Fritti had not been able to that day. But now, padding quietly through the great forest, he began to understand.

Days passed with the sameness of one tree to another as Fritti moved Vez'an-ward through Ratleaf. The words of the Firstborn led him on.

'*Follow your nose to your heart's desire*' Firefoot had told him in their last moment in the mound, '*through the great forest with the sun-birth in your eyes. Your way will lead you out, finally, and across the Pawdab Marshes, to arrive at last on the shores of Qu'cef – the Bigwater. You will follow the shore until you see a strange hill that shines at night . . . it rises from the waters themselves. This is the place that the M'an calls Villa-on-Mar, and there you will find what you seek.*'

*

Now the cycles of day and night, traveling and sleeping, all the othe
hunt-marks of the world above-ground came back to Tailchaser. H
had only himself to hunt for, and only himself to be responsible for
Like the silver pril fish that leaped and splashed upstream in th
heights of the Caterwaul, so the suns of Fritti's journey bounde
across the sky, one following closely upon the other. In this way h
journeyed through Ratleaf.

The old forest was slowly coming back to life. The cave-sleepin
Garrin came grumbling up from their rest. The graceful Tesri, buck
and does and a few stilting fawns, ran delicately on the drifts. Tail
chaser felt his affinity for this world come flowing back; the horror
of the mound began to recede. He was one of the earth's children
and even the long season below the ground could not destroy hi
knowledge of the dance. He reveled in every sign of fading winter
and of the return of life to once-haunted Ratleaf.

Twenty suns had risen and set since he had left his friends whe
Tailchaser at last found himself approaching the far edge of the forest
The last two days' journeying had brought him to a place where th
land began to slope gently downward, and the air beneath the grea
trees had a strange tang. Every breath was filled with moisture – no
hot, like the great Flume, but cool as stone, salty as blood. He ha
never scented anything like it. Every inhalation quickened his heart

Coming down the last highlands of Ratleaf one morning, Fritt
became aware of a great, slow sound. Like the contented purring o
the Allmother, it rose up through the vegetation below him, vast an
dignified. As he paused for a moment along the spare trees of th
Ratleaf fence, he could see something gleaming before him. A secon
sun, a twin to the herald of Smaller Shadows which hung low in th
sky, seemed to shine up at him through a gap in the uneven tootl
of the forest fringe.

Abandoning his grooming, Fritti climbed to his feet and padde
farther down, tail waving in the slight breeze like a willow limb. A
he neared the gap he saw that it was not another sun, but a reflectio
– impossibly huge. He stood between two ancient redwoods an
gazed out across the swiftly dropping slope, across the beginning o
the marshes. He caught his breath.

The Bigwater, burnished like wind-polished rock, stretched awa
to the horizon. Mighty Qu'cef, as red-golden as Fencewalker, hel
and returned the burning reflection of the sun like a glowing mote i

he eye of the Harar. Qu'cef's sounding call – patient and hugely calm – floated up to the promontory where he stood transfixed.

He watched all morning as the eye of the sun rose into the sky, and the Bigwater became in turn golden, then green, and finally at smaller Shadows took on the deep blue of a nighttime sky. Then, with Qu'cef's unanswerable voice still filling his ears and thoughts, he resumed his descent down into the marshes.

The Pawdab Marshes stretched from the shores of Qu'cef southward, flanking Ratleaf Forest on her Vez'an edge until they ended at last on the banks of the Caterwaul. The marshes were flat and chill, and the wet, spongy ground sank beneath Tailchaser's paws as he walked. Never, from the time that he entered Pawdab until he finally left it again, were his paws dry.

For days on end the salt-scent of the Bigwater was in his nose and its voice in his ears. Like the sound of his mother's purr when he had been a nursling, the call of Qu'cef was the first thing he heard when he woke up; the roaring of the waves lulled him to sleep at night, coming to him across the great marsh as he lay curled in a bed of reeds.

The marshes, too, had sensed the loosening grip of winter. Fritti was able to make many a meal on marsh-mouse and mudrat, and other, stranger creatures that proved nonetheless good to eat. Often at his approach unfamiliar birds would start up screaming from their nests hidden in the weeds, but Fritti – hunger sated – would only stand and watch them fly, marveling at their bright colors.

At the end of a fading afternoon, a successful hunt behind him, Fritti found himself walking beside a large, still pond that lay in the midst of the marshland, hemmed all about by tall grasses and reeds. The failing sun had turned the Qu'cef golden in the distance, and the pond itself seemed a pool of still fire.

Crouching down, Tailchaser scented the water. It smelled of salt; he did not drink. Fresh water was scarce on the Pawdab. Although he was well fed, he was often thirsty.

Now, leaning over the pond, he saw a strange thing: a cat, dark-furred, but with a star-mark like his own, looked up at him from underneath the water. Surprised, he leaped back – as he did, the water-cat took fright also, and disappeared. When he moved slowly back, the other peered cautiously up at him through the still waters. His hackles standing, Tailchaser hissed at the stranger – who did likewise – but as he crouched, a rock, dislodged by his paw, fell into the pond. Where it struck, circular ripples marred the surface of the pondwater in an ever-widening ring. Before his eyes the water-cat fell to pieces, floating shards, and was gone. Only when the face of the stranger re-formed, wearing a look of astonishment matching his own, did Fritti realize that it was no real beast, but a spirit or watershadow that mimicked his every movement.

Is this what I look like, then? he wondered. *This slender youngling is me?*

He sat for a long while staring silently at the pond-Fritti, until the sun's final disappearance blackened the surface of the pool. Meerclar's Eye appeared above, and the air was filled with the busy chaos of flying insects.

As if he were dreaming, he heard a sound, a low sound, above the distant murmur of the Bigwater. A voice was raised in droning song – an odd voice, deep yet small, charged with odd dissonances.

> ' . . . *Around it goes, then up and around around* . . .
> *Bugs blackly, bleakly bring the blinded, sing the sound*
> *Hope, the heart's hearth, now harshly, hardly has heard*
> *How round it goes, goes round, goes round the word* . . . '

Fritti stood wondering. Who could it be, singing such a song in the wilds of Pawdab? He walked quietly through the reeds circling the edge of the pond, following the voice to its source on the far side. As he crept through the waving stalks the song rose again:

> ' . . . *Goggle, they goggle, glaring at the gleaming goad,*
> *As wondering a-wander, they walk a-widdershins the winding road* . . .
> *Now the nameless notice how, not knowing, they had never heard.*
> *How round it goes, goes round, goes round, goes round the word* . . . '

As the chugging voice failed again, Tailchaser approached the spot that seemed to be its source. He could smell no unusual scent, only the marsh salts and the reek of mud. He waved away a crowd of hovering water-flies with his tail and pushed through the weeds.

Crouched at the edge of the pool was a great, green frog – throat swelling and shrinking, belly mired in the mud. As Tailchaser approached slowly from behind, the frog did not turn, but only said: 'Welcome, Tailchaser. Come to sit and talk.'

Bemused, Fritti walked around and sat on a mat of broken stems on the muddy shoal. It seemed *everybody* knew his name and business.

'I heard your song,' he said. 'How do you know me? Who are you?'

'Mother Rebum am I. My people are old. I am the oldest.' As she spoke she blinked her great eyes. 'Here in the marsh we Jugurum know all. Blood and water, stone and bone. My grandmother sat by this pond eating flies when dogs flew and cats swam.'

Without changing expression or moving from her crouch, Mother Rebum – as if in imitation of her ancestor – spat out a long gray tongue and – *snip!* – pulled in a gnat. Swallowing, she continued.

'Padding-paws, I have heard you in my marsh for five suns. The foolish seagulls have carried word of you as you walked up and down through the mudfields. Flea and fly will bring back mention of you when you have passed. Nothing that treads the Burum-gurgun escapes the attention of old Mother Rebum.'

Fritti stared at the immense frog. Silver Eye-light dappled her rough back. 'What song were you singing?' he asked.

Mother Rebum croaked a laugh. Legs straining, she lifted herself. After turning sideways to eye Fritti, she settled back down heavily.

'Ah,' she said. 'A song of power, that was. After the Days of Fire, the Jugurum used such strong melodies to keep the ocean down in its depth and the sky hanging safely above. My song was but a small one, though, and not so ambitious. 'Twas meant only to bring you traveler's luck.'

'Me?' Fritti asked. 'Why me? What have I ever done for you?'

'Why, less than nothing, my furry polliwog!' chugged the frog, amused. 'I did it as a service to another, to whom I owed a favor – one older even than Mother Rebum. He who asked me to aid you even walked the earth when Jargum the Great, father of my folk, strode the marshes of the elder world – or so I am told. A powerful protector you have, little cat.'

Tailchaser thought he could guess the meaning of her words. So, he was still beneath the guardian shadow. The thought took the cold edge from the wind that blew across the salt mere.

'Do not think, though,' Mother Rebum continued, 'to escape entirely free from obligation. Your friend told me that you have been part of the great doings to the northwest, yes?' Fritti assented. 'Good, then you shall tell me your story, for the feckless gulls have brought

me only snatches and shards. I cannot manage Burum-gurgun, the
Marsh at the Center of the World, in a proper fashion unless I am
kept informed of current events in the outlands.'

The Marsh at the Center of the World. Fritti smiled to himself
and began his long story.

It was almost the Hour of Deepest Quiet when he had finished.
Mother Rebum had sat still throughout the entire tale, her goggle
eyes watching him closely. As he ended she blinked several times,
then sat silent for a moment, her throat puffing in and out.

'Well,' she said finally, 'it sounds as though there have indeed been
many great splashings in the ponds of the cat-folk.' She paused to
pluck a low-flying insect from the night air. 'Hearteater was a force,
a great force, and his fall shall birth many ripples. I see now why
your spirit is troubled, little furback.'

'Troubled? Why do you say that?'

'Why?' Mother Rebum chugged. 'Because I know it. I watched
you when you saw the water-shadow. I have listened to you sing for
half the night. Your heart is in confusion.'

'It is?' Fritti was not sure he liked the turn the conversation had
taken.

'Oh, yes, my brave, questing tadpole . . . but fear not. If you but
take my advice you will find your way happily. Remember this one
thing, Tailchaser: all your troubles, all your searching, and wandering, struggling – they are as one small bubble in the world-pool.'

Fritti felt chastened, and a little angry. 'What do you mean? Many
important things have happened since I left my home. I was not
responsible for most of them, but I played a part. It is even possible
that things would have gone worse had it not been for me,' he finished
with some pride.

'That I will grant you. Please, don't bristle so!' chuckled the old
frog. 'But answer me this: has the snow covered Vastnir?'

'I suppose it has by now, yes. What of it? It will be spring soon.'

'Exactly, my minnow. Now, have the birds returned to Ratleaf?'

Tailchaser was not sure he saw the point. 'Many of the fla-fa'az
have made their way back . . . that is also true.'

Mother Rebum smiled a green, toothless smile. 'Very well, I shall
ask you no more questions. I can see for myself, here in my lily-pond
home, that the sun still crosses the sky each day. Do you understand
yet?'

'No,' said Fritti stubbornly.

'It is this. By the time another winter comes, and passes into another spring, Vastnir Mound and all the works of Hearteater will have disappeared entirely – lingering only in memory. Before too many more winters have come and departed, you and I also will have disappeared, leaving behind only our bones to be the home of tiny creatures. And do you know what, brave Tailchaser? The world-dance will falter not a step for any of these passings.'

She brought herself up heavily to her front legs. 'Now, friend cat, I must away and dunk these old bones in a mud bath. I thank you for the pleasure of your company.'

So saying, she hopped to the edge of the pond, half into the stagnant water, then turned and looked back. Her round eyes blinked sleepily.

'Never fear!' she said. 'I have woven my song well. If you need help you shall receive it – at least once. Look especially to things that move in water, for there lie most of my powers. Luck to you, Tailchaser!'

With a hop and a splash, Mother Rebum disappeared into the pool.

CHAPTER THIRTY-TWO

Wind over the lake: the image of inner truth.

– I Ching (The Book of Changes)

During his last night on the Pawdab, Fritti had a long, strange journey in the dream-fields.

His spirit soared like a fla-fa'az over the hills and trees and waters the night winds beating in his face. Like the great Akor that nested in the high mountains, he sailed up, up, up. The night-belly of Meerclar was his field, to travel in where he would.

As he sailed the wind spoke in his ear with the voices of many – Grassnestle, his mother; Bristlejaw and Stretchslow. They all called his name in the fierce howl of the breeze . . . but he flew on when Pouncequick's voice cried out to him, too – not in fear, but in a kind of wonder. As he heard it he swooped down, hurtling into blackness. The roaring airs became the mad yowls of Eatbugs and Scratchnail, the soft tones of Roofshadow intertwined with their screams, speaking his heart name over and over.

' . . . *Fritti Tailchaser* . . . *Fritti* . . . *Fritti* . . . *Fritti Tailchaser* . . .

Then the rushing sound of the winds changed, and became a great ceaseless roar. He was skimming above the Bigwater, so near to it that it seemed he could reach down a paw and skim it in the waves. Salt wind flattened his whiskers, and the night sky around him was empty but for the sounding of Qu'cef.

A bright flash, like Whitewind's star, appeared above the horizon. Carried rapidly nearer on the broad back of the wind, he could see the light gleam, then fade, then gleam again.

A great, gray tail stood up from the waters of Qu'cef. It towered

bove the waves, and at its summit the light he had seen burned like
sky-fire.

He was rushing toward it – helplessly, now – when he heard the
voice of Eyeshimmer the Far-senser echo down the wind:

'*The heart's desire . . . is found in an unexpected place . . . unexpected
. .*'

And suddenly the air currents carried him up again, past the
shining light . . . and the great, waving tail sank back down into the
waters, extinguishing the glow . . . and now . . . and now another,
softer light was kindling, spreading across the lower edge of the night
sky . . .

It was dawn. Fritti sat up in his bower of cordgrass, and the early-
morning marsh wind came moaning through the stalks and weeds.
He stood up and stretched, listening to the night insects singing a
final chorus.

So Fritti came up out of the marshlands, crossing the tiny stream –
a distant relative of the mighty Caterwaul – that flowed into the
southernmost tip of the Bigwater, marking the boundaries of the
Pawdab.

Sloping up from the shores of Qu'cef, windswept meadows with
green turf rose gradually on his right flank. Far away across the
grasslands he could see the dwellings of M'an: small, and isolated
from their neighbors. He was traveling U'ea-ward now, green fields
on his right side and the gravelly sea-strand on his left.

Woolly Erunor grazed all about the hummocky meadows. Their
fleecy bodies dotted the downs like fat, dirty clouds that had settled
to the ground, too heavy to stay aloft. They regarded him incuriously
as he passed, this small orange cat, and when he called out to them
they grimaced complacently with yellowed teeth, but did not answer.

When Tailchaser first saw the light he thought it was a star.

He had come down from the meadow-track to walk along the shore.
The Eye of Meerclar, rapidly approaching fullness, blued the sand
and silvered the waves. By its spirit light he had caught a crab, but
had been unable to force the wet and slippery shell. In disgust he
had watched it limp away – sideways, as if unwilling to turn its back
on him. For some time afterward he had paced hungrily up and down
the strand, in hopes of finding a more unprotected morsel.

Despairing of his ill-luck, he had looked up and seen the blossom-
ing glow on the northern horizon. After a moment's glare it was gone,

but as he stared into the darkness it returned once more. For a
moment it had illuminated the night sky. A heartbeat later, it had
vanished again.

Watching raptly, Fritti walked farther up the beach. The unusual
star repeated its cycle of brilliance and darkness. The words of the
Firstborn came back to Tailchaser: ' . . . a strange hill that shines at
night . . . '

The spot on the horizon flared again, and he remembered his
dream: the tail in the sea – the waving tail with the gleaming tip.
What was before him?

Dinner on the shore forgotten, he leaped up the rock-strewn slope.
Tonight, he wanted to walk.

That night and the next he followed the beckoning light; the morning
after he came finally into sight of the strange hill.

As Firefoot had said, it rose up from the midst of the Bigwater
itself, far from the gravel beach. It was a M'an-hill, Fritti could tell:
it climbed high, and unnaturally straight; it was as white as new
snow.

Tailchaser made his way out to a wooded peninsula of land that
reached out into the sea like an outstretched paw. From its farthest
tip he could make out the island on which the M'an-mountain grew.

The island sat in the lap of Qu'cef, rising up from the tumbling
waves. Its back was green with grass. Fritti could see tiny Erunor
moving slowly on the sward. At the base of the hill-thing – which
looked more like some great, white, branchless trunk – crouched a
M'an-dwelling of the kind Fritti had lived near, back at the Meeting
Wall, so long ago. This was his destination, so close that the scent of
the Erunor carried across to him, tickling his whiskers. But between
Tailchaser and his heart's desire stood a thousand jumps of the heaving blue Qu'cef.

Unfolding Dark came, and the blinding light sprang forth once more
from the top of the M'an-hill. Tailchaser felt it as a burning in his
heart.

Two more days passed. He remained on the peninsula, balked and
frustrated, hunting up what little game he could in the bracken and
shrubbery. As he patrolled the shore, thinking and scheming furiously, seabirds wheeled and dove in the sky above him. He thought

could hear their mocking voices calling: 'Fritti . . . Fritti . . .
itti . . . '

You are a bug-wit, he chided himself. *Why can't you solve this
oblem?*

He remembered the story that Earnotch had told him in the mound
out Lord Tangaloor.

Well, Harar's shining tail, he thought, *what good does it do me? The
-fa'az owe me no favors. They hover and laugh at me.*

He looked across the deep waters.

*I am not not too sure that I would be able to talk a great fish out of
ting me, either,* he decided. *Besides, they must all know of Firefoot's
mous trick by now.*

Depressed, he continued his vigil.

n the fourth day since coming to the little tongue of land, he saw
mething coming toward him over the waves.

Crouching low in the brush at land's end, he watched as the
ysterious object bobbed its way across the Qu'cef. It looked like
lf a walnut shell that had been cast away after a Rikchikchik's meal
but it was bigger. Much bigger.

Something moved inside it. When the shell came nearer to his
ninsula, he could see that the moving thing was one of the Big
nes – a M'an. The Big One was moving two long branches back
d forth in the water.

The shell, colored as gray as old tree bark, slid past Fritti's vantage
int and stopped at last on the shores of a small inlet at the base of
e peninsula. The M'an climbed out. After fussing for a while with
me sort of long vine, he stamped his feet and walked away across
e meadowlands toward the other M'an-dwellings.

Fritti ran excitedly down the peninsula, bounding over roots and
nes. When he reached the inlet, he looked cautiously about – the
g One had disappeared – then loped down to examine this strange
ing.

He sniffed it. It was obviously no walnut shell, but rather some-
ing M'an-built. It was twice as long as the Big One was tall. The
ay color was flaking off on its side, showing wood beneath. It
elled of the Qu'cef, and of M'an, and of fish, and other things he
uld not identify. For a long time Fritti walked around it, scenting
 strangeness, then leaped up inside. He nosed and probed, trying
 discover what made it swim like a great gray pril.

Perhaps it will swim for me, he thought, *and take me across the water.*

275

But it only lay on the rocky beach – no matter where Fritti stoo
or how hard he wished. He lay down on the bottom of the gre
shell-thing. He thought hard, trying to see a way to make it bear h
over to the hill that shined. He thought . . . and thought . . . and
the pondering, and the warm afternoon sun, made him f
drowsy . . .

He awoke with a start. Disoriented, he looked wildly around, b
could see nothing but the sides of the swimming walnut shell. Fo
steps crunched across the gravel toward him. Groggy and confuse
frightened of leaping up and revealing himself to the Big One,
dove beneath a pile of rough fabric. It scratched him as he squirm
beneath its comforting heaviness.

The footsteps of the M'an stopped, and then the whole shell v
sliding and scraping along the beach. Surprised, Fritti gripped t
wood beneath him with his claws. The scraping stopped abruptly,
be replaced by a sensation of smooth motion. Tailchaser heard t
Big One climb weightily over the edge, and then a regular sequer
of creaking and splashing.

After some time, Fritti worked up the courage to poke a pink ne
out of the enveloping folds of cloth. The massive back of the M'
was turned to him; the Big One was working the tree limbs back a
forth. The shell was entirely surrounded with water.

Mother Rebum did say 'things that move on water,' thought T*
chaser, *so if I succeed – and am not drowned in this strange nut hus*
I suppose I shall have her to thank.

He curled up in his hiding spot, tail over nose, and went back
sleep.

Time – he did not know how much – had passed. The shell thump
to a halt. Fritti heard the M'an rummaging about, but his haven v
not discovered. Finally the M'an got out and went thumping awa
Tailchaser lay silent for a while, then emerged to stretch and lo
about.

The island rose up before him. The shell had come to rest agai
a wooden walkway that stretched a short distance across the wat
then ended at a dirt path which wound away up the grassy slope.
the summit of this path Fritti could see the M'an-dwelling, and
looming above it like a white, limbless Vaka'az'me – the toweri
M'an-hill. The sun was still in the sky, and the white hill was da
Fritti made his way up the uneven path. The grass was sprin
beneath his feet. He stepped lightly. The wind off the Bigwater t

ressed his nose and whiskers made him feel as though he had
ached the top of the world.

A dark shape detached itself from the bulk of the M'an-nest, and
th plodding, unhurried steps, came partway down the hillside. It
as a large dog, deep of chest and heavy-legged.

Feeling curiously light-headed and confident, Tailchaser continued
s sedate walk up the grassy slope. Puzzled, the fik'az tilted his head
one shoulder and stared. After a moment's curious scrutiny, he
oke.

'You there!' the mastiff barked. 'Who be you? What be you doing?'
is voice was as deep and slow as distant thunder.

'I am Tailchaser, Master Fik'az. Good dancing to you. And whom
I have the pleasure of addressing?'

The dog squinted down at him. 'Huff-so-Gruff am I. You didna
swer question. What be you doing?'

'Oh, just looking about,' said Fritti, waving his tail in a disarming
anner. 'I just flew over from the other side of the water, and I
ought I'd look around. Quite a lovely place, isn't it?'

'Aye,' growled Huff-so-Gruff, 'but you shouldna be here. Be off,
u.' The dog glowered for a moment, muzzled lowered, then once
ore cocked his head to the side. 'Said you . . . "flew"?' he asked
wly. 'Cats dunna fly.'

As they talked, Tailchaser had been drawing steadily closer. Now,
rely five jumps away from the fik'az, Fritti sat, and began to groom
nchalantly.

'Oh yes, some do,' he said. 'As a matter of fact, my whole tribe
flying cats is thinking of making this spot our new nesting grounds.
e need a place to lay our eggs, you know.'

Tailchaser got up and began to walk in a wide circle around the
g. 'Yes, think of it,' he said, looking from side to side. 'Hundreds
flying cats . . . big ones, little ones . . . it's quite a marvelous idea,
1't it?'

He was almost safely past when a deep, rumbling snarl issued from
uff-so-Gruff. 'Cats canna fly! I willna have it!'

The mastiff leaped forward, baying, and Fritti turned and bolted
the hill. Within a few jumps he realized there were no trees to
imb, no fences to dodge behind; it was open grass to the top of the
se.

Well, he thought suddenly, *why should I bother to run? I have faced
rse dangers before, and survived*.

He whirled to face the great mastiff bearing down on him.

'Come on, dung-sniffer!' Tailchaser howled. 'Come and meet child of Firefoot!'

Huff-so-Gruff, in mid-bark, ran unsuspectingly into a faceful yowling, scratching cat. His deep baying turned to a yelp of surpr as sharp claws raked his jowls.

Like a small orange whirlwind, Fritti was suddenly all over Growler – claws and teeth and screeching voice. Shocked, Huff-Gruff pulled back, shaking his large head. In that second, Tailcha was off again, ears back and tail trailing.

As the dismayed Growler gingerly ran his tongue over his lacerat nose, Fritti reached the M'an-dwelling. With a leap and scrabble was up the low stone wall and onto the thatched roof. Standing the edge, he let out a cry of triumph.

'Don't take the Folk so lightly again, you great clumsy beast!'

Down on the ground below, Huff-so-Gruff grunted. 'Come y down and you be eaten, cat,' he said disgustedly.

'Hah!' sneezed Tailchaser. 'I will bring you an army of my F to settle here, and we will tweak your tail and smack your hang chops until you die from shame! Hah!'

Huff-so-Gruff turned and trudged away with heavy dignity.

Fritti walked softly back and forth across the thatch, his he gradually slowing to its usual pace. He felt wonderful.

After some searching – leaning out over the edge, wrinkling nose – he found an open window underneath the eaves of the ro He looked carefully around for the Growler, but Huff-so-Gruff v many jumps down the slope, nursing his wounds. Fritti sprang do to the stone wall, then quickly back up to the windowsill. He pau for a moment to gauge the distance to the floor inside, wavered the sill, then leaped down.

In the middle of the room, curled in a deep-furred ball, Hushpad.

CHAPTER THIRTY-THREE

certain recluse, I know not who, once said that no bonds attached
n to this life, and the only thing he would regret leaving was the
/.

– Yoshida Kenko

e did not appear to recognize him. He stood before her, back
hed and legs trembling, and could not speak.

Hushpad raised her head languidly and stared at him. 'Yes? What
you want?'

'Hushpad!' he choked. 'It's me! Tailchaser!'

The fela's eyes opened in surprise. For a long moment both cats
re still.

Hushpad shook her head wonderingly. 'Tailchaser? My little friend
ilchaser? Is it really you?' In a heartbeat she was on her paws, then
y were together, sniffing, rubbing noses and muzzles. Fritti felt a
at warmth in his breast. Soon the room was filled with the drowsy
nd of purring.

ter they lay nose to nose while Fritti told Hushpad of his travels
adventures. At first she was full of praise and wonder, but as the
ry wore on she asked fewer questions. Eventually she fell entirely
nt, grooming Fritti contentedly as he talked.

When he had completed his tale he rolled over to look at Hushpad.
'You must tell me how you came here!' he cried. 'I went down
o the depths to find you – yet here you are, safe. What happened?'

Hushpad arched her chin. 'It was very brave of you, Tailchaser,
lly – going after me like that. All those terrible creatures, too. I
quite impressed. My own story, I'm afraid, is nowhere near so
iting.'

279

'Please tell me!'

'Well, it's very simple, really. One day – it seems so long ago, n
– the M'an simply put me in a box. You know, like a sleeping b
but with the top covered. Well, he didn't really put me in the box
actually there was a little bit of pril fish in there. I am very fond
pril fish, of course, or I simply *never* would have gotten in. I was
the box for ever so long, but I could see out through some holes
it. We traveled and traveled, then came at last to the Bigwater. V
got into a shell-thing and swam across the water.'

'*I* rode in the shell-thing!' said Fritti excitedly. 'That's how I g
here.'

'Of course,' Hushpad said absently. 'Well, that's how I came
this place. I think it's very nice here, don't you?'

'But how about the Growler?' asked Tailchaser. 'Don't you ev
have trouble with him? It seems as though he would make thi
dangerous place to live.'

'Huff-so-Gruff?' She laughed. 'Oh, he's really just a big kitte
Besides, I don't go out much. It's so nice and warm in here . . . a
the M'an gives me such nice food. So nice and warm . . . ' She trai
off.

Fritti was disconcerted. Apparently Hushpad had never been
any danger.

'Did you think of me often?' he asked, but there was no rep
She was fast asleep.

When the Big One came into the room and found them lying togeth
Tailchaser sat up, bristling. The M'an approached slowly, maki
low noises. When Fritti did not run, the M'an leaned down a
stroked him gently. Tailchaser pulled away, but the Big One did
follow – only crouched with paw extended. Fritti moved hesitan
toward it. When he was close enough he gave it a cautious sniff. T
M'an-paw smelled, interestingly enough, of fish, and Fritti closed
eyes, nose wrinkling with pleasure.

The M'an placed something on the floor near him. He recogni
it instantly. It was a supper bowl. One scent of its contents a
Tailchaser's caution evaporated.

The Big One scratched behind Fritti's ear as he ate. Fritti did
mind.

Hushpad seemed different. The slenderness and grace of her pa
and tail were unchanged, but she had become a good deal plump

280

– round and soft beneath her glossy fur. Neither did she seem as energetic as she had once been – she preferred sleeping in the sun to running and jumping; Fritti could only entice her into games with great difficulty.

'You always were very *bouncy*, Tailchaser,' she said one day. He felt hurt.

She *was* pleased to see him, of course, and enjoyed having a companion to chat with, but Fritti felt unsatisfied. Hushpad just did not seem to understand all that he had gone through to find her. She did not pay much attention anymore when he told her of the wonders of Firsthome, or the majesty of the First-walkers.

The food was very good, though. The Big One gave them lovely meals, and was always kind to Tailchaser, stroking and scratching him, and allowing him to roam at will. Fritti did not get along so well with Huff-so-Gruff, the dog, but they maintained an uneasy truce. Fritti was careful never to get too far away from shelter.

So the days wore on in the place Firefoot had called Villa-on-Mar. Each sun was a little warmer than the one before. Flocks of migrating fla-fa'az stopped briefly on the island as they passed away to the north, and Fritti had great sport with them, although he was seldom hungry enough for serious hunting. Time passed smoothly as a quiet stream. Tailchaser grew plump himself, and restless.

One night in high spring, as Meerclar's Eye approached another fullness, several Big Ones came across the Qu'cef in a large shell to visit the M'an. The nest was full of Big Ones, and their booming voices echoed everywhere. Several of them tried to play with Fritti.

Big, grasping paws jerked him up in the air and squeezed him, and when they held him close to their faces their unpleasant breath made him squirm. When he pulled away the booming voices roared.

Fritti leaped to the window, but Huff-so-Gruff was stalking sentry outside, in an evil temper. Running between the legs of the bellowing, grabbing Big Ones, Tailchaser retreated to the room where Hushpad lay curled in sleep.

'Hushpad!' he cried, prodding her. 'Wake up! We have to leave this place!'

Yawning and stretching, the fela looked at him curiously. 'Whatever are you talking about, Tailchaser? Leave? Why?'

'This place is not right for us,' he said excitedly. 'The Big Ones

281

grab us and carry us, they feed us and stroke us . . . there is no place to run!'

'You are making no sense at all,' she told him coldly. 'We are treated very well.'

'They treat us like kittens. This is no life for a hunter. I might as well have never left my mother Grassnestle's nest!'

'You're right,' said Hushpad. 'You're right, because you're acting like a nervous newborn. Whatever do you mean, "leave"? Why should I go anywhere?'

'We can hide in the shell, as I did before. We can steal away and go back to the forest, the marshes, anywhere,' Fritti said desperately. 'We can run where we want. We can raise a family.'

'Oho, a family, is that it?' she said. 'Well, you just put it out of your mind right now. I've had enough of your pawing and sniffing, Skydancer knows. I've already told you I'm not the least bit interested in that sort of thing. I'm shocked to see you acting so ridiculous. The forest indeed! Leaves and burrs in my fur, and nothing to eat for days at a time! Visl and Garrin and . . . Harar knows what else! No, thank you.'

When she saw the hurt, startled expression on Fritti's face, her expression softened. 'Listen, dear Tailchaser,' she said. 'You're my friend, and I think you're very special. I think you're just upset. The Big Ones *can* be noisy and frightening sometimes. Just stay away from them, and tomorrow everything will be as calm and quiet as before.' She rubbed his muzzle with her nose. 'Now, just go to sleep. You'll see later that this is all very silly.' She laid her head down and closed her eyes.

Fritti sat and stared.

Why doesn't she understand? he wondered. *Something is wrong here, I can feel it.*

But what was it? Why should he feel as trapped as ever he did belowground?

Hushpad mewed in her sleep and flexed her claws.

I should be happy, Fritti thought. *Finding Hushpad was my heart's desire . . . wasn't it? Lord Firefoot said I would find my heart's desire here on Villa-on-Mar . . .*

Tailchaser walked slowly to the open window and bounded up onto the sill. The great light from the hill above the dwelling cast its bright beam out across the dark waters of Qu'cef. The air was warm, and full of the scents of growing things.

*

When the shell-thing bumped against the shore, Fritti emerged from his hiding place. He bounded past the startled Big Ones, out of the shell, and onto the gravelly beach. The M'an flock made noises of surprise. With a flirt of his orange tail he was up the slope and into the Eye-lit meadows.

He stood on a grassy hill and thought of all the things he would do. Pouncequick waited for him at Firsthome. He must see him again. And his friends at Meeting Wall, of course. What stories he had to tell! So many places left to see!

And Roofshadow, of course. Firsa Roofshadow, dark and slender as shade.

A night bird trilled. The world was so big, and the night sky was so full of glimmering light!

Like a fire, like a star that burned in his heart and head, it came to him then; he *understood*. He laughed and bounded, and then laughed again. He leaped and whirled on the hilltop, and his voice rose in delight.

When his dance was finished he sprang down the slope and ran singing into the fields, his tail waving behind him. Meerclar's Eye watched calmly as his bright form vanished into the tall grass.

AUTHOR'S NOTES

With a very few exceptions, all the unfamiliar words to be found in this story are in the Higher Singing of the Folk.

The Folk, like all their warm-blooded brothers and sisters, and some others, possess two languages. The everyday language, the one they share with most other mammals, is the Common Singing, made up mostly of gestures, scents and postures, with a few easily decipherable sounds and cries to round out the range of expression. The Common Singing has been represented by a rough translation into English in this story.

For special times, or for specific descriptive chores where the Common Singing falls short, the Higher Singing is employed. Almost all ritual – and certainly all storytelling – falls into this category.

The Higher Singing is a predominantly verbal language, although meaning can be shaped with posture and emphasis. So the reader needn't be constantly looking up words, much of the Higher Singing in use has been translated within the text; there is, however, a glossary at the back for the faint of heart.

A few notes on pronunciation.

'C' is always pronounced 'S': thus, Meerclar is pronounced 'Mereslar.'

In the instances where an 'S' has been used, it is only to clarify the pronunciation. For example, I felt that 'Vicl,' although the true spelling, was a little boggling; hence, 'Visl.'

'F' has a soft 'fth' sound.

Vowels tend to conform to Latinate 'ah-eh-ih-oh-ooh.'

CHARACTERS
APPENDIX

Allmother, Meerclar, *Creator of the Folk*

Bandyleg, *Firsthome cat*

Bast-Imret, *Boneguard*

Beetleswat, *young Meeting Wall tom*

Bitefast, Clawguard

Bite-then-Bark, Rauro, *Dog-king of Eatbugs' story*

Blueback, *a prince of the Folk*

Bobweave, *a First-walker*

Brightnail, *a prince of the Folk*

Brindleside, *Fritti Tailchaser's father*

Bristlejaw, *Meeting Wall Master-singer*

Brushstalker, *First-walker Thane*

Cleanwhisker, *a prince of the Folk*

Clearsong, Tirya, *Tailchaser's oldest sister*

Click, Master, *a squirrel*

Climbfast, *a prince of the Folk*

Cloudleaper, *Cat-queen of Eatbugs' story*

Crushgrass, *Clawguard chieftain*

Dandlegrass, *Firsthome cat*

Dayhunter, *companion of Fencewalker*

Dewtreader, Prince Sresla, *Prince Consort to Queen Sunback*

Earnotch, *Vastnir prisoner, storyteller*

Earpoint, *Meeting Wall elder, delegate*

Eatbugs, *mad cat, Tailchaser's companion*

Eyeshimmer, *Far-senser to the First-walkers*

Fencewalker, Prince, *son of Queen Sunback*

Firefoot, Tangaloor, *one of the Firstborn*

Fizz, Master, *a squirrel*

Fleetpaw, *young Meeting Wall tom*

Flickerswift, *sister of Jumptall*

Fumblefoot, *Vastnir prisoner*

Furscuff, *First-walker; Squakerbane's companion*

Glideswallow, *Firsthome cat*

Glitterfur, *a queen of the Folk*
Goldeneye, Harar, *father of the Folk*
Grassnestle, Indez, *Tailchaser's mother*
Hangbelly, *a First-walker*
Hearteater, Grizraz, *one of the Firstborn; lord of Vastnir*
Hissblood, *master of Toothguard*
Howlsong, *apprentice Master Old-singer*
Huff-so-Gruff, *Villa-on-Mar dog*
Hushpad, *Tailchaser's friend*
Jargum, *a mythological frog*
Jumptall, *young Meeting Wall tom; delegate*
Karthwine, *a fox*
Knet-Makri, *Boneguard*
Krelli, *a young raven*
Leafrustle, *a young Meeting Wall tom*
Longtooth, *Clawguard*
Lungeclaw, *ancestor of Quiverclaw*
Morningstripe, *a queen of the Folk*
Mudtracker, *cat from Beyond-Edge-Copse*
Nightcatcher, *companion of Fencewalker*
Ninebirds, *mythical prince, progenitor of the Big Ones*
Nipslither, *Toothguard*
Nuzzledark, *Toothguard*
Pawgentle, *Firsthome cat*
Pawgrip, *Vastnir prisoner*
Pfefirrit, *a prince of birds*
Plink, Master, *squirrel messenger*
Pokesnout, *Firsthome cat*
Pop, Lord, *squirrel-ruler*
Pouncequick, *Tailchaser's companion*
Quiverclaw, *First-walker Thane*
Rebum, Mother, *a frog*
Redlegs, *Cat-prince of Eatbugs' story*
Renred, *a mythological fox*
Riptalon, *Clawguard*
Roofshadow, Firsa, *Tailchaser's companion*
Rumblepurr, *Chamberlain of the Court of Harar*
Satinear, *a queen of the Folk*
Scratchnail, *Clawguard chieftain*
Scuffledig, *a First-walker*
Shredfang, *Clawguard*

Skinwretch, *Toothguard*

Skoggi, *raven father*

Skydancer, Fela, *mother of the Folk*

Skystone, Irao, *a prince of the Folk*

Sleekheart, *a prince of the Folk*

Slipwhisker, *Roofshadow's father*

Slitbelly, *Toothguard*

Smackbush, *Firsthome cat*

Snagrat, *cat in Hangbelly's song*

Snap, Lord, *squirrel-lord, brother of Lord Pop*

Snapjaw, *Clawguard*

Snaremouse, *Firsthome cat; dancer*

Snifflick, *Meeting Wall elder*

Snoutscar, *Clawguard overseer*

Snufflenose, *Roofshadow's brother*

Softwhisker, *Tailchaser's youngest sister*

Sourweed, *First-walker Thane*

Squeakerbane, *Ranking First-walker Thane*

Streamhopper, *Meeting Wall delegate*

Stretchslow, *Meeting Wall elder, Tailchaser's benefactor*

Strongclaw, *a prince of the Folk*

Sunback, Queen Mirmirsor, *the Queen of the Folk*

Tailchaser, Fritti, *our hero*

Thinbone, *Tailchaser's Meeting Wall friend*

Treesinger, *a princess of the Folk*

Twitchnose, *Snifflick's mate*

Volenibble, *Firsthome Master Old-singer*

Wavetail, *Meeting Wall elder*

Whir, Mistress, *mate of Master Fizz*

Whitewind, Viror, *one of the Firstborn*

Windflower, *strange cat in Squeakerbane's story*

Windruffle, *a queen of the Folk*

Wolf-friend, *a prince of the Folk*

GLOSSARY
APPENDIX

A, *to; at; toward*
Akor, *eagle*
An, *sun*
Ar, *yes*
Az, *cat; person*
Az-iri'le, *'we-cats:' the Folk*
Az'me, *'earth-cat:' tree*
Cef, *water*
Cef'az, *'water-cat:' fish*
Cir, *sing; speak*
Cu, *sibling*
Cu'nre, *'heart-brother:' friend*
E, *hot*
E'a, *'toward-hot:' south*
Erunor, *sheep*
Fa, *jump*
Fe, *mother*
Fela, *female*
Fik, *loud, frightening*
Fik'az, *'loud-cat:' dog*
Fikos, *'terrifying badness'*
Fla, *run*
Fla-fa'az, *'run-jump-cat:' bird*
Fri, *small*
Garrin, *bear*
Har, *father*
Hlizza, *snake*
Iri, *I; me*
Iri'le, *'many-me:' we*
Ka, *spirit; soul*
Krauka, *raven*
La, *birth*
Le, *many*

289

Ma, *away from; out of*
Me, *earth*
Mela, *'birth-ground:' nest*
Mela'an, *'sun-nest:' sky*
Me'mre, *'food-soil:' droppings*
Meskra, *hawk*
Mre, *eat; food*
Mre'az, *'food-cat:' mouse*
Mri, *sleep*
Mri'fa, *'sleep-jump:' dream*
Mri'fa-o, *'good dreaming:' good night*
Nre, *heart*
Nre'fa, *'heart-jump:' dance*
Nre'fa-o, *'good dancing:' hello; goodbye*
O, *good*
Oel, *master; chief*
Oel-cir'va, *'Master Old-singer'*
Oel-var'iz, *'master seer:' Far-senser*
Os, *bad, incorrect; wrong*
Praere, *rabbit*
Pril, *salmon*
Qu, *big*
Ri, *head*
Rikchikchik, *squirrel*
Ruhu, *owl*
Tesri, *deer*
Tom (ptom), *male*
Ue, *cold*
Ue'a, *'toward-cold:' north*
Va, *old*
Va'an, *'old-sun:' west*
Vaka'az'me, *'old-spirit-tree'*
Var, *sight; sense*
Vez, *young*
Vez'an, *'young-sun:' east*

£1 OFF

THE NEW
TAD WILLIAMS HARDBACK!

COMING APRIL 1993...
THE LONGEST AWAITED FANTASY
EVENT OF THE DECADE

TAD WILLIAMS'
TO GREEN ANGEL TOWER

Book 3 of the bestselling epic masterpiece
MEMORY, SORROW AND THORN

Tear out this page – present it to your bookseller
who will give you £1 off the published price of
To Green Angel Tower hardback

**Offer available in UK only,
and valid until 31st July 1993**

Dear Bookseller

When presented with this voucher, please send to the
address below **by 31st August 1993** to obtain your £1 credit.

"Tad Williams Offer", Arrow Sales Office, Random House,
20 Vauxhall Bridge Road, London SW1V 2SA